Dear Reader,

I love men of the desert. [...]
and dark hearts—and sex[...]
The two heroes you'll find in this book are both such
men—though their natures are very different.

In *Defiant in the Desert,* Suleiman Abd Al-Aziz has
been given an unwanted mission. He must return
reluctant bride Sara Williams to the desert, to marry
the Sultan of Qurhah. But Suleiman wants Sara for
himself—just as she wants him. *And both of them
know that their love is forbidden.*

This is a story of a couple who have all the odds
stacked against them. Who have to fight duty and
tradition, as well as their own desire. It is, if you like—
an *impossible* love story.

The Sheikh's Undoing is a complete contrast.
International tycoon Sheikh Tariq is a player—and
bedding women is his favorite pastime. Tariq's long-
suffering PA, Izzy Mulholland, hates the way he lives
his life, but at least she can turn her back on it at the
end of each working day.

That is, until Tariq has a prang in his sports car and
needs a week's respite in Izzy's country cottage.
Which is where she learns that you don't have to *like* a
man to want to share his bed....

I adored writing about these powerful, often infuriating
men—and the two feisty women who make them
question everything they'd previously thought about
life, and love.

Let me know which desert man captured *your* heart....

Love,

Sharon

Sharon Kendrick

—

Defiant in the Desert

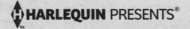

Recycling programs
for this product may
not exist in your area.

ISBN-13: 978-0-373-13199-0

First North American Publication 2013

DEFIANT IN THE DESERT
Copyright © 2013 by Sharon Kendrick

THE SHEIKH'S UNDOING
Copyright © 2012 by Sharon Kendrick

HARLEQUIN®
www.Harlequin.com

Printed in U.S.A.

CONTENTS

All about the author...
Sharon Kendrick

SHARON KENDRICK started storytelling at the age of eleven and has never really stopped. She likes to write fast-paced, feel-good romances with heroes who are so sexy they'll make your toes curl!

Born in west London, she now lives in the beautiful city of Winchester—where she can see the cathedral from her window (but only if she stands on tiptoe). She has two children, Celia and Patrick, and her passions include music, books, cooking and eating—and drifting off into wonderful daydreams while she works out new plots!

Visit Sharon at www.sharonkendrick.com.

Other titles by Sharon Kendrick available in ebook:

THE GREEK'S MARRIAGE BARGAIN
A WHISPER OF DISGRACE *(Sicily's Corretti Dynasty)*
A SCANDAL, A SECRET, A BABY
BACK IN THE HEADLINES *(Scandal in the Spotlight)*

Defiant in the Desert

To Peter O'Brien—the intrepid Irishman—who taught me some of the mysteries and miracles of desert life

CHAPTER ONE

'THERE'S A MAN downstairs in Reception who says he wants to see you.'

'Who is it?' questioned Sara, not bothering to lift her head from the drawing which was currently engrossing her.

'He wouldn't say.'

At this Sara did look up to find Alice, the office runner, staring at her with an odd sort of expression. Alice was young and very enthusiastic, but right now she looked almost *transported*. Her face was tight with excitement and disbelief—as if Santa Claus himself had arrived early with a full contingent of reindeer.

'It's Christmas Eve afternoon,' said Sara, glancing out of the window at the dark grey sky and wincing. No snow, unfortunately. Only a few heavy raindrops spattering against the glass. Pity. Snow might have helped boost her mood—to help shift off the inevitable feeling of *not quite fitting in* which always descended on her at this time of year. She never found it easy to enjoy Christmas—which was one of the main reasons why she tended to ignore the festival until it had gone away.

She pushed a smile to the corners of her mouth, try-ing to pick up on Alice's happy pre-holiday mood. 'And very soon I'm going to be packing up and going home. If it's a salesman, I'm not interested and if it's anyone else, then tell them to go away and make an appoint-ment to see me in the new year.'

'He says he's not going anywhere,' said Alice and then paused dramatically. 'Until he's seen you.'

Sara put her purple felt-tip pen down with fingers which had annoyingly started to tremble, telling herself not to be so stupid. Telling herself that she was perfectly safe here, in this bright, open-plan office of the highly successful advertising agency where she worked. That there was no reason for this dark feeling of foreboding which had started whispering over her skin.

But of course, there was…

'What do you mean—he's not going anywhere?' she demanded, trying to keep her voice from rising with panic. 'What exactly did he say?'

'That he wants to see you,' repeated Alice and now she made another face which Sara had never seen be-fore. 'And that he craves just a few minutes of your time.'

Craves.

It was a word which jarred like an ice cream eaten on a winter day. No modern Englishman would ever have used a word like that. Sara felt the cold clamp of fear tightening around her heart, like an iron band.

'What…what does he look like?' she asked, her voice a croaky-sounding husk.

Alice played with the pendant which was dangling

from her neck in an unconscious display of sexual awareness. 'He's…well, he's pretty unbelievable, if you must know. Not just because of the way he's built—though he must work out practically non-stop to get a body like *that*—but more…more…' Her voice tailed off. 'Well, it's his eyes really.'

'What about his eyes?' barked Sara, feeling her pulse begin to rocket.

'They were like…black. But like, *really* black. Like the sky when there's no moon or stars. Like—'

'Alice,' cut in Sara, desperately trying to inject a note of normality into the girl's uncharacteristically gushing description. Because at that stage she was still trying to fool herself into thinking that it wasn't happening. That it might all be some terrible mistake. A simple mix-up. Anything, but the one thing she most feared. 'Tell him—'

'Why don't you tell me yourself, Sara?'

A cold, accented voice cut through her words and Sara whirled round to see a man standing in the doorway of the office. Shock, pain and desire washed over her in rapid succession. She hadn't seen him for five long years and for a moment she almost didn't recognise him. He had always been dark and utterly gorgeous, gifted with a face and a mind which had captured her heart so completely. But now…

Now…

Her heart pounded.

Something about him had changed.

His dark head was bare and he wore a custom-made suit instead of his usual robes. The charcoal jacket defined his honed torso just as well as any folds of flowing silk and the immaculately cut trousers emphasised the endless length of his powerful thighs. He had always carried the cachet which came from being the Sultan of Qurhah's closest advisor, but now his natural air of authority seemed to be underpinned with a steely layer Sara had never seen before. And suddenly she recognised it for what it was.

Power.

It seemed to crackle from every pore of his body. To pervade the screne office environment like high-voltage electricity. It made her wary—warier than she felt already, with her heart beating so fast it felt as if it might burst right out of her chest.

'Suleiman,' she said, her voice unsteady and a little unsure. 'What are you doing here?'

He smiled, but it was the coldest smile she had ever seen. Even colder than the one which he had iced into her the last time they'd been together. When he had torn himself away from her passionate embrace and looked down at her as if she was the lowest of the low.

'I think you can probably work that one out for yourself, can't you, Sara?'

He stepped into the office, his clever black eyes narrowing.

'You are an intelligent woman, if a somewhat misguided one,' he continued. 'You have been ignoring repeated requests from the Sultan to return to Qurhah to become his wife. Haven't you?'

'And if I have?'

He looked at her, but there was nothing but indifference in his eyes and, stupidly, that hurt.

'If you have, then you have been behaving like a fool.'

His phrase was coated with an implicit threat which made her skin turn to ice and Sara heard Alice gasp. She turned her head slightly, expecting to see horror on the face of the trendy office runner, with her pink streaked hair and bottom-hugging skirt. Because it wasn't cool for men to talk that way, was it? But she saw nothing like horror there. Instead, the bohemian youngster was staring at Suleiman with a look of rapt adoration.

Sara swallowed. Cool obviously flew straight out of the window when you had a towering black-haired male standing in your office just oozing testosterone. Why wouldn't Alice acknowledge the presence of a man unlike any other she had probably met? Despite all the attractive hunks who worked in Gabe Steel's advertising empire—didn't Suleiman Abd al-Aziz stand out like a spot of black oil on a white linen dress? Didn't he redefine the very concept of masculinity and make it a hundred times more meaningful?

For her, he had always had the ability to make every other man fade into insignificance—even royal princes and sultans—but now something about him had changed. There was an indefinable quality about him. Something *dangerous*.

Gone was the affection with which he always used to regard her. The man who had drifted in and out of her childhood and taught her to ride seemed to have been replaced by someone else. The black eyes were flat and cold; his lips unsmiling. It wasn't exactly *hatred* she could see on his face—for his expression implied that she wasn't worthy of an emotion as strong as hate. It was more as if she was a *hindrance*. As if he was here under sufferance, in the very last place he wanted to be.

And she had only herself to blame. She knew that. If she hadn't flung herself at him. If she hadn't allowed him to kiss her and then silently invited him to do so much more than that. To…

She tried a smile, though she wasn't sure how convincing a smile it was. She had done everything in her power to forget about Suleiman and the way he'd made her feel, but wasn't it funny how just one glimpse of him could stir up all those familiar emotions? Suddenly her heart was turning over with that painful clench of feeling she'd once thought was love. She could feel the sink of her stomach as she was reminded that he could never be hers.

Well, he would never know that. He wouldn't ever guess that he could still make her feel this way. She wasn't going to give him the chance to humiliate her and reject her. Not again.

'Nice of you to drop in so unexpectedly, Suleiman,' she said, her voice as airy as she could manage. 'But I'm afraid I'm pretty busy at the moment. It *is* Christmas Eve, you know.'

'But you don't celebrate Christmas, Sara. Or at least, I wasn't aware that you did. Have you really changed so much that you have adopted, wholesale, the values of the West?'

He was looking around the large, open-plan office

with an expression of distaste curving his carved lips which he didn't bother to hide. His flat black eyes were registering the garish tinsel which was looped over posters depicting some of the company's many successful advertising campaigns. His gaze rested briefly on the old-fashioned fir tree, complete with flashing lights and a glittering star at the top, which had been erected as a kind of passé tribute to Christmases past. His expression darkened.

Sara put her fingers in her lap, horribly aware that they were trembling, and it suddenly became terribly important that he shouldn't see that, either. She didn't want him to think she was scared, even if that moment she was feeling something very close to scared. And she couldn't quite work out what she was afraid of—her, or him.

'Look, I really am *very* busy,' she said. 'And Alice doesn't want to hear—'

'Alice doesn't have to hear anything because she is about to leave us alone to continue this conversation in private,' he said instantly. Turning towards the office junior, he produced a slow smile, like a magician producing a rabbit from a hat. 'Aren't you, Alice?'

Sara watched, unwillingly fascinated as Alice almost melted under the impact of his smile. She even—and Sara had never witnessed this happen before—she even *blushed.* In a single moment, the streetwise girl from London had been transformed into a gushing stereotype from another age. Any minute now and she might actually *swoon.*

'Of course.' Alice fluttered her eyelashes in a way

which was also new. 'Though I could get you a cup of coffee first if you like?'

'I am not in the mood for coffee,' said Suleiman and Sara wondered how he managed to make his refusal sound like he was talking about sex. Or was that just her projecting yet more stupid fantasies about him?

He was smiling at the runner and she was smiling right back. 'Even though I imagine that yours would be excellent coffee,' he purred.

'Oh, for heaven's sake! Alice buys coffee from the deli next door,' snapped Sara. 'She wasn't planning on travelling to Brazil and bringing back the beans herself!'

'Then that is Brazil's loss,' murmured Suleiman.

Sara could have screamed at the cheesy line which had the office runner beaming from ear to ear. 'That will be all, thanks, Alice,' she said sharply. 'You can go home now. And have…have a happy Christmas.'

'Thanks,' said Alice, clearly reluctant to leave. 'I'll see you in the new year. Happy Christmas!'

There was complete silence for a moment while they watched the girl gather up her oversized bag, which was crammed with one of the large and expensive presents which had been handed out earlier by Gabe Steel, their boss. Or rather, by his office manager. But it was only after her footsteps had echoed down the corridor towards the lift that Suleiman turned to Sara, his black eyes hard and mocking.

'Quite the little executive these days, aren't you, Sara?'

Sara swallowed. She hated the way he said her name.

Or rather, she hated the effect it had on her. The way it made her want to expel a long and shuddering breath and to snake her tongue over lips which had suddenly grown dry. It reminded her too much of the time he had kissed her. When he had overstepped the mark and done the one thing which had been forbidden to him. And to her.

The memory came back as vivid and as real as if it had happened only yesterday. It had been on the night of her brother's coronation—when Haroun had been crowned King of Dhi'ban, a day which many had thought would never come because of the volatile relations between the desert states. All the dignitaries from the neighbouring countries had attended the ceremony—including the infamous Sultan of nearby Qurhah, along with his chief emissary, Suleiman.

Sara remembered being cool and almost non-committal towards the Sultan, to whom she was betrothed. But who could blame her? Her hand in marriage had been the price paid for a financial bail-out for her country. In essence, she had been sold by her father like a piece of human merchandise!

That night she had barely made eye contact with the powerful Sultan who had seemed so forbidding, but her careless attitude seemed to amuse rather than to irritate the potentate. And anyway, he had spent most of the time locked away in meetings with all the other sultans and sheikhs.

But Sara had been eager to be reunited with the Sultan's emissary. She had been filled with pleasure at the thought of seeing Suleiman again, after six long years away at an English boarding school. Suleiman, who had taught her to ride and made her laugh during those two long summers when the Sultan had been negotiating with her father about a financial bail-out. Two summers which had occupied a special place in her heart ever since, even though on that final summer—her marital fate had been sealed.

During the coronation fireworks, she had somehow managed to manoeuvre herself into a position to watch them with Suleiman by her side. The crowds had been so huge that nobody had noticed them standing together and Sara was thrilled just to be in his company again.

The night was soft and warm, but in between the explosions and the roar of the onlookers the conversation between them was as easy as it had always been, even if initially Suleiman had seemed startled by the dramatic change that six years had wrought on her appearance.

'How old are you now?' he'd questioned, after he'd looked her up and down for a distractingly long moment.

'I'm eighteen.' She had smiled straight into his eyes, successfully hiding the hurt that he hadn't even remembered her age. 'And all grown up.'

'All grown up,' he had repeated slowly, as if she'd just said something which had never occurred to him before.

The conversation had moved on to other topics, though she had still been conscious of the curious expression in his eyes. He had asked her about her life at boarding school and she'd told him that she was planning to go to art school.

'In England?'

'Of course in England. There is no equivalent here in Dhi'ban.'

'But Dhi'ban isn't the same without you here, Sara.'

It was a strangely emotional thing for Suleiman to say and maybe the unexpectedness of that was what made her reach up to touch her fingertips to his cheek. 'Is that in a good way, or a bad way?' she teased.

A look passed between them and she felt him stiffen.

The fireworks seemed to stop—or maybe that was because the crashing of her heart was as deafening as any man-made explosion in the sky.

He caught hold of her hand and moved it away from his face, and suddenly Sara could feel a terrible yearning as he looked down at her. The normally authoritative Suleiman seemed frozen with indecision and he shook his head, as if he was trying to deny something. And then, almost in slow motion—he lowered his head to brush his lips over hers in a kiss.

It was just like all the books said it should be.

Her world splintered into something magical as their lips met. Suddenly there were rainbows and starlight and a deep, wild hunger. And the realisation that this was her darling, darling Suleiman and he was *kissing* her. Her lips opened beneath his and he circled her waist with his hands as he pulled her closer. She clung to him as her breasts pressed against his broad chest. She heard him groan. She felt the growing tension in his body as his hands moved down to cup her buttocks.

'Oh, Suleiman,' she whispered against his mouth— and the words must have broken the spell, for suddenly he tore himself away from her and held her at arm's length.

For a long moment he just stared at her, his breathing hard and laboured—looking as if he had just been shaken by something profound. Something which made a wild little flicker of hope flare in her heart. But then the look disappeared and was replaced with an expression of self-contempt. It seemed to take a moment or two before he could speak.

'Is this how you behave when you are in England?' he demanded, his voice as deadly as snake poison. 'Offering yourself as freely as a whore when you are promised to the Sultan? What kind of woman are you, Sara?'

It was a question she couldn't answer because she didn't know. Right then, she didn't seem to know anything because her whole belief system seemed to have been shattered. She hadn't been expecting to kiss him, nor to respond to him like that. She hadn't been expecting to want him to touch her in a way she'd never been touched before—yet now he was looking at her as if she'd done something unspeakable.

Filled with shame, she had turned on her heel and fled—her eyes so blurred with tears that she could barely see. And it wasn't until the next day that she heard indulgent tales of the princess weeping with joy for her newly crowned brother.

The memory cleared and Sara found herself in the uncomfortable present, looking into Suleiman's mocking eyes and realising that he was waiting for some sort of answer to his question. Struggling to remember what he'd asked, she shrugged—as if she could shrug off those feelings of humiliation and rejection she had suffered at his hands.

'I hardly describe being a "creative" in an advertising agency as being an executive,' she said.

'You are *creative* in many fields,' he observed. 'Particularly with your choice of clothes. Such revealing, western clothes, I cannot help but notice.'

Sara felt herself stiffen as he began to study her. *Don't look at me that way,* she wanted to scream. Because it was making her body ache as his gaze swept over the sweater dress which came halfway down her thighs, and the high boots whose soft leather curved over her knees.

'I'm glad you like them,' she said flippantly.

'I didn't say I liked them,' he growled. 'In fact, I wholeheartedly disapprove of them, as no doubt would the Sultan. Your dress is ridiculously short, though I suppose that is deliberate.'

'But everyone wears short skirts round here, Suleiman. It's the fashion. And the thick tights and boots almost cancel out the length of the dress, don't you think?'

His eyes were implacable as they met hers. 'I have not come here to discuss the length of your clothes and the way you seem to flaunt your body like the whore we both know you are!'

'No? Then why are you here?'

There was a pause and now his eyes were deadly as they iced into her.

'I think you know the answer to that. But since you seem to have trouble facing up to your responsibilities, maybe I'd better spell it out for you so that there can be no more confusion. You can no longer ignore your destiny, for the time has come.'

'It's not my destiny!' she flared.

'I have come to take you to Qurhah to be married,' he said coldly. 'To fulfil the promise which was made many moons ago by your father. You were sold to the Sultan and the Sultan wants you. And what is more, he is beginning to grow impatient—for this long-awaited alliance between your two countries to go ahead and bring lasting peace in the region.'

Sara froze. The hands which were still concealed in her lap now clenched into two tight fists. She felt beads of sweat break out on her brow and for a moment she thought she might pass out. Because hadn't she thought that if she just ignored the dark cloud which hung over her future for long enough, one day it might just fade away?

'You can't mean that,' she said, hating her voice for sounding so croaky. *So get some strength back. Find the resources within you to stand up to this ridiculous regime which buys women as if they were simply objects of desire lined up on a market stall.* She drew in a deep breath. 'But even if you do mean it, I'm not coming back with you, Suleiman. No way. I live in England now and I regard myself as an English citizen, with all the corresponding freedom that brings. And nothing in the world you can do or say will induce me to go to Qurhah. I don't want to marry the Sultan, and I won't do it. And what is more, you can't make me.'

'I am hoping to do this without a fight, Sara.'

His voice was smooth. As smooth as treacle—and

just as dark. But nobody could have mistaken the steely intent which ran through his words. She looked into the flatness of his eyes. She looked at the hard, compromising lines of his lips and she felt another whisper of foreboding shivering its way down her spine. 'You think I'm just going to docilely agree to your plans? That I'm going to nod my head and accompany you to Qurhah?'

'I'm hoping you will, since that would be the most sensible outcome for all concerned.'

'In your dreams, Suleiman.'

There was silence for a moment as Suleiman met the belligerent glitter of her eyes, and the slow rage which had been simmering all day now threatened to boil over. Had he thought that this would be easy?

No, of course he hadn't.

Inside he had known that this would be the most difficult assignment of his life—even though he had experienced battle and torture and real hardship. He had tried to turn the job down—for all kinds of reasons. He'd told the Sultan that he was busy with his new life—and that much was true. But loyalty and affection for his erstwhile employer had proved too persuasive. And who else possessed the right amount of determination to bring the feisty Sara Williams back to marry the royal ruler? His mouth hardened and he felt the twist of something like regret. Who else knew her the way that he did?

'You speak with such insolence that I can only assume you have been influenced by the louche values of the West,' he snapped.

'Embracing freedom, you mean?'

'Embracing disrespect would be a more accurate description.' He drew in a deep breath and forced his lips into something resembling a smile. 'Look, Sara—I understand that you needed to…what is it that you women say? Ah yes, to *find yourself.*' He gave a low laugh. 'Fortunately, the male of the species rarely loses himself in the first place and so such recovery is seldom deemed necessary.'

'Why, you arrogant piece of—'

'Now we can do this one of two ways.' His words cut through her insult like a honed Qurhahian knife. 'The easy way, or the hard way.'

'You mean we do it your way, rather than mine?'

'Bravo—that is exactly what I mean. If you behave reasonably—like a woman who wishes to bring no shame onto her own royal house, or the one you will embrace after your marriage to the Sultan—then everyone is happy.'

'Happy?' she echoed. 'Are you out of your mind?'

'There is no need for hysteria,' he said repressively. 'Our journey to Qurhah may not be an expedition which either of us would choose, but I don't see why we can't conduct ourselves in a relatively civilised manner if we put our minds to it.'

'Civilised?' Sara stood up and pushed herself away from the desk so violently that a whole pile of coloured felt-tips fell clattering to the ground. But she barely registered the noise or the mess. She certainly didn't bend down to pick them up and not just because her skirt was so short. She felt a flare of rage and *impotence*—that Suleiman could just march in here as if he owned the place. Start flexing his muscles and telling her—*telling* her—that she must go back and marry a man she barely knew, didn't particularly like and certainly didn't *love*.

'You think it's civilised to hold a woman to a promise of marriage made when she was little more than a child? A forced marriage in which she had no say?'

'Your father himself agreed to this marriage,' said Suleiman implacably. 'You know that.'

'My father had no choice!' she flared. 'He was almost bankrupt by that point!'

'I'm afraid that your father's weakness and profligacy put him in that position. And let us not forget that it was the Sultan's father who saved him from certain bankruptcy!'

'By demanding my hand for his only son, in return?' she demanded. 'What kind of a man could do that, Suleiman?'

She saw that her heartfelt appeal had momentarily stilled him. That his flat black eyes had narrowed and were now partially obscured by the thick ebony lashes which had shuttered down to veil them. Had she been able to make him see the sheer lunacy of his proposal in this day and age? Couldn't he see that it was barbaric for a woman of twenty-three to be taken back to a desert kingdom—no matter how fabled—and to be married against her will?

Once Suleiman had regarded her fondly—she knew that. If he allowed himself to forget that stupid kiss— that single lapse which should never have happened— then surely there still existed in his heart some of that same fondness. Surely he wasn't happy for her to enter into such a barbaric union.

'These dynastic marriages have always taken place,' he said slowly. 'It will not be as bad as you envisage, Sara—'

'Really? How do you work that out?'

'It is a great honour to marry such a man as the Sultan,' he said, but he seemed to be having to force some kind of conviction into his words. He gave a heavy sigh. 'Do you have any idea of the number of women who would long to become his Sultana—'

'A sultana is something I put on my muesli every morning!' she spat back.

'You will be prized above all women,' he continued. 'And given the honour of bearing His Imperial Majesty's sons and heirs. What woman could ask for more?'

For a moment Sara didn't speak, she was so angry. The idea of such a marriage sounded completely abhorrent to her now, but, as Suleiman had just said, she had grown up in a world where such a barter was considered normal. She had been living in England for so long that it was easy to forget that she was herself a royal princess. That her English mother had married a desert king and produced a son and a much younger daughter.

If her mother had been alive she would have stopped this ludicrous marriage from happening, Sara was sure of that. But her mother had been dead for a long time— her father, too. And now the Sultan wanted to claim what was rightfully his.

She thought of the man who awaited her and she shivered. She knew that a lot of women thought of him as a swarthy sex-god, but she wasn't among them. During their three, heavily chaperoned meetings—she had felt nothing for him. Nada.

But mightn't that have had something to do with the fact that Suleiman had been present all those times? Suleiman with his glittering black eyes and his hard, honed body who had distracted her so badly that she couldn't think straight

She glared at him. 'Doesn't it strike at your conscience to take a woman back to Qurhah *against her will*? Do you always do whatever the Sultan asks you, without questioning it? His tame puppet!'

A nerve flickered at his temple. 'I no longer work for the Sultan.'

For a moment she stared at him in disbelief. 'What... what are you talking about? The Sultan values you above all other men. Everyone knows that. You are his prized emissary and the man on whom he relies.'

He shook his head. 'Not any longer. I have returned to my own land, where I have built a different kind of life for myself.'

She wanted to ask him what kind of life that was, but she reminded herself that what Suleiman did was none of her business. *He doesn't want you. He doesn't even seem to like you any more.* 'Then why are you here?'

'As a favour to Murat. He thought that you might prove too much of a challenge for most of his staff.'

'But not for you, I suppose?'

'Not for me,' he agreed.

She wanted to tell him to wipe that smug smile off his face and get out of her office and if he didn't, then she would call security and get them to remove him. But was that such a good idea? Her eyes flickered doubtfully over his powerful body and immovable stance. Was she seriously suggesting that *anyone* could budge him if he didn't want to go?

She thought about her boss. Wouldn't Gabe Steel have Suleiman evicted from the building if she asked him? Though when she stopped to think about it—did she really want to go bleating to her boss for help? She had no desire to blight her perfect working record by bringing her private life into the workplace. Because wouldn't Gabe—and all her colleagues—be amazed to discover that she wasn't just someone called Sara Williams, but a half-blood desert princess from the desert country of Dhi'ban? That she had capitalised on her mother's English looks and used her mother's English surname to blend in since she'd been working here in London. And blend in, she had—adopting the fashions and the attitudes of other English women her age.

No, this was not a time for opposition—or at least, not a time for *open* opposition. She didn't want Suleiman's suspicions alerted. She needed to lull him. To let him think that he had won. That she would go with him—not *too* meekly or he would suspect that something was amiss, but that she *would* go with him.

She shrugged her shoulders as if she were reluctantly conceding victory and backed it up with a resigned sigh. 'I suppose there's no point in me trying to change your mind?'

His smile was cold. 'Do you really think you could?'

'No, I suppose not,' she said, as if his indifference didn't matter. As if she didn't care what he thought of her.

But she felt as if somebody had just taken her dreams and trampled on them. He was the only man she had ever wanted. The only man she'd ever loved. Yet Suleiman thought so little of her that he could just hand her over to another man, as if she were a parcel he was delivering.

'Don't look like that, Sara.' His black eyes narrowed and she saw that little muscle flicker at his temple once more. 'If you open your mind a little—you might find that you can actually enjoy your new life. That you can be a good wife. You will have strong sons and beautiful daughters and this will make the people of Qurhah very happy.'

For a moment, Sara thought she heard the hint of uncertainty in his voice. As if he was trotting out the official line without really believing it. Was he? Or was it true what they said—that something in his own upbringing had hardened his heart so that it was made of stone? So that he didn't care about other people's feelings—because he didn't have any of his own.

Well, Suleiman's feelings were none of her business. She didn't care about them because she couldn't afford to. She needed to know what his plans were—and how to react to them accordingly.

'So what happens now?' she asked casually. 'Do I give a month's notice here and then fly out to Qurhah towards the end of January?'

His mouth twisted, as if she had just said something uniquely funny. 'You think that you are free to continue to make the Sultan wait for your presence?' he questioned. 'I'm afraid that those days are over. You will fly out to Qurhah tonight. And you are leaving this building with me, right now.'

Panic—pure and simple—overwhelmed her. She could feel the doors of the prison clanging to a close. Suleiman's dark features blurred for a second, before clicking back into sharp focus, and she tried to pull herself together.

'I'll…I'll need to pack first,' she said.

'Of course.' He inclined his dark head but not before she could see the sudden glint of fire in his eyes. 'Though I doubt whether your mini-skirt will cut it in your new role as Sultana. A far more suitable wardrobe will be provided for you, so why bother?'

'I'm not talking about my clothes!' she flared back. 'Surely you won't deny me my trinkets and keepsakes? The jewellery my mother left me and the book my father published after her death?'

For a moment she wondered if she had imagined the faint look of disquiet which briefly flickered in his eyes. But it was gone as quickly as it had appeared and she told herself to stop attributing thoughts and feelings to him, just because she wanted him to have them. Because he didn't.

'Very well,' he said. 'That can be arranged. Now let's go—I have a car waiting downstairs.'

Sara's heart missed a beat. Of course he had a car waiting. Probably with a couple of heavies inside. That feeling of being trapped closed in on her again and suddenly she knew that she wasn't going to take this lying down. She would not go meekly with Suleiman Abd al-Aziz—she would slip through his hands like an eel plucked from an icy river.

'I have to finish up in here,' she said. 'I can't just walk out for ever without putting my work in some kind of order.'

His face was unreadable. 'How long will it take?'

Sara felt her mouth dry as she wondered realistically how much time she could plead to play with. 'A few hours?'

'Don't test my patience, Sara. Two hours will be more than adequate for what you need to do. I will be waiting with my men at your apartment.' He walked over to the door and paused. 'And don't be late,' he said softly.

With one final warning flickering from his black eyes, he was gone. She waited until she heard the ping of the lift in the corridor and the sound of the elevator doors closing—but she was still paranoid enough to poke her head outside the office to check that he really *had* gone. That he wasn't standing in the shadows spying on her and waiting to see what she would do next.

She shut the office door and walked over to one of the giant windows which overlooked the dark glitter of the river, feeling a stab of pain in her heart. She had loved working here. She had loved the freedom and the creativity of being part of Gabe Steel's enormous organisation.

But now it was all coming to an end, whether she wanted it to or not.

Like hell it was.

An idea began to form in her mind. A plan so audacious that for a moment she wondered if she dared go
ahead with it. Yet what choice did she have? To go with
Suleiman, like a sheep to the slaughter? To be forced
to share a bed with the hawk-faced Sultan—a man for
whom she had felt not one whisper of chemistry?

She picked up the office phone instead of her own
mobile phone. Because if they'd had bodyguards watching her all this time—who was to say they hadn't
bugged her phone?

It didn't take her long to get the information she
wanted from the Business Development Director, who
was in charge of the company's public relations. Judging
by the noise in the background, he was clearly at some
sort of Christmas party and gave her a list of journalists without asking any questions.

Her fingers were trembling as she dialled the first
number and listened to the ring tone. Maybe nobody
would pick up. Maybe they'd all set off home for Christmas—all going to some storybook destination with a
wreath on the door and a roaring log fire, with the smell
of chestnuts and pine scenting the air.

They wouldn't be spending their Christmas Eve like
her—with a car full of cold-faced men sitting outside
the building, waiting to take her away to an unknown
and unwanted future.

'Hello?'

She took a deep breath. 'Look, I know this is going
to sound crazy—but I've got a story you might be interested in.' Her fingers dug into the phone as she listened.
'Details? Sure I can give you details. How about the pro-

posed kidnap of a woman, who is being taken against her will to the desert country of Qurhah to marry a man she doesn't want to marry? You like that? I rather thought you might—and it's all yours. An exclusive. But we haven't got long. I need to leave London before six o' clock.'

CHAPTER TWO

SULEIMAN BROUGHT THE car to a halt so that it was hidden beneath the shadows of the trees, but still within sight of the cottage. The other cars all waited in darkness at various intervals down the country lane, as he had instructed them to do.

He turned off the lights. Rain spattered relentlessly across the windscreen, running in thick rivulets down the glass. For a moment he sat watching the lighted windows of the house. He saw Sara's unmistakable silhouette going around, pulling the drapes tightly shut, and he felt a potent combination of anger and satisfaction. But alongside his triumph at having tracked her down, a deep disquiet ran through his veins like slow poison.

He should have refused this job.

He should have told Murat that his schedule did not allow him time to travel to England and deal with the princess.

But the Sultan did not ask favours of many men and the bonds of loyalty and gratitude ran deeper than Suleiman had anticipated. And although he would have given anything to have avoided this particular task, somehow he had found himself accepting it. Yet just one sight of her today had reinforced what a fool he had been. Better to have thrown himself to the mercy of a starving lion, than to have willingly closeted himself with the temptress Sara.

He remembered the honeyed taste of her lips and her intoxicating perfume of jasmine mixed with patchouli. He remembered the pert thrust of her breast beneath his questing fingers and the way his body had ached for her afterwards. The frustrated lust which seemed to have gone on for months.

His hands tightened around the steering wheel. Women like her were born to create trouble. To make men want them and then to use their sexual power to destroy them. Hadn't her own mother—a fabled beauty in her time—brought down the king who had spent his life in slavish devotion to her? A husband who had spent so much time enthralled by her that he had barely noticed his country slipping into bankruptcy.

He drew in a deep, meditative breath, forcing all the frustrating thoughts from his mind. He must go and do what he needed to do and then leave and never see her again.

With a stealth nurtured by years of undercover work, he waited until he was certain the coast was clear before he got out of the car and silently pulled the door shut behind him. He saw one of the limousines parked further down the lane flash its lights at him.

Avoiding the crunch of the gravel path, he felt his shoes sink into the sodden mud of the lawn which ran alongside it. But the night was fearsome and the weather atrocious and he was soaked within seconds, despite his long-legged stride towards the front door.

He was half tempted to break in by one of the back windows and then to walk in and confront her to show just how vulnerable she really was. But that would be cruel and he had no desire to be cruel to her.

Did he?

His mouth hardened as he lifted one rain-soaked hand to the door handle and knocked.

If she was sensible, she wouldn't answer. Instead, she would phone the local police station and tell them she had an intruder banging on the door of this isolated cottage on Christmas Eve.

But clearly she wasn't being sensible because he could hear the sound of her approaching footsteps and his body tensed as adrenalin flooded through him.

She pulled open the door, her violet eyes widening as she registered his identity. For a split second she reacted quickly, trying desperately to shut the door again—but her reactions were not as fast as his. Few people's were. He placed the flat of his hand on the weathered knocker and blocked her move until she had the sense to step back as he entered the hallway, pushing the door shut behind him.

For a moment there was silence in that small hallway, other than the soft drip of rainwater onto the stone tiles. He could see that she was too stunned to speak—and so was he, but for very different reasons. She might be regarding him with horror but no such feelings were dominating his own mind right then.

She had changed from the provocative dress she'd been wearing in her office earlier. Her hair was loose and her jeans and pink sweater were not particularly clingy, yet still they managed to showcase the magnificence of her body.

He knew it was wrong but he couldn't stop himself from drinking her in, like a man lost in the desert who had just been handed a jug of cool water. Was she aware of her beauty? Of the fact that she looked like a goddess? A goddess in blue jeans.

'Suleiman!' Her voice sounded startled and her violet eyes were dark.

'Surprised?' he questioned.

'You could say that! And horrified.' She glared at him. 'What do you think you're doing—pushing your way in here like some sort of heavy?'

'I thought we had an appointment to meet at six, but since it is now almost eight, you appear to have broken it. Shockingly bad manners, Sara. Especially for a future queen of the desert.'

'Tough!' she retorted. 'And I'm not going to be a queen of the desert. I already told you that I have no intention of getting married. Not to Murat and not to anyone! So why waste everybody's time by turning up? Can't you just go back to the Sultan and tell him to forget the whole idea?'

Suleiman heard the determination in her voice and felt an unwilling flare of admiration for her unashamed—and very stupid—defiance. Such open insubordination was unheard of from a woman from the desert lands and it was rather magnificent to observe her spirited rebellion. But he didn't let it show. Instead, he injected a note of disapproval into his voice. 'I am waiting for an explanation about why you failed to show.'

'Do you realise you sound exactly like a school-teacher? I don't really think you'd need to be a detective to work out my no-show. I don't like having my arm twisted.'

'Clearly you hadn't thought things through properly, if you imagined it was going to be that easy to shake me off,' he said. 'But you're here now.'

She eyed him speculatively 'I could knock you over the back of the head and make a run for it.'

His mouth quirked at the corners, despite all his best efforts not to smile. 'And if you did, you would run straight into the men I have positioned all the way down the lane. Don't even think about it, Sara. And please don't imagine that I haven't thought of every eventuality, because I have.'

He pulled off his dripping coat and hung it on a peg.

She glared at him. 'I don't remember asking you to take your coat off!'

'I don't require your permission.'

'You are impossible!' she hissed.

'I have never denied that.'

'Oh,' she said, her voice frustrated as she turned round and marched towards a room where he could see a fire blazing.

He followed her into a room which had none of the ornaments the English were so fond of cramming into their country homes. There were no china dogs or hang-

ings made of brass. No jumbled oil paintings of ships
which hinted at a naval past. Instead, the walls were pale
and contrasted with the weathered beams of wood in the
ceiling. The furniture was quirky but looked comfortable and the few contemporary paintings worked well,
though in theory they shouldn't have done. Whoever
owned this had taste, as well as money.

'Whose cottage is this?' he questioned.

'My lover's.'

He took a step forward, so that his shadow fell over
her defiant features. 'Please don't jest with me, Sara.
I'm not in the mood for it.'

'How do you know I'm jesting?'

'I hope you are. Because if I thought for a moment
that you had been intimate with another man—then I
would seek him out and tear him from limb to limb.'

As she heard his venomous but undoubtedly truthful
words Sara swallowed, reminding herself that it wasn't
a question of Suleiman being jealous. He had only ut-
tered the threat out of loyalty to the Sultan.

She wished he hadn't turned up and yet if she'd
stopped to think about it for more than a second—she
must have known he would follow her. If Suleiman
took on a task, then Suleiman would see it through. No
matter what obstacles were put before him, he would
conquer them. *That* was why the Sultan had asked
him—and why he was so respected and feared within
the desert nations.

She had driven here without really thinking about
the consequences of her action, only about her urgent
need to get away. Not just from the dark certainty of

her future, but from this man. The man who had rejected her, yet could still make her heart race with desire and longing.

But his face was as cold as a stone mask. His body language was tense and forbidding. Suleiman's feelings towards her had clearly not changed since the night he'd kissed her and then thrust her away from him. She swallowed. How could she bear to spend hours travelling with him, towards a dark fate which seemed unendurable?

'It's my boss, Gabe Steel's cottage,' she said. 'And how did you find me?'

'It wasn't difficult,' he said. 'You forget that I have tracked down quarry far more elusive than a stubborn princess. Actually, it was your sudden unexpected consent to my plan which alerted my suspicions. It is not like you to be so *acquiescent,* Sara. I suspected that you would try to give my men the slip so I hid outside the side entrance to your office block and followed you to the car park.'

'You *hid*? Outside my office block?'

'You find that so bizarre?'

'Of course I do!' Her heart was hammering in her chest. 'I live in England now and I live an English life, Suleiman. One where men don't usually lurk in shadows, following women who don't want to be followed. Why, you could have been arrested for trespass—especially if my boss had any idea that you were *stalking* me.'

'Unlikely—for I am never seen if I do not wish to be seen,' he said arrogantly. 'You must have known it was a futile attempt to try to escape, so why do it, Sara? Did you really think you could get away with it?'

'Go to hell!'

'I'm not going anywhere and certainly not without you.'

She hated the ruthless tone of his voice. She hated the unresponsive look on his hard face. Suddenly she wanted to shake him. To provoke him. To get some sort of reaction which would make her feel as if she was dealing with a real person, instead of a cold block of stone. 'I was waiting here,' she said deliberately. 'For my lover.'

'I don't think so.'

'And why not?' she demanded. 'Am I so repulsive that you can't imagine that a man might actually want to take me to bed?'

For a moment Suleiman stilled, telling himself that he wouldn't fall into the trap she was so obviously laying for him. She was trying to rile him. Trying to get him to admit to something he was not prepared to admit. Even to himself. Concentrate on the facts, he told himself fiercely—and not on her blonde-haired beauty, or her soft curves which nature must have invented with the intention of sending any man crazy with longing.

'I think you know the answer to that question—and I'm not going to flatter your ego by answering it. Your desirability has never been in question, but you seem to imply that your virtue is.'

'What if it is?' she challenged, her voice growing reckless. 'But I don't have to explain myself to you and

I'm certainly not going to take orders from you. Do you want to know why?'

'Not really,' he said, in a bored tone.

'I think you might.' She licked her lips in a cat-got-the-cream expression and then smiled. 'It might interest you to know that in between your invasion of my office and following me here, I have spoken to a journalist.'

There was a pause. Suleiman's eyes narrowed. 'I hope that's a joke.'

'It's not.'

There was another moment of silence before he could bring himself to speak. 'And what did you tell the journalist?'

She scraped her fingers back through her blonde hair and smirked. 'I told him the truth. No need to look so scared, Suleiman. I mean, who in their right mind could possibly object to the truth?'

'Let's get one thing straight,' he said, biting the words out from between gritted teeth. 'I am not scared—of anyone or anything. I think you may be in danger of mistaking my anger for fear, though perhaps you would do well to feel fear yourself. Because if the Sultan finds out that you have spoken to the western press, then things are going to get very tricky. So I shall ask you again and this time I want a straight answer—what exactly did you tell the journalist?'

Sara stared into the spitting blackness of his eyes and some of her bravado wavered, until she told herself that she wasn't going to be intimidated. She had worked too hard and too long to forge a new life to allow these powerful men to control her. These desert men who would crush your very spirit if you allowed them to do so. So she wouldn't let them.

Even her own mother—who had married a desert king and had loved him—had felt imprisoned by ancient royal rules which hadn't changed for centuries and probably never would. Sara had witnessed for herself that sometimes love just wasn't enough. So what chance would a marriage have if there was no love at all?

Her mother's unhappiness had been the cause of her father's ruination—and had ultimately governed Sara's own fate. She hadn't known that Papa was so obsessed by his English wife that he hadn't paid proper attention to governing his country. Sara remembered that all too vividly. The Queen had been his possession and nothing else had really existed for him, apart from that.

He had taken his eye off the ball. Poor investments and a border war which went on too long meant that his country was left bankrupt. The late Sultan of Qurhah had come up with a deal for a bail-out plan and the price had been Sara's hand in marriage.

When Sara's mother had died and she had been allowed to go off to boarding school—hadn't she thought that her father's debt would just be allowed to fade with time? Hadn't she been naïve and hopeful enough to think that the Sultan might just forget all about marrying her, as his own father had decreed he should?

Blinking back the sudden threat of tears, Sara tried to ignore the fierce expression on Suleiman's face. She was *not* going to be made to feel guilty—when all she was doing was trying to save her own skin. And ultimately she would be doing the Sultan a favour—for surely it would damage the ego of such a powerful man if she was forced kicking and screaming to the altar.

'I am waiting,' he said, with silky venom, 'for you to enlighten me. What did you tell the journalist, Sara?'

She met the accusation in his eyes. 'I told him everything.'

'Everything?'

'Yes! I thought it would make a good story,' she said. 'At a time of year when newspapers are traditionally very light on news and—'

'What did you tell him?' he raged.

'I told him the truth! That I was a half-blood princess—half English and half Dhi'banese. You know the papers—they just love any kind of royal connection!' She forced a mocking smile, knowing that it would irritate him and wondering if irritating him was only a feeble attempt to suppress her desire for him. Because if it was, it wasn't working. 'I told him that my mother travelled as an artist to Dhi'ban, to paint the beautiful desert landscape—and that my father, the king, had fallen in love with her.'

'Why did you feel it necessary to parade your private family history to a complete stranger?'

'I'm just providing the backstory, Suleiman,' she said. 'Everyone knows you need a good backstory if you want an entertaining read. Anyway, it's all there on record.'

'You are severely testing my patience,' he said. 'You had no right to divulge these things!'

'Surely the Sultan wouldn't mind me discussing it?' she questioned innocently. 'This is a marriage we're talking about, Suleiman—and marriages are supposed to be happy occasions. I say *supposed* to be, but that's quite a difficult concept to pull off when the bride is being kidnapped! I have to say that the journalist seemed quite surprised when I told him that I had no say in this marriage. No, when I come to think of it— surprise is the wrong word. I'd say that astonished covered it better. And deeply shocked, of course.'

'Shocked?'

'Mmm. He seemed to find it odd—abhorrent, even— that the Sultan of Qurhah should want to marry a woman who had been bought for him by his own father!'

She saw his fists clench.

'That is the way of the world you were brought into,' he said unequivocably. 'None of us can change the circumstances of our birth.'

'No, we can't. But that doesn't mean we have to be made prisoners by it. We can use everything in our power to change our destinies! Can't you see that, Suleiman?'

'No!'

'Yes,' she argued passionately. 'Yes and a thousand times yes!' Her heart began to race as she saw something written on his carved features which made her stomach turn to jelly. Was it anger? Was it?

But anger would not have made him shake his head, as if he was trying to shake off thoughts of madness. Nor to make that little nerve flicker so violently at his olive-skinned temple. He took a step towards her and, for one heart-stopping moment, she thought he was about to pull her into his arms, the way he'd done on the night of her brother's coronation.

And didn't she want that? Wasn't she longing for him to do just that, only this time not stop? This time they were alone and he could lie her down in front of that log fire and loosen her clothes and...

But he didn't touch her. He stood a tantalisingly close distance away while his eyes sparked dark fire at her. She could see him swallowing, as if he had something bitter lodged in his throat.

'You must accept your destiny,' he said. 'As I have accepted mine.'

'Have you? Did "accepting your destiny" include kissing me on the night my brother was crowned, even though you knew I was promised to another?'

'Don't say that!'

The strangled words sounded almost *powerless* and Sara realised she'd never heard Suleiman sound like that before. Not even after he'd returned from his undercover duties in the Qurhah army, when he'd been thirty pounds lighter with a scar zigzagging down his neck. People said he'd been tortured, but if he had he never spoke of it—well, never to her. She remembered being profoundly shocked by his appearance and she felt a similar kind of shock washing over her now.

For it was not like looking at Suleiman she knew of old. It was like looking at a stranger. A repressed and forbidding stranger. His features had closed up and his eyes were hooded. Had she really thought he was about to kiss her? Why, kissing looked like the furthest thing on his mind.

'We will not speak of that night again,' he said.

'But it's true, isn't it?' she questioned. 'You weren't so moralistic when you touched me like that.'

'Because most men would have died rather than resist you that night,' he admitted bitterly. 'And I chose not to die. I hadn't seen you for six long years and then I saw you, with your big painted eyes and your silver gown, shining like the moon.'

Briefly, Suleiman closed his eyes, because that kiss had been like no other, no matter how much he had tried to deny it. It hadn't just been about sex or lust. It had been much more powerful than that, and infinitely more dangerous. It had been about feeding a hunger as fundamental as the need to eat or drink. It had felt as necessary as breathing. And yet it had angered him, because it had seemed outside his control. Up until that moment he had regarded the young princess with nothing more than indulgent friendship. What had happened that night had taken him completely by surprise. He swallowed. Perhaps that was why it had been the most unforgettable kiss of his life.

'Didn't you realise how much I wanted you that night, Sara, even though you were promised to the Sultan? Were you not aware of your own power?'

'So it was all my fault?'

'No. It is not your "fault" that you looked beautiful enough to test the appetites of a saint. I blame no one but myself for my unforgivable weakness. But it is a weakness which will never be repeated,' he ground out.

'And yes, I blame you if you have now given an interview which will bring shame on the reputation of the Sultan and his royal house.'

'Then ask him to set me free,' she said simply. 'To let me go. Please, Suleiman.'

Suleiman met the appeal in her big violet eyes and for a moment he almost wavered. For wasn't it a terrible crime to see the beautiful and spirited Sara forced to marry a man she did not love? Could he really imagine her lying in the marital bed and submitting to the embraces of a man she claimed not to want? And then he told himself that Murat was a legendary lover. And even though it made him feel sick to acknowledge it—it was unlikely that Sara would lie unresponsive in Murat's bed for too long.

'I can't do that,' he said, but the words felt like stone as he let them fall from his lips. 'I can't allow you to reject the Sultan; I would be failing in my duty if I did. It is a question of pride.'

'Pride!' Angrily, she shook her head. 'What price pride? What if I refuse to allow him to consummate the marriage?' she challenged. 'What then? Won't he skulk away to his harem and take his pleasure elsewhere?'

He flinched as if she had hit him. 'This discussion has become completely inappropriate,' he bit out angrily. 'But you would be wise to consider the effect of your actions on your brother, the King—even though I know you never bother to visit him. There are some in your country who wonder whether the King still has a sister, so rarely does she set foot in her homeland.'

'My relationship with my brother is none of your business—and neither are my trips home!'

'Maybe not. But you would do well to remember that Qurhah continues to shoulder some of your country's national debt. How would your brother feel if the Sultan were to withdraw his financial support because of your behaviour?'

'You *bastard*,' she hissed, but she might as well have been whispering on the wind, for all the notice he took.

'My skin is thick enough to withstand your barbed comments, princess. I am delivering you to the Sultan and nothing will prevent that. But first, I want the name of the journalist you've been dealing with.'

She made one last stab at rebellion. 'And if I won't tell you?'

'Then I will find out for myself,' he said, in a tone which made a shiver trickle down her spine. 'Why not save me the time and yourself my anger?'

'You're a brute,' she breathed. 'An egocentric brute.'

'No, Sara, I just want the story spiked.'

Frustration washed over her as she recognised that he meant business. And that she was fighting a useless battle here.

'His name is Jason Cresswell,' she said sulkily. 'He works for the *Daily View.*'

'Good. Perhaps you are finally beginning to see sense. You might learn that co-operation is infinitely more preferable to rebellion. Now leave me while I speak with him in private.' He glanced at her as he pulled his mobile phone from his pocket.

'Go and get your coat on. Because after I've finished with the journalist we're heading for the airfield, where the plane is waiting to take you to your new life in Qurhah.'

CHAPTER THREE

THE FLIGHT WAS smooth and the aircraft supremely comfortable but Suleiman couldn't sleep. For the past seven hours during the journey to Qurhah, he had been kept awake by the tormenting thoughts of what he was doing.

He felt his heart clench. What *was* he doing?

Taking a woman to a man she did not love.

A woman he wanted for himself.

Restlessly, he moved noiselessly around the craft, wishing that there were somewhere to look other than at the sleeping Sara. But although he could have joined the two pilots in the cockpit or tried to rest in the sealed-off section at the far end of the plane, neither option appealed. He couldn't seem to tear his eyes away from her.

He wondered if the silent female servants who were sitting sentry had noticed the irresistible direction of his gaze. Or the fact that he had not left the side of the sleeping princess. But he didn't care—for who would dare challenge him?

He had fulfilled the first part of his task by getting Sara on board the plane. He just wished he could shake off this damned feeling of *guilt*.

Their late exit from the cottage into the driving rain had left her soaking wet for she had stubbornly refused to use the umbrella he'd opened for her. And as she had sat shivering beside him in the car he'd fought the powerful urge to pull her into his arms and to rub at her cold flesh until she was warm again. But he had vowed that he would not touch her again.

He could never touch her again.

He let his eyes drift over her.

Stretched out in the wide aircraft seat in her crumpled jeans and sweater, she should have looked unremarkable but that was the very last thing she looked. He felt his gut tighten. The sculpted angles of her bone structure hinted at her aristocratic lineage and her eyelashes were naturally dark. Even her blonde hair, which had dried into tousled strands, looked like layered starlight.

She was beautiful.

The most beautiful woman he'd ever seen.

His heart clenched as he turned away, but his troubled thoughts continued to plague him.

He knew the Sultan's reputation. He knew that he was a charismatic man where women were concerned and that most of his former lovers still yearned for him. But Murat the Mighty was a desert man and he believed in destiny. He would marry the princess who had been chosen for him, for to do otherwise would be to renege on an ancient pact. He would marry and take his new bride back to the Qurhahian palace. He would think nothing of it.

Suleiman winced as he tried to imagine Sara being

closed off for ever in the Sultan's gilded world and felt a terrible darkness enter his heart.

He heard the small sound she made as she stirred, blinking open her eyes to look at him so that he found himself staring into dark pools of violet ink.

Sitting up, she pushed her tousled hair away from her face. Was she aware that he had been watching her while she slept, and that it had felt unbelievably intimate to do so? Would she be shocked to know that he had imagined moving aside the cashmere blanket and climbing in beside her?

She lifted her arms above her head to yawn and in that moment she looked so *free* that another wave of guilt washed over him.

What would she be like when she'd had her wings clipped by the pressures and the demands of her new position as Sultana? Did she realise that never again would she wear her faded blue jeans or move around anonymously as she had done in London? Did she realize—as he now did—that this trip was the last time he would ever be permitted to be alone with her?

'You're awake,' he said.

'Top marks for observation,' she said, raking her fingers back through her hair to subdue it. 'Gosh, the Sultan must miss having you around if you come out with inspirational gems like that, Suleiman.'

'Are you going to be impertinent for the rest of the journey?'

'I might. If I feel like it.'

'Would a little tea lighten your mood, princess?'

Sara shrugged, wondering whether anything could

lighten her mood at that precise moment. Because this was fast becoming like her worst nightmare. She had been bundled onto the plane, with the Sultan's staff bowing and curtseying to her as soon as she had set foot on the private jet. These days she wasn't used to being treated like a princess and it made her feel uncomfortable. She had seen the surreptitious glances which had come shooting her way. Were they thinking: *Here's the princess who ran away?* Or were they thinking what an unworthy wife she would make for their beloved Sultan?

But the most troubling aspect was not that she was being taken somewhere against her will, to marry a man she didn't love. It was the stupid yearning feeling she got whenever she looked at Suleiman's shuttered features and found herself wishing that he would lose the uptight look and just kiss her. She found herself longing for the closeness of yesteryear, instead of this strange new tenseness which surrounded him.

She could guess *why* he was behaving so coolly towards her, but that didn't seem to alleviate this terrible *aching* which was gnawing away at her heart, despite all her anger and confusion.

'So. How did your "chat" with the journalist go?' she asked. 'Did he agree to kill the story?'

'He did.' He slanted her a triumphant look. 'I managed to convince him that your words were simply a heightened version of the normal nerves of a bride-to-be.'

'So you bribed him, I suppose? Offered him riches beyond his wildest dreams not to publish?'

Suleiman smiled. 'I'm afraid so.'

Frustratedly, Sara sank back against the cushions and watched Suleiman raise his hand in command, instantly bringing one of the servants scurrying over to take his order for tea. He was so *easy* with power, she thought. He acted as if he'd been born to it—which as far as she knew, he hadn't. She knew that he'd been schooled alongside the Sultan, but that was all she *did* know—because he was notoriously cagy about his past. He'd once told her that the strongest men were those who kept their past locked away from prying eyes—and while she could see the logic in that, it had always maddened her that she hadn't known more about what made him tick.

She took a sip of the fragrant camomile brew she was handed before putting her cup down to study him. 'You say you're no longer working for the Sultan?'

'That's right.'

'So what are you doing instead? Doesn't your new boss mind you flitting off to England like this?'

'I don't have a boss. I don't answer to anyone, Sara. I work for myself.'

'Doing what—providing bespoke kidnap services for reluctant brides?'

'I thought we'd agreed to lose the hysteria.'

'Doing what?' she persisted.

Suleiman cracked the knuckles of his fists and stared down at the whitened bones because that was a far less distracting sight than confronting the spark of interest in those beautiful violet eyes. 'I own an oil refinery and several very lucrative wells.'

'You own an oil refinery?' she repeated in disbelief. 'A baby one?'

'Quite a big one, actually.'

'How on earth can you afford to do that?'

He lifted his head and met the confusion in her gaze. He thought how inevitably skewed her idea of the world was—a world where kingdoms were lost and bought and bartered. His investigations into her London life had assured him that her job for Gabe Steel was bona fide, but he knew that she'd inherited her luxury apartment from her mother. Sara was a princess, he reminded himself grimly. She'd never wanted for anything.

'I played the stock market,' he said.

'Oh, come on—Suleiman. It can't be as simple as that. Loads of people play the stock market, but they don't all end up with oil refineries.'

He leaned back against the silken pile of cushions, an ill-thought-out move, since it put his eye-line on a level with her breasts. Instead, he fixed his gaze on her violet eyes.

'Even as a boy, I was always good with numbers,' he said. 'And later on, I found it almost *creative* to watch the movement of the markets and predict what was going to happen next. It was, if you like, a hobby— a consuming as well as a very profitable one. Over the years I managed to accrue a considerable amount of wealth, which I invested. I bought shares along the way which flourished. Some property here and there.'

'Where?'

'Some in Samahan and some in the Caribbean. But I was looking for something more challenging. On the hunch of a geologist I met on a plane to San Francisco, I began drilling in an area of my homeland which, up until that moment, everyone had thought was barren land. It provided one of the richest oil wells in Middle Eastern history.' He shrugged. 'I was lucky.'

Sara blinked at him, as if there was a fundamental part of the story missing. 'So you had all this money in the bank, yet you continued to work for the Sultan?'

'Why not? There is nothing to match the buzz of being in politics and I'd always enjoyed my role as his envoy.'

'So you did,' she agreed slowly. 'Until one day, something made you leave and start up on your own.'

'If you hadn't been a princess, you could have been a detective,' he said sardonically.

'So what was it, Suleiman? Why the big lifestyle change?'

'Isn't it right and natural that a man should have ambition?' he questioned, taking a sip of his own tea. 'That he should wish to be his own master?'

'What was it, Suleiman?' she repeated quietly.

Suleiman felt his body tense. Should he tell her? Would the truth weaken him in her eyes, or would it make her realise why this damned attraction which still sizzled between them could never be acted upon?

'It was you,' he said. 'You were the catalyst.'

'Me?'

'Yes, you. And why the innocent look of surprise? Haven't you yet learned that every action has a consequence, Sara? Think about it. The night you offered yourself to me—'

'It was a kiss, for heavens sake!' she croaked.

'It was more than a kiss and we both know it,' he continued remorselessly. 'Or are you saying that, if I had pushed you against the shadowed palace wall for yet more intimacy, you would have stopped me?'

'Suleiman!'

'Are you saying that?' he repeated, but he found her blush deeply satisfying—for it spoke of an innocence he had begun to question. And wouldn't it be better to air all his bitterness and frustration so that he could let it out and move on, as he needed to move on? As they both did.

'No,' she said, the word a flat, small admission. 'How can I deny it?'

'I felt shame,' he continued. 'Not so much for what I had done, but for what I wanted to do. I had betrayed the Sultan in the worst way imaginable and I could no longer count myself as his most loyal aide.'

She was looking at him in disbelief. 'So one kiss made you resign?'

He nearly told her the rest, but he stopped himself in time. If he admitted that he couldn't bear to think of her in another man's arms and that he found it intolerable to contemplate her being married to the Sultan and being forced to look on from the sidelines. If he explained that the thought of another man thrusting deep inside her body made him feel sick—then wouldn't that reveal more than it was safe to reveal? Wouldn't it make temptation creep out from behind the shadows?

'It would have been impossible for me to work alongside your new husband with you as his wife,' he said.

'I see.'

And she did see. Or rather, she saw some of it. Sara stared at the black-haired man sitting before her, because now the pieces of the puzzle were beginning to form a more coherent shape. Suleiman had *wanted* her. Really wanted her. And now she was beginning to suspect that he still did. Behind the rigid pose he presented and the wall of disapproval, there still burned *something*. He had all but admitted it just now.

Didn't that explain the way his body tensed whenever she grew close? Why his dark eyes had grown stormy and opaque when he'd studied her short skirt that day in the office. It was not indifference towards her as she had first thought.

It was Suleiman trying to hide the fact that he still wanted her.

She licked her dry lips and saw his eyes follow the movement of her tongue, as if he was being compelled to do something against his will. Was he remembering—as she was—when his own tongue had entered her mouth and made her moan with pleasure?

Her head was spinning; her thoughts were confused but as they began to clear she saw a possible solution to her dilemma. What if she used Suleiman's desire for her to her own advantage? What if she tempted him beyond endurance and *seduced* him, what then? If they finished off what they had started all those years ago, wasn't that a way out for her? He was a single-minded man, yes, and a determined one, but there was no way he could present her to Murat if he had been intimate with her himself.

Could she do it? Could she? She was certainly no seductress, but how difficult could it be to beguile the only man she had ever really wanted?

She rose to her feet. 'Where's the bathroom?' she asked.

'Through there,' he said—pointing towards the door at the far end of the cabin.

She reached up towards the rack to retrieve the bag she'd brought with her and Suleiman moved forward to help, but she shook her head with a sudden fierce show of independence. She might want him, but she didn't need him. She didn't need any man. Wasn't that the whole point of her carefree life in London? That she didn't have to be tied down and trapped. 'I'm perfectly capable of doing it myself.'

She disappeared into the bathroom, emerging a short while later with her blonde hair brushed and woven into a neat chignon. She had changed from her jeans and sweater and replaced them with clothes more suited to the desert climate of Qurhah.

Her slim-fitting linen trousers and long-sleeved silk shirt now covered most of her flesh, but, despite the concealing outfit, she felt curiously *exposed* as she walked back towards him. Her legs were unsteady and her stomach was tying itself up in knots as she sat down. For a moment she couldn't quite bring herself to meet Suleiman's eyes, terrified that he might discover the subversive nature of her thoughts.

'So what happens when we arrive?' she questioned. 'Will an armed guard be taking over from you? Will I be handcuffed, perhaps?'

'We are landing at one of the military airbases,' he said. 'That way, your arrival won't be marred by the curiosity of onlookers at Qurhah's international airport.'

'In case I make a break for freedom, you mean?'

'I thought we'd discounted this rather hysterical approach of yours?' he said. 'And since the threat of desert storms has been brewing for days, it is considered unsafe for us to use a helicopter to get you to the Sultan's summer residence. So it might interest you to know that we will be travelling there by traditional means.'

At this, Sara's head jerked up in surprise. 'You don't mean an old-fashioned camel caravan?'

Suleiman smiled. 'Indeed I do. A little-used means of desert travel nowadays, but many of the nomadic people still claim it is the most efficient.'

'And who's to say they aren't right? Gosh, I haven't been on one since I was a child.' Sara looked at him, her violet eyes shining with excitement. 'And of course, this means that there will be horses, too.'

Suleiman felt his throat tighten. Was it wrong that he found the look on her face utterly captivating? That her smile would have warmed a tent on the coldest desert night. 'I had forgotten how much you enjoyed riding,' he said.

'Well, you shouldn't—because it's thanks to you that I ride so well.'

'You were an exemplary pupil,' he said gruffly.

She inclined her head, as if she was acknowledging the sudden cessation in hostilities between them. 'Thank you. But your lessons were what gave me my confidence and my ability.'

'Do you still ride?'

She shook her head. 'There aren't too many stables in the middle of London.' She looked at him. 'But I miss it.'

Something about the vulnerable pout of her lips made him ask the indulgent question, despite his own silent protestations that their conversation was becoming much too intimate. 'And what do you miss about it?'

She wriggled her shoulders. 'It's the time when I feel most free, I guess.'

Their eyes met and Suleiman saw a sudden shadow cross her face. It was almost as if she'd just remembered something—something which made her face take on a new and determined expression.

He watched as she smoothed down the silk of her blouse, her fingers whispering over the delicate material which covered her ribcage. Why did she insist on doing that, he wondered furiously—when all it was doing was making him focus on her body? And he must *stop* thinking of her body. And her violet eyes. He must think of her only as the woman who would soon be married to the Sultan—the man for whom he would lay down his life.

'We're nearly there,' he said, his sudden lust tempered by relief as the powerful jet began its descent.

Their arrival at the airbase had been kept deliberately low-key, since all celebrations had been put on hold until the wedding. Suleiman watched the natural grace with which Sara walked down the aircraft steps and then moved along the small line of officials who were assembled to meet her. She had lowered her lashes to a demure level, in order to conceal the brilliant gleam of her eyes, and her lips were curved into a serene and highly appropriate little smile. She could easily become an exemplary Sultana, he thought, despising himself for the dull ache of disappointment which followed this thought.

Afterwards, he watched her look around her, as if she was reacquainting herself with the vastness and beauty of the desert. He saw the admiration in her eyes as she gazed up at the mighty herd of camels standing at the edge of the airstrip, where the land was always waiting to encroach. And wasn't she only reflecting his own feelings about this particular form of transport?

A camel caravan could consist of a hundred and fifty animals, but since this endeavour was mainly ceremonial there were no more than eighteen beasts. Some were topped with lavishly fringed tents while others carried necessary provisions for the journey. Men on horseback moved up and down the line, riding some of the finest Akhal-Teke horses in the world, their distinctive coats gleaming metallic in the bright sun.

'It's pretty spectacular, isn't it?' he observed.

'It's more than that. I think it's one of the most beautiful sights in the world,' she said softly.

He turned to her and suddenly he didn't care if he was breaking protocol in the eyes of the onlookers. Wasn't this his opportunity to make amends for having let his lust override his duty to the Sultan, on the night of her brother's coronation? Couldn't he say the *right* thing to her now? The thing she needed to hear, rather than the impure thoughts which were still making him hard whenever he was near her.

'That is genuine passion I hear in your voice, Sara,' he said. 'Can't you piece together the many things you love about the desert? Then you could flick through them as you would a precious photo album—and be grateful for the many beauties of the life which will be yours when you marry.'

'But they won't be mine, will they?' she demanded. 'Everything will belong to my husband—including me! Because we both know that, by law, women in Qurhah are not allowed ownership of anything. I'll just be there, some bored figurehead, sitting robed and trapped. Free only to communicate with my husband and my female servants—apart from at official functions, and even then the guests to whom I will be introduced will be highly vetted. I don't know how the Sultan's sister stands it.'

'The Princess Leila is deeply contented in her royal role,' said Suleiman.

Sara closed her lips together. That wasn't what she'd heard. Apparently, at the famous Qurhah Gold Cup races, Leila had been seen looking glum—but it was hardly her place to drop the princess in it.

'I'll probably have to fight to be able to ride a horse,' she continued. 'And only when any stray man has been cleared away from the scene in case he dares *look* at me. *And* I'll probably be forced to ride side-saddle.'

'You do not have to be bored,' he argued. 'Boredom is simply a question of attitude. You could use your good fortune and good health to make Qurhah a better place. You could do important work for charity.'

'That goes without saying,' she said. 'I'm more than happy to do that. But am I to be consigned to a love-less marriage, simply because my country got itself into debt?'

Suleiman felt a terrible conflict raging within him. The conflict of believing what was right and knowing what was wrong. The conflict of duty versus desire. He wanted nothing more than to rescue her from her fate. To tell her that she need not marry a man she did not love. And then to drag her off to some dark cor-ner and slide those silken robes from her lush young body. He wanted to rub the nub of his thumb between her legs, to feel the moist flowering of her sex as her body prepared itself for his entry. He wanted to bite at her breasts. To leave the dark indentation of his teeth behind. His mark. So that no other man would be able to touch her...

With an effort he closed his mind to the torture of his erotic thoughts—for that way lay madness. He could do nothing other than what he had promised to do. He would deliver Sara to the Sultan and he would forget her, just as he had forgotten every woman he had ever lain with.

'This is your destiny,' he breathed. 'And you can-not escape it.'

'No?'

He watched, fascinated and appalled as the rosy tip of her tongue emerged from her lips and began to trace a featherlight path around their cupid's bow. And suddenly all he could think about was the exquisite gleam of those lips.

'You can't think of any alternative solution to my dilemma?' she questioned softly.

For a moment he thought of entering eagerly into the madness which was nudging at the edges of his mind. Of telling her that the two of them would fly away and he would spend the rest of his life protecting her and making love to her. That they would create a future together with children of their own. And they would build the kind of home that neither of them had ever known.

He shook his head, as if emerging from an unexpected dream.

'The solution to your *dilemma*,' he said coldly, 'is to shake off your feelings of self-pity—and start counting your blessings instead. Be grateful that you will soon be the wife of His Imperial Majesty. And now, let us join the caravan and begin our journey—for the Sultan grows impatient. You will take the second camel in the train.'

'I will not,' she said.

'I beg your pardon?'

'You heard—and glaring at me like that won't make any difference, Suleiman,' she said. 'I want to ride one of those beautiful horses.'

'You will not be riding anywhere.'

'Oh, but I will,' she argued stubbornly. 'Because either you let me have my own mount, or I'll refuse to get on one of the camels—and I'd like to see any of you trying to get a woman on top of a camel if she doesn't want to go. Apart from the glaring problem of propriety—I have a very healthy pair of lungs and I doubt whether screaming is considered appropriate behaviour for a princess. You know how much the servants gossip.'

Suleiman could feel a growing frustration as he acknowledged the fierce look on her face. 'Are you calling my bluff?' he demanded.

'No. I'm just telling you that I don't intend to spend the next three days sitting on a camel. I get travel-sick on camels— you know that!'

'You have been allocated the strongest and yet most docile beast in the caravan,' he defended.

'I don't care if he's fluent in seven languages—I'm not getting on him. Please, Suleiman,' she coaxed. 'Let me ride. I've got my eye on that sweet-looking palomino over there.'

'But you told me you haven't been on a horse for years,' he growled.

'I know. And that's precisely why I need the practice. So either you let me ride there, or I shall refuse to come.'

He met her obstinate expression, knowing she had him beat. Imagine the dishonour to her reputation if he tried to force her onto the back of a camel. 'If I agree— *if* I agree…you will stay close beside me at all times!' he ordered.

'If you insist.'

'I do. And you will not do anything reckless. Is that understood?'

'Perfectly,' she said.

Frustratedly, he shook his head—wondering how the Sultan was going to be able to cope with such a *headstrong* woman.

But a far more pressing problem was how he was going to get through the next couple of days without succumbing to the temptation of making love to her.

CHAPTER FOUR

SARA GAVE A small sigh of satisfaction as she submitted to the ministrations of the female attendant. Luxuriously, she wriggled her toes and rested her head against the back of the small bath tub. It was strange being waited on like this again after so long. On the plane she had decided she didn't like being treated like a princess, but that wasn't quite true. Because nobody could deny that it felt wonderful to have your body washed in cool water, especially when you had been on horseback all day beneath the baking heat of the desert sun.

They had spent hours travelling across the Mekathasinian Sands towards the Sultan's summer palace and until a few moments ago she had been hot and tired. But according to Suleiman they had made good progress—and hadn't it felt wonderful to be back in the saddle again after so long?

She had stubbornly ignored his suggestion that she ride side-saddle. Instead, she had lightly swung up onto her beautiful Akhal-Teke mount with its distinctive metallic golden coat, before going for a gentle trot with the black-eyed emissary close by. When she'd been going for a couple of hours, he had grudgingly agreed to let her canter. She suspected that he was testing her competence in the saddle and she must have passed the test—for it had taken very little persuasion for him to agree to a short gallop with her across the desert plain.

And that bit. That bit had been bliss...

She closed her eyes as the cool water washed away the sand which still clung to her skin. Today had been one of the best days she could remember—and how crazy was that? Shouldn't pleasure be the last thing which a woman in her position should be feeling?

Yet the freedom of riding with Suleiman beneath the hot desert sun had been powerful enough to make her forget that she was getting ever closer to a destiny which filled her with horror.

It had felt fantastic to be back on a horse again. She had eagerly agreed to his offer of a race, although at one point she'd been lagging behind him as they were galloping towards the sand dune. Suleiman had turned to look at her and had slowed his horse to match her pace.

'Are you okay, Sara? Not feeling too tired?'

'Oh, I'm okay.' Without warning, she had dug her knees into the horse and had surged ahead. And of course she reached the dune first—laughing at the frustration and admiration which were warring in his dark eyes.

'You little cheat,' he murmured.

'It's called tactics, Suleiman.' Her answer had been insouciant, but she had been unable to hide her instinctive glee at having beaten him. 'Just plain old tactics.'

It was only now, with the relaxation which followed

hours of physical exertion, that her thoughts were slowing down enough to let her dwell on the inevitable.

One day down and time was ticking away. Soon she would never be alone with him again.

The thought of that was hard to bear. Within a few short hours, all those feelings she'd repressed for so long had come flooding back with all the force of a burst dam. He was the only man she'd ever felt anything for and he still was. She couldn't believe how badly she had underestimated the impact of being in his company again.

She had been planning to use him as her means of escape, yes. What she hadn't been planning was to fall deeper under his spell. To imagine herself still in love with him, as she'd been all those years ago. Had she forgotten the power of the heart to yearn for the impossible? Or had she just forgotten that Suleiman was her fantasy man, who had now come to vibrant life before her eyes?

On horseback, he looked like a dream. He had changed into his desert clothes and the result had been breathtaking. Sara had forgotten how good a man could look in flowing robes and had spent most of the day trying not to stare at him, with varying degrees of success. The fluid fabric had clung to his body and moulded the powerful thrust of his thighs as they'd gripped the flanks of his stallion. His headdress had streamed behind him like a pale banner in the warm air. His rugged profile had been dark and commanding—his lips firmly closed against the clouds of fine sand which billowed up around him.

She lay back as the servant continued to wash her with a mixture of rose water, infused with jasmine blossom. Next, her ears would be anointed with oil of sandalwood, a process which would be repeated on her toes. After that, her hair would be woven with fragrant leaves which had been brought from the gardens of the Sultan's palace and the intention was for her to be completely perfumed by the time she was presented to him at court.

Sara shuddered as she imagined the swarthy potentate stripping her of her bridal finery, before lowering his powerful body on hers.

She could not go through with it.

She would not go through with it.

For the Sultan's sake and for all their sakes—she could not become his wife.

And deep down she knew that the only way to ensure her freedom was with the seduction of Suleiman.

Yet the nagging question remained about how she was going to accomplish that. How could such a scenario be possible when silent servants hovered within the shadows of the camels and the tents? When the eyes of the bodyguards were so sharp it was said they could see a snake move from a hundred yards away.

The light was fading by the time she emerged from the tasselled tent for the evening meal. Against the clear, cobalt sky the giant desert sun looked like a fiery giant beach-ball as it sank slowly into the horizon. She found herself remembering the week she'd spent in Ibiza last year—when, bikini-clad, she'd frolicked in the waves with two girlfriends from the office, enjoying the kind of freedom she'd only ever dreamed of. Would she ever do something like that again? Would she ever be able to wander down to the deli near Gabe's offices and buy herself a cappuccino, with an extra shot?

Her silken robes fluttered in the gentle breeze and tiny silver bells adorned the jewellery she wore. They jangled at her wrists and her ankles as she moved—and apart from their decorative qualities, that was the whole point of wearing them—to warn others that the Sultan's fiancée was in the vicinity. As soon as the sound was heard the servants would bow their heads and the male members of the group would quickly avert their eyes.

All except Suleiman.

He had been standing talking to one of the bodyguards but he must have heard her for he glanced up, his eyes narrowing. It was impossible to know what was on his mind but she knew she hadn't imagined the sudden tension which had stiffened his body. She saw his mouth harden and the skin stretching tautly over his cheekbones—as if he was mentally preparing himself for some sort of endurance test.

The bodyguards had melted away into the shadows and even though the temporary camp was humming with the unseen life of servants, it felt as if it were just her and him, alone beneath the vast canopy of the darkening sky, which would soon give way to starry night.

He, too, had changed for dinner. Soft robes of dark crimson silk made him look as if he were part of the setting sun himself. His ebony hair was covered with a headdress which was held in place by a woven circlet of silver cord. There was no aristocratic blood in his veins—that much she knew about a childhood of which he rarely spoke—but at that moment he looked as proud and patrician as any king.

He bowed his head as she approached, but not quickly enough to hide the sudden flash of hunger in his eyes.

'You look like a true desert princess tonight,' he said.

'I can't make up my mind whether or not that's a compliment.'

'It is,' he said, looking for all the world as if he now regretted his choice of words. 'It signals that you are accepting your fate—outwardly, at least. Are you hungry?'

She nodded. The sight of Suleiman was enough to make food seem inconsequential, but she could smell cooking. The familiar concoction of sweet herbs and spices drifting towards her was making her mouth water and it was a long time since she had eaten a feast in the desert. 'Starving.'

He laughed. 'Don't they say that a hungry woman is a dangerous woman?'

'And don't they also say that some women remain dangerous even when their bellies are full?'

'Is that a threat or a promise?'

She looked into his eyes. So black, she thought. So very black. 'Which would you like it to be, Suleiman?'

There was a split second of a pause, when she thought he might respond in a similar, teasing style. But then something about his countenance changed and his face darkened. She could see him swallow—as if something jagged had lodged itself in his throat. And was it a terrible thing to admit that she found herself almost *enjoying* his obvious discomfort?

Well, it might be terrible, but it was also human nature—and right now, nothing else seemed to matter. She was achingly aware that beneath their supposedly polite banter thrummed the unmistakable tremor of sexual desire. She wanted to break down the walls that he had built around himself—to claw away at the bricks with her bare hands. She wanted to seduce him to guarantee her freedom, yes—but it was more than that. Because she wanted him.

She had never stopped wanting him.

But this could never be anything more than sex. She knew that. If she seduced Suleiman, then she needed to have the strength to walk away. Because no happy ending was possible. She knew that, too.

'It's dinner time,' he said abruptly, glancing at the sun, which she knew he could read as accurately as any clock.

Sara said nothing as they walked over to the camp-fire, where a special dining area had been laid out for the two of them. She saw the fleeting disquiet which had darkened Suleiman's face and realised that this faux-intimacy was probably the last thing he wanted. But protocol being what it was—there was really no alternative. Of course she would be expected to eat with him, rather than alone—while the servants ate their own rations out of sight.

It was a long time since she had enjoyed a meal in the desert and, inevitably, the experience had a story-book feel to it. The giant bulk of the camels was silhouetted against the darkening sky, where the first stars were beginning to glimmer. The crackling flames glowed golden and the smell of the traditional Qurhah stew was rich with the scent of oranges and cinnamon.

Sara sank down onto a pile of brocade cushions while Suleiman adopted a position on the opposite side of the low table, on which thick, creamy candles burned. It was as if an outdoor dining room had been erected in the middle of the sands and it looked spectacular. She'd forgotten how much could be loaded onto the backs of the camels and how it was a Qurhah custom to make every desert trip feel like a home-from-home.

She accepted a beaker of pomegranate juice and smiled her thanks at the servant who ladled out a portion of the stew onto each of the silver platters, before leaving the two of them alone.

The food was delicious and Sara ate several mouthfuls but her hunger soon began to ebb away. It was too distracting to think about eating when Suleiman was sitting opposite her, his face growing shadowed in the dying light. She noticed he was watching her closely—his intelligent eyes narrowed and gleaming—and she knew that she must approach this very carefully. He could not be played with and toyed with. If she went about her proposed seduction in a crass and obvious manner, then mightn't he see through it?

So try to get underneath his skin—without him realising what you're doing.

'You do realise that I've known you for years and yet you're still something of a mystery to me,' she said conversationally.

'Good. That's the way I like it.'

'I mean, I know practically nothing about your past,' she continued, as if he hadn't made that terse interruption.

'How many times have I told you, Sara? My past is irrelevant.'

'I don't agree. Surely our past is what defines us. It makes us what we are today. And you've never told me how you first got to know the Sultan—or to be regarded so highly by him. When I was a child you said I wouldn't understand—and when I became an adult, well…' She shrugged, not wanting to spell it out. Not needing to say that once sexual attraction had reared its powerful head, any kind of intimacy had seemed too dangerous. She put her fork down and looked at him.

'It isn't relevant,' he said.

'Well, what else are we going to talk about? And if I am to be the Sultan's wife…' She hesitated as she noticed him flinch. 'Then surely it must be relevant. Am I to know nothing about the background of the man who was my future husband's aide for so long? You must admit that it is highly unusual for such a powerful man as the Sultan to entrust so much to someone who has no aristocratic blood of their own.'

'I had no idea that you were such a snob, Sara,' he mocked.

'I'm not a snob,' she corrected. 'Just someone seeking the facts. That's one of the side effects of having had a western education. I was taught to question things, rather than just to accept what I was told or be fobbed off with some bland reply designed to put me in my place.'

'Then maybe your western education has not served you well,' he said, before suddenly stilling. He shook his head. 'What am I saying?' he said, almost to himself. 'How unforgivable of me to try to damn your education and in so doing—to damn knowledge itself. Forget that I ever said that.'

'Does that mean you'll answer my question?'

'That is not what I meant at all.'

'Please, Suleiman.'

He gave an exasperated sigh as he looked at her. But she thought she saw affection in his eyes too as he lowered his voice and began to speak in English, even though Sara was certain that none of the servants or bodyguards were within earshot.

'You know that I was born into poverty?' he said. 'Real and abject poverty?'

'I heard the rumours,' Sara answered. 'Though you'd never guess that from your general bearing and manner.'

'I learn very quickly. Adaption is the first lesson of survival,' he said drily. 'And believe me, it's easier to absorb the behaviour of the rich, than it is the other way round.'

'So how did you—a boy from the wrong side of the tracks—ever come into contact with someone as important as the Sultan?'

There was silence for a moment. Sara thought she saw a sudden darkness cross his face. And there was bitterness, too.

'I grew up in a place called Tymahan, a small area

of Samahan, where the land is at its most desolate and people eke out what living they can. To be honest, there was never much of a living to be made—even before the last war, when much blood was shed. But you, of course—in your pampered palace in Dhi'ban—would have known nothing of those hardships.'

'You cannot blame me for the way I was protected as a princess,' she protested. 'Would you sooner I had cut off my hair and pretended to be a boy, in order to do battle?'

'No.' He shook his head. 'Of course not.'

'Carry on with your story,' she urged, leaning forward a little.

He seemed to draw in a quick breath as she grew closer.

'The Sultan's father was touring the region,' he said. 'He wanted to witness the aftermath of the wars and to see whether any insurrection remained.'

Sara watched as he took a sip from his beaker and then put the drink back down on the low table.

'My mother had been ill—and grieving,' he continued. 'My father had been killed in the uprisings and as a consequence she was vulnerable—struck down by a scourge known to many at that time.' His mouth twisted with pain and bitterness. 'A scourge known as starvation.'

Sara flinched as guilt suddenly washed over her. Earlier, he had accused her of self-pity and didn't he have a point? She had moaned about her position as a princess—yet despite the many unsatisfactory areas of her life, she had certainly never experienced anything as fundamental as a lack of food. She'd never had to face a problem as pressing as basic *survival*. She looked into his black eyes, which were now clouded with pain, and her heart went out to him.

'Oh, Suleiman,' she said softly.

His mouth hardened, as if her sympathy was unwelcome. 'The Sultan was being entertained by a group of local dignitaries and there was enough food groaning on those tables to feed our village for a month,' he said, his voice growing harsh. 'I was lurking in the shadows, for that was my particular skill—to see and yet not be seen. And on this night I saw a pomegranate—as big as a man's fist and as golden as the midday sun. My mother had always loved pomegranates and I...'

'You stole it?' she guessed as his words faded away.

He gave her a tight smile. 'If I had been old enough to articulate my thoughts I would have called it a fair distribution of goods, but my motives were irrelevant since I was caught, red-handed. I may have been good at hiding in the shadows, but I was no match for the Sultan's elite bodyguards.'

Sara shivered, recognising the magnitude of such a crime and wondering how he was still alive to tell the tale.

'And they let you off?'

He gave a short laugh. 'The Sultan's guards are not in the habit of granting clemency to common thieves and I was moments away from losing my head to one of their scimitars, when I saw a young boy about the same age as me running from within one of the royal tents and shouting at them to stop. It was the Sultan's son, Murat.' He paused. 'Your future husband.'

Sara flinched, for she knew that his heavy reminder had been deliberate. 'And what did he do?'

'He saved my life.'

She stared at him in bewilderment. 'How?'

'It was simple. Murat was protected and pampered—but lonely and bored. He wanted a playmate—and a boy hungry enough to steal from the royal table was deemed a charitable cause to rescue. My mother was offered a large sum of money—'

'She took it?'

'She had no choice other than to take it!' he snapped. 'I was to be washed and dressed in fine clothes. To be removed from my own country and taken back to the royal palace of Qurhah, where I was to be educated alongside the young Sultan. In most things, we two boys would be as equals.'

There was silence while she digested this. She could see how completely Suleiman's life would have been transformed. Why sometimes he unconsciously acted with the arrogance known to all royals, though his was tempered by a certain *edge*. But his mother had *sold* him. And there was something he had omitted to mention. 'Your…mother? What happened to her?'

This time the twist of pain on his face was so raw that she could hardly bear to observe it.

'She was given the best food and the best medicines,' he said. 'And a new dwelling place was built for her and my two younger brothers. I was taken away to the palace, intending to return to Samahan to see my family

in the summer. But her illness had taken an irrevers-
ible toll and my mother died that springtime. I never…
I never saw her again.'

'Oh, Suleiman,' she said, her heart going out to him.
His mother's sacrifice had been phenomenal and yet she
had died without seeing her eldest son. How terrible for
them both. She wanted to go to him and take him in
her arms, but the unseen presence of the servants and
the expression on his face warned her not to try. Only
words could convey her empathy and her sorrow and
she picked the simplest and most heartfelt of all. 'I'm
sorry,' she said. 'So very sorry.'

'It happened a long time ago,' he said harshly. 'It's
all in the past. And that's where it should stay. Like I
said, the past is irrelevant. Now perhaps you will understand why I prefer not to talk of it?'

She looked at him. All these years she'd known
him—or, rather, had thought she'd known him. But
she had only seen the bits he had allowed her to see.
He had kept this vital part of himself locked away, until
now—when it had poured from his lips and made him
seem strangely vulnerable. It made her understand a
little more about why he was the kind of man he was.
Why he kept his feelings bottled away and sometimes
seemed so stubborn and inflexible. It explained why he
had always been so unquestioningly loyal to the Sultan
who had saved his life. He was so driven by duty—because duty was all he knew.

Suddenly she realised why he had rejected her on the
night of her brother's coronation. Again, because it was
his *duty*. Because she had been betrothed to the Sultan.

Yet the price of duty had been to never see his mother again. No wonder he had always seemed so proud and so alone. Because essentially he was.

And suddenly Sara knew that she could not seduce him as some cynical game-plan of her own. She could not use Suleiman Abd al-Aziz to help her escape from this particular prison. She could not place him in any position of danger, because if the Sultan were ever to discover that his bride-to-be had slept with the man he most trusted in all the world—then all hell would be let loose.

No. She lifted her hand to brush a strand of hair away from her cheek and she saw his eyes narrow as the bells on her silver bangles tinkled. She was going to have to be strong and take responsibility for herself.

She could not use sex as an instrument of barter, not when she cared about Suleiman so much. If she wanted to get out of here, then she was going to have to use more traditional means. But she was resourceful, wasn't she? There was nothing stopping her.

She needed to make her bid for freedom without implicating Suleiman. Even if he was blamed for her departure, he should not be party to it. Somehow she needed to escape without him knowing—and escape she would. She would return to the military airfield and *demand* to be put on a plane back to England— promising them a sure-fire international outcry if they failed to comply with her wishes. They kept wanting to remind her that she was a princess—well, maybe it was time she started behaving like one!

She rose to her feet but Suleiman was shadowing her every move and was by her side in an instant.

'I must turn in for the night,' she said, giving a huge yawn and wondering if it looked as staged as it felt. 'The effects of the desert heat are very wearying and I'm no longer used to it.'

He inclined his head. 'Very well. Then I accompany you to your tent.'

'There's no need for you to do that.'

'There is every need, Sara—for we both know that snakes and scorpions can lurk within the shadows.'

She wanted to tell him that she knew the terrain as well as he did. That she had been taught to understand and respect its mysteries and its dangers, because he had taught them to her. But perhaps now was not a good time to remind him that at heart she was a child of the desert—for mightn't that alert him to all the possibilities which still lay beneath her fingertips?

The beauty of the night seemed to mock her. The sky was a vast dark dome, pinpricked by the brightest stars a person was ever likely to see. The moon brightened the indigo depths like a giant silver dish which had been superimposed there—the shadows on its face disturbingly clear. For a moment she wished that she had supernatural powers—that she could leap into the air and fly to the moon, like the most famous of all the Dhi'banese fables she had heard as a child.

But her sandaled feet were firmly on the ground as she walked through the soft sand, her eyes taking in her surroundings. She looked at the layout of the camp as she walked. She saw where the horses were tethered and where the bodyguards had been stationed. Obviously they were close enough to keep her from harm, but far enough away for propriety to be observed.

They reached the tasselled entrance of her tent and she wanted to reach up and touch Suleiman's face, aware that the sands of time were running out for them. If she could have just one wish, it would be to run her fingers through the thick ebony of his hair and then to kiss him. But nothing more. She'd changed her mind about that. She suspected that to have sex with him would rob her of all the strength she possessed, and leave her yearning for him for the rest of her life. Perhaps it was best all round that making love was an option which was no longer open to her. But oh, to be able to kiss him...

Would it be so very wrong to bid him goodnight, as she had done to male friends in England countless times before?

On impulse, she rose on tiptoe and brushed her lips over first one of his cheeks, and then the other. It could not have been misinterpreted by anyone. Even the Sultan—if he had been standing there—would have recognised it as a very unthreatening form of western greeting, or farewell. He might not have liked it, but he would have understood it.

Except that this time, that quick brush of her lips was threatening her very sanity. She could feel the hammering of her heart and the hot flush of colour to her face. She could feel the whisper of her breath on his cheeks as she kissed each one in turn. And she could hear, too, the startled intake of breath he took in response. It should have been innocent and yet it felt light years from innocence. How could that be? How could one innocuous touch feel so powerful that it seemed to have rocked her to the core of her being?

Their eyes met and clashed in the indigo light as silent messages of desire and need passed between them. Her skin screamed out for him to touch it. The thrum of sexual tension was now so loud that it almost deafened her.

Slowly, his gaze travelled from her face, all the way down her lavishly embroidered gown, until it lingered at last on the swell of her bodice. The sensation of him looking so openly at her breasts was so *exciting*. It was making her nipples prickle with hunger and frustration. She sucked in an unsteady breath which made her chest rise and fall, and she heard him utter a soft groan.

For a moment he seemed about to move towards her and she prayed that he would. Kiss me, she prayed silently. Just kiss me one more time and I will never ask again.

But the suggestion of movement was arrested as quickly as it had begun for suddenly he stiffened, his face hardening into a granite-like mask. His eyes deadened into dull ebony and when he spoke, his voice was ragged and tinged with self-disgust.

'Get to bed, Sara,' he bit out harshly. 'For God's sake, just get to bed.'

CHAPTER FIVE

SARA AWOKE EARLY. Before even the early light they called the 'false dawn' had begun to brighten the arid desert landscape outside her tent. She lay there in the silence for a moment or two, collecting her thoughts and wondering whether she had the nerve to go through with her plan. But then she thought about reality. About needing to get away from Suleiman just as badly as she needed to get away from her forced marriage to the Sultan.

She had no choice.

She *had* to escape.

Silently, she slipped from beneath the covers of her bedding, still wearing the clothes she had slept in all night. Just before dismissing the servant last evening, she had asked one of them to bring her a large water-bottle as well as a tray of mint tea and a bowl of sugar cubes. The girl had looked a little surprised but had done as requested—no doubt putting Sara's odd request down to the vagaries of being a princess.

Now she wrapped a soft, silken veil around her head before peeping out from behind the flaps of the tent, and her heart lifted with relief. All was quiet. Not a soul around. She glanced upwards at the sky. It looked clear enough. Soon it would be properly light and with light came danger. The animals would grow restless and all the bodyguards would waken. She cocked her head as she heard a faint but unmistakable noise. Did that mean one of the guards was already awake? Her heart began to pound. She must be off, with not a second more to be wasted.

Stealthily, she moved across the sand to where the horses were tethered. The Akhal-Teke palomino she had been riding earlier greeted her with a soft whinny and she shushed him by feeding him a sugar cube, which he crunched eagerly with his big teeth. Her heart was thumping as she mounted him and then urged him forward on a walk going with the direction of the wind, not giving him his head and letting him gallop until they were well out of earshot of the campsite.

Her first feelings were of exhilaration and delight that she had got away without being seen. That she had escaped the dark-eyed scrutiny of Suleiman and had not implicated him in her flight. The pale sky was becoming bluer by the second and the sand was a pleasing shade of deep gold. Suddenly, this felt like an adventure and her life in London seemed a long way away.

She made good progress before the sun grew too high, when she stopped beside a rock to relieve herself and then to drink sparingly from her water bottle. When she remounted her horse it was noticeably hotter and she was glad of the veil which shielded her head from the increasingly strong rays. And at least the camel trail was easy enough to follow back towards the airbase. The tread of the heavy beasts was deep and there had been none of the threatened sandstorms overnight to sweep away the evidence of their route.

Did she stop paying attention?

Did her ever-present thoughts of Suleiman distract her for long enough to make her stray from the deep line of animal footprints she'd been following so intently?

Was that why one minute she seemed so secure in her direction, while the next…?

Blinking, Sara looked around like someone who had just awoken from a dream, telling herself that the trail was still there if she looked for it and she had probably just wandered a little way from it.

It took only a couple of minutes for her to realise that her self-reassurance was about as real as a mirage.

Because there was nothing. Nothing to be seen.

She blinked again. No indentations. No little tell-tale heaps where a frisky camel might have kicked out at the sand.

Panic rose in her throat like bile but she fought to keep it at bay. Because panicking would not help. Most emphatically it would not. It would make her start to lose her nerve and she couldn't afford to lose anything else—losing her way was bad enough.

She didn't even have a compass with her.

She dismounted from her horse, trying to remember the laws of survival as she took a thirsty gulp of water from her bottle. She should retrace her steps. That was what she should do. Find where she'd lost the path and then pick up the camel trail again. Bending, she lifted a small pebble out of the sand. Sucking it would remind her to keep her mouth closed and prevent it from drying out.

She patted the horse before swinging lightly into the saddle again. It was going to be all right, she told herself. Of course it was going to be all right. It had only been a couple of minutes since she'd missed the path and she couldn't possibly be lost.

It took her about an hour of fruitless riding to accept that she was.

'What do you mean, she's not there?'

His voice distorted with anger, Suleiman stared at the bent head of the female servant who stood trembling before him.

'Tell me!' he raged.

The girl began to babble. They had thought that the princess was sleeping late, so they did not wish to disturb her.

'So you left the princess's tent until now?'

'Y-yes, sir.'

Suleiman forced himself to suck in a deep breath, only just managing to keep his hot rage from erupting as he surveyed the bodyguards who were milling around nervously. 'And not one of you thought to wonder why one of the horses was missing?' he demanded.

But their shamefaced excuses were quelled with a furious wave of his hand as Suleiman marched over to the horses, with the most senior bodyguard close behind him. Because deep down he knew that he was not really in any position to criticise—not when he was as culpable as they.

Why hadn't *he* been watching her?

His mouth hardened as he swung himself up onto the biggest and most powerful stallion.

Because he was a coward, that was why.

Despite his supposedly exemplary military record and all the awards which had been heaped upon him—he had selected a tent as far away from hers as possible. Too unsure of his reaction to her proximity, he had not dared risk being close. Not trusting himself—and not trusting her either.

He hadn't imagined the white-hot feeling of lust which had flared between them last night and he was too experienced a lover to mistake the look of sexual yearning which had darkened her violet eyes. When she was standing in front of him in her embroidered robes—her hair woven with fragrant leaves—he had never wanted her quite so much.

Hadn't he wondered whether her western sensibilities might make her take the initiative? Hadn't he wondered whether she might boldly arrive naked at his tent under cover of darkness and slip into his bed without invitation, as so many women had done before?

He stared down at the senior bodyguard. 'You have checked her trail?'

'Yes, boss. She has headed due north—taking the same path by which we came, back towards the airbase.'

Suleiman nodded. It was as he had thought. She was trying to get back to England on her own—oh, most stubborn and impetuous of women! 'Very well,' he said.

'I will follow her trail. And you will assign three men to take up the other three points of the compass and to set off immediately. But no more than three. I don't want the desert paths disturbed any more than they need be. I don't want any clues churned up by the damned horses.'

'Yes, boss.'

'You will also send someone to find a high enough vantage point to try to get a mobile phone signal. I want the military base informed and I want every damned plane at their disposal out looking for her. Understand?'

The bodyguard nodded. 'Understood.'

'And believe me when I tell you that you have not heard the last of this!'

With his final, angry words ringing Suleiman galloped off at a furious pace, the warm wind streaming against his face as he followed the mixed track of the camels and the newer footprints of Sara's horse.

He had already realised that there would be repercussions. By involving the military, word would inevitably get back to the Sultan that the princess was missing. But he didn't care what criticism or punishment came his way for having lost the future Sultana of Qurhah. They could exile him or imprison him and he wouldn't care.

He didn't care about anything other than finding her safe and well.

He had never known such raw fear as he travelled beneath the heat of a sun which was growing ever more blistering. Even though she was out of practice, he knew that she was a sound horsewoman—a fact which had always been a source of pride since he had been the one to tutor her, but which now gave him only comfort.

And he found himself clinging to that one small comfort. Please let her ride safely, he prayed. Please not let something have frightened the horse so that Sara might be lying there buckled and broken on the sand. Alone and scared while the sun beat down on her and the vultures waited to peck out her beautiful violet eyes...

He sucked in a breath of hot air which felt raw as it travelled down his throat. He should not think the worst. He would not think the worst. Think positive, he told himself. At least no snake or brown scorpion could touch her when she was high up on her horse.

But knowing that did not help him locate her, did it?

Where was she? Where *was* she?

His eyes trained unblinkingly on the ground before him—he saw the exact point where her path had veered off from the main route. Had something distracted the horse? Distracted her?

He pushed forward now, letting the powerful stallion stream across the sands until Suleiman urged it to a halt and then opened his mouth to call across the desolate landscape.

'Sara! Sa-ra!'

But the ensuing response was nothing but an empty silence and his heart gave a painful lurch.

He forced himself to take a drink from one of the water-bottles he carried, for dehydration would be good for neither of them if he found her.

When he found her.

He had to find her.

The position of the sun and his wristwatch told him that he had been searching for her for over four hours.

He could feel his heart pumping painfully in his chest. The heat of the midday sun was a tough enough combatant but darkness was a whole different ball-game.

He thought of the nocturnal creatures which came out in the cold of the desert night—dangerous animals which populated this inhospitable terrain.

'Sara!' he called again and then the horse's ears pricked up and Suleiman strained to hear a sound that was almost lost in the distance. He listened again.

It *was* a sound. The smallest sound in the world. The sound of a voice. If it had been anyone else's voice, he might not have recognised it—but Suleiman had heard Sara's voice in many guises. He'd heard it as a child. He'd heard its hesitancy in puberty and its breathlessness in passion. But he had never heard it sound quite so broken nor so lost as it did right now.

'Sara!' he yelled, the word spilling from his lips as if it had been ripped from the very base of his lungs.

And then the shout again. Due east a little. He pressed his thighs against the flanks of the horse and urged it forward in a gallop in the direction of the sound. He heard nothing more and as the silence grew, so too did his fear that he had simply imagined it. An aural version of a desert mirage…

Until he saw the shape of a rock up ahead. A dark red rock which soared up revealing a dark cool cave underneath against which gleamed the metallic golden sheen of an Akhal-Teke palomino. He narrowed his eyes, for the horse carried no rider, and he galloped forward to see Sara leaning back against the rock. Its shadow consumed her with its terracotta light but he could see that her face was white with fear and her eyes looked like two deep pools of violet ink.

Grabbing a water-bottle, he jumped from the horse's back and was beside her in a moment. He held the vessel to her lips and she sucked on it greedily, like a small animal being bottle-fed. He put the bottle down and as he watched the colour and the strength return to her all his own fear and anger bubbled up inside him.

'What the hell did you think you were doing?' he demanded, levering her up against him so that her face was inches away from his.

'Isn't it obvious?' Her voice sounded weak. 'I was trying to get away.'

'You could have died!'

'I'm not...I'm not that easy to get rid of,' she said, her lips trying for a smile but he noticed she didn't quite achieve it—though nothing could disguise the flash of relief which flared briefly in her eyes.

'Where were you headed for?' he demanded, watching as he saw her face assume a look of sudden wariness.

She looked at him from the shuttered forest of her lashes. 'Where do you think? Back to the airport.'

'To the military base?'

'Yes, to the military base. To demand to be taken back to England. I...I came to my senses, Suleiman. I realised that I couldn't go through with it after all— no matter what you or the Sultan threatened me with, I don't care. I don't care about political dynasties or forging an alliance between my country and his. My brother will have to find someone else to offer up as a human sacrifice.'

Furiously, he stood up and pulled out his mobile phone and started barking into it in Qurhahian. Sara could hear him telling the military that the search should be called off. That the princess had been found and she was safely in his charge.

But when he terminated the call the look on his face didn't make Sara feel in the least bit safe. In fact, it made her feel the opposite of safe. His black eyes were filled with fury as he slowly advanced towards her again.

'So let me get this straight,' he said, and she could tell that he was only just holding onto his temper. 'You took off on your own into one of the most hostile territories in the world—even though you have not ridden for years and have been living a pampered life in London—is that right?'

Her gaze was defiant as she met the accusation in his eyes.

'Yes,' she said fiercely. 'That's exactly right.'

The absurdity of her quest infuriated him. He thought about the danger she'd put herself in and he felt the clench of anger—and fear too, at the thought of what could have happened to her. He intended to give her a piece of his mind. To tell her that he felt like putting her across his knee and smacking her. At least, that was what he thought he intended. But somehow it didn't work out like that.

Maybe it was the sight of all that tousled blonde hair, or the violet glitter of her beautiful eyes. Maybe it was because he'd always wanted her and had never stopped wanting her. His desire for her had been like an endless hunger which had eaten him up from the inside out and suddenly there was no controlling it any longer.

He made one last attempt to fight it but his resistance was gone. He'd never felt so powerless in his life as he stared down into her beautiful face and caught hold of her by the shoulders again. Only this time he was pulling her towards him.

'Damn you, Sara,' he whispered. 'Just *damn you.*'

And that was when he started to kiss her.

CHAPTER SIX

SARA GASPED AS Suleiman's mouth drove down on hers. She told herself that this was crazy. That it was only going to lead to heartbreak and tears. She told herself that if she tore herself out of his embrace, then he would let her go. But her body was refusing to listen.

Her body was on fire.

His mouth explored hers and it felt like a dream. Or some hot, X-rated mirage. It surpassed every hope she'd nurtured during these desperate last few hours. Long, grim hours, as she'd realised the full extent of her plight—that she was hopelessly lost in the unforgiving desert. Until the stern-faced emissary had appeared on the empty horizon, astride a gleaming black stallion like her greatest fantasy come true.

And then he had taken the fantasy and given it a sexy embellishment, by pulling her into his arms and giving her this hard and seeking kiss.

Yet this was dangerous, wasn't it? Dangerous for her heart. Dangerous for her soul. She couldn't afford to love this man, no matter how much she wanted him.

She meant to push him away but he pulled her closer,

so that she could smell his raw, male smell. He smelt of sandalwood and salt. The hard sinews of his body were pressed against hers and the proximity of his tight, taut flesh made her want to melt into him. His lips were hard and soft in turn as they kissed her. One minute they were cajoling, the next they were masterfully stating their intent to make love to her.

'Suleiman.' It didn't come out like the protest she intended it to be—it sounded more like a plea.

'Sara,' he said, drawing his mouth away from hers and cupping her face with both his hands. 'Foolish, beautiful, hot-headed Sara.' His gaze raked over her with a mixture of exasperation and lust. 'Why the hell did you take off like that? Why take such a risk?'

'You know why,' she whispered, moving her head fractionally as she sought out another kiss. 'Because I wanted to escape.'

He brushed his lips over hers. Back and forth in a teasing graze. 'Do you still want to escape?'

She nodded her head. 'Yes.'

'Do you?'

She closed her eyes. 'Stop it.'

'I'm waiting for an answer to my question.'

She shook her head. 'N-not any more. At least, not right now. Not if you keep on kissing me like that.'

'That sounds very much like an invitation.' He gave another groan as their mouths meshed together and his breath was warm in her mouth. 'I should put you straight back on that horse and ride you back into camp.'

'Then why are you unbuttoning my tunic?'

'Because I want to taste your nipples.'

'Oh.'

She tipped her head back as his lips trailed a fiery path over her neck, closing her eyes as sensation washed over her. His fingers felt hard and calloused against her delicate flesh. She could feel the slick, wet heat of her sex overwhelming her as he lowered his mouth to trail his tongue over one hardened nipple.

Her mouth grew dry as her lashes fluttered open to watch him. He kissed each breast in turn and then turned his attention to her tunic, peeling it off entirely— along with her slim-fitting trousers. He freed her aching body so that at last her skin was bared to the warm desert air. And to his eyes.

She heard him suck in a ragged breath as he looked down at her and she was glad she was wearing the provocative underwear she'd brought from England. The balcony bra in electric-blue lace and matching thong were both pretty racy, but she'd discovered a while back that she liked wearing expensive lingerie. It had been another aspect of the freedom she'd relished—that she could go into any department store and stock up on X-rated undies and nobody was going to tell her she couldn't.

He said something she couldn't quite make out and the expression in his slitted eyes was suddenly forbidding.

'Is something wrong?' she questioned tentatively.

'Who buys your lingerie for you?' His voice was dark with some unnamed emotion.

'I do.'

'But you buy it for you? Or do you buy it for the men

who will enjoy watching you wearing it?' he persisted, slithering his finger inside her thong where she was so wet and so sensitive that she bucked beneath his touch and gave a little cry. His finger stilled. 'Do you?'

Sara nodded, so strung out with pleasure that she barely knew what she was agreeing to. But men liked women to indulge in fantasy, didn't they? She'd read enough erotic literature to know that. Men liked you to pretend to *be* things and to do things. She read that normality was the killer in the bedroom.

Not that they were anywhere near a bedroom, of course—but who cared about that? Why not feed into his fantasies—and her own? Why shouldn't she make love with Suleiman in the wild desert which had spawned her, on this shaded patch of sand? She might not like all the restrictions of life here, but she was sensitive enough to appreciate its beauty. And if Suleiman wanted her to play the femme fatale, then play it she would.

'I'm enjoying wearing it for you,' she answered coyly, her finger moving to trace the curving satin trim of her bra. 'Do you like it?'

He made a sound mid-way between hunger and anger as he pulled off his crimson robes with impatient disregard, until he was also naked. She let her gaze drift over him, her eyes widening as her gaze locked onto the most intimate part of his aroused body—and suddenly she was a little daunted by what she saw.

'Suleiman…' she whispered, but her words faded because he was back in her arms and was touching her again. Moving his hand intimately against her sex and stroking her with pinpoint accuracy. She could smell the scent of her arousal on the air. She could feel the warm rush of blood flooding through her veins. And shouldn't she be touching *him*? She reached down to whisper her fingertips against his silken length, but he stilled her movement by the abrupt clamp of his hand around her wrist.

'No,' he said.

She looked into his eyes, confused. 'Why not?'

'Because I'm too close to coming, that's why. And I want to come when I'm inside you. I want to watch your face as I enter and hear the sounds you make when I move inside you.'

It was the most erotic thing she'd ever heard. Sara swallowed. Suleiman deep inside the one place where she had always longed for him to be. She could feel her skin burning as he spread his robes down on the shaded sand, like a silken blanket for them to lie on. His face was dark and taut as he peeled off her electric-blue underwear, until she lay before him like a naked sacrifice.

She could see the hardness of his erection and the dark whorls of hair from which it sprang. His olive skin gleamed softly in the terracotta light and his dark eyes were as black as tar as he reached for her, bending his lips to hers. The kiss which followed made her gasp with pleasure. It seemed to unlock something deep within her, but when he lifted his head she could see that his eyes were dark with pain.

'My greatest fantasy and my greatest sin,' he said, his voice shaking. 'And it is wrong. We both know that.'

Suddenly Sara was terrified he was going to stop.

That she would never know what it was like to have Suleiman Abd al-Aziz make love to her. And she couldn't bear it. She thought she could pretty much bear anything else, but not that. Not now.

Her hand reached up to touch the blackness of his hair, letting her fingers slide beneath the silken strands. 'How can it possibly be wrong, when it feels so right?'

'Don't ask disingenuous questions, Sara. And don't look at me with those big violet eyes, a colour which I've never seen on any woman other than you. Just stop me from doing this. Stop me before it goes any further because I don't have the strength to stop myself.'

'I *can't*,' she whispered. 'Because I...' She nearly said *I love you*, but just in time she bit back the words. 'Because I've wanted this for so long. We both want it. You know that. Please, Suleiman. Make love to me.'

He tilted up her chin and gazed down at her. 'Oh, Sara,' he said, saying her name like an unwilling surrender.

He entered her slowly. So slowly that she thought she would die with the pleasure. She cried out as he made that first thrust—a cry which was disbelieving and exultant.

Suleiman was inside her.

Suleiman was filling her.

Suleiman was...

He groaned as he found his rhythm, moving deeper with each stroke. And Sara suddenly felt as if she had been born for this moment. She wrapped her legs around his back as he splayed his hands over her bare buttocks to drive even deeper. Her breath was coming in shuddered little gasps as he moved inside her. She'd had sex before, but never like this. *Never like this*. It was like everyone said it should be. It was...

And then she stopped thinking. Stopped everything except listening to the demands of her body and letting the pleasure pile on, layer by sensual layer.

She felt it build—desperately sweet, yet tantalisingly elusive. She felt the warmth flood through her as Suleiman's movements became more urgent and she was so locked into his passionate kiss that the first spasms of her orgasm took her almost by surprise. Like a feather which had been lifted by a storm and then tossed around by it, she just went with the flow. She cried out his name as his own body suddenly tensed, and he shuddered violently as he came.

But it was over all too quickly. Abruptly, he pulled out of her—so that all she was aware of was a warmth spurting over her belly. He had *withdrawn* from her! It took a couple of disconcerting moments before she felt together enough to open her eyes and to look at him and when she did she felt almost *embarrassed*. As if the sudden ending had wiped out the magic of what had gone before.

'Why...why did you do that?'

His voice was flat. 'I realised that in our haste to consummate our lust, we hadn't even discussed contraception.'

Sara did her best not to flinch, but it seemed a particularly emotionless thing to say in view of what just happened. Consummate their *lust*? Was that it? 'I suppose we didn't.'

'Are you on the pill?'

She shook her head. 'No.'

'So we add a baby into the equation and make the situation a million times worse than it already is,' he said bitterly. 'Is that what you wanted?'

She flushed, knowing he was right—and wasn't it the most appalling thing that she found herself wishing that he *had* made her pregnant? How weird was it that some primitive part of her was wishing that Suleiman had planted his seed inside her belly. So that now there would be a baby growing beneath her heart. *His* baby. 'No, of course it wasn't what I wanted.' She met his eyes. 'Why are you being like this?'

'Like what?'

'So...*cold.*'

'Why do you think? Because I've just betrayed the man who saved my life. Because I've behaved like the worst kind of friend.' His gaze swept over her and somehow she knew what he was going to say, almost before the words had left his lips. 'And you weren't even a virgin.'

It was the 'even' which made it worse. As if she'd been nothing but a poor consolation prize. 'Were you expecting me to be?'

'Yes,' he bit out. 'Of course I was!'

'I'm twenty-three years old, Suleiman. I've been living an independent life in London. What did you expect?'

'But you were brought up as a desert princess! To respect your body and cherish your maidenhood. To save your purity for your bridegroom. Your royal bridegroom.' He shook his head. 'Oh, I know you spoke freely of sex and that beneath your clothes you were wearing the kind of lingerie which only a truly liberated woman would wear. But even though I had my suspicions, deep down I thought you remained untouched!'

'Even though you had your suspicions?' she repeated, in disbelief. 'What are you now—some sort of detective?'

'You are destined to be a royal bride,' he flared back. 'And your virginity was an essential part of that agreement. Or at least, that's what I thought.'

'No, Suleiman, that's where you're wrong.' Sitting up, she angrily brushed a heavy spill of hair away from her flushed face. 'You don't think—you just *react*. You don't see me as an individual with my own unique history. You didn't stop to think that I might have desires and needs of my own, just as you do—and presumably just as Murat does. You simply see me as a stereotype. You see what I am *supposed* to be and what I am *supposed* to stand for. The virgin princess who has been bought for the Sultan. Only I am not that person and I will never be!'

'And didn't it occur to you to have made some attempt to communicate your thoughts with the Sultan, *before* he was forced to take matters into his own hand?' Suleiman demanded. 'Didn't it occur to you that running away just wasn't the answer? But you've spent your whole life running away, haven't you, Sara?'

'And you've spent your whole life denying your feelings!'

'I have never denied that!' he flared back. 'It's a pity

that more people don't stop neurotically asking themselves whether or not they are "happy"—and just get out there and *do* something instead!'

'Like you've just done, you mean?' she challenged. 'What, did you think to yourself? "Now, how can I punish the princess for running off? I know—I'll seduce her!"'

For a moment there was nothing other than the sound of them struggling to control their breathing and Suleiman felt the cold coil of anger twisting at his gut as he looked at her.

He swallowed but the action did little to ease the burning sensation which scorched his throat. The acrid taste of guilt couldn't be washed away so easily, he thought bitterly.

He had just seduced the woman who was to marry the Sultan.

He had just committed the ultimate betrayal against his sovereign—and wasn't treason punishable by death?

Had she used him to facilitate her escape? Had she? Had this been a trap into which he had all-too-willingly fallen?

'How many men have you had?' he demanded suddenly.

She stared at him in disbelief. 'Have you heard a word I've just been saying? How many women have *you* had?'

'That's irrelevant!' he snapped. 'So I shall ask you again, Sara—and this time I want an answer. How many?'

'Oh, hundreds,' she retorted, but the expression on

his face made her backtrack and even though she despised herself for wanting to salvage her reputation—it didn't stop her from doing it. 'If you must know—I've had one experience before you. One—and it was awful. An ill-judged foray into the sexual arena with a man I'd convinced myself could mean something to me, but I was wrong.' Just as she'd been wrong about so many things at the time.

'Who was he?'

'You think I'm crazy enough to tell you his name?' She shook her head, not wanting to reveal any more than she had to. She didn't want Suleiman to know that at the time she'd been on a mission—trying to convince herself that there were men other than him. That she'd wanted another man to make her feel the way he did. But she had been hoping in vain because no man had even come close. He affected her in a way she had no control over. Even now, with this terrible atmosphere which had descended upon them, he was still making her *feel* stuff, wasn't he? He still made her feel totally *alive* whenever she was near him.

'I was experimenting,' she said. 'Trying to experience the same things as other women my age, but it didn't work.'

'So you conveniently forgot about your planned marriage?'

'You didn't seem to have much difficulty forgetting it, did you? And surely that's the most glaring hypocrisy of all. It wasn't just me who broke the rules. It took two of us to make love just now, and you were one very willing partner. I'm wondering how that registers on your particular scale of loyalty?'

Something in the atmosphere shifted and changed and his face tightened as he nodded.

'You are right, of course. Thank you for reminding me that my own behaviour certainly doesn't give me the right to censure yours. But before we go, just answer me one thing. Did you set out to seduce me, knowing that having sex with me would put an end to your betrothal?'

She hesitated, but only for a moment. 'No,' she said and then, because it felt like a heavy burden, she told him the truth. 'I planned to do something like that, but in the end I couldn't go through with it.'

'Why not?'

She shrugged and suddenly the threat of tears seemed very real as she thought of the boy who had been sold by his mother. 'Because of what you told me about how you and Murat met. How he'd saved your life and how close you'd been when you were growing up. I realised what a big deal your friendship was and how much it meant to you. That's why I ran away.'

'Only I came after you,' he said slowly. 'And seduced you anyway.'

'Yes.' She kept swallowing—the way they told you to do in aircraft, to stop your ears from popping. But this was to stop the welling tears from falling down over her face. Because tears wouldn't help anyone, would they? They made a woman look weak and a man take control. And she wasn't going to be that woman. 'Yes, you did.'

'I appreciate your honesty,' he said. 'And at least

you've concentrated my mind on what needs to happen next.'

She heard the finality in his tone and guessed what was coming next. 'You mean you'll take me to the airfield?'

'So that you can run away again? I don't think so. Isn't it time that you stopped running and faced up to the consequences of your actions? Maybe it's time we both did.' He gave a grim smile and stood up, magnificent and unashamed in his nakedness. 'My brief was to deliver you to the Sultan and that's exactly what I'm going to do.'

She stared at him in bewilderment and then in fear as his body blocked out the fierce light of the sun. All she could see was the powerful shape of his silhouette and suddenly he seemed more than a little intimidating. 'You're still planning to take me to the Sultan?'

'I am.'

'You can't do that.'

'Just watch me.'

She licked her lips. 'He'll kill me.'

'He'll have to kill me first. Don't be absurd, Sara.' He flicked her a glance. 'And don't move. At least, not yet.'

She didn't know what he meant until he walked over to his horse and took a bottle from his saddle-bag, dousing his headdress with a generous slug of water before coming back to her. His face was grave as he crouched down to wipe her belly clean and Sara felt her cheeks flame, because the peculiar intimacy of having Suleiman removing his dried seed from her skin was curiously poignant.

'Removing all traces of yourself?' she questioned.

'You think it's that easy? I wish.' His bitter tone matched hers and she could see the angry gleam of his eyes. 'Now get dressed, Sara—and we will ride together to the palace.'

CHAPTER SEVEN

THE SUN WAS low in the sky when Sara and Suleiman brought their horses to a dusty halt outside the gates of the Sultan's summer residence. Before them, the vast palace towered majestically—its golden hues reflecting the endless desert sands which surrounded it. It was the first time Sara had ever seen the fabled building, and on any other occasion she might have taken time to admire the magnificent architecture with all its soaring turrets and domes. But today her heart was full of dread as she thought of what lay ahead.

What on earth was she going to say to the man she had now spurned in the most dramatic way possible? She had never loved the Sultan, nor wanted him—but never in a million years had she wanted it to turn out this way. She didn't want to hurt him, or—which was much more likely—hurt his pride.

Would he want to punish her? Punish her brother and his kingdom?

The reality began to soak into her skin, which was still glowing after her passionate encounter with the man who had ridden by her side. No matter what happened next—she wasn't going to regret what had just taken place. It might have been wrong, but the words she had whispered to Suleiman just before he had thrust into her had been true. It had felt so right.

She shot a glance at him as he brought his horse to a halt but his stony profile gave nothing away and she suspected that his body language was deliberately forbidding. He hadn't spoken a word to her since that uncomfortable showdown after they'd made love. He had kept busy with the practicalities of preparing to return. And then he had turned on her and hissed that she was nothing but a temptation, silencing her protests with an angry wave of his hand before phoning ahead to let the Sultan's staff know that they were on their way.

Sara looked up at the wide blue bowl of the desert sky as another band of fear gripped her. If ever she had thought she'd felt trapped before—she was quickly discovering a whole new meaning to the word. Here was one hostile man taking her to confront another—and she had no idea of what the outcome would be.

Her instinct was to turn and head in the opposite direction—but during the ride she had thought about what Suleiman had said.

You've spent your whole life running away?

Had she? It was weird seeing yourself through somebody else's eyes. She'd always thought that she was an intrepid sort of person. That she had shown true backbone by setting up on her own in London, far away from her pampered life. It was disturbing to think that maybe there was a kernel of truth in Suleiman's accusation.

Their approach had obviously been observed from

within the palace complex, for the tall gates silently opened and they walked their horses through onto the gravelled forecourt. Sara became aware of the massed blooms of white flowers and their powerful scent which pervaded the air. A white-robed servant came towards them, briefly bowing to her before turning to Suleiman and speaking to him in Qurhahian.

'The Sultan wishes to extend his warmest greeting, Suleiman Abd al-Aziz. He has instructed me to tell you that your chambers are fully prepared—and that you will both rest and recuperate before joining him for dinner later.'

'No.'

Suleiman's denial rang out so emphatically that Sara was startled, for she knew that the language of the desert was couched in much more formal—sometimes flowery—tones. She saw the look of surprise on the servant's face.

'The princess may wish to avail herself of the Sultan's hospitality,' said Suleiman. 'But it is imperative that I speak to His Imperial Majesty without further delay. Please take me to him now.'

Sara could see the servant's confusion but such was the force of Suleiman's personality that the man merely nodded in bewildered consent. He led them through the huge carved doors, speaking rapidly into an incongruously modern walkie-talkie handset which he pulled from his white robes.

Once inside, where several female servants had gathered together in a small group, Suleiman turned to her, his features shadowed and unreadable. 'You will go with these women and they will bathe you,' he instructed.

'But—'

'No buts, Sara. I mean it. This is my territory, not yours. Let me deal with it.'

Sara opened her mouth, then shut it again as she felt a wave of relief wash over her. Was it cowardly of her to want to lean on Suleiman and him to take over? 'Thank you,' she said.

'For what?' he questioned in English, his sudden switch of language seeming to emphasise the bitterness of his tone. 'For taking what was never mine to take? Just go. *Go.*'

He stood perfectly still as she turned away, watching her retreat across the wide, marble entrance hall— his feelings in turmoil; his heart sick with dread. He found himself taking in the unruliness of her hair and the crumpled disorder of her robes. He swallowed. If the Sultan had seen her flushed face, then mightn't he guess the cause of her untidy appearance?

He turned to follow the servant, his heart heavy.

How was he going to be able to tell Murat? How could he possibly admit what had been done? The worst betrayal in the world, from the two people who should have been most loyal to the sovereign.

He was ushered into one of the informal ante-rooms which he recognised from times past. He lifted his gaze to the high, arched ceiling with its intricate mosaic, before the Sultan swept in, alone—his black eyes inscrutable as he subjected his erstwhile emissary to a long, hard look.

'So, Suleiman,' he said. 'This is indeed an unconventional meeting. I was disturbed from playing backgammon at a crucial point in the game, to be told that you wished to see me immediately. Is this true?'

His eyes were questioning and Suleiman felt a terrible wave of sadness wash over him. Once their relationship had been so close that he might have made a joke about his supposed insubordination. And the Sultan would have laughed softly and made a retort in the same vein. But this was no laughing matter.

'Yes, it's true,' he said heavily.

'And may I ask what has provoked this extraordinary break with protocol?'

Suleiman swallowed. 'I have come to tell you that the Princess Sara will not marry you,' he said.

For a moment, the Sultan did not reply. His hawk-like features gave nothing away. 'And should not the princess have told me this herself?' he questioned softly.

Suleiman felt his heart clench as he realised that years of loyalty and friendship now lay threatened by his one stupid act of disloyalty and lust. He had accused Sara of being headstrong—but was not his own behaviour equally reprehensible?

'Sire, I must tell you that I have—'

'No!' The word cracked from Murat's mouth like the sound of a whip and he held up his palm for silence. 'Hold your tongue, Suleiman. If you tell me something I should not hear, then I will have no option than to have you tried for treason.'

'Then so be it!' declared Suleiman, his heart pounding like a piston. 'If that is to be my fate, then I will accept it like a man.'

The Sultan's mouth hardened but he shook his head. 'You think I would do that? You think that a woman—*any woman*—is worth destroying a rare friendship between two men? One which has endured the test of time and all the challenges of hierarchy?'

'I will accept whatever punishment you see fit to bestow on me.'

'You want to slug it out? Is that it?'

Suleiman stared at Murat and, for a moment, the years melted away. Suddenly they were no longer two powerful men with all the burdens and responsibilities which had come with age, but two eight-year-old boys squaring up to each other in the baked dust of the palace stables. It had been soon after Suleiman had been brought from Samahan and he had punched the young Sultan at the height of an argument which had long since been forgotten.

He remembered seeing the shock on Murat's face. The realisation that here was someone who was prepared to take him on. Even to beat him. Murat had waved away the angry courtiers. But he had gone away and taken boxing lessons and, two weeks later, had fought again and soundly beaten Suleiman. After that, the fight victory rate had been spread out evenly.

Suleiman found himself wondering which of them would win, if they fought now. 'No, I don't want to fight you, Sire,' he said. 'But I am concerned about the fall-out, if this scheduled marriage doesn't go ahead.'

'As well you should be concerned!' said Murat furiously. 'For you know as well as I do that the union was intended as an alliance between the two countries.'

Suleiman nodded. 'Couldn't an alternative solution be offered instead? A new peace agreement drawn up between Qurhah and Dhi'ban—which could finally banish all the years of unrest. After all, a diplomatic solution is surely more modern and appropriate than an old-fashioned dynastic marriage.'

Murat gave a soft laugh. 'Oh, how I miss your skills of diplomacy, Suleiman. As well as your unerring ability to pick out the most beautiful women on our foreign tours.' He gave a reminiscent sigh. 'Some pretty unforgettable women, as I recall.'

But Suleiman's head was too full of concern to be distracted by memories of the sexual shenanigans of the past. 'Is this a feasible plan, do you think, Sire?'

Murat shrugged. 'It's feasible. It's going to take a lot of backroom work and manoeuvring. But it's do-able, yes.'

The two men stared at one another and Suleiman clenched his teeth. 'Now give me my punishment,' he ground out.

There was a brief silence. 'Oh, that's easy. My punishment is for you to take her,' said Murat silkily. 'Take her away with you and do what you will with her. Because I know you—and I know how your mind operates. Countless times I have watched as you grow bored with the inevitable clinginess of the female of the species. She will drive you mad within the month, Suleiman—that much I can guarantee.'

Murat's words were still ringing in Suleiman's ears

as he waited in the sunlit palace courtyard for Sara to emerge from her ablutions. And when she did, with her blonde hair still damp and tightly plaited, he could not prevent the instinctive kick of lust which was quickly followed by the equally potent feeling of regret.

Her face was pale and her eyes dark with anxiety as she looked up at him. 'What did he say?'

'He accepts the situation. The wedding is off.'

'Just like that?'

Suleiman's mouth hardened. What would she say if he told her the truth? That Murat had spoken of her as if she'd been a poisoned chalice he was passing to his former aide. That his punishment was to have her, not to lose her.

He suspected she would never speak to him again. And he wasn't prepared for that to happen.

Not yet.

'He has agreed to make way for a diplomatic solution instead.'

'He has?' Her eyes were filled with confusion as if she found something about his reaction difficult to understand. 'But that's good, isn't it?'

'It is an acceptable compromise, considering the circumstances,' said Suleiman, holding up a jangling set of keys which sparked silver in the bright sunlight. 'Now let's go. We're leaving the horses here and taking one of the Sultan's cars.'

Sara tried to keep up with his long-legged stride as she followed him into the courtyard, but it wasn't until they were sitting in the blessed cool of the air-conditioned car that she could pluck up enough courage to ask him.

'Where are we going?'

He didn't answer straight away. In fact, he didn't answer for a good while. Not until they had left the palace far behind them and all that surrounded them was sand and emptiness. Pulling over onto the side of the wide and deserted road, he unfastened his seat belt before leaning over and undoing hers.

'What…are you doing?' she asked.

'I want to kiss you.'

'Suleiman—'

His mouth was hard and hungry and she could feel his anger coming off him in waves. He slid towards her on the front seat of the luxury car, one hand capturing her breast, while the other began to ruck up the slithery silk of her dress. He stopped kissing her long enough to slide his hand up her bare thigh and stare down at her face.

'Suleiman,' she said again—as if saying his name would make some kind of sense of the situation. As if it would remind her that this was dangerous—in so many ways.

'All I can think of is you,' he said. 'All I want is to touch you again. You're driving me crazy.'

She swallowed as he edged his fingertip inside her panties. 'This isn't the answer.'

'Isn't it?'

He had reached her core now, touching her exquisitely aroused flesh so that the scent of her sex overrode the subtle perfume of the rose petals in which she'd bathed.

'No. It's…oh, Suleiman. That's not fair.'

'Who said anything about fairness?'

His finger brushed against the sensitive nub. 'Oh,' she breathed. And again. *'Oh.'*

'Still think this isn't the answer?'

She shook her head and Suleiman felt an undeniable burst of triumph as she fell back against the leather seat and spread her legs for him. But his mouth was grim as he rubbed his finger against her sex and all kinds of dark emotions stirred within him.

He distracted himself by watching her writhe with pleasure. He watched the flush of colour which spread over her skin like wildfire and felt the change in her body as her back began to arch. Her little cries became louder. Her legs stiffened as they stretched out in front of her and he saw a flash of something—was it anger or regret? —before her eyelids fluttered to a close and she cried out his name, even though he got the idea she was trying very hard not to.

Afterwards she smoothed down her tunic with trembling fingers and turned to him and there was a look on her face he'd never seen before. She looked satiated yes, but determined too—her eyes flashing violet fire as she lifted up his robes.

'Now what are you doing?' he questioned.

'You ask too many questions.'

She freed an erection which was so hard that it hurt—and sucked him until he came in her mouth almost immediately. And he had never felt so powerless in his life. Nor so turned on. Afterwards, he opened his eyes to look at her but she was staring straight ahead, her shoulders stiff with tension and her jaw set.

'Sara?' he questioned.

She turned her head and he was shocked by the pallor of her face, which made her eyes look like two glittering violet jewels. 'What?'

He picked up one of her hands, which was lying limply in her lap, and raised it to his lips and kissed it. 'You didn't enjoy that?'

She shrugged. 'On one level, yes, of course I did—as, I imagine, did you. But that wasn't about sex, was it, Suleiman? That seemed to be more about anger than anything else. I think I can understand why you're feeling it, but I don't particularly like it.'

'You were angry too,' he said softly.

She turned her head to look at the endless stretch of sand outside the window. 'I was feeling things other than anger,' she said.

'What things?'

'Oh, you know. Stupid things. Regret. Sadness. The realisation that nothing ever stays the same.' She turned back to him, telling herself to be strong. Telling herself that the friendship they'd shared so long ago had been broken by time and circumstance. And now by desire. And that made her want to bury her face in her hands and weep.

She forced a smile. 'So now we're done—are you going to take me to the airfield so I can go back to England?'

He reached his hand out to touch her face, sliding

his thumb against her parted lips so that they trembled. Leaning over, he hovered his lips over hers. *'Are we done?'*

Briefly, Sara closed her eyes. *Say yes,* she told herself. *It's the only sane solution. You've escaped the marriage and you know there's no future in this.* Her lashes fluttered open to stare straight into the obsidian gleam of his eyes. His mouth was still close enough for her to feel the warmth of his breath and she struggled against the temptation to kiss him.

Were they done?

In her heart, she thought they were.

She ought to go back to England and start again. She should go back to her job at Gabe's—if he would have her—and carry on as before. As if nothing had happened.

She bit her lip, because it wasn't that easy. Because something *had* happened and how could she go back to the way she'd been before? She felt different now because she *was* different. Inevitably. She had been freed from a marriage in which she'd had no say, but she was confused. Her future looked just as bewildering as before and it was all because of Suleiman.

She had tried burying memories of him, but that hadn't worked. And now that she'd made love with him, it had stirred up all the feelings she had repressed for so long. It had stirred up a sexual hunger which was eating away at her even now—minutes after he'd just brought her to orgasm in the front seat of the Sultan's car. It didn't matter what she *thought* she should do—

because, when push came to shove, she was putty in his hands. When Suleiman touched her, he set her on fire.

And maybe that was the answer. Maybe she just needed time to convince herself that his arrogance would be intolerable in the long term. If she tore herself away from him now—before she'd had her fill of him—wouldn't she be caught in the same old cycle of forever wanting him?

'Do you have a better suggestion?' she questioned.

'I do. A much better one.' He stroked his hand down over her plaited hair. 'We could take my plane and fly off somewhere.'

'Where?'

'Anywhere you like. As long as there's a degree of comfort. I'm done with desert sand and making out in the front seat, like a couple of teenagers. I want to take you to bed and stay there for a week.'

CHAPTER EIGHT

'So why Paris?' Sara questioned, her mouth full of croissant.

Suleiman leaned across the rumpled sheets and used the tip of his finger to rescue a stray fragment of pastry which had fallen onto her bare breast. He lifted the finger to his mouth and sucked on it, his dark eyes not leaving her face.

And Sara wanted to kiss him all over again. She wanted to fling her arms around him and press her body against him and close her eyes and have him colour her world wonderful. Because that was what it was like whenever he touched her.

'It's my favourite hotel,' he said. 'And there is a reason why it's known as the city of lovers. We can lie in bed all day and nobody bats an eyelid. We need never set foot outside the door if we don't want to.'

'Well, that's convenient,' said Sara drily. 'Because that's exactly what we've being doing. We've hardly seen any of the sights. In fact, we've been here for three days and I haven't even been up the Eiffel Tower.'

He kissed her nipple. 'And do you want to go up the Eiffel Tower?'

'Maybe.' Sara put her plate down and leant back against the snowy bank of pillows. That thing he was doing to her nipple with his tongue was distracting her from her indolent breakfast in bed, but there were other things on her mind. Questions which kept flitting into her mind and which, no matter how hard she tried, wouldn't seem to flit away again. She had told herself that there was a good reason why you were supposed to live in the present—but sometimes you just couldn't prevent thoughts of the future from starting to darken the edges of your mind. Or the past, come to that...

She kept her voice light and airy. As if she were asking him nothing more uncomplicated than would he please order her a coffee from room service. 'Have you brought other women here?'

There was a pause. The fingers which had been playing with her nipple stilled against the puckered flesh. He slanted her a look which she found more rueful than reassuring. 'What do you want me to say? That you're the first?'

'No, of course not,' she said stiffly. 'I didn't imagine for a moment that I was.'

But the thought of other women lying where she was lying unsettled her more than it should have done. Actually, it didn't unsettle her—it hurt. The thought of Suleiman licking someone *else's* breasts made dark and hateful thoughts crowd into her head. The image of him sliding his tongue between another woman's legs made her feel almost dizzy with rage. And jealousy. And a million other things she had no right to feel.

She should have known this would happen. She should have listened to all the doubts she'd refused to listen to that day in the desert. When she'd been so hungry for him and so impressed—yes, impressed—when he'd offered to fly her anywhere in the world that she'd smiled the smile of a besotted woman and said yes.

And now look what had happened. Her feelings for him hadn't died, that was for sure. She still cared for him more than she wanted to care for him and more than it was safe to care. Yet deep down she knew that this trip was supposed to be about getting the whole *passion* thing out of their system. For both of them. Something which had begun so messily needed to have a clean ending so that they could both move on; she knew that, too.

So what had happened?

Suleiman had pulled out all the stops—that was what had happened. He was a man she had always adored, and now he had an added wow factor, because his vast self-made wealth gave him an undeniable glamour. And glamour mixed with desire made for a very powerful cocktail indeed.

He had whisked her onto his own, private jet—and she'd got the distinct feeling that he had enjoyed showing it off—and flown her to a city she'd never got around to visiting before. That was the first mistake. Was it a good idea to go to the city of romance if you were trying to convince yourself that you weren't still in love with a man?

He had booked them into the presidential suite at the Georges V, where the staff all seemed to know him by name. Sara had been brought up in a palace, so she knew pretty much everything there was to know about luxury, but she fell in love with the iconic Parisian hotel.

Next he took her shopping. Not just, as he said, because she had brought only a very inappropriate wardrobe with her—but because he wanted to buy her things. She told him that she would prefer to buy things for herself. He told her that simply wasn't acceptable. There was a short stand-off, followed by a making-up session which had involved a bowl of whipped cream and a lot of imagination. And because she felt weak from all their love-making and dizzy just with the sense of *being* there—she went ahead and let him buy her the stuff anyway.

The crisp January weather was cold so he splashed out on an ankle-length sheepskin coat and some thigh-high leather boots.

'But you disapproved when I was wearing a very similar pair back in England,' she had objected.

'Yes, but these are for my eyes only,' he'd purred, pillowing his head against his folded arms as he'd leaned back against the sofa to watch her slide them on when they had arrived back at the hotel with their purchases. 'And they will look very good when worn with nothing but a pair of panties.'

Ah, yes. Panties. That seemed to be another area of his expertise. He indulged her taste for lingerie with tiny, wispy bras designed to highlight her nipples. He bought her an outrageous pair of crotchless panties and later on that day proved just what a time-effective purchase they could be. Silky camiknickers and matching suspender belts were added to the costly pile he accumulated in the city's most exclusive store, with Suleiman displaying an uncanny knack of knowing just what would suit her.

Sara sat up in bed and brushed away the last few crumbs of croissant. 'How many?' she questioned, getting out of bed and feeling acutely aware that he was watching her.

He frowned. 'How many what?'

'Women.' She walked across the room towards the windows, wondering why she had gone ahead and asked him a question she had vowed not to ask.

'Sara,' he said softly. 'It's knowing women as I do which allows me to give you so much pleasure.'

'Yes,' she said, staring fixedly out of the giant windows which commanded a stunning view of the city, where the Eiffel Tower dominated a landscape made light by the shimmering waters of the Seine. 'I imagine it is.'

She listened to the sudden sound of silence which had descended on the room. One of those silences between two people which she'd realised could say so much. Or rather, so little. Silences when she had to fight to bite back the words which were bursting to come out. Words which had been building up inside her for days— years—and which she knew he wouldn't want to hear.

Instead, she stared out at the cityscape in front of her as if it was the most wonderful thing she'd ever seen, which wasn't easy when her vision was starting to get all blurred.

'Sara?'

She shook her head, praying that he wouldn't pursue it. *Leave me alone. Let me get over it in my own time.*

'Sara, look at me.'

It took a moment or two before she had composed herself enough to turn around and curve him a bright smile. 'What?'

His eyes were narrowed and speculative. 'Are those *tears* I see?'

'No, of course it isn't,' she said, dabbing furiously at her eyes with a bunched fist. 'And if it is, then it's only my damned hormones. You must know all about those.'

'Come here.'

'I don't want to. I'm enjoying the view.'

His gaze slid over her naked body. 'I'm enjoying the view too, but I want you to come back to bed and tell me what's wrong.'

She considered refusing—but what else was she going to do in this vast arena of the bedroom, with Suleiman watching her like that? She felt vulnerable—and not just because she was naked. She felt vulnerable with each hour of every day, knowing she was losing her heart to him.

He held out his arms and she felt as if she'd lost some kind of battle as she went to him, loving the way the flat of his hand smoothed down the spill of her hair as she climbed into bed beside him. She loved the feel of his naked body entwined with hers. She snuggled up to him, hoping that her closeness would distract him enough to stop asking questions she had no desire to answer. But no. He tilted up her chin, so that there was nowhere to look except into the ebony gleam of his eyes.

'Want to talk about it, princess?'

She shook her head. 'Not really.'

'Shall I guess?'

'Please don't, Suleiman. It's not important.'

'I think it is. You're falling in love with me.'

Sara flinched. Maybe she wasn't as good at hiding her feelings as she'd thought. But then, neither was Suleiman as clever as *he* thought. He'd got the sentiment right—but the tense was wrong. She wasn't 'falling' in love with him—she'd *always* been in love with him. Fancy him not knowing that. She gave him a cool smile. 'That's an occupational hazard for you, I expect?'

'Yes,' he said seriously. 'I'm afraid it is.'

She shook her head, laughing in spite of everything. 'You really are the most arrogant man I've ever known.'

'I have never denied my arrogance.'

'Admitting that doesn't make it all right!'

She was trying to wriggle out of his arms, but he was having none of it. He captured both her wrists in his hands, stilling her so that their eyes were on a collision course.

'I can't help who I am, Sara. And I have enough experience—'

'And then some.'

'To recognise when a woman starts to lose her heart to me. Sweetheart, will you please stop wriggling—and glaring—and listen to what I have to say?'

'I don't want to listen.'

'I think you need to.'

She stilled in his arms, aware of the loud thunder of her heart. His hard thigh was levered between her own and a sadness suddenly swept over her—because wasn't she going to miss being in bed with him like this? Cuddled up in his arms and feeling as if the rest of the world didn't exist. 'I don't want to turn this into a long goodbye,' she whispered.

'And neither do I.' He tucked a strand of hair behind her ear and sighed. 'I thought I did.'

'What do you mean, you thought you did?'

Suleiman stared at her, as if unsure how much to tell her. But this was Sara—and hadn't his relationship with her always been special and unique? The usual rules didn't apply to this blonde-haired beauty he'd known since she was a mixed-up little kid. 'Usually when a woman reaches this stage, I begin to grow wary. Bored.'

'This *stage*?' she spluttered indignantly. 'You mean, as if this is some kind of infectious disease you're incubating!'

He laughed. 'I know that sounds like more arrogance but I'm trying to tell you the truth,' he said. 'Or would you rather me dress it up with lavish compliments and make like you're the only woman I've ever been intimate with?'

'No,' she said, unable to keep the slight sulk from her voice.

'At this stage of an affair,' he said, though his mocking smile didn't lessen the impact of his words, 'I usually recognise that it must come to an end, no matter how much desire I'm feeling. Because an inequality of affection can prove volatile—and I have never wished to play games of emotional cruelty.'

'Good of you,' she said sarcastically. Her heart was beating painfully against her ribcage as she waited to hear what was coming next. But she kept her face as impassive as possible because she wasn't going to give him the chance to reject her. Not a second time. And if that made it seem as if all she cared about was her pride—so what? What else was she going to be left with in the long, lonely hours when he'd gone?

She forced a smile, hoping that she seemed all grown up and reasonable. Because she was not going to be the woman with the red eyes, clinging to his legs as he walked out of the door. 'Look, Suleiman—you've been very honest with me, so let me return the compliment. I've always had a crush on you—ever since I was a young girl. We both know that. That's one of the reasons that kiss when I was eighteen turned into so much more.'

'That kiss changed my life,' he said simply.

Sara felt the clamp of pain around her heart. *Don't tell me things like that, because I'll read into them more than you want me to.* 'This time in Paris has been… great. You know it has. You're the most amazing lover. I'm sure I'm not the first woman to have told you that.' She sucked in a deep breath, because she was sure she wouldn't be the last, either. 'But we both know this isn't going anywhere—and we mustn't make it into more than it is, because that will spoil it. We both know that when something is put out of reach, it makes that something seem much more tantalising. That's why—'

He silenced her by placing his finger over her lips and his black eyes burned into hers. 'I think I love you.'

Sara froze. Wasn't it funny how you could dream of a man saying those words to you? And then he did and it was nothing like how you thought it would be. For a start, he had qualified them. He *thought* he loved her? That was the kind of thing someone said when they took an umbrella out on a sunny day. *I thought it might rain.* She didn't believe him. She didn't dare believe him.

'Don't say that,' she hissed.

He looked startled. 'Even if it's true?'

'Especially if it's true,' she said, and burst into tears.

Perplexed, Suleiman stared at her and tightened his arms around her waist as he felt her tears dripping down his neck. 'What have I done wrong?'

'Nothing!'

'Then why are you crying?'

She shook her head, her words coming out between gulps of swallowed air. Words he could hardly make out but which included 'always', quickly contradicted by 'never' and then, when she'd managed to snatch enough breath back, finishing rather inexplicably with 'hopeless'.

Eventually, she raised a tear-stained face to his. 'Don't you understand, you stupid man?' she whispered. 'I think I love you too.'

'Then why are you crying like that?'

'Because it can never work!' she said fiercely. 'How could it?'

'Why not?'

'Because our lives are totally incompatible, that's

why.' She rubbed her hand over her wet cheek. 'You live in Samahan and I live in London. You are an oil baron and I'm a flaky artist.'

'You think those things are insurmountable?' he demanded. 'You don't imagine these are the kind of logistical problems which other couples might have overcome?'

Sara shook her head as all her old fears came crowding back. She thought of her own mother. Love certainly hadn't brought *her* happiness, had it? Because love was just a feeling. A feeling which had no guarantee of lasting. She and Suleiman had both experienced something when they were fixed at a time and in a place which was light years away from their normal lives. How could something like that possibly survive if it was transplanted into the separate worlds which they both inhabited?

'Listen to me, Suleiman,' she said. 'We don't really *know* one another.'

'That's completely untrue. I have known you since you were seven years old. I certainly know you better than I know any other woman.'

'Not as adults. Not properly. We have no idea if we're compatible.'

His hand tightened around her waist; his thumb traced a provocative little circle. 'I think we're *ve-ry* compatible.'

'That's not the kind of compatibility I was talking about.'

'No?'

'No. I'm not talking about snatched moments of forbidden passion beneath the shade of a rock in the desert. Or sex-filled weekends at one of the best hotels in the world. I'm talking about normal life, Suleiman. Everyday life. The kind of life we all have to lead—whether we're a princess or an oil magnate, or the man who drives the grocery truck.' She pulled away from him so she could look at him properly. 'Tell me what your dream scenario would be. Where you'd like us to go from here—if you had the choice.'

'Well, that bit's easy.' He tugged at the end of a long strand of hair which was tickling his chest. 'You no longer have a job, do you?'

'Not officially, no. I left Gabe a letter on Christmas Eve, saying I'd had to go away suddenly and I wasn't sure when I was coming back. It's not the kind of thing his employees usually do and I'm not sure if he'd ever employ me again. There's a long list of people desperate to fill my shoes. He's the best in the business who could get anyone to work for him. I doubt whether he'd give another chance to someone who could let him down without any warning.'

But if she was hoping to see some sort of remorse on Suleiman's face, she was in for a disappointment. The slow smile which curved his lips made the little hairs on the back of her neck stand up, because she suspected she wasn't going to like what she heard next.

'Perfect,' he said.

'I fail to see what's perfect about leaving my boss in the lurch and not having any kind of secure future to go back to.'

'But that's the point, Sara. You do have a secure future—just a different kind of future from the one you envisaged.' He smiled at her as if he had just discovered that all his shares had risen by ten per cent while they'd been in bed. 'You don't have to go back to working for a large organisation. All that— what do they say?—clocking in and clocking out. Buying your lunch in a paper bag and eating it at your desk.'

'Gabe happens to run a very large staff canteen,' she said coldly. 'And insists on all his staff taking a proper lunch break. And I think it's you who are missing the point. I *want* to go back to work. It's what I do. What else do you suggest I do?'

He tugged on another strand of blonde hair and began to wind it around his finger. 'Simple. You come back to Samahan, with me.'

She stared at him in disbelief. 'Samahan?'

His eyes narrowed. 'The expression on your face looks as if I have suggested that you make your home in Hades. But I think you will find yourself greatly surprised. Samahan has improved greatly since the cross-border wars. The discovery of oil has brought with it much wealth and we are ploughing some of that wealth back into the land.'

He let go of the twisted strand of hair and it dangled in front of her bare breast, in a perfect blonde ringlet.

'My home will not disappoint you, Sara—for it is as vast as any palace and just as beautiful. A world-class architect from Uruguay designed it for me, and I flew in a rose expert from the west coast of America to design my gardens. I stable my horses there—two of them won medals in the last Olympics. I have a great team around me.'

Sara recognised what he was doing. This was the modern equivalent of a male gorilla beating his chest. He was showing her how much he had achieved against the odds—he, the poor boy whose own mother had sold him. He was trying to reassure her that he would treat her like a princess, but that was just what she didn't want. She had hated her life as a princess, which was why she had left it far behind.

'And what would I do all day in this beautiful house of yours?'

'You would make love to me.'

'Obviously that's extremely tempting.' Her smile didn't slip. 'But how about when you're not around? When you're jetting off to the States or swanning off somewhere being an oil baron?'

'You can amuse yourself, for there is much that you will enjoy. Swim in the pool. Explore my extensive library.'

'Just like one long holiday, you mean?' she questioned brightly.

'Not necessarily. You will find a role for yourself there, Sara. I know you will. I think you will find that the desert lands are changing. How long is it since you visited the region?'

'Years,' she said distractedly. 'And I think you'd better stop right there. It's very sweet of you and I'm sure your home is perfectly lovely, but I don't want to go to Samahan. I want to go back to London because there are still loose ends to tie up. I owe Gabe an explanation about what happened and I want to finish up the project I was working on.' Her eyes met his. She realised that she wanted him and loved him enough to want to try to make it work. So why not reverse his question to her? 'But you could come back with me, if you like.'

'With you?' His black eyes were hooded.

'Why not? We can see if we can exist compatibly there and if we can, then I'll think about giving Samahan a try. Does that sound reasonable?'

She saw the sudden hardening of his lips and realised that 'reasonable' was not on the top of Suleiman's agenda. He wasn't used to having his wishes thwarted, particularly not by a woman. He had expected her to fall in with his plans—without stopping to think that she might have plans of her own.

But was he seriously suggesting she might be happy being ensconced in what sounded like the luxury prison of his desert home? Hadn't that been what she'd spent her whole life rebelling against?

'What do you think?' she questioned tentatively.

He slipped his hand between her legs. 'I think we have wasted enough time talking about geographical escape.'

'Suleiman—'

He bent his head to her neck and kissed it.

'You want me to stop?'

'That's the last thing I want.'

She thought she heard soft triumph in his laugh as he sheathed himself in a condom and then lay back against the mattress with a look of satisfaction on his face. *Like a conquering hero,* she thought as he lifted her up like a trophy, hating the part of her which enjoyed that.

His moan echoed hers as he slid her down slowly onto his erection. With each angled thrust of her hips she took him deeper and deeper and she wondered what he was thinking. She knew he was watching her as her blonde hair swung wild and free—and suddenly she found herself *performing* for him.

Was she trying to prove that she was a match for all those women who had preceded her—by playing with her breasts and biting her lips, her eyes closed as if she was indulging in some wild and secret fantasy?

Whatever it was, it seemed to work because he went crazy for her. Crazier than she'd ever known him. He splayed his dark hands possessively over her hips as he made the penetration deeper still. And each time she was close to orgasm, he stopped. Stopped so that once she actually screamed out loud with pent-up frustration, because he made her build it up all over again.

He did it to her over and over again. Until she begged him to release her and then at last he slid her onto the floor and drove into her, as if it were the very first time all over again. She felt her body shatter with the most powerful orgasm she'd ever known but once it began to recede, she felt a sudden sense of unease.

An unease which grew stronger with every second. Because that had been all about power, hadn't it? Suleiman was a man who was used to getting his own way and by refusing to conform to his wishes she had taken control of the situation. She had taken control and he would use whatever it took to get it back.

Sex.

Power.

Palaces.

Even words of love which sounded wonderful, until you wondered if he actually knew what they meant. Were they just another lever to get her to see things his way? she wondered.

He'd never even seen her in her usual environment. He didn't *know* that very important side of her personality.

'I want to go back to London,' she said stubbornly. 'Do you want to come with me or not?'

CHAPTER NINE

'Say that again.'

Bathed in the light which flooded into Gabe Steel's enormous penthouse office, Sara met her boss's eyes as he drawled his question. He was leaning back in his chair with a look of curiosity in his grey eyes. And Gabe didn't usually do curiosity. At least, not with his employees. She guessed that leaving him a rather dramatic letter saying she was going away and then asking to be reinstated just a few weeks later was enough to stir anyone's interest. Even your incredibly high-powered and often cynical boss.

'I know it sounds incredible,' she said.

He laughed. 'Incredible is something of an understatement, Sara. How come you kept it a secret for so long?'

She shrugged. 'Oh, you know. I'd hate to make out that I'm some poor little rich girl—but everyone treats you differently once they know you're a princess.'

'I guess they do.' His pewter eyes narrowed as he twirled a solid gold pen between his long fingers. 'So what's brought about the sudden change of heart?'

Change of heart.

She wondered if Gabe had any idea of how uncannily accurate that particular phrase was. Probably. You didn't get to be head of one of the world's biggest advertising agencies without having a finely tuned degree of insight.

'I was...' She wondered what he would say if she told him the truth. *I was due to get married to a Sultan, but I put a stop to that particular arrangement by having sex with his closest friend.* Probably not a good idea. Men could be notoriously tribal about that kind of thing and she didn't want to portray Suleiman as some sort of bad guy. And anyway, that wasn't the whole truth, was it? Suleiman wasn't the *reason* behind the cancelled wedding. He was just a symptom.

She stared sightlessly out of the penthouse window. A symptom who was currently prowling around her London apartment and making her feel as if she had imprisoned a tiger there.

It was a big apartment—everyone said so. So how come the rooms seemed to have shrunk to the size of matchboxes since Suleiman had accompanied her back from Paris and moved in with her? It had been her mother's apartment and Sara loved every inch of it, a feeling clearly not shared by her lover.

He had walked through the three huge—or so she'd thought—reception rooms, had barely deigned to look at the kitchen and had given the bedrooms only a cursory glance, before turning to demand where the garden was.

She had hated the way her voice had sounded all defensive. 'There isn't one.'

'No garden?' He had sounded incredulous, while all her explanations about the convenience of having a nearby park had fallen on deaf ears.

He had complained about the plumbing—which admittedly *was* fairly ancient—and insisted on having black-out blinds installed in her bedroom. He had commandeered the second bedroom as some kind of makeshift office. Suddenly emails began arriving at odd times of the day and night. Important documents from the US and the Middle East were delivered daily, while a series of efficient sounding staff would ring and she would hear him speaking in his native tongue. She told him it was like living at the United Nations.

He said he was trying to decide whether or not to set up a London headquarters. But that was a big decision which couldn't be made in a hurry, while Sara seemed to get stuck with the smaller, niggling ones.

She'd been forced to find some kind of laundry service since it seemed that Suleiman liked to change his shirt at least twice a day. It helped explain why he always looked so immaculate, but the practicalities of such high sartorial standards were a pain.

But she tried to tell herself that these were just glitches which could easily be sorted out. That Suleiman had never lived with anyone before and neither had she. She convinced herself that all these problems were solvable, but quickly realised there was one which wasn't—and that was the problem of time management. Or rather, *her* time management. Suleiman was obviously used to having women at his beck and call. He didn't like it when she got up at seven each morning to get ready for work. Sometimes it seemed as if he was almost *jealous* of her job.

And that scared her.

It scared her even more than her growing feelings for him.

It was as if the love she felt for Suleiman had started out as a tiny seed, which was in danger of becoming a rampant plant and spreading its tentacles everywhere. His presence was so pervasive and his character so compelling that she felt as if she was being taken over by him. That if she allowed him to, he would take over her whole life and completely dominate her and she would become invisible. And she couldn't allow him to do that.

She didn't dare do that.

So even though she had to fight every loving and lustful instinct in her body, she didn't give in to Suleiman's repeated attempts to push her job into second place.

'Come back to bed,' he would purr, with that tiger-hasn't-been-fed look on his face, as he patted the empty space on the bed beside him.

And Sara would pull on her silk wrap and move to a safe distance away from him. 'I can't do that or I'll be late,' she'd said primly, the third time it happened. 'Haven't you ever been out with a working woman before—and if so, how on earth did you cope?'

His answering smile had been infuriating. Almost, she thought—*smug.*

'Most women can be persuaded to take a sabbatical, if you make it worth their while.'

Sara had felt sick at the lengths to which her sex

would go to in order to hang onto a man. Which, of course, made her even more determined not to weaken. Her job meant independence and she'd fought long and hard for it.

She realised that Gabe was still looking at her from the other side of the desk. Still waiting for some kind of explanation. She flashed him a slightly self-conscious smile.

'Actually, it's a man.'

'It usually is,' he offered drily. 'Would that be the reason why you had your skirt on inside out yesterday morning?'

'Oh, Gabe!' She clapped her palms to her flaming cheeks. 'I'm so sorry. I only realised when I came out of the meeting and Alice pointed it out.'

'Forget it. I only mention it because the client did— so perhaps best not to repeat it. Anyway.' He smiled. 'What's his name? This man.'

She could hear her voice softening as she said it. 'It's Suleiman Abd al-Aziz—'

Gabe's eyes narrowed 'The oil baron?'

'You've heard of him?'

He smiled. 'Unlike princesses, global magnates tend not to stay anonymous for very long.'

'No, I suppose not. The thing is, I was thinking…' She twisted her fingers together in her lap and wondered what was making her feel so nervous. Actually, that wasn't true. She knew exactly what was making her nervous. On some instinctive level, she was terrified of Suleiman meeting her powerful and very sexy boss. 'I wanted Suleiman to get a bit of an idea about what my job's about. I told him about the massive campaign we did for that new art gallery in Whitechapel—and I thought that I might bring him along to the opening tonight. If that's all right.'

'Excellent. You do that.' Gabe looked at her expectantly. 'And now, if we're through with all the personal details—can you get me the drawings for the Hudson account?'

Noting the slight reprimand, Sara opened up the folder she'd carried in with her and worked hard on the account for the rest of the afternoon. She sent Alice out for coffee and tried ringing Suleiman to tell him about the gallery opening, but he wasn't answering his phone.

It was gone six by the time she arrived back home to find the apartment filled with the smell of cinnamon and oranges. She wondered if Suleiman had ordered something in and whether he'd just forgotten that she had the opening tonight.

Because mealtimes had proved another stumbling block, mainly because Suleiman was used to having servants cater to his every whim. He liked food to arrive when he wanted it—usually after sex. He was not interested in the mechanics of getting it, not of shopping for it nor having Sara rustle him up a meal. So far they had compromised by eating out every night, but sometimes she just wanted to kick off her shoes and scoff toast on the sofa.

She followed the direction of the aroma out to the kitchen, and blinked in surprise to see Suleiman leaning over the hob, adding something to a pot. It was such an incongruous sight—and so rare to see him in jeans—

that for a moment she just stood there, feasting her eyes on his powerful frame and thick dark hair. The denim clung to his narrow hips, it hugged the muscular shaft of his long legs and she had to swallow down her instant feeling of lust.

'Wow. This is a sight for sore eyes,' she said softly. 'What are you doing?'

'Wondering why it's so difficult to buy fresh apricots in central London.' He turned round, his black eyes glittering as he curved her a smile. 'Actually, I'm trying to impress my liberated princess by producing a meal, after she's spent a hard day at the office.'

Putting her handbag down on the counter, she walked over to him and looped her arms around his neck. 'I didn't know you cooked.'

'That's because I rarely do these days. But as you know, I once served in the Qurhahian army,' he said, bending to brush his mouth over hers. 'Where even men who had been spoilt by living in palaces were taught the basics of food prep.'

She laughed, lifting her lips for a proper kiss and within seconds she was lost in it. And so was he. Suddenly food was forgotten. Everything was forgotten, except the need to have him as close to her as possible. Her fingers tugged at his shirt, pulling it open to reveal his bare chest—not caring that several buttons went bouncing all over the stone tiles of the kitchen floor.

She tugged impatiently at his belt and he gave a low laugh as he pushed her up against the door. Rucking up her dress, he ripped her panties apart and her muffled protest was stifled with a hungry kiss. She could hear the rasp of his zip and the buoyant weight of his erection as it sprang free. She reached down to touch him, her fingertips skating over his silken hardness before he removed her hand. Cushioning the weight of her bottom with his hands, he positioned himself where she was hot and wet for him and thrust deep inside her.

Her legs wrapped tightly around his hips, Sara clung to him as they rocked in rhythm, but it was over very quickly. Her head wilted like a cut flower as she leaned it against his shoulder and her voice was sleepy in his ear.

'Nice,' she murmured.

'Is that the best you can do? I was hoping for something a little more lyrical than "nice".'

'Would stupendous work better?'

'Stupendous is a good word,' he said.

'Listen.' She kissed his neck. 'Do you want to go to the opening of that gallery in Whitechapel? The one I told you about? It's tonight.'

He lifted up a handful of hair and brushed his lips against her neck. 'No, I don't—and neither do you. Let's just stay home. I'm making dinner and afterwards I'm sure we can find ways to amuse ourselves.'

Sara could feel the warmth of her orgasm beginning to ebb away. 'Suleiman, I have to go.'

'No, you don't. You don't *have* to go anywhere. You've been working all day as it is.'

'I know I have. But this is my job. Remember?' She thought of her mother and the way she'd let all her options slide away from her. She thought of the way that men could manoeuvre women into a corner, if you let them. *And she wasn't going to let Suleiman do that to her.* She bent down to pick up the tattered lace which had once been her panties. 'I've been a major part of the whole campaign from the get-go and I want to see the launch. It's expected of me and it would look very odd if I wasn't there. But I asked Gabe whether I could bring you along—and he said yes.'

There was a pause. 'How very generous of him,' he said acidly. 'And you didn't think to give me any notice?'

'Actually, I did.' She tried to ignore the dangerous note in his voice, telling herself that she *had* sprung this on him at the last minute. And why had that been? Because she'd feared just this kind of reaction if she'd said anything about it sooner? 'I tried ringing, but you weren't picking up. Look, you really don't have to go to this, Suleiman, but I do. So I'm going to take a shower and get ready.'

Without another word, she walked into the bedroom and stripped off her clothes before hitting the shower. She half expected Suleiman to follow her, but he didn't.

She was *not* going to feel guilty. Furiously, she lathered shampoo into her hair. If he loved her—as he said he loved her—then shouldn't he be making more of an effort to integrate into her world, and her life?

He could meet Gabe and he'd see Alice again—as well as some of the other graphic designers she'd spoken about. Wasn't that what modern coupledom was all about?

But as she blow-dried her hair in front of the bedroom mirror her fears just wouldn't seem to leave her.

She found herself wondering if they were just *playing* at being modern. Pretending that everything was fine, when deep down nothing had really been addressed. At heart, wasn't Suleiman just another old-fashioned desert warrior who was incapable of any real change?

Knowing that the press would be there, as well as the usual smattering of celebrity guests, she was extra generous with the mascara. She could hear the sound of water running in the bathroom next door and moments later Suleiman walked into the bedroom, a towel wrapped around his hips.

He rubbed at his damp hair with a second towel and she thought how powerful his body looked. The whiteness of the towel contrasted against the deep olive of his skin and droplets of water gleamed there, as if he'd been showered with tiny diamonds.

'Oh, good,' she said, and smiled. 'You've decided to come.'

'Reluctantly,' he growled as he pulled a white shirt from the wardrobe.

She watched him from the mirror as she finished fiddling around with her make-up. He looked heartstoppingly gorgeous in that dark suit which emphasised the blackness of his hair and eyes. She wondered what Alice would say when she saw his name on the guest list. She wondered how he would fit in with all her work colleagues. But her heart was suddenly ridiculously light. He was coming, wasn't he? How could they fail to love him, as she loved him?

She had just slithered her dress over her head, when his words whispered through the air and startled her.

'You're not wearing that?'

She felt the clench of her heart, but she turned round to face him, a sanguine expression on her face. She smoothed her fingers down over the fine gold mesh and smiled. 'I am. Do you like it?'

'No.'

'Well, that's a pity. It's made by one of London's top designers, so it's eminently suitable for tonight's party.'

'It may be, but it is also much too short. You're practically showing your panties.'

The tone of his voice made her heart contract, but she was determined not to back down. She'd thought that they were over all this.

'Don't exaggerate, Suleiman—and please don't come over all heavy on me. The dress is a fashionable length and I'm wearing it. End of story.'

Their eyes met and she became aware of the silent war being waged between them and she tried to see it from his point of view. In Suleiman's world, a woman going out in public wearing a dress this short was sending out a very definite message.

'Look, I know it's the way you've been brought up,' she said. 'But you've really got to lose this idea that women are either saints or scrubbers. I'm wearing gold tights and long boots with it. The boots you bought me in Paris, actually—'

'And I bought those for you to wear in the bedroom.'

'Yes. Well, it may have missed your notice—' she lifted up her leg to reveal the sole of the boot '—but they have real heels made for walking. They weren't designed just for the bedroom! So are you going to lighten up and enjoy the evening?' Her gold bangles jangling, she walked over to him, placing one hand on his shoulder as she tilted her head to one side. 'Are you?'

There was a moment while their eyes fought another silent, clashing battle before Suleiman gave a low growl which was almost a laugh. 'No other woman would dare speak to me the way that you do, Sara.'

'That's why you love me, isn't it?'

'Maybe.' He slid his hand possessively around her waist. 'Come on. Let's go.'

CHAPTER TEN

MOODILY, SULEIMAN GLANCED around the vast art gallery. The cavernous space and endlessly high ceilings made him think that this might have been a warehouse in a former life, though the place certainly bore no resemblance to its humbler origins.

On white walls hung vast canvases sporting naïve splashes of colour which a five-year-old child could have achieved—all bearing price tags far beyond the reach of most ordinary mortals. Stick-thin women and geeky-looking men in glasses stood gazing up at them in rapt concentration, while waitresses dressed like extravagant birds offered trays of exotically coloured cocktails.

He still couldn't believe he was here. He couldn't believe that Sara had brought him here to look at these dull paintings and meet dull people, when she could have been in bed with him instead. He had been cooking her a meal. Didn't she realise that he'd never cooked for a woman before? But instead of switching off her phone and treating him with a little gratitude, she had brought him to this pretentious place. Had given him a plastic glass of very mediocre wine and then had disappeared to greet someone with one of those ridiculous air-kisses he so despised.

She needed to work, she had told him. Just as it seemed she always needed to work. She never stopped. It was as if she couldn't bear to get off the treadmill she'd leapt back on with such enthusiasm when they'd returned from Paris.

He watched her cross the room. The shimmer of her golden dress caressed her body as she moved, while the sinful blonde hair streamed over her shoulders in a silken cascade. Men were watching her, as they had been watching from the moment they'd arrived—even the geeky ones, who didn't particularly look as if they were into women. He wondered if she was aware of that. Was that why she had worn that skimpy little dress—to draw attention to her beauty? Was that what made her walk with such a seductive sway, or was that simply a consequence of wearing those indecently sexy boots?

Why had he bought her those damned boots?

She had stopped to talk to someone and her head was tilted upwards as she listened to what he was saying to her—a tall man with cold grey eyes and a chiselled face. They seemed to be having some kind of animated discussion. They acted as if they knew each other well and Suleiman's eyes narrowed. Who was he? He smiled with polite dismissal at the woman who had attached herself to his side like glue, and walked across the gallery until he had reached them.

Sara looked up as he approached and he noticed that her cheeks had gone very pink. Had her male companion made her blush? he wondered. He felt the twist of something unfamiliar in his gut. Something dark and nebulous.

'Oh, Suleiman.' She smiled. 'There you are.'

'Here I am.' He looked at the man who stood beside her, with a questioning expression. 'Hello.'

He saw the way Sara's teeth had begun to dig into her bottom lip. Was she nervous, he wondered—and if so, why?

'I'd like to introduce you to my boss,' she was saying. 'This is Gabe Steel and he owns the best and biggest advertising agency in London. Gabe—this is Suleiman Abd al-Aziz and I've known…' She began to blush. 'Well, I've known Suleiman ever since I was a little girl.'

There was a split second as the two men eyed one another before briefly shaking hands and Suleiman found his fingers grasped with a bone-crushing strength which equalled his own. So this was her boss. The tycoon he had heard so much about and the man who had lent her his cottage at Christmas. A man with cold grey eyes and the kind of presence which was attracting almost as much attention from the women in the room as Suleiman himself.

One thought jarred uncomfortably in his head.

Why *had* he lent her his cottage?

'Good to meet you, Suleiman,' said Gabe. 'So tell me, was she a good little girl—or was she very naughty?'

Suleiman froze. He tried telling himself that this was the normal, jokey kind of statement which existed among work colleagues in the west—but his heart was stubbornly refusing to listen to reason. Instead, his years of conditioning, which had resulted in a very rigid way of thinking, now demanded to be heard. Instead of joining in with the banter, he found himself thinking that this man Steel—no matter how exalted his position—was speaking most impertinently about the Princess of Dhi'ban.

Unless…

Suleiman's heart began to hammer painfully against his ribcage. Unless the relationship went deeper than that of mere workmates. He swallowed. Was it possible that Gabe Steel was the other man she had slept with— the man who had taken her virginity? Hadn't she told him on Christmas Eve that it was Gabe Steel's cottage and that she was *waiting for her lover*?

Had Gabe Steel been her lover?

For a moment he was so overcome by a sweep of jealousy so powerful that he couldn't speak, and when he did his words felt like little splinters of metal being expelled from his mouth.

'I don't think that the princess would wish me to divulge secrets from her past,' he said repressively.

'No, of course not.' Gabe looked startled, before flashing him an easy smile. 'So tell me, what do you think of the paintings?'

'You want my honest opinion?' Suleiman questioned.

'Suleiman's not a great connoisseur of art,' put in Sara hastily, before shooting him a furious look. She put her hand on his arm and pressed it—the sharp dig undeniably warning him not to elaborate. 'Are you, darling?'

Suleiman felt a cold fury begin to rise within him.

She was speaking to him as if he were some tame little lapdog she had brought along with her. But he could see that causing a scene here would serve no purpose, except to delay their departure and ensure her fury. Clearly she danced obediently to this man Steel's tune—and when they got home he would do her the favour of pointing it out.

So he merely gave a bland smile as he reached out and drew her against him, a proprietorial thumb moving very deliberately over her ribcage. He felt her shiver beneath his touch and he allowed himself a small smile of satisfaction as he looked at her boss.

'Sara's right, of course. I have never been able to understand the penchant for spending vast sums of money on modern art. Call me old-fashioned—but I prefer something which doesn't look as if a cat has regurgitated its supper all over the canvas.'

'Oh, I think we could certainly call you old-fashioned, Suleiman,' said Sara in a high, bright voice.

'But I can see that your campaign has been successful,' conceded Suleiman, forcing a smile. 'Judging by the amount of people here tonight.'

'Yes, we're very pleased with the turnout,' said Gabe. 'Much of which is down to the talent of your girlfriend, of course. It was her artwork which made people sit up and start taking notice.' He smiled. 'Sara's one of the best creatives I have.'

'I'm sure she is. I just hope you have a good replacement ready to step in to fill her shoes,' said Suleiman.

He could see the look of surprise on Gabe Steel's face and the sudden draining of colour from Sara's.

'Something you're not telling me?' questioned Gabe lightly.

'Nothing that I know of,' she answered as her boss gave a brief nod of his head and walked across the art gallery to talk to a woman on the other side of the room.

'Shall we go home?' questioned Suleiman.

'I think we'd better,' said Sara quietly. 'Before I smash one of those very expensive "regurgitated cat supper" canvasses over your arrogant head.'

'Are you saying you'd like one of those hanging in your living room?'

'I do happen to like some of them, yes, but I'm not going to have a conversation about the artwork.'

Suleiman kept his hand firmly on her waist as he steered her towards the cloakroom, so that she could collect her wrap.

She didn't speak until they were outside and neither did he, but just before he opened the door of the waiting cab he leaned into her, breathing in her scent of jasmine and patchouli oil. 'Just what is your relationship with Steel?'

'*Don't*,' she snapped back. 'Don't you dare say another word, until we're back at my apartment.' She began speaking to him in Qurhahian then, her heated words coming out in a furious tirade. 'I don't want the cab driver thinking I'm out with some kind of *Neanderthal*!'

She made no attempt to hide her anger all the way through the constant stop-starting of traffic lights but Suleiman felt nothing but the slow build of sexual hunger in response. The stubborn profile she presented made him want her. Her defiantly tilted chin made him want her even more. He felt the hardening at his groin. He would subdue her fire in the most satisfying way. Subdue her so completely and utterly that she wouldn't ever defy him again. She wouldn't want to...

Feeling more frustrated than he could ever remember, he watched as the orange, green and red of the traffic lights flickered over her face. The flickering kaleidoscope of colour and the sparkle of her golden dress only added to her beauty.

If it had been any other woman, he would have just pulled her in his arms and kissed her. Maybe even brought her to gasping orgasm on the back seat of the cab. But this was not any other woman. It was Sara. Fiery and beautiful Princess Sara. Stubborn and sensual Sara.

The elevator ride up to her apartment was torture. The heat at his groin almost too painful to endure. All he could see was the glimmer of gold as her dress highlighted every curve of her magnificent body, but her shoulders were stiff with tension and her face was still furious.

It seemed to take for ever before the lift pinged to a halt and they were back in her apartment again. The front door had barely closed behind them before she turned on him. 'How *dare* you behave like that?'

'Like what?'

'Coming over all possessive and squaring up to my boss like that!'

'So why the sudden defence of Steel, Sara? Was he your lover? The man to whom you lost your innocence?'

'*Oh!*' Frustratedly, she stared at him for a piercing moment before turning her back and marching into the sitting room, just the way she'd done on Christmas Eve at the cottage. And just like then, he followed her—mesmerised by the shimmering sway of her bottom, until she turned round to glare at him again.

The violet flash in her eyes warned him not to continue with his line of questioning, but Suleiman found he was in the grip of an emotion far bigger than reason. '*Was* he?' he demanded hotly. 'Is that why he lent you his cottage? Why you were so keen to get to the party tonight?'

She shook her head. 'You just don't *get* it, do you? You don't seem to realise that I've been living in England for all these years and I'm just not used to men behaving like this. It's *primitive*. And it's inappropriate.'

'I don't think it's inappropriate,' he ground out. 'You told me that night that you were waiting for your lover and that it was Steel's cottage. Then I discovered that you were not a virgin and so I put two and two together—'

'And came up with a number which seems to have reached triple figures!' she flared, before taking a deep breath as if she was trying to get her own feelings under control. 'Look, I shouldn't have said that about Gabe that night. I was trying to make you angry—and it seems that I have far exceeded my own expectations. I was hurling out stuff and hoping to get a reaction. But I said all that before we became…involved. For the record, Gabe has never been my lover. But even if he had… *even if he had*…that does not give you the right to just march up to him like that in public and start playing the jealousy card. I just don't get it.'

'What don't you get?' he demanded. 'That a man should feel possessive about the woman he loves? Isn't that a mark of the way he feels about her?'

She shook her head. 'It's got nothing to do with the way he feels about her—it's more a mark of wanting to *own* her! Before you became Mr Oil Baron, you travelled for years on Murat's behalf. Are you trying to tell me that this is the way you behaved whenever you met with some diplomat or politician whose ideas you didn't happen to agree with? Going in with all guns blazing?'

His eyes narrowed. 'On the contrary. One of the reasons I excel at card games is because I have the ability to conceal what I'm thinking.'

Slowly, she nodded her head 'So what happened tonight?'

'You did,' he said. 'You happened.'

'You mean it's something I did?'

He shook his head. 'I'm having trouble working it out for myself. I've never *felt* this way about a woman before, and sometimes it scares the hell out of me. I've never wanted a woman in the way I want you, Sara.'

'But wanting me doesn't give you permission to behave like that towards Gabe. It doesn't give you the right to start treating me like a *thing*. Like a valuable painting or some vase that you own, which nobody else is allowed to look at, because it's *all yours*. I don't want that.'

For a moment there was silence as he looked at her.

'Then just what *do* you want, Sara?' he questioned.

'Because you don't seem to want a normal relationship. Not from where I'm standing.'

'That's funny. A normal relationship? I don't think you'd recognise one if you tripped over it in the street!' she said. 'And how could you? You're possessive and demanding and insanely jealous.'

'And you don't think that you might have fed my instinct to be jealous?'

'I've already explained about Gabe.'

'I'm not talking about Gabe! I'm talking about the fact that ever since I've moved in here, you seem to be pushing me away. It's like you've surrounded yourself with a glass wall and I just can't get through to you.'

She felt the fear licking at the edges of her skin. Was that true—or did Suleiman just want to make her completely his, and to stamp out all her natural fire and independence?

She couldn't risk it.

'Oh, what's the point?' she said tiredly. 'There is no point. We've shone the light on what we've got and seen all the gaping great cracks.'

'I think you've made up your mind that it isn't going to work,' he said. 'And maybe that's the way it has to be. But since you've had your say, then let me have mine. And yes, I hold my hands up to all the charges you've just levelled at me. Yes, I've been "possessive and demanding and insanely jealous". I'm not proud of the way I behaved earlier and I'm sorry. It's been bubbling away for a while now and tonight it just seemed to spill over. But I wonder if you've stopped for a minute to ask yourself why?'

'Because you're still living in the Dark Ages? A typical desert male who will never change?'

He shook his head. 'Let me tell you something else, Sara—that I may have failed to live up to your ideal of the ideal lover tonight, but I've sure as hell tried in other ways.'

'How?' She felt stupid standing there in her golden dress with her bangles dangling from her limp wrist. Like a butterfly which had been speared by a pin. 'How have you tried?'

'*How?* For a start, I have relocated into your poky London apartment—'

'It is *not* poky!'

'Oh, believe me,' he said grimly, 'it is. I've been trying to run a global business from the second bedroom and all I get from you is complaints about the phone ringing at odd hours.'

'Is that *all* you get from me, Suleiman?'

He heard the unconsciously sultry note which had entered her voice and wondered if their angry words had scared her. And turned her on. Because didn't women like to push a man to the brink—even though sometimes they didn't like what happened when they got there?

'No,' he said. 'I get a lot of good stuff, too. The best stuff ever, if you must know—but what we have is not sustainable.'

'Not *sustainable*?'

He hardened his heart against the sudden darkening of her eyes and, even though he wanted to cross the room and pull her into his arms, he stood his ground.

'You think I'm content to continue to be treated as some kind of mild irrelevance, while your job dominates everything?'

'I told you that I needed to work.'

'And I accepted that. I just hadn't realised that you would be living at the office, virtually 24/7—as if you had to prove yourself. I don't know if it was to me, or to your boss—to reassure him that you weren't going to take off again. Or to show me that you're an independent woman in your own right. But whatever it is—you aren't facing up to the truth behind your actions.'

'And you are, right?'

'Maybe I am. And I'll tell you what you seem so determined to ignore, if that's what you want, Sara. Or even if it's not what you want. Because I think you need to hear it.'

'Oh, do you?' She walked over to one of the squashy pink velvet sofas and sat down on it, leaning back with her arms crossed over her chest and a defiant expression on her face. 'Go on, then. I can hardly wait.'

His eyes narrowed, because he could hear the vulnerability she was trying so hard to hide. But he needed to say this. No matter what the consequences. 'I get it that you grew up in an unhappy home and that your mother felt trapped. But you are not your mother. Your circumstances are completely different.'

'Not that different,' she whispered. 'Not when you treated me like that tonight. Like your possession.'

'I've held up my hands for that. I've said sorry. I would tell you truthfully that I would never behave in that way again, but it's too late.'

Her arms fell to her side. 'What do you mean, too late?'

'For us. I've tried to change and to adapt to being with you. I may not have instantly succeeded, but at least I gave it a go. But not you. You've stayed locked inside your own fear. You're scared, Sara. You're scared of who you really are. That's what made you run away from Dhi'ban. That's why you let your job consume you.'

'My father gave me permission to go away to board-ing school—I didn't *run away*.'

'But you never go back, do you?'

'Because my life is here.'

'I know it is. But you have family. Your only fam-ily, in fact. When did you last see your brother? I heard that you were at his wedding celebrations for less than twenty-four hours.'

Briefly she wondered how he knew something like that. Had he been *spying* on her? 'I couldn't stay for long…I was in the middle of an important job.'

'Sure you were. Just like you always are. But you have vacations like other people, don't you, Sara? Couldn't you have gone over to see him from time to time? Didn't you ever think that being a king can be a lonely job? Hasn't his wife had a baby? Have you even *seen* your niece?'

'I sent them a gift when she was born,' she said de-fensively, and saw his mouth harden with an expres-sion which suddenly made her feel very uncomfortable.

'You might want to reject your past,' he grated. 'But you can't deny the effect it's had on you. You may hate some things about desert life—but half of you *is* of the desert. Hide from that and you're hiding from yourself—and that's a scary place to be. I know that. You were one of the reasons I knew I could no longer work for Murat, but what happened between us that night made me re-examine my life. I realised that I couldn't continue playing a subordinate role out of some lingering sense of gratitude to a man who had plucked me from poverty.' He looked at her. 'But that's all irrelevant now. I need to pack.'

Her head jerked up as if she were a puppet and somebody had just given the string a particularly violent tug. 'Pack? What for?' She could hear the rising note of panic in her voice. 'What are you packing for?'

'I'm going.' His voice was almost gentle. 'It's over, Sara. We've had good times and bad times, but it's over. I recognise that and sooner or later you will, too. And I don't want to destroy all the good memories by continuing to slug it out, so I'm leaving now.'

She was swallowing convulsively. 'But it's late.'

'I know it is.'

'You could… Couldn't you stay tonight and go in the morning?'

'I can't do that, Sara.'

'No.' She shrugged as if it didn't matter. As if she didn't care. 'No, I guess you can't.'

Her lips were trembling as she watched him turn round and walk from the sitting room. She could hear the sounds he made as he clattered around in the bathroom, presumably clearing away that lethal-looking razor he always used. A terrible sense of sadness—and an even greater sense of failure—washed over her as he appeared in the doorway, carrying his leather overnight bag.

'I'll collect the rest of my stuff tomorrow, while you're at work.'

She stood up. Her legs were unsteady. She wanted to run over to him and tell him to stop. That it had all been a horrible mistake. Like a bad dream which you woke from and discovered that none of it had been real. But this *was* real. Real and very painful.

She wasn't going to be that red-eyed woman clinging onto his leg as he walked out of the door, she reminded herself. *Was she?* And surely they could say goodbye properly. A lifetime of friendship didn't have to end like *this*.

'A last kiss?' she said lightly, sounding like some vacuous socialite he'd just met at a cocktail party.

His mouth hardened. He looked...*appalled*. As if she had just suggested holding an all-night rave on someone's grave.

'I don't think so,' he said grimly, before turning to slam his way out of her apartment—leaving only a terrible echoing emptiness behind.

CHAPTER ELEVEN

THE APARTMENT FELT bare without him.

Her life felt bare without him.

Sara felt as if she'd woken up on a different planet.

It reminded her of when she'd arrived at her boarding school in England, at the impressionable age of twelve. It had been a bitter September day, and the contrast to the hot desert country she'd left behind couldn't have been more different. She remembered shivering as the leaves began to be ripped from the trees by the wind, and she'd had to get used to the unspeakably stodgy food and cold, dark mornings. And even though she had known that here in England lay the future she had wanted—it had still felt like being on an alien planet for a while.

But that was nothing to the way she felt now that Suleiman had gone.

Hadn't she thought—prayed—that he hadn't meant it? That he would have cooled off by morning. That he would come back and they could make up. She could say sorry, as he had done. They could learn from their mistakes, and work out what they both wanted from their lives and walk forward into the future together.

He didn't come back.

She watched the clock. She checked her phone. She waited in.

And even though her pride tried to stop her—eventually she dialled his number. She was clutching a golden pen she'd found on the floor of the second bedroom—the only reminder that Suleiman had ever used the room as an office. He had loved this pen and would miss it, she convinced herself, even though she knew he had a dozen other pens he could use.

But he didn't pick up. The phone rang through to a brisk-sounding male assistant, who told her that Suleiman was travelling. In as casual a tone as she could manage, she found herself asking where—only to suffer the humiliation of the assistant telling her that security issues meant that he would rather not say.

Where was he travelling to? Sara wondered—as she put the phone down with a trembling hand. Had he gone back to Paris? Was he lying in that penthouse suite with another blonde climbing all over him wearing kinky boots and tiny knickers?

With a shaking hand she put the gold pen down carefully on the desk and then she forced herself to dress and went into the office.

But for the first time in her life, she couldn't concentrate on work.

Alice asked her several questions, which she had to repeat because Sara wasn't paying attention. Then she spilt her coffee over a drawing she'd been working on and completely ruined it. The days seemed to rush past her in a dark stream of heartache. Her thoughts wouldn't focus. She couldn't seem to allocate her time into anything resembling *order*. Everything seemed a mess.

At the end of the week, Gabe called her into the office and asked her to sit down and she could see from his face that he wasn't happy.

'What's wrong?' he questioned bluntly.

'Nothing's wrong.'

'Sara,' he said. 'If you can't do your job properly, then you really shouldn't come to work.'

She swallowed. 'That bad, huh?'

He shrugged. 'Do you want to talk about it?'

Miserably, she shook her head. Gabe was a good boss in many ways but she knew what they said about him—steely by name and steely by nature. 'Not really.'

'Look, take a week off,' he said. 'And for God's sake, sort it out.'

She nodded, thinking that men really *were* very different from women. It was all so black and white to them. What if it couldn't be sorted out? What if Suleiman had gone from her life for good?

She left the building and walked out into the fresh air, where a gust of wind seemed to blow right through her. She hugged her sheepskin coat closer and began to walk, thinking about the things Suleiman had said to her.

Thoughts she'd been trying to block out were now given free rein as she examined them. *Had* she run away from her old life and tried to deny it? Pretended that part of her didn't exist?

Yes, she had.

Had she behaved thoughtlessly, neglecting the only family she had? Rushing away from the wedding celebrations and not even bothering to get on a plane to go and see her new niece?

She closed her eyes.

Yes, again.

She'd thought of herself as so independent and mature, and yet the first thing she had done was to lift up the phone to Suleiman. What had she been planning to say to him? Start whining that she missed him and wanted him to come back to make her feel better?

That wasn't independence, was it? That was more like co-dependence. And you couldn't rely on somebody else to make you feel better about yourself.

She needed to face up to the stuff she'd locked away for so long. She'd been so busy playing the part of Sara Williams who had integrated so well into English life and making sure she fitted in that she had forgotten the other Sara.

The desert princess. The sister. The auntie.

And that other Sara was just as important.

A lump came into her throat as she lifted her hand to hail a cab and during the drive to her apartment she started making plans to try to put it right.

She managed to get a flight out to Dhi'ban later that evening. It meant she would have a two-hour stopover in Qurhah, but she could cope with that. Oddly enough, she wasn't tempted to ask her brother to send a plane to Qurhah to collect her—and she would sooner walk bare-footed across the desert than ask Suleiman to come to her aid.

She spent the intervening hours shopping and packing and then she dressed as conservatively and as unobtrusively as possible, because she didn't want anyone getting wind of her spontaneous visit.

The journey was long and tiring and she blinked with surprise when eventually she arrived at Dhi'ban's main airport, because she hardly recognised it. The terminal buildings had been extended and were now gleaming and modern. There were loads of shops selling cosmetics and beautiful Dhi'banese jewellery and clothes. And there…

She looked up to see a portrait of her brother, the King, and she thought how stern he looked. Sterner than she'd ever seen him, wearing the crown that her father had worn.

Inevitably, she was recognised as she went through Customs, but she waved aside the troubled protestations of the officials, telling them that she had no desire for a red carpet.

'I didn't want any kind of fuss or reception,' she said, smiling as she held up the large pink parcel she had purchased at Qurhah's airport. 'I want this to be a surprise. For my niece, the princess Ayesha.'

The palm-fringed road was reassuringly familiar and when she saw her childhood home appear in the distance, with the morning light bouncing off the white marble, she felt her heart twist with a mixture of pleasure and pain.

She'd never seen the guards outside the main gates

look more surprised than when she stepped from the airport cab into the bright sunshine. But today she wasn't impatient when they bowed deeply. Today she recognised that they were just doing their job. They respected her position as Princess—and maybe it was about time that she started respecting it, too.

She walked through the grounds and into the palace. Her watch told her that it was almost two o'clock and she wondered if her brother was working. She realised that she didn't know anything about his life and she barely knew Ella, his wife.

But before she could decide what to do next, there was Haroun walking towards her. His features—a stronger, more masculine version of her own—were initially perplexed and then he broke into a wide smile as he held out his arms.

'Is it really you, Sara?'

'It really is me,' she whispered, glad that he chose that moment to gather her in his arms in a most un-Kingly bear-hug, which meant that she had time to blink away her tears and compose herself.

Within the hour she was sitting with Haroun and his wife Ella and begging their forgiveness. She told them she felt guilty about her absence, but if they were prepared to forgive her—she would like to be part of their lives. And could she please see her niece?

The royal couple looked at one another and smiled with deep satisfaction, before Ella hugged her tightly and said Ayesha was sleeping, and that Sara could see her once they had taken tea.

The three of them sat in the scented bower of the

rose garden and drank mint tea. She started to tell them about the Sultan, but of course Haroun knew about the cancelled wedding, because the politicians and diplomats from the two countries were working on a new alliance.

'So you've *seen* Murat?' she asked cautiously.

'I have.'

'And did he…did he seem upset?'

'Not unless your idea of upset is being photographed with a stunning woman,' laughed Haroun.

It was only after gentle prompting that she was persuaded to tell them about Suleiman and how much she loved him. Her voice was shaky as she said it, because she'd realised that the truth was something she couldn't keep running from either.

'But it's over,' she said.

Ella looked at Haroun, and frowned. 'You *like* Suleiman, don't you, darling?'

'I don't like him when I'm playing backgammon,' Haroun growled.

Sara was shown to her old room and there, set between the two gold-framed portraits of her late mother and father, was a book about horses, which Suleiman had bought for her twelfth birthday, just before she'd left for England.

For the brave and fearless Sara, he had written. *Your friend, Suleiman. Always*.

And that was when the sobs began to erupt from her throat, because she had been none of those things, had she? She had not been brave and fearless—she had been a coward who had run away and hidden and neglected

her family. She hadn't lived up to Suleiman's expectations of her. She hadn't been a real friend. She hadn't
fulfilled her potential in so many ways.

She bathed and changed and dried her eyes and Ella
knocked on the door, to take her to the nursery. And that
was poignant, too. Shielded from the light by swathed
swags of softest tulle lay a sleeping baby in the large,
rocking cot she had slept in herself. For a moment Sara
touched the side and felt it sway, watching as Ella lifted
out the sleepy infant.

Ayesha was soft and smiling, with a mop of silken
curls and a pair of deep violet eyes. Sara felt her heart
fill with love as she touched her fingertip to the baby's
plump and rosy cheek.

'Oh, she's beautiful,' she said. 'How old is she now?'

'Nine months,' said Ella. 'I know. Time flies and all
that. And by the way—they say she looks just like you.'

'Do they?'

Ella smiled. 'Check out your baby photos if you don't
believe me.'

Sara stared into the baby's eyes and felt the sharp
twist of pain. Was it normal to feel wistful for what
might have been, but now never would? To imagine
what kind of baby she and Suleiman might have produced?

'I wonder if she'd come to me,' she said, pulling a
smiley face at the baby as she held out her arms.

But Ayesha wriggled and turned her face away and
started to cry.

'Don't worry,' said Ella. 'She'll get used to you.'

It took four days before Ayesha would consent to

have her auntie hold her, but once she had—she seemed reluctant to ever let her go. Sara wondered if the baby instinctively guessed how badly she needed the cuddles. Or maybe there was some kind of inbuilt recognition— the primitive bond of shared blood.

She fitted in with Haroun and Ella's routine, and began to relax as she reacquainted herself with Dhi'ban and life at court. She went riding with her brother. She helped Ella with the baby and quickly grew to love her sister-in-law.

One afternoon the two women were wheeling the pram through the palace gardens, their heads covered with shady hats. The week off work which Gabe had given her was almost up and Sara knew that she needed to give some serious thought to her future.

She just hadn't decided what she wanted that future to be.

'Shall we go back now?' questioned Ella, her soft voice breaking into Sara's thoughts.

'Yes, let's.'

Along the scented paths they walked, back towards the palace, but as they grew closer Sara saw a dark figure silhouetted against the white marble building. For a moment her eyes widened, until she forced her troubled mind to listen to reason. *Please stop this,* she prayed silently. *Stop conjuring up hallucinations which make me think I can actually see him.*

She ran her hand across her eyelids, but when she opened them again he was still there and her steps faltered.

'Is something wrong?'

Did Ella's voice contain suppressed laughter—or was she imagining *that*, too?

'For a minute then, I thought I saw Suleiman.'

'Well, that's because you did,' said Ella gently. 'He's here. Suleiman's here.'

The ground seemed suddenly to shift beneath Sara's feet—the way it did when you stepped onto a large ship which looked motionless. She was aware of the rush of blood to her ears and the pounding of her heart in her chest. Questions streamed into her mind but her lips seemed too dry to do anything other than stumble out one bewildered word. 'How?'

But Ella was walking away, wheeling the pram towards one of the side entrances, and Sara was left standing there, feeling exposed and scared and impossibly vulnerable. Now her legs felt heavy. As if her feet had suddenly turned to stone and it was going to be impossible for her to walk. But she *had* to walk. Independent women walked. They didn't stumble—weak-kneed and hopeless—because the man they dreamed of had just appeared, like a blazing dark comet which had fallen to earth.

He didn't move as she went towards him and it was impossible to read the expression on his dark face. Even as she grew closer she still couldn't tell what he was thinking. But hadn't he told her himself that he was famous at the card table for being able to keep a poker-straight face?

She was trying to quell the hope which had risen up inside her—because dashed hopes were surely worse than no hope at all. But she couldn't keep her voice steady as she stood before him, and the pain of wanting to hold him again was almost physical.

'Suleiman,' she said and her voice sounded croaky and unsure. 'What are you doing here?'

'I've come to speak to your brother about the possibility of drilling for oil in Dhi'ban.'

Her heart plummeted. 'Are you being serious?'

He looked at her, an expression of exasperation on his face. 'Of course I'm not being serious. Why do you *think* I might be here, Sara?'

'I don't *know*!'

She was shaking her head and, for the first time, Suleiman saw that she had changed—even if for a moment he couldn't quite work out what that change was. Her skin was a little paler than usual and her lips looked as if they had been bitten into—but beneath all that he could see something else. Something which had been missing for a long time. He swallowed down the sudden lump in his throat as he realised that something was peace. That there was a new strength and resolution which shone out from her shadowed eyes as she looked at him.

And now he began to have doubts of his own. Had Sara found true contentment—*without* him? For a moment he acknowledged that his motives for being here today were entirely selfish. What if she would be better off without him? Had he stopped to consider *that*? Was her need for independence such that she considered a man like him to be an impediment?

His heart turning over with love and pain, he looked into her beautiful face and suddenly he didn't care. He knew there were no guarantees in this life, but that didn't mean you shouldn't strike out for the things which really mattered. Let Sara tell him that she didn't want him if that was what she truly believed—but let her be in no doubt about his feelings for her.

'I think you do know,' he said softly. 'I'm here because I love you and I can't seem to stop loving you.'

'Did you try?' she questioned, her voice full of pain. 'Is that why you walked away? Why you left my life so utterly when you walked out of my apartment?'

There was a silence for a moment, broken only by the sound of a bird calling from high up in one of the trees. 'I couldn't stay when you were like that,' he told her truthfully. 'When you were too scared to let go and be the woman you really wanted to be. You were pushing me away, Sara—and I couldn't stand that. I knew you needed to come home before you could think about making any kind of home of your own.' He smiled. 'Then I heard on the desert grapevine that you'd come back to Dhi'ban. And I thought that was probably the best thing I'd heard in a long time.'

She turned big violet eyes up at him. 'Did you?'

'Mmm.' He wanted to go to her. To cup her chin in the palm of his hand and hold it safe. To run the edge of his thumb over the tremble of her lips. But he needed her to hear these words before he could touch her again. He owed her his honesty.

'As for the answer to your question. I'm here because you make me feel stuff—stuff I've spent a lifetime trying not to feel.'

'What kind of stuff?'

'Love.'

'Oh. You *think* you love me?' she questioned, echoing the words he had used in Paris.

'No.' His voice was quiet. 'I *love* you—without qualification. I love you fully, completely, utterly and for ever. I'm here because although I'm perfectly capable of living without you, I don't want to. No. That's not entirely true. If you want the truth, I can't bear the thought of living without you, Sara. Because without you I am only half the man I'm capable of being and I want to be whole.'

There was silence for a moment. She lowered her gaze, as if she had found something of immense interest on the gravelled palace forecourt. For a moment he wondered if she was plucking up the courage to tell him that his journey here had been wasted, but when she lifted her face again, Suleiman could see the shimmer of tears in her violet eyes.

'And without you I'm only half the woman I'm capable of being,' she said shakily. 'You've made me whole again, too. You've made me realise that only by facing our biggest fears can we overcome them. You've made me realise that independence is a good thing—but it can never be at the expense of love. Nothing can. Because love is the most important thing of all. And you are the most important thing of all, Suleiman—someone so precious who I thought I'd lost through my own stupidity.'

'Sara,' he said and the word was distorted by the shudder of his breath. 'Sweet Sara. My only love.'

And that was all it took. A declaration torn from

somewhere deep inside him. A declaration she returned over and over again in between their frantic kisses, although Suleiman first took the precaution of walking her further into the gardens, away from the natural interest of the servants' eyes.

By the time they returned to the palace—where Ella and Haroun had perceptively put a bottle of champagne on ice—Sara was wearing an enormous emerald engagement ring.

And she couldn't seem to stop smiling.

EPILOGUE

'YOU DO REALISE,' said Sara as she removed her filmy tulle veil and placed it next to the emerald and diamond tiara, which her sister-in-law had lent her, 'that I'm not going to be a traditional desert wife.'

'Shouldn't you have mentioned this *before* we got married?' murmured Suleiman. He was lying naked waiting for his bride to join him on her old childhood bed, and had decided that there was something gloriously decadent about that.

'I did.' She stepped out of her ivory lace gown and hung it over the back of the chair, revelling in the look in his eyes as he ran his gaze over her bridal lingerie. 'Just as long as you know that I meant it.'

'And I meant it when I said that I didn't expect you to be. Just as I did when I said that I will not be a traditional desert husband. I will not try to possess you, Sara—not ever again. I will give you all the freedom you need.'

She gave a happy sigh as she smiled at him. Wasn't it a strange thing that when somebody gave you freedom, it meant you no longer wanted it quite so much?

Suleiman had told her that of course she could carry on working for Gabe—just as long as they came to some compromise over her long hours. The crazy thing was that she no longer wanted to work there—or, at least, not as she'd done before. She had loved her job, but it was part of her past and part of her life as a single woman. She had a different life now and different opportunities. Which was why she had agreed to carry on working for the Steel organisation on a freelance basis. That way, she could travel with her husband and everyone was happy.

She gave a contented sigh. Their wedding had been the best wedding she'd ever been to—although Suleiman told her she was biased. Alice from the office had been invited—and her expression as she'd been shown around the Dhi'ban palace had been priceless. Gabe had been there too—and Sara thought that even her cynical boss had enjoyed all the ancient ritual and ceremony which accompanied the joining of her hand to Suleiman's.

The best bit had been the Sultan's surprise appearance, because it signified that he had forgiven Suleiman—and her—for so radically changing the course of desert history.

'Murat seemed to get on well with Gabe, don't you think?' she questioned as she slid her diamond bracelet onto the dressing table, where it lay coiled like a glittery snake. 'What do you suppose they were talking about?'

'Right now I don't care,' Suleiman murmured. 'About anything other than kissing you again. It seems like an eternity since I had you in my bed.'

'It's almost a week since you had me in your bed—palace protocol being what it is,' she agreed. 'But less than eight hours since you *had* me. *In* the stables, no less—on the eve of my wedding. And I wasn't allowed to make a sound.'

'That was part of the thrill,' he drawled, watching as she kicked off her high-heeled shoes. 'Not very much keeps you quiet, but it seems that at last I've found something which does. Which means that we are going to be indulging in lots of illicit sex in the future, my darling wife.'

She walked over to the bed to join him, still wearing her panties, her bra and her white lace suspender belt and stockings. It felt warm in his embrace, and safe. So very safe.

They were going to honeymoon in Samahan and she was going to learn all about the land of Suleiman's birth. Afterwards, they would decide where they wanted to make their main base.

'It can be anywhere,' he had promised her. 'Anywhere at all.'

She closed her eyes as he tightened his arms around her, because where they lived didn't matter.

This was home.

* * * * *

The Sheikh's Undoing

CHAPTER ONE

THE SOUND OF the telephone woke her, but Isobel didn't need to see the name flashing on the screen to know who was ringing. Who else would call her at this time of night but the man who thought he had the right to do pretty much whatever he wanted? And frequently did.

Tariq, the so-called 'Playboy Prince'. Or Prince Tariq Kadar al Hakam, Sheikh of Khayarzah—to give him his full and rather impressive title. And the boss if not exactly from hell then certainly from some equally dark and complicated place.

She glanced at the clock. Four in the morning was early even by *his* standards. Yawning, she picked up the phone, wondering what the hell he had been up to this time.

Had some new story about him emerged, as it so often did, sparked by gossip about his latest audacious take-over bid? Or had he simply got himself tied up with a new blonde—they were always blonde—and wanted Isobel to juggle his early morning meetings for him? Would he walk into the office later on with yesterday's growth darkening his strong jaw and a smug smile curving the edges of his sensual lips? And the scent of someone's perfume still lingering on his skin…

It wouldn't be the first time it had happened, that was for sure. With a frown, Isobel recalled some of his more famous sexual conquests, before reminding herself that she was employed as his personal assistant— not his moral guardian.

Friends sometimes asked whether she ever tired of having a boss who demanded so much of her. Or whether she was tempted to tell him exactly what she thought of his outrageously chauvinistic behaviour— and the answer was yes. Sometimes. But the generous amount of money he paid her soon put a stop to her disapproval. Because money like that provided security—the kind of security which you could never get from another person. Isobel knew that better than anyone. Hadn't her mother taught her that the most important lesson a woman could learn was to be completely independent of men? Men could just walk away whenever they wanted…and because they could, they frequently did.

She answered the call. 'Hello?'

'I-Isobel?'

Her senses were instantly alerted when she heard the deep voice of her employer—because there was something very different about it. Either he was in some kind of post-coital daze or something was wrong. Because he sounded…*weird.*

She'd never heard Tariq hesitate before. Never heard him as anything other than the confident and charismatic Prince—the darling of London's casinos and international gossip columns. The man most women couldn't resist, even when—as seemed inevitable—he was destined to break their heart into tiny little pieces.

'Tariq?' Isobel's voice took on a sudden note of urgency. 'Is something wrong?'

From amid a painful throbbing, which felt as if a thousand hammers were beating against his skull, Tariq registered the familiar voice of his assistant. His first brush with reality after what seemed like hours of chaos and confusion. Almost imperceptibly he let out a low sigh of relief as his lashes parted by a fraction. Izzy was his anchor. Izzy would sort this out for him. A ceiling swam into view, and quickly he shut his eyes against its harsh brightness.

'Accident,' he mumbled.

'Accident?' Isobel sat up in bed, her heart thundering as she heard the unmistakable twist of pain in his voice. 'What kind of accident? Tariq, where are you? What's *happened*?'

'I…'

'Tariq?' Isobel could hear someone indignantly telling him that he shouldn't be using his phone, and then a rustling noise before a woman's voice came on the line.

'Hello?' the strange voice said. 'Who is this, please?'

Isobel felt fear begin to whisper over her as she recognised the sound of officialdom, and it took an almighty effort just to stop her voice from shaking. 'M-my name is Isobel Mulholland and I work for Sheikh al Hakam—would you please tell me what's going on?'

There was a pause before the woman spoke again. 'This is one of the staff nurses at the Accident and

Emergency department of St Mark's hospital in Chislehurst. I'm afraid that the Sheikh has been involved in
a car crash—'

'Is he okay?' Isobel interrupted.

'I'm afraid I can't give out any more information at
the moment.'

Hearing inflexible resistance in the woman's voice,
Isobel swung her legs over the side of the bed. 'I'm on
my way,' she said grimly, and cut the connection.

Pulling on a pair of jeans, she grabbed the first warm
sweater which came to hand and then, after shoving her
still-bare feet into sheepskin boots, took the elevator
down to the underground car park of her small London apartment.

Thank heavens for sat-nav, she thought as she tapped
in the name of the hospital and waited for a map to
appear on the screen. She peered at it. It seemed that
Chislehurst was on the edge of the Kent countryside—
less than an hour from here, especially at this time in
the morning.

But, even though there was barely any traffic around,
Isobel had to force herself to concentrate on the road
ahead and not focus on the frightened thoughts which
were crowding into her mind.

What the hell was Tariq doing driving around at this
time in the morning? And what was he doing *crashing
his car*—he who was normally as adept at driving as
he was at riding one of his polo ponies?

Her fingers tightened around the steering wheel as
she tried and failed to imagine her powerful boss lying
injured. But it was an image which stubbornly failed to

materialise, for he was a man who was larger than life in every sense of the word.

Tall and striking, with distinctive golden-dark colouring, Sheikh Tariq al Hakam commanded attention wherever he was. Complete strangers stopped to watch him walk by in the street. Women pressed their phone numbers into his hand in restaurants. She'd seen it happen time and time again. His proud and sometimes cruel features had often been compared to those of a fallen angel. And he exuded such passion and energy that it was impossible to imagine anything inhibiting those qualities—even for a second.

What if...? Isobel swallowed down the acrid taste of fear. What if her charismatic boss was in *danger?* What would she do if he was in a life-threatening condition? If he...he...

She'd never thought of Tariq as mortal before, and now she could think of nothing else. Her heart missed a beat as she registered the blaring horn of a passing car and she tightened her fingers on the steering wheel. There was no point in thinking negatively. Whatever it was, he would pull through—just like he always did. Because Tariq was as strong as a lion, and she couldn't imagine anything dimming that magnificent strength of his.

A dull rain was spattering against the windscreen as she pulled into the hospital car park. It was still so early that the morning staff hadn't yet arrived. The whole building seemed eerily quiet as she entered it, which only increased her growing sense of foreboding.

Noiselessly, she sped down the bright corridors towards the A&E department until she reached the main desk.

A nurse glanced up at her. 'Can I help you?'

Isobel wiped a raindrop from her cheek. 'I've come… I'm here about one of your patients. His name is Tariq al Hakam and I understand he's been involved in a car crash.'

'And you are?' enquired the nurse, her carefully plucked eyebrows disappearing beneath her fringe.

'I work for him.'

'I'm afraid I can't tell you anything,' said the nurse, with a dismissive smile. 'You aren't his next of kin, are you?'

Isobel shook her head. 'His next of kin lives in the Middle East,' she said. Swallowing down her frustration, she realised that she'd crammed her thick curls into a ponytail and thrown on a pair of old jeans and a sweater. Did she look unbelievably scruffy? The last kind of person who would be associated with the powerful Sheikh? Was that the reason the nurse was being so…so…*officious?* 'I work closely with the Prince and have done for the past five years,' she continued urgently. 'Please let me see him. I'm…I'm…'

For one stupid moment she was about to say *I'm all he's got.* Until she realised that the shock of hearing he was injured must have temporarily unhinged her mind. Why, Tariq had a whole *stable* of women he could call upon in an instant. Women who were far closer to him than Isobel had ever been or ever would be.

'I'm the person he rang just over an hour ago,' she

said, her voice full of appeal. 'It was…it was me he turned to.'

The nurse looked at her steadily, and then seemed to take pity on her.

'He has a concussion,' she said quietly, and then shook her head as if in answer to the silent question in Isobel's eyes. 'His CT scan shows no sign of haemorrhaging, but we're putting him under observation just to be sure.'

No sign of haemorrhaging. A breath of relief shuddered from Isobel's lips, and for a moment she had to lean on the nurses' station for support. 'Thank you,' she whispered. 'Can I *see* him? Please? Would that be okay? Just for a moment.'

There was a moment's assessment, and then the nurse nodded. 'Well, as long as it *is* a moment. A familiar face is often reassuring. But you're not to excite him—do you understand?'

Isobel gave a wry smile. 'Oh, there's no danger of that happening,' she answered because Tariq thought she was about as exciting as watching paint dry.

He'd often described her as the most practical and sensible woman he knew—citing those as the reasons he employed her. Once, she'd even overheard him saying that it was a relief to find a woman under thirty who wasn't a *distraction,* and although it had hurt at the time, she could live with it. She'd always known her place in his life and that wasn't about to change now. Her job was to soothe his ruffled feathers, not to excite him. There were plenty of other contenders for *that* category.

She followed the rhythmical squishing of the nurse's rubber-soled shoes into a side-room at the far end of the unit, and the unbelievable sight that confronted her there made her heart skip a painful beat.

Shrouded in the bleached cotton of a single sheet lay the prone figure of her boss. He looked too long and too broad for the narrow hospital bed, and he was lying perfectly still. The stark white bedlinen threw his darkly golden colouring into relief—and even from here she could see the dark red stain of blood which had matted his thick black hair.

Waves of dizziness washed over her at the sight of the seemingly indestructible Tariq looking so stricken, and Isobel had to quash a stupid instinct to run over to his side and touch her fingers to his cheek. But the nurse had warned her not to excite him, and so she mustered up her usual level-headed attitude and walked quietly towards him.

His eyes were closed—two ebony feathered arcs of lashes were lying against a face which she could see was unusually blanched, despite the natural darkness of his olive skin.

She swallowed down the acid taste of fear. She had seen Tariq in many different guises during the five eventful years she'd been working for him. She'd seen him looking sharp and urbanely suited as he dominated the boardroom during the meetings which filled his life. She'd seen him hollow-eyed from lack of sleep when he'd spent most of the night gambling and had come straight into the office brandishing a thick wad of notes and a careless smile.

Once she'd started remembering Isobel couldn't stop. Other images crowded into her mind. Tariq in jodhpurs as he played polo with such breathtaking flair, and the faint sheen of sweat that made his muddy jodhpurs stick to his powerful thighs. Tariq in jeans and a T-shirt when he was dressed down and casual. Or looking like a movie idol in a sharply tailored tuxedo before he went out to dinner. She'd even seen him in the flowing white robes and headdress of his homeland, when he was leaving on one of his rare visits to the oil-rich kingdom of Khayarzah—where his brother Zahid was King.

But she had never seen her powerful boss looking so defenceless before, and something inside her softened and melted. At that moment she felt almost *tender* towards him—as if she'd like to cradle him in her arms and comfort him. Poor, vulnerable Tariq she thought bleakly.

Until the reality of the situation came slamming home to her and she forced herself to confront it. Tariq was looking vulnerable because right at this moment he *was.* Very vulnerable. Lying injured on a hospital bed. Beneath the wool of her sweater she could feel the crash of her heart—and she had to fight back a feeling of panic, and nausea.

'Tariq,' she breathed softly. 'Oh, Tariq.'

Tariq screwed up his eyes. Through the mists of hammering pain he was aware of something familiar and yet curiously different about the woman who was speaking to him. It was a voice he knew well. A voice which exemplified the small area of calm which lay at the centre of his crazy life. It was…*Izzy's* voice, he realised—but not as he'd ever heard it before. Normally it was crisp and matter-of-fact, sometimes cool and disapproving, but he'd never heard it all soft and trembling before.

His eyes opened, surprising a look of such darkened fear in her gaze that he was momentarily taken aback. He studied the soft quiver of her lips and felt the tiptoeing of something unfamiliar on his skin. Was that really Izzy?

'Don't worry. I'm not about to die,' he drawled. And then, despite the terrible aching at his temples, he allowed just the right pause for maximum effect before directing a mocking question at the woman in uniform who was standing beside his bed, her fingertips counting the hammering of his pulse. 'Am I, Nurse?'

Inexplicably, Isobel felt angry at Tariq for being as arrogant as only he knew how. He could have killed himself, and all he could do was flirt with the damned nurse! Why had she wasted even a second being sentimental about him when she should have realised that he was as indestructible as a rock? And with about as much emotion as a rock, too! She wanted to tell him not to dare be so flippant—but, recognising that might fall into the category of exciting him, she bit back the words.

'What happened?' she questioned, still having to fight the stupid desire to touch him.

Bunching her wistful fingers into a tight fist by her side, she stared down at the hawkish lines of his autocratic face.

'You may not be the slowest driver in the world, but you're usually careful,' she said. And then seeing the nurse glare at her, Isobel remembered that she was supposed to be calming him, not quizzing him. 'No, don't bother answering that,' she added hastily. 'In fact, don't even think about it. Just lie there—and rest.'

Black brows were elevated in disbelief. 'You aren't usually quite so agreeable,' he observed caustically.

'Well, these aren't usual circumstances, are they?'

Isobel gave what she hoped was a reassuring smile — but it wasn't easy to keep the panic at bay. Not when all she wanted to do was take him in her arms and tell him that everything was going to be all right. To rest his cheek against the mad racing of her heart and lace her fingers through the inky silk of his hair and stroke it. What on earth was the *matter* with her?

'You've just got to lie there quietly and let the nurses take care of you and check that you're in one p-piece.'

That unfamiliar tremble in her voice was back, and Tariq's eyes narrowed as her face swam in and out of focus. Funny. He couldn't really remember looking at Izzy's face before. Or maybe he had—just not like this. In the normal progression of a day you never really stared at a woman for a long time. Not unless you were planning to seduce her.

But for once there was nowhere else to look. He could see the freckles standing out like sentries against her pale skin, and her amber eyes looked as if they would be more at home on a startled kitten. She looked *soft,* he thought suddenly. *Cute.* As if she might curl into the crook of his arm and lie there purring all afternoon.

Shaking his head in order to rid himself of this temporary hallucination, he glared at her.

'It'll take more than a car crash or a nurse to make
me lie quietly,' he said, impatiently moving one leg—
which had started to itch like no itch he could remember. As he bent his knee, the sheet concertinaed down
to his groin and one hair-roughened thigh was revealed.
And despite the pain and the bizarre circumstances he
could not resist the flicker of a smile as both the nurse
and Isobel gave an involuntary little gasp before quickly
averting their eyes.

'Lets just cover you up, shall we?' questioned the
nurse briskly, her cheeks growing bright pink as she
tugged the sheet back in place.

Isobel felt similarly hot and bothered as she realised
that her handsome boss was completely naked beneath
the sheet. That, unless she was very much mistaken, the
sheet seemed to be moving of its own accord around
his groin area. She wasn't the most experienced cookie
in the tin but even she knew what *that* meant. It was a
shockingly intimate experience, which started a heated
prickling of her skin in response. And that was a first.

Because—unlike just about every other female with
a pulse—she was immune to Tariq al Hakam and his
sex appeal. His hard, muscular body left her completely
cold—as did those hawk-like features and the ebony
glitter of his dark-lashed eyes. She didn't go for men
who were self-professed playboys—sexy, dangerous
men who knew exactly the kind of effect they had on
women. Who could walk away from the women who
loved them without a backward glance. In fact, those
were precisely the men she tended to despise. The ones
her mother had warned her against. Men like her own

father—who could shrug off emotion and responsibility so easily...

Composing herself with a huge effort of will, she turned to the nurse. 'What happens now?' she asked but Tariq answered before the woman in uniform had a chance to.

'I get off this damned bed and you drive me to the office. That's what happens,' he snapped. But as he tried to sit up the stupid shooting pain made him slump back against the bed again, and he groaned and then glared at her again as if it was all *her* fault.

'Will you please *lie still,* Prince al Hakam?' ordered the nurse crisply, before turning to Isobel. 'The doctors would like to keep the Sheikh in for twenty-four hours' observation.'

'Izzy,' said Tariq, and as Isobel turned to him his black eyes glinted with the kind of steely determination she recognised so well. 'Sort this out for me, will you? There's no way I'm staying in this damned hospital for a minute longer.'

For a moment Isobel didn't speak. There were many times when she admired her boss—because nobody could deny his drive, his determination, his unerring nose for success. But his arrogance and sheer self-belief sometimes had the potential to be his downfall. Like now.

'Look, this isn't some business deal you're masterminding,' she said crossly. 'This is your *health* we're talking about—and you're not the expert here, Tariq, the doctors and nurses are. They don't want to keep you in because it's some sort of *fun*—I can't imagine it's much fun having *you* as a patient—but because it's necessary. And if you don't start listening to them and doing what they say, then I'm going to walk out of here right now and leave you to get on with it.'

There was a pause as Tariq's eyes narrowed angrily. 'But I have meetings—'

'I know precisely what meetings you have,' she interrupted, her voice gentling suddenly as she registered the strain which was etched on his face. 'I organise your diary, don't I? I'll sort everything out back at the office and you're not to worry about a thing. Do you…?' She found herself staring down at the white hospital sheet which now seemed to be stretched uncomfortably tight across the muscular expanse of his torso. 'Do you want me to get hold of some pyjamas for you?'

'Pyjamas?' His mouth curved into a smile which mocked her almost as much as the lazy glitter of his eyes. 'You think I'm the kind of man who wears pyjamas, do you, Izzy?'

Inexplicably, her heart began to pound with unwilling excitement—and Isobel was furious at her reaction. Had he seen it—and was that why his smile had now widened into an arrogant smirk? 'Your choice of nightwear isn't something I've given a lot of thought to,' she answered crossly. 'But I'll take that as a no. Is there anything else you want?'

Tariq winced as he recalled the blood-stained and crumpled clothing which was stuffed into a plastic bag in the locker next to his bed. 'Just bring me some clean clothes, can you? And a razor?'

'Of course. And as soon as the doctors give you the thumbs-up I'll come and get you. Is that okay?'

There was a pause as their gazes met. 'You don't really want me to answer that, do you?' he questioned, closing his eyes as a sudden and powerful fatigue washed over him. It was like no feeling he'd ever experienced and it left him feeling debilitated. Weak. The last thing he wanted was for his assistant to see him looking weak. 'Just go, will you, Izzy?' he added wearily.

Slipping silently from the room, Isobel walked until she stepped out into the brightening light of the spring morning. Sucking in a deep breath, she felt a powerful sense of relief washing over her. Tariq was alive. That was the main thing. He might have had a nasty knock to the head, but hopefully he hadn't done any lasting damage. And yet… She bit her lip as she climbed into her car and started up the engine, her thoughts still in turmoil. How *alone* he had looked on that narrow hospital bed.

The loud tooting of a car made her glance into the driving mirror, where she caught a glimpse of her pale and unwashed face. A touch of reality began to return.

Alone?

Tariq?

Why, there were innumerable women who would queue around the block to put paid to that particular myth with no more incentive than the elevation of one black and arrogant eyebrow and that mocking smile. Tariq had plenty of people to take care of him, she reminded herself. He didn't need *her*.

Arriving back in London, she spent the rest of the

day cancelling meetings and dealing with the calls which flooded in from his associates. She worked steadily until eight, then went over to his apartment— a vast penthouse in a tall building which overlooked Green Park. Although she held a spare set of keys, she'd only ever been there once before, when she had delivered a package which the Sheikh had been expecting and which had arrived very late at the office, while she'd still been working. Rather than having it couriered round to him, Isobel had decided to take it there herself.

It had been one of the most embarrassing occasions of her life, because a tousle-headed Tariq had answered the door wearing what was clearly a hastily pulled on silk dressing gown. His face had been faintly flushed as he'd taken the package from her, and she hadn't needed to hear the breathless female voice calling his name to realise that he had company.

But it had been his almost *helpless* shrug which had infuriated her more than anything. The way his black eyes had met hers and he'd bestowed on her one of his careless smiles. As if he was inviting her to join him in a silent conspiracy of wondering why he was just so irresistible to women. She remembered thrusting the package into his hands and stomping off home to an empty apartment, cursing the arrogance of the Playboy Prince.

Closing her mind to the disturbing memory, Isobel let herself into the apartment using the complicated trio of keys. Experience made her listen for a moment. But everything was silent—which meant that his servants had all gone home for the evening.

In his dressing room she found jeans, cashmere

sweaters and a leather jacket—and added a warm scarf. But when it came to selecting some boxer shorts from the silken pile which were heaped neatly in a drawer, she found herself blushing for the second time that day. How...*intimate* it was to be rifling through Tariq's underwear. Underwear which had clung to the oiled silk of his olive skin...

Frustrated with the wayward trajectory of her thoughts, she threw the clothes into an overnight bag and let herself out. Then she phoned the hospital, to be told that the Sheikh's condition was satisfactory and that if he continued to improve then he could be discharged the next day.

But the press had got wind of his crash—despite the reassuring statement which Isobel had asked his PR people to issue. Fabulously wealthy injured sheikhs always provided fascinating copy, and by the time she arrived back at the hospital the following morning there were photographers hanging around the main entrance.

Tariq had been transferred to a different side ward, and Isobel walked in to see a small gaggle of doctors gathered around the foot of his bed. There was an unmistakable air of tension in the room.

She shot a glance at her boss, who was sitting up in bed, unshaven and unashamedly bare-chested—the vulnerability of yesterday nothing but a distant memory. His black eyes glittered with displeasure as he saw her, and his voice was cool.

'Ah, Izzy. At last.'

'Is something wrong?' she asked.

'Damned right there is.'

A tall, bespectacled man detached himself from the group, extending his hand and introducing himself as the consultant. 'You're his partner?' he asked Isobel, as he glanced down at the overnight bag she was carrying.

Isobel went bright red, and she couldn't miss the narrow-eyed look which Tariq angled in her direction. But for some reason she was glad that she wasn't the same wild-haired scarecrow she'd been in the middle of the night. That she'd taken the care to wash and tame her hair and put on her favourite russet-coloured jacket.

Just because the Sheikh never looked at her in the way he looked at other women it didn't mean she was immune to a little masculine attention from time to time, did it? She gave the doctor a quick smile. 'No, Doctor. I'm Isobel Mulholland. The Sheikh's assistant.'

'Well, perhaps you could manage to talk some sense into your boss, Isobel,' said the consultant, meeting her eyes with a resigned expression. 'He's had a nasty bang to the head and a general shock to the system—but he seems to think that he can walk out of here and carry on as normal.' The doctor continued to hold her gaze. 'It sounds like a punishing regime at the best of times, but especially so in the circumstances. Unless he agrees to take things easy for the next week—'

'I can't,' interrupted Tariq testily, wondering if his perception had been altered by the bump on the head he'd received. Was the doctor *flirting with Isobel?* And was she—the woman he'd never known as anything other than a brisk and efficient machine—*flirting back?* He had never found her in the least bit attractive himself, but Tariq was unused to being overlooked for another man, and his mouth thinned as he subjected the medic to an icy look. 'I need to fly to the States tomorrow.'

'That's where you're wrong. You need rest,' contradicted the consultant. 'Complete rest. Away from work and the world—and away from the media, who have been plaguing my office all morning. You've been driving yourself too hard and you need to recuperate. Otherwise I'll have no alternative but to keep you in.'

'You can't keep me in against my will,' objected Tariq.

Isobel recognised that a stand-off between the two men was about to be reached—and she knew that Tariq would refuse to back down if it got to that stage. Diplomatically, she offered the consultant another polite smile. 'Does he need any particular medical care, Doctor?'

'Will you stop talking about me as if I'm not here?' growled Tariq.

'Just calm and quiet observation,' said the doctor. 'And a guarantee that he won't go anywhere near his office for at least seven days.'

Isobel's mind began to race. He could go to a clinic, yes—but even the most discreet of clinics could never be relied on to be *that* discreet, could they? Especially when they were dealing with billionaire patients who were being hunted by the tabloids. Tariq didn't need expensive clinics where people would no doubt seek to exploit his wealth and influence. He needed that thing which always seemed to elude him.

Peace.

She thought about the strange flash of vulnerability she'd seen on his face and an idea began to form in her mind.

'I have a little cottage in the countryside,' she said slowly, looking straight into a pair of black and disbelieving eyes. 'You could come and stay there for a week, if you like. My mother used to be a nurse, and I picked up some basic first aid from her. I could keep my eye on you, Tariq.'

CHAPTER TWO

'WHERE THE HELL are you going, Izzy?'

For a moment Isobel didn't answer Tariq's growled question as she turned the small car into a narrow country lane edged with budding hedgerows. Why couldn't he just settle down and relax—and be grateful she'd managed to get him out of the hospital? Maybe even sit back and appreciate the beauty of the spring day instead of haranguing her all the time?

It wasn't until she was bowling along at a steady pace that she risked a quick glance and saw the still-dreadful pallor of his face, which showed no signs of shifting. He was in *pain,* she reminded herself—and besides, he was a man who rarely expressed gratitude.

Already she'd had to bite back her words several times that morning. They had left by a staff exit at the back of the hospital, and although he had initially refused to travel in a wheelchair she had persuaded him that it would help elude any waiting press. Which of course, it had. The photographers were looking for the muscular stride of a powerful sheikh—not a man being pushed along by a woman. She remembered her mother

telling her that nobody ever looked at people in wheel-
chairs—how society was often too busy to care about
those who were not able-bodied. And it seemed that
her mother was right.

'You know very well where I'm going,' she answered
calmly. 'To my cottage in the country, where you are
going to recuperate after your crash. That was the agreement we made with the doctor before he would agree
to discharge you. Remember?'

He made a small sound of displeasure beneath his
breath. His head was throbbing, his throat felt as dry
as parchment, and now Izzy was being infuriatingly
stubborn. 'That's the doctor you were flirting with so
outrageously?' he questioned coolly.

Isobel's eyes narrowed as she acknowledged her
boss's accusation. In truth, she'd been so worried about
him that she'd barely given a thought to the crinkly-
eyed consultant. But even if she *had* fallen in love at
first sight and decided to slip the doctor her phone number—well, it was none of Tariq's business. Wasn't she
doing enough for him already, without him attempting
to police her private life for her?

'And what if I was?' she retorted.

He shrugged. 'I would have thought that extremely
unprofessional behaviour on his part.'

'I hardly think that you're in any position to pass
judgement on flirting,' she murmured.

Tariq drummed his fingers against one tense thigh.
It was not the response he'd been expecting. A firm as-
sertion that the doctor had been wasting his time would
have been infinitely more desirable. Isobel was reso-

lutely single, and that was the way he liked it. It meant that she could devote herself to *his* needs and be there whenever *he* wanted her.

'I thought you only told him all that stuff about taking me to your cottage to get him off my back,' he objected.

'But that would have been dishonest.'

'Do you always have to be so damned *moral?*'

'One of us has to have morals.'

His eyes narrowed. 'Is that supposed to be a criticism?'

'No, Tariq,' she answered calmly. 'It's merely an observation.'

He stared at her set profile and inexplicably began to notice the way the pale spring sunshine was picking out the lights in her hair, turning it a glowing shade of amber. Had the doctor also noticed its subtle fire? he wondered. Would that explain his behaviour? 'I don't know why you're dragging me out to the back of beyond,' he said, 'when I can rest perfectly well at home.'

'In central London?' She gave a dry laugh. 'With the press baying at your door like hounds and all your ex-girlfriends lining up to offer to come and mop your brow for you? I don't think so. You'll be much safer at my cottage. Anyway, it's a done deal. I've informed the office that you'll be incommunicado for a week, and that all calls are to come through me. Fiona in the PR office is perfectly capable of running things until we get back. I've had your housekeeper pack a week's worth of clothes, which are being couriered down. And I haven't told anybody about your exact whereabouts.'

'My brother—'

'Except for your brother,' she concurred, remembering the brief conversation she'd had earlier that day with the ruler of Khayarzah. 'I telephoned the palace and spoke to the King myself—told him that you're on the mend but that you needed to recuperate. He wanted you flown to Khayarzah, but I said that you would be fine with me.' She shot him a glance. 'That was the right thing to do, wasn't it?'

'I suppose so,' he answered moodily, but as usual she had done exactly the right thing. The last thing he needed was the formality of palace life—with all the strictures that came with it. He'd done his level best to escape from the attendant attention which came with being the brother of the King—a role which had been thrust on him when his brother had suddenly inherited the crown. A role which had threatened his freedom— something he had always guarded jealously. Because wasn't his freedom the only good thing to have emerged from the terrible isolation of his childhood?

He fixed her with a cool and curious stare. 'You seem to have it all worked out, Izzy.'

'Well, that's what you pay me for.' She glanced in the driving mirror and let a speedy white van overtake them before starting to speak again. 'Do you want to tell me what happened? About why one of the most careful drivers I know should crash his car?'

Tariq closed his eyes. Wasn't it frustrating that a split-second decision could impact so dramatically on your life? If he hadn't been beguiled by a pair of blue eyes and a dynamite body then he wouldn't be facing the rather grim prospect of being stuck in some remote cottage with his assistant for a week.

'I went for dinner with a woman,' he said.

'No—' Isobel started to say something and then changed her mind, but Tariq seized on her swallowed words like a cat capturing a mouse.

His thick lashes parted by a fraction. 'No what, Izzy?'

'It doesn't matter.'

'Oh, but it does,' he answered stubbornly.

'I was about to say no change there. You having dinner with a woman is hardly remarkable, Tariq. Blonde, was she?'

'Actually, she was.' Reluctantly, his lips curved into a smile. Sometimes Izzy was so damned sharp he was surprised she didn't cut herself. Maybe that was what less attractive women did—they made up for their shortcomings by developing a more sophisticated sense of humour. 'But she wasn't all she seemed to be.'

'Not a transvestite, I hope?'

'Very funny.' But despite the smile which her flippant comment produced Tariq was irritated with himself. He had been stressed out, and had intended to relax by playing poker until the small hours. He hadn't really been in the mood for any kind of liaison, or the effort of chatting someone up. But the woman had been very beautiful, and he'd found himself inviting her for a late dinner. And then she had started to question him. Wanting to know the kind of things which suggested that she might have done more than a little background research on him.

Tariq had some rules which were entirely his own.

He didn't like being interrogated.

He didn't trust people who knew too much about him.

And he never slept with a woman on a first date.

At heart, he was a deeply old-fashioned man, with plenty of contradictory values. For him sex had always been laughably easy—yet he didn't respect a woman who let him too close, too soon. Especially as he had a very short attention span when it came to the opposite sex. He liked the slow burn of anticipation—to prolong the ache of desire until it became unbearable. So when the blonde had made it very clear that she was his for the taking—some primitive sense of prudery had reared its head. Who wanted something which was so easily obtained? With a jaded yawn, he had declined her offer and reached for his jacket.

And that was when the woman's story had come blurting out. It seemed that it hadn't been fate which had brought her into his life, but cunning and subterfuge.

'She was a journalist,' he bit out. He'd been so angry with himself because he hadn't seen through her flimsy cover. Furious that he had fallen for one of the oldest tricks of all. He'd stormed out, wondering if he was losing his touch, and for those few seconds when his attention had wandered so had his powerful sports car. 'She wanted the inside story on the takeover bid,' he finished.

Isobel shrugged as her little car took a bend in the road. 'Well, if you *will* try and buy into the Premier League, what do you expect? You know the English are crazy about football—and it's a really big deal if some power-hungry Sheikh adds a major team to his portfolio.'

'There's nothing wrong with being hungry for power, Izzy.'

'Only if it becomes addictive,' she countered.

'You think I'm a power junkie?'

'That's not for me to say.'

His black eyes narrowed. 'I notice you didn't deny it, though.'

'I'm glad you're paying attention to what I say, Tariq.'

With a small click of irritation, he attempted, without much success, to stretch his legs. Some lurid looking air-freshener in the shape of a blue daisy hung from the driving mirror and danced infuriatingly in front of the windscreen. Other than the occasional childhood ride on a camel in his homeland, he could never remember enduring such an uncomfortable form of transport as this. Rather longingly, he thought about the dented bonnet of his smooth and gleaming sports car and wondered how long before it would be roadworthy again.

'Is your cottage as cramped as your car?' he demanded.

'You don't like my car?'

'Not really. I don't like second-hand cars which don't go above fifty.'

'Then why don't you give me a pay raise?' she suggested sweetly. 'And I'll buy myself a newer one.'

For a moment Tariq acknowledged the brief flicker of discord which made his pulse quicken. Wasn't it strange how a little tension between a man and a woman could instantly begin to heat a man's blood and make him start thinking of...

But the smile left his face as he realised that this was *Izzy* he was about to start fantasising about. Safe and sensible Izzy. The plain stalwart of his office—and the very last candidate for any erotic thoughts. So how was it that he suddenly found his attention riveted on a pair of slender thighs which were outlined with delectable precision beneath the blue of her denim skirt?

With an effort, he dragged his gaze away and settled back in the seat. 'I pay you enough already—as well you know,' he said. 'How far is it?'

'Far enough,' said Isobel softly, 'for you to close your eyes and sleep.' *And stop annoying me with your infuriating comments.*

'I'm not sleepy.'

'Sure?'

'Quite sure,' he mumbled, but something in her voice was oddly soothing, so he found himself yawning—and seconds later he was fast asleep.

Isobel drove in a silence punctuated only by the low, steady sound of Tariq's breathing. She tried to concentrate on her driving and on the new green buds which were pushing through the hedgerows—but it wasn't easy. Her attention kept wandering and she felt oddly light-headed. She kept telling herself it was because her usual routine had been thrown out of kilter—and not because of the disturbing proximity of her boss.

But that wouldn't have been true. Something had happened to her and she couldn't work out what it was. Why should she suddenly start feeling self-conscious and *peculiar* in Tariq's company? Why couldn't she seem to stop her eyes from straying to the powerful shafts of his thighs and then drifting upwards to the narrow jut of his hips?

She shook her head. She'd been alone with Tariq many, many times before. She had shared train, plane and car journeys with him on various business trips. But never like this. Not in such cramped and humble confines, with him fast asleep beside her, his legs spread out in front of him. Almost as if they were any normal couple, just driving along.

Impatiently, she shook her head.

Normal? That was the last adjective which could ever be applied to Tariq. He was a royal sheikh from the ancient House of Khayarzah and one of the wealthiest men on the planet.

Sometimes it still seemed incredible to Isobel that someone like her should have ended up working so closely for such a powerful man. She could tell that people were often surprised when she told them what she did for a living. That he who could have anyone should have chosen her. What did *she* have that a thousand more well-connected women didn't have? That was what everyone always wanted to know.

Deep down, she suspected it was because he trusted her in a way that he trusted few people. And why did he trust her? Hard to say. Probably because she had met him when he was young—at school—before the true extent of his power and position had really sunk in. Before he'd realised the influence he wielded.

She'd been just ten at the time—a solitary and rather

serious child. Her mother, Anna, had been the school nurse at one of England's most prestigious boarding schools—a job she'd been lucky to get since it provided a place to live as well as a steady income. Anna was a single mother and her daughter Isobel illegitimate. Times had changed, and not having a father no longer carried any stigma, but it certainly had back then— back in the day.

Isobel had borne the brunt of it, of course. She remembered the way she'd always flinched with embarrassment whenever the question had been asked: *What does your father do?* There had been a thousand ways she had sought to answer without giving away the shaming fact that she *didn't actually know.*

As a consequence, she'd always felt slightly *less than*—a feeling which hadn't been helped by growing up surrounded by some of the wealthiest children in the world. She'd been educated among them, but she had never really been one of them—those pampered products of the privileged classes.

But Tariq had been different from all the other pupils. His olive skin and black eyes had made him stand out like a handful of sparkling jewels thrown down onto a sheet of plain white paper. Sent to the west to be educated by his father, he had excelled in everything he'd done. He'd swum and ridden and played tennis—and he spoke five languages with native fluency.

Sometimes, Isobel had gazed at him with wistful wonder from afar. Had watched as he was surrounded by natural blondes with tiny-boned bodies and swish flats in Chelsea.

Until the day he had spoken to her and made a lonely little girl's day.

He'd have been about seventeen at the time, and had come to the sanatorium to ask about a malaria injection for a forthcoming trip he was taking. Her mother had been busy with one of the other pupils and had asked Isobel to keep the young Prince entertained.

Initially Isobel had been tongue-tied—wondering what on earth she could say to him. But she couldn't just leave him looking rather impatiently at his golden wristwatch, could she? Why, her mother might get into trouble for daring to keep the young royal waiting.

Shyly, she had asked him about his homeland. At first he had frowned—as if her question was an intrusion. But a brief and assessing look had followed, and then he had sat down so that he was on her level before starting to talk. The precise words she had long forgotten, but she would never forget the dreamy way he had spoken of desert sands like fine gold and rivers like streams of silver. And then, when her mother had appeared—looking a little flustered—he had immediately switched to the persona of confident royal pupil. He hadn't said another word to her—but Isobel had never forgotten that brief encounter.

It had been over a decade later before their paths crossed again. She had gone back to the school for the opening of a magnificent extension to the library and Tariq had been there, still surrounded by adoring women. For one brief moment Isobel had looked at him with adult eyes. Had registered that he was still as gorgeous as he was unobtainable and that her schoolgirl crush should sensibly die a death. With a resigned little shrug of her shoulders she had turned away and put him right out of her mind as of that moment.

The new library was fabulous, with softly gleaming carved wooden panels. Tooled leather tables sat at its centre, and the long, leaded arched windows looked out onto the cool beauty of the north gardens.

By then Isobel had been a secretary—working in a dusty office for a rather dry bunch of lawyers in London. It hadn't been the most exciting work in the world, but it had been well paid, and had provided her with the security she had always craved.

There'd been no one in the library that she knew well enough to go up and talk to, but she'd been determined to enjoy her time there, because secretly she'd been delighted to get an invitation to the prestigious opening. Just because she'd been educated at the school free, it didn't mean she'd been overlooked! She'd drunk a cup of tea and then begun to look at the books, noting with interest that there was a whole section on Khayarzah. Picking up a beautifully bound volume, she'd begun to flick through the pages, and had soon been lost in the pictures and descriptions of the land which Tariq had once made come alive with his words.

She'd just got to a bit about the source of the Jamanah River when she'd heard a deep voice behind her.

'You seem very engrossed in that book.'

And, turning round, she'd found herself imprisoned in the Sheikh's curious gaze. She'd thought that his face was harder and colder than she remembered—and that there was a certain air of detachment about him. But then Isobel recalled the sixth-former who'd been so kind to her, and had smiled.

'That's because it's a very engrossing book,' she said. 'Though I'm surprised there's such a big section on your country.'

'Really?' A pair of jet eyebrows was elevated. 'One of the benefits of donating a library is that you get to choose some of its contents.'

Isobel blinked. '*You* donated the new library?'

'Of course.' His voice took on a faintly cynical air. 'Didn't you realise that wealthy old boys—particularly foreign ones—are expected to play benefactor at some point in their lives?'

'No, I didn't.'

Afterwards, Isobel thought that his question might have been some sort of test—to see if she was one of those people who were impressed by wealth. And if that *was* the case then she'd probably passed it. Because she genuinely didn't care about money. She had enough for her needs and that was plenty. What had her mother always told her? *Don't aim too high; just high enough.*

'I just wanted to know if it was as beautiful as...' Her words tailed off. As if he could *possibly* be interested!

But he was looking at her curiously, as if he *was* interested.

'As beautiful as what?'

She swallowed. 'As the way you described it. You once told me all about Khayarzah. You were very... passionate about it. You said the sand was like fine gold and the rivers like streams of silver. You probably don't remember.'

Tariq stared at her, as if he was trying to place her, but shook his head.

'No, I don't remember,' he admitted, and then, as he glanced up to see a determined-looking blonde making her way towards them, he took Isobel's elbow. 'So why don't you refresh my memory for me?' And he led her away to a quieter section of the room.

And that was that. An unexpected meeting between two people who had both felt like outsiders within the privileged walls of an English public school. What was more it seemed that Tariq happened to have a need, and that Isobel could be just the person to answer that need. He was looking for someone to be his assistant. Someone he could talk to without her being fazed by who he was and what he represented. Someone he could trust.

The salary he was offering made it madness for her even to consider refusing, so Isobel accepted his offer and quickly realised that no job description in the world could have prepared her for working for *him*.

He wanted honesty, yes—but he also demanded deference, as and when it suited him.

He was fair, but he was also a powerful sheikh who had untold wealth at his fingertips—so he could also be highly unreasonable, too.

And he was sexy. As sexy as any man was ever likely to be. Everyone said so—even Isobel's more feminist friends, who disapproved of him. But Isobel's strength was that she simply refused to see it. After that meeting in the library she had trained herself to be immune to his appeal as if she was training for a marathon. Even if she considered herself to be in his league—which she didn't—she still wouldn't have been foolish enough to fancy him.

Because men like Tariq were trouble—too aware of their power over the opposite sex and not afraid to use it. She'd watched as women who fell in love with him were discarded once he'd tired of them. And she knew from her own background how lives could be ruined if passion was allowed to rule the roost. Hadn't her mother bitterly regretted falling for a charmer like Tariq? Telling her that the brief liaison had affected her whole life?

No, he was definitely not on Isobel's wish-list of men. His strong, muscular body and hard, hawkish features didn't fill her with longing, but with an instinctive wariness which had always served her well.

Because she wouldn't have lasted five minutes—let alone five years—if she had lost her heart to the Sheikh.

She steered the car up a narrow lane and came to a halt outside her beloved little cottage. The March sunshine was clear and pale, illuminating the purple, white and yellow crocuses which were pushing through the earth. She loved this time of year, with all its new beginnings and endless possibilities. Opening the car door a fraction, she could hear birds tweeting their jubilant celebration of springtime—but still Tariq didn't stir.

She turned to look at him—at the ebony arcs of his feathered lashes which were the only soft component to make up his formidable face. She had never seen him asleep before, and it was like looking at a very different man. The hard planes and angles of his features threw shadows over his olive skin, and for once his sensual lips were relaxed. Once again she saw an unfamiliar trace of vulnerability etched on his features, and once again she felt that little stab of awareness at her heart.

He was so *still,* she thought wonderingly. Remarkably still for a man who rarely stopped. Who drove himself remorselessly in the way that successful men always did. Why, it seemed almost a shame to wake him…and to have him face the reality of his convalescence in her humble home.

Racking her brain, she thought back to how she'd left the place last weekend, and realised that there was no fresh food or milk. Stuff she would normally have brought down with her from London.

Reaching out her hand, she touched his shoulder lightly—but his eyelashes moved instantly, the black eyes suspicious and alert as they snapped open.

For a moment Tariq stayed perfectly still, his memory filtering back in jigsaw pieces. What was he doing sitting in an uncomfortably cramped and strange car, while Izzy frowned down at him, her breathing slightly quickened and her amber eyes dark with concern?

And then he remembered. She had offered to play nursemaid for the next week—just not the kind of nursemaid which would have been *his* preference. His mouth hardened as he dispelled an instant fantasy of a woman with creamy curves busting out of a little uniform which ill concealed the black silk stockings beneath. Because Isobel was not that woman. And under the circumstances wasn't that best?

'We're here!' said Isobel brightly, even though her heart had inexplicably started thudding at some dangerous and unknown quality she'd read in his black eyes. 'Welcome to my home.'

CHAPTER THREE

'CAREFUL,' WARNED ISOBEL.

'Please don't state the obvious,' Tariq snapped, as he bent his head to avoid the low front door.

'I was only trying to help,' she protested, as he walked straight past her.

Stepping into the cluttered sitting room was no better, and Tariq quickly discovered that the abundance of overhanging beams was nothing short of a health hazard. 'I've already had one knock to the head, and I don't particularly want another,' he growled. 'Why is your damned ceiling so low?'

'Because men didn't stand at over six feet when these houses were built!' she retorted, thinking that he had to be the most ungrateful man ever to have drawn breath. Here she was, putting herself out by giving him house-space for a week, and all he could do was come out with a litany of complaints.

But some of her exasperation dissolved as she closed the front door, so that the two of them were enclosed in a room which up until that moment she had always thought of as a safe and cosy sanctuary. But not any more. Suddenly it didn't seem safe at all…

She felt hot blood begin to flood through her veins—because the reality of having Tariq standing here was having a bizarre effect on her senses. Had the dimensions magically shrunk? Or was it just his towering physique which dwarfed everything else around him?

Even in jeans and the soft swathing of a grey cashmere sweater he seemed to exude a charisma which drew the eye like nothing else. His faded jeans were stretched over powerful thighs and the sweater hinted at honed muscle beneath. Somehow he managed to make her cottage look like a prop from Toytown, and the thick and solid walls suddenly seemed insubstantial. Come to think of it, didn't she feel a little insubstantial herself?

She remembered that uncomfortable feeling of awareness which had come over her in the hospital—when she'd looked down at him and something inside her had melted. It was as if in that moment she had suddenly given herself permission to see him as other women saw him—and the impact of that had rocked her. And now it was rocking her all over again. Something about the way he was standing there was making her heart slam hard against her ribcage, and an aching feeling began to tug at her belly.

Isobel swallowed, willing this temporary madness to subside. Because acknowledging Tariq's charisma was the last thing she needed right now. Arrogant playboys were not number one on her list of emotional requirements. And even if they were…as if he would ever look at a woman like *her*.

She flashed him a quick smile, even as she became aware of the peculiar prickle of her breasts. 'Look, why don't you sit down and I'll make you some tea?'

'I don't want any tea,' he said. 'But I'd quite like to avoid getting frostbite. It's absolutely freezing in here. Give me some matches and I'll light a fire.'

Isobel shook her head. 'You aren't supposed to be lighting fires. In fact, you aren't supposed to be doing anything but resting. I can manage perfectly well—so will you please sit down on the sofa and put your feet up and let me look after you?'

Tariq's eyes narrowed as her protective command washed over him. His first instinct was to resist. He wasn't used to *care* from the fairer sex. His experience of women usually involved the rapid removal of their clothing and them gasping out their pleasure when he touched them. Big eyes clouded with concern tended to be outside his experience.

'And if I don't?' he challenged softly.

Their gazes clashed in a way which made Isobel's stomach perform a peculiar little flip. She saw the mocking curve of his lips and suddenly she felt almost *weak*—as if she were the invalid, not him. Clamping down the sudden rise of longing, she shook her head— because she was damned if he was going to manipulate her the way other women let him manipulate *them*. 'I don't think you're in any position to object,' she answered coolly. 'And if you did I could always threaten to hand my notice in.'

'You wouldn't do that, Izzy.'

'Oh, wouldn't I?' she returned fiercely, because now

she could see a hint of that awful pallor returning to his face, and a horrifying thought occurred to her. Yes, her mother had been a nurse, and she had learned lots of basic first aid through her. She had managed to convince the hospital doctor that she could cope. But what if she had taken on more than she could handle? What if Tariq began to have side-effects from his head injury? She thought about the hospital leaflet in her handbag and decided that she'd better consult it. 'Now, will you please *sit down?*'

Unexpectedly, Tariq gave a low laugh. 'You can be a fierce little tiger at times, can't you?'

Something about his very obvious approval made her cheeks grow warm with pleasure. 'I can if I need to be.'

'Okay, you win.' Sinking down onto a chintzy and over-stuffed sofa, he batted her a sardonic look. 'Is that better, *Nurse?*'

Trying not to laugh, Isobel nodded. 'Marginally. Do you think you could just try sitting there quietly while I light the fire?'

'I can try.'

Tariq leaned back against a heap of cushions and watched as she busied herself with matches and kindling. Funny, really—he'd never really pictured Izzy in a cottage which was distinctly chocolate-boxy despite the sub-zero temperatures. Not that he'd given very much thought at all as to how his assistant lived her life.

Stifling a yawn, he looked around. The sitting room had those tiny windows which didn't let in very much light, and a big, recessed fireplace—the kind you saw on the front of Christmas cards. She was crouching down in front of the grate, and he watched as she began to blow on the flames to coax them into life. He found his eyes drawn to the denim skirt, which now stretched tightly over the curves of her buttocks.

He swallowed down a sudden, debilitating leap of desire which made him harden in a way he hadn't been expecting. In five years of close contact with his highly efficient assistant he couldn't remember ever noticing her bottom before. And it was actually a rather fine bottom. Firm and high and beautifully rounded. The kind of bottom which a man liked to cup in the palms of his hands as he…

'What?' Isobel turned round and frowned.

'I didn't…' Tariq swallowed. What the hell was going on? Did bumps to the head make men lose their senses, so that they started imagining all kinds of inappropriate things? 'I didn't say anything.'

'But you made a funny sort of noise.' Her eyes narrowed as she looked at him. 'Are you all right? Your eyes have gone all glazed.'

'Are you surprised?' Shifting his position, Tariq glared at her, willing his erection to subside. 'I've just had to endure your driving.'

Isobel turned back to the now leaping flames, an unseen smile playing around her lips. If he was jumping down her throat like that, then there couldn't be very much wrong with him.

She waited until the fire was properly alight and then went into the kitchen and made his favourite mint tea—bringing it back into the sitting room on a tray set with bone china cups and a jar of farm honey.

To her relief, she could see that he had taken her at her word. He'd kicked off his hand-made Italian shoes and was lying stretched out on the sofa, despite it being slightly too small to accommodate his lengthy frame. His thick black hair was outlined by a chintz cushion and his powerful thighs were splayed indolently against the faded velvet. It made an incongruous image, she realised—to see the *über*-masculine Sheikh in such a domestic setting as this.

She poured tea for them both, added honey to his, and put it down on a small table beside him, her gaze straying to his face as she sat on the floor beside the fire. Tariq was known for his faintly unshaven buccaneering look, but today the deep shadowing which outlined the hard definition of his jaw made him look like a study in brooding testosterone.

Now it was Isobel's turn to feel vulnerable. That faint butterflies-in-the-stomach feeling was back, bigtime. And so was that sudden sensitive prickling of her breasts. She swallowed. 'How are you feeling?'

His eyes narrowed. 'Will you stop talking to me as if I'm an invalid?'

'But that's what you are, Tariq—otherwise you wouldn't be here, would you? Just put my mind at rest. I'm not asking you to divulge the secrets of your heart— just answer the question.'

For the first time he became aware of the faint shadows beneath her eyes. She must be tired, he realised suddenly, and frowned. Hadn't he woken her at the crack of dawn yesterday? Called her and known she would come running to his aid without a second thought—because that was what she always did? Safe, reliable Izzy, who was always there when he needed her—often before he even realised he did. It wasn't an observation which would have normally occurred to him, and the novelty of that made him consider her question instead of batting it away with his habitual impatience.

Oddly—apart from the lessening ache in his head and the woolly feeling which came from his having been inactive for over a day—he felt strangely relaxed. Usually he was alert and driven, restlessly looking ahead to the next challenge. He was also constantly on his guard, knowing that his royal blood made him a target for all kinds of social climbers. Or journalists masquerading as dinner-dates.

Since his brother had unexpectedly acceded to the throne it had grown worse—placing him firmly in the public eye. He was bitterly aware that his words were always listened to, often distorted and then repeated—so he used them with caution.

Yet right now he felt a rush of unfamiliar *contentment* which was completely alien to him. For the first time in his adult life he found himself alone in a confined space with a woman who wasn't intent on removing his clothes....

'I have a slight ache in my...' he shifted his position as she tucked her surprisingly long legs beneath her and he felt another sharp kick of awareness '...head. But other than that I feel okay.'

The gleam in his black eyes was making Isobel feel uncomfortable. She wished he'd stop *looking* at her like that. Rather unnecessarily, she gave the fire a quick poke. 'Good.'

Tariq sipped at his tea, noting the sudden tension in her shoulders. Was she feeling it too? he wondered. This powerful sexual awareness which was simmering in the air around them?

With an effort, he pushed it from his mind and sought refuge in the conventional. 'I didn't realise you had a place like this. I thought you lived in town.'

Isobel laid the poker back down in the grate, his question making her realise the one-sided quality of their relationship. She knew all about *his* life—but he knew next to nothing about hers, did he?

'I do live in town. I just keep this as a weekend place—which is a bit of a luxury. I really ought to sell it and buy myself something larger than the shoebox I currently inhabit in London, but I can't quite bring myself to let it go. My mother worked hard to buy it, you see. She lived rent-free at the school, of course, and when she retired she moved here.' She read the question in his eyes, took a deep breath and faced it full-on. 'She died six years ago and left it to me.'

'And what about your father?'

All her old defensiveness sprang into place. 'What about him?'

'You never talk about him.'

'That's because you never ask.'

'No. You're right. I don't.' And the reason he never asked was because he wasn't particularly interested in the private lives of his staff. The less you knew about the people who worked for you, the less complication all round.

But surely these circumstances were unusual enough to allow him to break certain rules? And didn't Izzy's hesitancy alert his interest? Arouse his natural hunter instincts? Tariq leaned back against the pillow of his folded elbows and studied her. 'I'm asking now.'

Isobel met the curiosity in his eyes. If it had been anyone else she might have told them to mind their own business, or used the evasive tactics she'd employed all her life. She was protective of her private life and her past—and hated being judged or pitied. But that was the trouble with having a personal conversation with your boss—you weren't exactly on equal terms, were you? And Tariq wasn't just *any* boss. His authority was enriched with the sense of entitlement which came with his princely title and his innate belief that he was always right. Would he be shocked to learn of her illegitimacy?

She shrugged her shoulders, as if what she was about to say didn't matter. 'I don't know my father.'

'What do you mean, you don't know him?'

'Just that. I never saw him, nor met him. To me, he was just a man my mother had a relationship with. Only it turned out that he was actually married to someone else at the time.'

He narrowed his eyes. 'So what happened?'

She remembered all the different emotions which had crossed her mother's face when she had recounted her tale. Hurt. Resentment. And a deep and enduring sense of anger and betrayal. Men were the enemy, who could so easily walk away from their responsibilities, Anna

Mulholland had said. Had that negativity brushed off on her only daughter and contributed to Isobel's own poor record with men? Maybe it had—for she'd never let anyone close enough to really start to care about them.

'He didn't want to know about a baby,' she answered slowly. 'Said he didn't want anything to do with it. My mother thought it was shock making him talk that way. She gave him a few days to think about it. Only when she tried to contact him again—he'd gone.'

'Gone?' Tariq raised his eyebrows. 'Gone where?'

'That's the whole point—she never knew. He'd completely vanished.' She met the look of disbelief in his eyes and shook her head. 'It was only a quarter of a century ago, but it was a different kind of world back then. There were no computers you could use to track people down. No Facebook or cellphones. A man and his wife could just disappear off the face of the earth and you would never see them again.'

Tariq's frown deepened. 'So he never saw you?'

'Nope. Not once. He doesn't even know I exist,' she answered, as if she didn't care—and sometimes she actually managed to convince herself that she didn't. Wasn't it better to have an absent father rather than one who resented you, or didn't match up to your expectations? But deep down Isobel knew that wasn't the whole story. There was always a bitter ache in her heart when she thought about the parent she'd never had.

For a moment Tariq tensed, as an unwilling sense of identification washed over him. Her childhood sounded sterile and lonely—and wasn't that territory he was painfully familiar with? The little boy sent far away from home to endure a rigid system where his royal blood made him the victim of envy? And, like her, he had never known what it was to be part of a 'normal' family.

Suddenly, he found his voice dipping in empathy. 'That's a pretty tough thing to happen,' he said.

Isobel heard the softness of his tone but shook her head, determined to shield herself from his unexpected sympathy—because sympathy made you weak. It made regret and yearning wash over you. Made you start wishing things could have been different. And everyone knew you could never rewrite the past.

'It is what it is. Some people have to contend with far worse. My childhood was comfortable and safe— and you can't knock something like that. Now, would you like some more tea before it gets cold?' she questioned briskly.

He could tell from the brightness in her voice that she wanted to change the subject, and suddenly he found he was relieved. It had been his mistake to encourage too much introspection—especially about the past. Because didn't it open up memories which did no one any good? Memories which were best avoided because they took you to dark places?

He shook his head. 'No thanks. Just show me which bathroom you want me to use.'

'Right.' Isobel hesitated. Why hadn't she thought of this? 'The thing is that there's only one bathroom, I'm afraid.' She bit her lip. 'We're going to have to… well, share.'

There was a pause. 'Share?' he repeated.

She met the disbelief in his eyes. He's a *prince,* she reminded herself. He won't be used to sharing and making do. But it might do him some good to see how the other half lived—to see there were places other than the luxurious penthouses and palaces he'd always called home.

'My cottage is fairly basic, but it's comfortable,' she said proudly. 'I've never had the need or the money to incorporate an *en-suite* bathroom—so I'm afraid you'll just have to get used to it. Now, would you like me to show you where you'll be sleeping?'

Tariq gave a mirthless smile, acknowledging that it was the first time he'd ever been asked that particular question without the involvement of some kind of foreplay. Wordlessly he nodded as he rose from the sofa to follow her out into the hall and up a very old wooden staircase. The trouble was that her movements showcased her bottom even more than before. Because this time he was closer—and every mounting step made the blue denim cling like honey to each magnificent globe.

How could he have been so blind never to have noticed it before? His gaze travelled downwards. Or to have registered the fact that her legs were really very shapely—the ankles slim enough to be circled by his finger and his thumb...?

'This is the bathroom,' Isobel was saying. 'And right next door is your room. See?'

She pushed open a door and Tariq stepped inside and looked around, glad to be distracted by something other than the erotic nature of his thoughts.

It was a room like no room he'd ever seen. A modestly sized iron bedstead was covered with flower-sprigged bedlinen, and on top of one of the pillows sat a faded teddy bear. In the corner was an old-fashioned dressing table and a dark, rickety-looking wardrobe—other than that, the room was bare.

Yet as Tariq walked over to the window he could see that the view was incredible—overlooking nothing but unadulterated countryside. Hedgerows lined the narrow lane, and primroses grew in thick lemon clusters along the banks. Beyond that lay field after field—until eventually the land met the sky. There was absolutely no sound, he realised. Not a car, nor a plane—nor the distant trill of someone's phone.

The silence was all-enveloping, and a strange sense of peace settled on him. It crept over his skin like the first sun after a long winter and he gave a sigh of unfamiliar contentment. Turning around, he became aware that Izzy had walked over to the window to join him. And she was looking up at him, her eyes wide and faintly uncertain.

'Do you think you could be comfortable here?' she questioned.

Contentment forgotten now, he watched as she bit her lip and her teeth left behind a tiny indentation. He saw the sudden gleam as the tip of her tongue moistened the spot. Her tawny eyes were slitted against the sunlight which illuminated the magnificent Titian fire of her hair. Wasn't it peculiar that before today he'd never really noticed that her hair was such an amazing colour? And that, coupled with the proximity of her newly discovered curvaceous body, made a powerful impulse come over him.

He forgot that she was sensible Isobel—the reliable and rather sexless assistant who organised his life for him. He forgot everything other than the aching throb at his groin, which was tempting him with an insistence he was finding difficult to ignore. He wanted to kiss her. To plunder those unpainted lips with a fierce kind of hunger. To cup those delicious globes of her bottom and find if they were covered with cotton or lace. And then...

He felt the rapid escalation of desire as his sexual fantasy took on a vivid life of its own and the deep pulse of hunger began a primitive beat in his blood. For a moment he let its tempting warmth steal into his body, and he almost gave in to its powerful lure.

But Tariq prided himself on his formidable willpower, and his ability to turn his back on temptation. Because the truth was that there wasn't a woman in the world who couldn't be replaced.

What would be the point of seducing Isobel when the potential fall-out from that seduction could have far-reaching consequences? She'd probably fall in love with him—as women so often did—and when he ended it, what then?

When she'd told him about her father he'd seen a streak of steel and determination which might indicate that she wasn't a total marshmallow—but still he couldn't risk it. She was far more valuable to him as a member of staff than as a temporary lover.

He saw that she was still waiting for an answer to her

question, the anxious hostess eager for reassurance, and he gave her a careless smile. 'I think it will be perfectly *adequate* for my needs,' he answered.

Isobel nodded. Not the most heartfelt of thanks, it was true—but who cared? She was feeling so disorientated that she could barely think straight. Had she imagined that almost *electric* feeling which had sizzled between them just now? When something unknown and tantalising had shimmered in the air around them, making her blood grow thick with desire? When she'd longed for him to pull her into his arms and just *kiss* her?

Apprehension skittered over her skin as she tried to tell herself that she didn't find Tariq attractive. She *didn't*. Her innate fear of feckless men had always protected her from his undeniable charisma.

So what had happened to that precious immunity now? Was it because they were in *her* home, and on *her* territory instead of his, that she felt so shockingly vulnerable in his presence? Or because she'd been stupid enough to blurt out parts of her life which she'd always kept tucked away, and in so doing had opened up a vulnerable side of herself?

Suddenly she was achingly aware of his proximity. Every taut sinew of his powerful body seemed to tantalise her and send a thousand questions racing through her mind. What would it be like to be held by him? To be pressed against that muscular physique while his fingertips touched her aching breasts?

Aware that her cheeks had grown flushed, she lifted

her eyes to his, wondering what had happened to all her certainties. 'Is there…is there anything else you need?'

He wondered what she would do if he answered that question honestly, and a wry smile curved the edges of his lips as he noted her sudden rise in colour. Would her lips fall open with shock if he told her that he longed for her to fall to her knees, to take him in her mouth and suck him? Or would she simply comply with the easy efficiency she showed in all other elements of their working relationship? Would she *swallow?* he found himself wondering irreverently.

His desire rocketed, frustrating him with a heavy throbbing at his aching groin. He needed her out of here. Now. Before he did or said something he might later regret.

'Leave me now, Izzy,' he commanded unsteadily. 'Unless you're planning to stay and watch while I shower?'

CHAPTER FOUR

SOMEHOW, ISOBEL MANAGED to hold onto her composure until she'd closed the bedroom door, and then she rushed back down the creaky staircase to the kitchen. Once there, she leaned against one of the cupboards, her eyes squeezed tight shut as she tried not to think about the Sheikh's powerful body, which would soon be acquainting itself with her ancient little bathroom. Her heart was hammering as an imagination she hadn't known she possessed began to taunt her with vivid images.

She thought about Tariq naked. With little droplets of water gleaming against his flesh.

She thought about Tariq drying—the towel lingering on his damp, golden flesh as he rubbed himself all over.

Swallowing down the sudden lump which had risen in her throat, she shook her head. Weaving erotic fantasies about him would lead to nothing but trouble—and so would baring her soul. Taking Tariq into her confidence would only add to the vulnerability she was already experiencing. She wondered what had made her confide in him about her father, and the fact that she'd never known him.

She knew she had to pull herself together. *She* had been the one who'd invited him to stay, and he was going to be here for the next few days whether she liked it or not. Just because her feelings towards him seemed to have changed—what mattered was that she didn't let it show.

Because Tariq was no fool. He was a master of experience when it came to the opposite sex, and he was bound to start noticing her reaction if she wasn't careful. If she dissolved into mush every time he came near, or her fingers started trembling just like they were doing now, wouldn't that give the game away? Wouldn't he guess that her senses had been shaken into life and she'd become acutely attracted to him? And just how embarrassing would that be?

She needed a plan. Something to stop him from dominating her mind with arousing thoughts.

Opening the door of the freezer, she peered inside and began to devise a crash course in displacement therapy which would see her through the days ahead. She would make sure she had plenty to occupy her. She would be as brisk and efficient as she was at work, and maybe this crazy *awareness* of him would go away.

But that was easier said than done. By the time Tariq came back downstairs she was busy chopping up ingredients for a risotto, but she made the mistake of lifting her head to look at him. And then found herself mesmerised by the intimate image of her boss fresh from the bath. His hair was damp and ruffled, and he carried with him the faint tang of her ginger and lemon gel.

Isobel swallowed. 'Bath okay?'

He raised his eyebrows. 'You didn't bother telling me that you don't have a shower.'

'I guessed you find out soon enough.'

'So I did,' he growled. 'It's the most ancient bathroom I've used in years—and the water was tepid.'

'Don't they say that tepid baths are healthier?'

'Do they?' He looked around. 'Where's your TV?'

'I don't have one.'

'You don't have a TV?'

Isobel shot him a defensive look. 'It isn't mandatory, you know. There's a whole wall of books over there. Help yourself to one of those.'

'You mean *read*?'

'That *is* what people usually do with books.'

With a short sigh of impatience, Tariq wandered over to examine the neat rows of titles which lined an entire wall of her sitting room.

The only things he ever read were financial papers or contracts, or business-related articles he caught up with when he was travelling. Occasionally his attention would be caught by some glossy car magazine, which would lure him into changing his latest model for something even more powerful. But he never read books. He had neither the time nor the inclination to lose himself in the world of fiction. He remembered that stupid story he'd read at school—about some animal which had been abandoned. He remembered the tears which had welled up in his eyes when its mother had been shot and the way he'd slammed the volume shut. Books made you *feel* things—and the only thing he wanted to feel right now were the tantalising curves of Izzy's body.

But that was a *bad* idea. And he needed something to occupy his thoughts other than musing about what kind of underwear a woman like that would wear beneath her rather frumpy clothes.

In the end he forced himself to read a thriller—grateful for the novel's rapid pace, which somehow seemed to suck him into an entirely believable story of a one-time lap dancer successfully nailing a high-profile banker for fraud. He was so engrossed in the tale that Izzy's voice startled him, and he looked up to find her standing over him, her face all pink and shiny.

'Mmm?' he questioned, thinking how soft and kissable her lips looked.

'Supper's ready.'

'Supper?'

'You *do* eat supper?'

Actually he usually ate *dinner*—an elegant feast of a meal rather than a large spoonful of glossy rice slapped on the centre of an earthy-looking plate. But to Tariq's surprise he realised that he was hungry—and he enjoyed it more than he had expected. Afterwards Izzy heaped more logs on the fire, and they sat there in companionable silence while he picked up his novel and began to race through it again.

For Tariq, the days which followed his accident were unique. He'd been brought up in a closeted world of palaces and privilege, but now he found himself catapulted into an existence which seemed far more bizarre.

His nights were spent alone, in an old and lumpy bed, yet he found he was sleeping late—something he rarely did, not even when he was jet-lagged. And the lack of a shower meant that he'd lie daydreaming in the bath in the mornings. In the cooling water of the rather cramped tub he would stretch out his long frame and listen to the sounds of birds singing outside the window. So that by the time he wandered downstairs it was to find his Titian-haired assistant bustling around with milk jugs and muesli, or asking him if he wanted to try the eggs from the local farm.

For the first time in a long time he felt *relaxed*—even if Izzy seemed so busy that she never seemed to stop. She was always doing *something*—cooking or cleaning or dealing with the e-mails which flooded in from the office, shielding him from all but the most necessary requests.

'Why don't you loosen up a little?' he questioned one morning, glancing up from his latest thriller to see her cleaning out the grate, a fine cloud of coal dust billowing around her.

Izzy pushed a stray strand of hair from out of her eyes with her elbow. Because action distracted her from obsessing about his general gorgeousness, that was why. And because she was afraid that if she allowed herself to stop then she might never get going again.

What did he expect her to do all day? Sit staring as he sprawled over her sofa, subjecting her to a closer-than-was comfortable view of his muscular body? Watch as he shifted one powerful thigh onto the other, thus drawing attention to the mysterious bulge at the crotch of his jeans? A place she knew she shouldn't be looking—which, of course, made it all the more difficult not to.

She felt guilty and ashamed at the wayward path of her thoughts, and began to wonder if he had cast some kind of spell on her. Suddenly the clingy behaviour of some of his ex-lovers became a little more understandable.

Her nights weren't much better. How could they be when she knew that Tariq was lying in bed in the room next door? Hadn't she already experienced the disturbing episode of him wandering out of the bathroom one morning with nothing but a small towel strung low around his hips?

Tiny droplets of water had clung to his hard, olive-skinned torso, and Isobel's heart had thumped like a piston as she'd surveyed his perfect physique. She'd briefly thought of suggesting that perhaps he ought to be using a bigger towel. But wouldn't that have sounded awfully presumptuous? In the end, she had just mumbled, 'Good morning...' and hurried past him, terrified that he would see the telltale flush of desire in her cheeks.

Almost overnight the cool neutrality she'd felt towards her boss had been replaced with new and scary sensations. She felt almost molten with longing whenever she looked at him—yet at the same time she resented these disturbing new feelings. Why couldn't she have felt this sharp sense of desire with other men? Decent, reliable men? The kind of men she usually dated and who inevitably left her completely cold? Why the hell did it have to be *him?*

'Izzy?' His deep voice broke into her disturbed thoughts. 'Why don't you sit down and relax?'

'Oh, I'm happier when I'm working,' she hedged,

as she swept more dust out of the fireplace. 'Anyway, we're going back to London tomorrow.'

'We are?' He put his book down and frowned. 'Has it really been a week?'

'Well, five days, actually—but you certainly seem better.'

'I feel better,' he said, acknowledging that this was something of an understatement. He hadn't felt like this in years—as if every one of his senses had been retuned and polished. He was looking forward to getting back to London and hitting the ground running.

But his last night in Izzy's little cottage was restless, and the sound sleep he'd previously enjoyed seemed to elude him. Inexplicably, he found himself experiencing a kind of regret that he wouldn't ever sleep in this old-fashioned bed again, beneath the flower-sprigged linen. He lay awake, wondering if he was imagining the sound of Izzy moving in her sleep next door, her slim, pale limbs tossing and turning. Maybe he was—but he certainly wasn't imagining his reaction to those thoughts.

With a small groan he turned onto his side, and then onto his stomach—feeling the rising heat of yet another erection pressing against the mattress. It had been like this for most of the week, and it had been hell. Night after night he'd imagined parting Izzy's pale thighs and sliding his hot, hard heat into her exquisite warmth. He swallowed as the tightness increased. Was his body so starved of physical pleasure that he should become fixated on a woman simply because she happened to be *around*? Yet what other explanation could there be for this inexplicable lust he was experiencing?

In the darkness of the bedroom he heard the distant hoot of an owl in the otherwise silent countryside and his mouth thinned. He needed a lover, that was for sure—and the moment he got back to London he'd do something about it. Maybe contact that beautiful Swedish model who had been coming on to him so strong...

Resisting the urge to satisfy himself, he buried his cheek against a pillow which smelt of lavender, and yawned as he fantasised about a few more likely candidates.

But sleep still eluded him, and at first light he gave up the fight, tugged on a pair of jeans and went downstairs—still yawning. He made strong coffee in Izzy's outdated percolator, and after he'd drunk it settled down to finish his thriller.

And that was where Isobel found him a couple of hours later—stretched out on the sofa, the book open against the gentle rise and fall of his chest. The feathery dark arcs of his lashes did not move when she walked in, and she realised that he was fast asleep.

Her barefooted tread was silent as she padded across the room towards him, unable to resist the temptation to observe him at closer quarters—telling herself that she only wanted to see if he looked rested and recovered. To see whether it really was a good idea for him to go back to London later that day.

But that was a lie and she knew it. Deep down she knew she was going to miss this crazy domestic arrangement. Despite the pressure of wanting him, she had enjoyed sharing her living space with her boss. Even if it had been an artificial intimacy which they'd created between them, it didn't seem to matter. She'd seen another side to him—a more *human* side—and she couldn't help wondering what it would be like once they were back in the office.

Yet, despite her mixed thoughts, she felt a quiet moment of pride as she looked down at him—because he was certainly back to his usual robust self. If anything, he looked better than she could ever remember seeing him. Less strained. More relaxed. His olive skin was highlighted with a glorious golden glow, and his lips were softened at the edges.

But the hard beating of her heart made her realise that her new-found feelings for him hadn't gone away. That stupid softness hadn't hardened into her habitual indifference towards him. Something had changed—or maybe the feeling had always been there, deep down. Maybe it was a left-over crush from her schooldays and she'd only buried it rather than abandoning it. But, either way, she didn't know what she was going to do about it.

She continued to stare at him, willing herself to feel nothing—but to no avail. She was itching to touch him, even in the most innocent of ways. Because what other way did she know? A thick ebony lock of hair had curled onto his forehead, and she had to resist the impulse to smooth it away with the tips of her fingers.

But maybe she moved anyway—if only fractionally—because his lashes suddenly fluttered open to reveal the watchful black gleam of his eyes.

Did she suck in a sudden breath and then expel it with a sigh which shuddered out from somewhere deep in her lungs? The kind of sigh which could easily be mistaken for longing? Was that why his arm suddenly snaked up without warning, effortlessly curling around her waist before bringing her down onto his bare chest in one fluid movement?

'T-Tariq!' she gasped, feeling the delicious impact as their bodies made unexpected contact.

'Izzy,' he growled, as every fantasy he'd been concocting over the last few days burst into rampant life.

Izzy with her hair loose and cascading around her shoulders. Izzy wearing some ridiculously old-fashioned pair of pyjamas. Izzy warm and soft and smelling of toothpaste, just begging to be kissed. Reaching up, he tangled his fingers in the rich spill of her curls and brought her mouth down on his.

'Oh!' Her startled exclamation was muffled by his kiss, and it only partially blotted out the urgent clamour of her thoughts. She ought to stop him. She knew that. A whole lifetime of conditioning told her so.

But Isobel didn't stop him, and the words which her mother had once drummed into her floated straight out of her mind. It no longer mattered that Tariq was the worst possible person to let make love to her. Because her body was on fire—a fire created by the blazing heat of his. She wanted him, and she wanted his kiss. She wanted it enough to turn her back on all her so-called principles, and now she gave in to it with greedy fervour, her mouth opening hungrily beneath his.

She could hear the small moan he made as the kiss deepened. He crushed his lips against hers and a fierce heat began to flood through her body, from breast to belly and beyond.

Frantically, her fingers slithered over his chest and began to knead at the silken flesh, feeling the mad hammer of his heart against her palm. She moaned into his mouth as his hand skimmed down from the base of her throat to her breast, slipping his fingers inside her pyjama jacket and capturing the aching mound with proprietorial skill. She could feel him stroking one pinpoint nipple between finger and thumb until she gasped aloud, wriggling uselessly as she felt the flagrant ridge at his groin pressing against her belly.

Tariq groaned. She tasted of mint, and her hair tickled him as the thick curls cascaded down the side of her face. She felt *amazing*. Was that because this had come at him out of the blue? Or was it novelty value because she was the last person in the world he could imagine responding with such easy passion? My God, she was *hot*.

He kissed her until he had barely any breath left in his lungs, and it became apparent that her narrow sofa was hopelessly inadequate for two people who were exploring each other's bodies for the first time.

'This is getting a little crowded,' he managed, pulling his lips away from hers with an effort.

He slid them both to the ground, barely noticing the hard flagstones beneath the thin rug. All that concerned him was the gasping beauty in his arms, her hair spilling out all over the floor like tendrils of pale fire and her eyes as tawny as a tiger's.

'Comfortable?' he questioned, as he smoothed some of the wiry corkscrews away from the pink flush of her cheeks.

Heart thundering, Isobel gazed up at him, wondering why she didn't feel shyer than she did. Was it because Tariq was staring down at her with such gleaming hunger in his eyes that in that moment she felt utterly desirable? As if almost *anything* was possible? 'Oddly enough, yes, I am.'

'Me too. Deliciously comfortable. Perhaps I can help make you more comfortable still, *anisah bahiya*.' Pulling open her dressing gown, he began to unbutton her pyjamas—until two rosy-peaked breasts were thrusting towards him. Unable to resist their silent plea, he bent his head to suckle one. Slicking his tongue against the tight bud, he felt the responsive jerk of her hips and heard her gasp his name. 'I've never seduced a woman in pyjamas before,' he whispered against the puckered flesh.

'Are you...are you going to seduce me, then?'

'What do you think? That I've got you down here because I want to discuss my diary for next week?'

Thinking was the last thing Isobel wanted to do—because if she did that then surely she would realise that what they were doing was crazy. Wouldn't thinking remind her that Tariq was a cavalier playboy, and that there was a reason why men like him should be avoided like the plague? Wouldn't it prompt her into doing the only sensible thing—which was to tear herself away from him and rush upstairs to her room, away from temptation?

She felt the graze of his teeth against her nipple and shut her eyes. Far better to feel. To allow these amaz-

ing sensations to skate over her skin and fill her with an
urgent longing which was fast spiralling out of control.

'Oh!' she breathed, eagerly squirming her hips beneath him and feeling a warm, wild heat building up inside her. And he answered her voiceless plea by slipping
his hand inside the elasticated waistband of her pyjamas.

She held her breath as his warm palm navigated its
way down her belly, tiptoeing tantalisingly to the fuzz
of hair which lay beyond. Still she held her breath as
he stroked at the sensitive skin of her inner thigh, and
then gasped as his fingertips seared over her moist heat.

'Oh!' she said again.

'You're very wet.'

'A-am I?'

'Mmm…' Tariq's mouth brushed over hers as his
finger strayed to the tight bud at the very core of her
desire. Her instant compliance didn't surprise him—he
was capable of reducing a woman to a boneless state
of longing no matter what the circumstances. But the
sheer and urgent spontaneity of what they were doing
made him tense—just for a moment. And that moment
was enough for him to remember one vital omission.

He froze, before snatching his hand away from her.
Damn and damn and *damn!*

'I don't have any protection with me,' he ground out.

For one stupid moment Isobel thought he was talking
about the bodyguards he sometimes used, and then she
saw the look of dark frustration on his face and realised
what he meant. A wave of insecurity washed over her.

Should she tell him?

Of *course* she should tell him—they were on the

brink of making love, and now was not the time for coyness.

'Actually, I'm...' Isobel swallowed, wanting his fingers back on her aching flesh. 'I'm on the pill.'

Her admission dampened his ardour fractionally. He drew away from her, his black eyes slitted in a cool question. 'The pill?'

Isobel heard the unmistakable disapproval in his voice. 'Lots of women are.'

There was a pause. 'Yes. I imagine that they are.'

Suddenly she shrank from the truth in his hard black eyes, indignant words tumbling from her lips before she could stop them. 'I suppose you think that the kind of woman who happens to have contraception covered is easy?'

Tariq shrugged. 'You must agree that it does imply a certain degree of *accessibility*.'

'Well, you couldn't be more wrong, Tariq,' she declared hotly. 'Because...because I've never had a lover before!'

He stared at her, genuinely confused. 'What the hell are you talking about?'

'I was prescribed the pill because my periods are heavy, and that's the only reason. I've... Well, I've never had any other reason to take it.'

This commonplace and unexpected disclosure highlighted the unusual degree of intimacy between them, and Tariq frowned. He brushed a corkscrew lock of hair away from her forehead, trying to make sense of her words. 'You're trying to tell me you're—?'

'Yes, I'm a virgin,' she said, as if it didn't matter.

Because surely it didn't? What mattered was Tariq kissing her and transporting her back to that heavenly place he'd taken her to before. Just because she had waited a long time for a man to turn her on as much as this, it didn't mean that she should be treated as some kind of leper, did it?

Sliding her arms around his neck, she lifted her face to his, hungry for him. 'Now, kiss me again,' she whispered.

How could he refuse her soft entreaty? Tariq groaned as he tasted her trembling lips and a shaft of pure desire shot through him. He could feel the softness of her breasts yielding against his bare chest, their taut tips firing at him like little arrows towards his heart. Irresistibly, his fingers slipped inside the waistband of her pyjama trousers again, and he heard her little gurgle of anticipation.

For one moment he was about to peel them right off. Then his hand paused, mid-motion, as he forced himself to recall the unbelievable facts.

She was a virgin!

And more importantly…

She was his assistant!

'No!' he thundered, dragging his lips away from hers. 'I will not do this!'

Her body screaming out its protest, Isobel looked up at him in confusion. 'Will not do what?'

'I will not rob you of your innocence!'

She stared at him, still not understanding. 'Why not?'

'Are you crazy? Because a woman's purity is her greatest gift. And it's a one-off—you don't get to use it again. So save it for a man who will give you more than I ever can, Izzy. Don't throw it away on someone like me.'

For a moment he cupped her chin between his palms, looking down at her with a regret which only compounded her intense feeling of rejection. She jerked her face away—as if to allow him continued contact might in some way contaminate her.

'Then w-would you mind moving away from me and letting me get up?' she said, trembling hurt distorting her words.

'I can try.' With a grimace, he rose to his feet, the heavy throb at his groin making movement both difficult and uncomfortable.

Despite the scene he now rather grimly anticipated he couldn't help a flicker of admiration as he looked at Isobel clambering to her feet, tugging furiously at the jacket of her pyjamas. Passion always changed a woman, he mused, but in Izzy's case it had practically *transformed* her. Her hair was falling in snake-like tendrils all around her slender shoulders and she stood before him like some bright and unrecognisable sorceress. For a moment he experienced a deep sense of regret and frustration—and then he steeled his heart against his foolishness and turned his back on her.

With shaking fingers Isobel began to do up her pyjamas, realising that she had let herself down—and in so many ways. She had shown Tariq how much she wanted him and he had pushed her away, leaving her feeling guilty that she'd been prepared to 'throw away' her virginity on someone like him. How did you ever get back from something like that? The dull truth washed over her. The answer was that you didn't.

Biting her lip, she watched as he turned away to adjust his jeans, trying to ignore the sense of having missed out on something wonderful. Of having been on the brink of some amazing discovery. Inevitably she was now going to lose her job, and she didn't even have the compensation of having known him as a lover. But surely it was better to face up to the consequences of her behaviour than to wait for him to put the knife in?

'You want me to hand my notice in?' she asked quietly.

This was enough to make Tariq turn back and scrutinise her, steeling himself against the enduring kissability of her darkened lips, knowing that if he didn't get out of there soon he'd go back on everything he'd just said and thrust deep and hard inside her, tear her precious membrane and leave his mark on her for ever. He shook his head. 'Actually, that's precisely what I *don't* want. That's one of the reasons I pulled back. I value you far too much to want to lose you, Izzy.'

In spite of everything, his words took Isobel aback. In five years of working for him it was the first time he'd ever said anything remotely like that. She screwed her face up, wondering how to react to the unfamiliar compliment. 'You do?'

'Of course I do—and this week has shown me just how much. I have a lot to thank you for. You're a hardworking, loyal member of my staff, and I've come to rely on you a great deal. And believe me—I'd have a lot of trouble replacing you.'

Isobel kept her face expressionless as something inside her withered and died. 'I see.'

'And just because of this one uncharacteristic lapse...'

She grimaced as his voice tailed off. Now he was making her sound like a docile family dog which had unexpectedly jumped up and bitten the postman.

'I don't see why it should have to change anything,' he continued.

'So you want that we should just forget what has happened and carry on as normal?'

'In theory, yes.' His black eyes bored into her. 'Do you think you can do that?'

It was the patronising tone of the question which swung it. Isobel had been on the verge of telling him that she didn't think there was any going back—or forward—but his arrogant assumption that she might struggle with resuming their professional relationship made her blood boil.

'Oh, I don't think *I'd* have a problem with it,' she answered sweetly. 'How about you?'

Tariq's eyes narrowed as she tossed him the throwaway question. Was she now implying that she was some sort of irresistible little sex-bomb who was going to test his formidable powers of self-control once they were back in the office? He gave a slow smile. He thought she might be forgetting herself.

Once she was back in her usual environment, with her hair scraped back and her rather frumpy clothes in place, there would be no reoccurrence of that inexplicable burst of lust. There would be no flower-sprigged pyjamas and soft curves to send out such sizzling and mixed messages, threatening to make a man lose his head.

'I wouldn't over-estimate your appeal, if I were you,' he said coolly. 'Because that would be a big mistake. I can resist you any time I like.'

CHAPTER FIVE

How COULD HE have been so damned *stupid?*

Tariq stared out of the window at the darkening London skyscape which gave his office its magnificent views. Stars were twinkling in the indigo sky, and in the distance he could see the stately dome of St Paul's Cathedral.

He should have been on top of the world.

The doctor had given him the all-clear, his car was in the garage being painstakingly mended, and his acquisition of the Premiership team looked almost certain. Khayarzah oil revenues were at an all-time high, and he had received an unexpected windfall from some media shares he'd scooped up last year. It seemed that everything he turned his hand to in the world of commerce flourished. In short, business was booming.

He turned away from the magnificent view, trying to put his finger on what was wrong. Wondering why this infuriating air of discontentment simply would not leave him—no matter how hard he tried to alleviate it.

He gave a ragged sigh, knowing all too well what lay at the heart of his irritation yet strangely reluctant to acknowledge its source. Its sweet and unexpected source…

Izzy.

His rescuer and tormentor. His calm and efficient assistant, with all her contradictory qualities, who had somehow—against all the odds—managed to capture his imagination.

Had it been pure arrogance which had made him so certain that his lust for her would dissolve the moment they were back in the office? He'd decided that the crash had weakened him in all ways—mentally, physically *and* emotionally. He'd thought that was why he had been so curiously susceptible to a woman he had never found in the least bit attractive. An insanity, yes—but a temporary one.

But he had been wrong.

Since being back at work he'd been unable to stop fantasising about her. Or to stop thinking about those prudish pyjamas which had covered up the red-hot body beneath. His mind kept taking him back to their tangled bodies on the floor of her cottage, reminding him of just how close they'd got. If common sense hadn't forced him to call a halt to what was happening he would have…would have…

But it was more than just frustrated lust which was sending his blood pressure soaring. His desire was compounded by knowing that she was a virgin. That she had never known a man's lovemaking before and she had wanted *him*. Just as he had wanted *her*.

He swallowed. The fact that she worked for him and that it was entirely inappropriate did little to lessen his appetite. On the contrary, the thought of making love to her excited him beyond belief—perhaps because it was his first ever taste of the forbidden. And for a man like Tariq very few things in life were forbidden...

His erotic thoughts were interrupted by the cause of his frustration as Izzy walked in, bearing a tiny cup of inky coffee which she deposited in front of him with a smile. Not the kind of smile he would have expected, in the circumstances. It was not tinged with longing, nor was it edged with a frustration similar to the one he was experiencing. No, it was a bright and infuriatingly sunny smile—a sort of pre-weekend kind of smile. As if she had forgotten all about those passion-fuelled moments back in her country cottage.

Had she?

'You aren't changing?' she questioned.

Tariq blinked at her, her question arrowing into the confusing swirl of his thoughts. 'Changing?' he growled. 'What's wrong with the way I am?'

Isobel felt her heart hammer in response. Oh, but he was edgy this evening! Even edgier than he'd been all week. Mind you, she'd been feeling similarly jumpy— just determined not to show it. Her pride had been shattered by his rejection, and she was determined to salvage what was left of it by maintaining a cool air of composure. But it was difficult trying to pretend that nothing had happened when your boss had fondled your naked breasts and part of you was longing for him to do it all over again.

She tipped her head to one side and pretended to consider his question. 'How long have you got?'

'Izzy—'

'I meant *changing* in a literal sense,' she clarified, with a quick glance at her watch. 'Aren't you due for a party at the Maraban Embassy at seven? And don't you usually wear something dark and tailored instead of…?' Her bravado suddenly evaporated, her voice tailing off as she was momentarily distracted by his physical presence. *Why* had she allowed her eyes to linger on his physique, when she had determinedly been avoiding it all week?

'Instead of what, Izzy?' he questioned silkily, for he had noticed the sudden. rapid blinking of her eyes.

'Instead of…' She realised that he must have removed his tie at some point during the afternoon, and loosened at least two buttons of his shirt. Because rather more of his chest was on show than usual—and it reminded her of his warm, bare flesh beneath her fingertips on the floor of her cottage.

She could see the lush, dark whorls of hair growing there—which added texture to the olive glow of his skin and invited the eye on an inevitable path downwards…

Keep your mind on the job, she urged herself fiercely. *You're not supposed to be lusting after him—remember?*

'It's…it's a formal event, isn't it?' she finished helplessly.

Tariq felt a brief moment of triumph as he saw her eyes darken. So she was *not* completely immune to him—despite the way she'd been behaving all week. His mouth hardened with grudging respect—for Izzy had shown herself to be made of sterner stuff than he would have thought. Since they'd been back in the

office she had treated him with exactly the same blend
of roguish yet respectful attitude as she'd done all
through their professional relationship. As if his being
moments away from penetrating her body had left her
completely cold. So was that true? Or was it all some
kind of act?

He let his eyes drift over her, wondering if she had
decided to showcase the dullest items in her wardrobe.
Maybe he'd seen that skirt before—and her pale sweater
certainly wasn't new—but she looked dowdier than he
could ever remember. Was that deliberate? Or was it
because now he knew more about her he was looking
at her more closely? Comparing how she looked now to
how she'd looked when she had been writhing around
beneath him? And he couldn't rid himself of the un-
settling knowledge of the magnificent rose-tipped and
creamy breasts which lay beneath her insipid armour.

'Yes, it's a formal event,' he drawled. 'And, to be
truthful, I don't feel like going.'

'But you have to go, Tariq.'

'Have to?' He raised his brows. 'Is that an order?'

'No, of course it isn't.'

He began to walk towards her, noticing the tip of her
tongue as it snaked out to moisten her lips 'Why do I
have to?' he queried softly.

'Well, your two countries are neighbours, and you've
just signed that big trade agreement, and it will look
very b-bad if…if…'

He heard her stumbled words with a triumphant kick
of pleasure. 'If what?'

Isobel swallowed. What was going on? What was he

doing? The gap between them was closing, and instinct made her step backwards—away from his inexorable path towards her. But there was no escaping him despite the massive dimensions of his office. Nowhere to go until she reached a wall and felt its smooth, cool surface at her back. She stared up at him with widened eyes. Wasn't he breaking the agreement they'd made?

'T-Tariq! What do you think you're doing?'

Pushing one hand against the wall right beside her head, he leaned forward and looked deep into her tawny eyes. 'I'm wondering why you're trying to give me lessons in protocol I neither want nor need. But mostly I'm wondering whether you're feeling as frustrated as I am.'

Perhaps if he'd put it any other way than that Isobel might have given his question some consideration—or allowed her feelings to sway her. Because hadn't she been teetering on a knife-edge of wanting him and yet terrified of letting him know that? Hadn't it been as much as she could do each morning not to gaze wistfully at the sensual curve of his cynical lips? Not to wish that they were subjecting her to another of those hard and passionate kisses?

But his question had been more mechanical than emotional. No woman wanted to feel like an itch which a man needed to scratch, did she? And hadn't she told herself over and over again that no matter how much she wanted him no good would come of any kind of liaison? She *knew* about his track record with women. And only someone who was completely insane would lay herself open to an inevitable hurt like that.

'We aren't supposed to be discussing this,' she said flatly.

'Aren't we? Says who?'

'Said *you!* And me! That's what we agreed on back at the cottage. We agreed that it was a mistake. We're supposed to be carrying on as normal and forgetting it ever happened.'

'Maybe we are. But the trouble is…' And now he leaned in a little further towards her, so that he could feel the warm fan of her rapid breathing. 'The trouble is that I'm finding it difficult to forget it ever happened. In fact, it's proving impossible. I keep thinking about how it felt to have you in my arms. About how wild your hair looks when you let it down. I keep remembering what it was like to kiss you, and how your breasts felt when I was touching them.'

'Tariq,' she whispered, as his words made her body spring into instant life and her mouth dried as she stared into his darkening eyes. 'You were the one who stopped it. Remember?'

'And I did that because you're a virgin!' he said, letting his hand fall by his side. 'I decided I had no right to take your innocence from you. That you deserved a man who would cherish you more than I could ever do.'

'Well, that much hasn't changed. I haven't rushed out and leapt into bed with someone else in the meantime. I'm still a virgin, Tariq.'

'I realise that.' Their gazes clashed as he fought to do the decent thing. 'And I still don't think it's the right thing to do.'

She bit her lip. Was he playing games with her? 'So why are we even *having* this conversation?'

For a moment he clenched his fists savagely by his thighs, telling himself that he had no right to take an innocence which would be better given to another man. A man who would love her and cherish her. Who was capable of giving her the things that every woman wanted.

But the soft, sweet tremble of her lips defeated his best intentions, and a ragged sigh shuddered from between his lips. 'Because I'm finding resisting you harder than I anticipated.'

She stared into the heated gleam of his black eyes as a blend of frustration and emotion began to bubble up inside her and that sweet, terrible aching started all over again. 'And what about what *I* think?' she questioned quietly. 'What if I'm finding resisting *you* harder than I thought?'

Once again he fought with his conscience, but this time it was even more difficult because he realised that Izzy was enchantingly unique. An innocent who was up-front about her needs. A woman who wasn't playing coy games. The fists at his sides relaxed, and he lifted his hand and began to trace a light line around the butterfly tremble of her lips.

'You know I can't offer you anything in the way of commitment? That nothing long-term is going to come out of this? Three weeks is about my limit with any woman—you know that better than anyone, Izzy.'

She heard the stark warning in his words, but she wanted him too much to pay them any attention. And she was wise enough not to question him about why he was so adamant about short-term relationships. Maybe she'd ask him another time...just not now. Now she was fighting for something she wasn't prepared to give up on.

'You think that all virgins expect marriage from the first man they sleep with? Er, hello—and welcome to the twenty-first century! Aren't I allowed to do something just because I want to—the way you always seem to do? Just for the hell of it?'

Tariq felt his resistance trickling away. Nobody could say he hadn't tried—but it seemed that Izzy was intent on fighting him every inch of the way. Maybe this *was* the only solution to the otherwise unendurable prospect of the two of them dancing around each other every day, aching with frustrated need. And wasn't there something about making love to her which appealed to him on a very fundamental level? Something which he had never done with any other woman...

'For the hell of it? I think you're selling yourself short. Why don't we try a taste of heaven instead?' he said, and he pulled her into his arms and let his mouth make a slow motion journey to meet hers.

She actually cried out with pleasure as he began to kiss her, the taste and feel of his mouth seeming gloriously familiar. Gripping his shoulders, she dug her fingers into his suit jacket, afraid that her knees might give way if she didn't have something to cling onto. And as the kiss grew deeper she could feel the hard jut of his hips, which framed the unmistakable evidence of his arousal. Recklessly she pressed her body closer still, making no protest when he began to ruck her skirt up, urging him on with a guttural little sound of hunger which didn't sound a bit like her.

'Damn tights,' he ground out as his fingers met the least erotic piece of clothing ever designed by man. But he could feel the heat searing through them at the apex of her thighs, and the restless circling of her hips as he touched her there.

With practised ease he yanked them down, slithering them over her knees to her ankles. He knelt to slide off first one shoe and then the other—tossing them aside with the tights, so that they lay discarded. And then he rose again to take her in his arms.

Maybe he should have carried her across to one of the plush sofas which comprised the more casual meeting area of his office. Stripped her off slowly and provocatively as she doubtlessly deserved. But for the first time in his life Tariq couldn't bear the thought of delaying this for a second longer than was necessary. Her wide eyes and quickened breath were doing something inexplicable to him. He felt unaccountably *primitive*… as if his desire to possess her was urging him along on a dark and unstoppable tide.

He touched her against her panties, heard her make some yelping little sound of pleasure and frustration as he ripped them apart. Then he unzipped himself with a shaking hand, freeing the leaden spring of his erection with a ragged sigh of relief.

She was wet and ready for him, clinging to him eagerly as he thrust into her—hard and deep and without warning. Yet it still came as a shock as he encountered a momentary resistance, and he stilled as he heard her make a little moan of discomfort.

'*Aludra!*' he choked out, stopping inside her to give her the chance to acclimatise herself to these new sensations. Holding her close, he bent his lips to her ear. 'Did I hurt you, little Izzy?'

She shook her head. 'If you did, then I've forgotten. Please don't stop,' she whispered back, giving a little yelp of pleasure as he began to move inside her. 'It feels…' She closed her eyes and expelled a shuddering breath. 'Oh, Tariq, it feels…*incredible.*'

It felt pretty incredible for him, too. Especially when she wrapped her legs around his back with athletic skill. But it was more than that. He'd never done it like this before. Had never felt this free. This *powerful.* Was that because it was Izzy? A woman who knew him better than any other woman? Didn't that add an extra piquant layer of desire? Or was it because there was no infernal covering of thin rubber between them? He could feel the soft squash of her buttocks as he cupped them, and the deep molten tightness of her body as it welcomed him. He could hear her soft exclamations of pleasure and astonishment, and that too reminded him of the reality.

She's never done this with anyone else.

That possessive thought only sharpened his hunger, and he shuddered with pleasure as he drove deeper and deeper inside her. He spoke to her in half-forgotten words of Khayarzahian as they moved in ancient rhythm, until he heard her make a helpless little cry and felt her begin to convulse around him.

She gasped his name and clutched at his shoulders

like a woman who was drowning, and then at last he let go. And it was like nothing he'd ever experienced. One sweet and erotic spasm after another racked through him, until he felt as if he'd been wrung out and left to dry. Her head fell against his shoulder and he could feel the quiver of her unsteady breath as she panted against his neck. Her legs slipped down from his waist and he wrapped his arms around hers and held her very close.

He didn't know how long they stayed like that—just that it seemed like warm and satiated bliss. As if they were in their own private and very erotic bubble. Until he felt himself begin to harden again inside her and knew that he had to move.

Reluctantly he withdrew from her, tilting her face upwards with his hand. Her cheeks were flushed, and some of the Titian corkscrew curls had come loose and were falling untidily around her shoulders. She looked as wanton as any woman could—and light-years away from the woman who had placed a cup of coffee in front of him not long ago.

He felt...*dazed*. And for the first time in his life slightly *bewildered*. That had been *incredible*. And yet slightly perturbing too, for he could never remember being so out of control before.

Pushing away any remaining doubts, he brushed a dancing corkscrew strand away from her lips, recognising that a latent sense of guilt would serve no useful purpose. 'Well, I don't remember *that* being in your job description,' he murmured.

Isobel took her lead from him. She was obviously supposed to keep it light. Her lips curved into a coquettish smile she'd never used before. 'And did I perform the task to your satisfaction...*sir?*'

Softly, he laughed. 'Well, there'll need to be a repeat session, of course. I can't possibly judge after just one performance.'

Performance? The word cut through her heightened senses and Isobel bit her lip, suddenly feeling way out of her depth. 'And was I...?'

'You were amazing,' he reassured her softly. 'In fact you were more than amazing.'

He stared down into her face as if he was seeing it for the first time—though this was the face that greeted him each day. This was Izzy—who told him the truth when he asked her. And sometimes when he didn't ask her. Would sex destroy some of the unique rapport which existed between them? he wondered, as even more questions began to flood into his mind.

'Let's go and sit down,' he said abruptly.

Tugging her skirt back over her naked hips, he led her over to one of the low sofas on the far side of the office. Gently, he pushed her down on it, then slid next to her, his black eyes narrowed and questioning.

'So why?' he queried softly.

She guessed she could have pretended to misunderstand him, but she knew exactly what he meant. And that was the trouble—she knew Tariq far too well to play games with him. 'Why am I a virgin, you mean?'

'Wrong tense,' he corrected acidly.

Slightly flustered, she looked at him, seeking refuge in flippancy. 'Because you make me work such long hours that I hardly ever have the opportunity to meet any other men?'

'Izzy. I'm serious. Why?'

She sighed. 'Because… Oh, Tariq. Why do you think?'

Because no man had ever come close to the way he'd made her feel. Because it had been impossible *not* to let him make love to her once they'd started down that path. He'd warned her that there was going to be no long-term or commitment, and she wasn't holding out for any. But that didn't mean she couldn't be honest, did it? Just as long as she kept it cool.

'Because nobody has ever turned me on as much as you do.'

He found himself slightly shocked to hear her talking to him in that way—but that was what he wanted, wasn't it? The fact that she could see their lovemaking for what it was and not construct some romantic fantasy about it the way that women always did?

'It was like that for me too,' he admitted softly. 'In fact…' Hot and erotic memories flooded back. Of skin on skin as she welcomed him into her hot, slick body. He swallowed, acknowledging the potency of what had happened between them. And because of her innocence he felt he owed her the truth. 'It was the best sex of my life.'

Isobel drew away from him, hating the sudden leap of her heart, angry with herself for wanting to buy into what was clearly a lie. And angry with him for feeling that she needed to be placated with a lie as whopping as that one. 'Oh, come on, Tariq—with all the lovers you've had, you're honestly expecting me to believe that?'

'But it is true.' He stared into her now smoky tawny eyes, wondering how much of the truth she could bear. 'You see, never before have I made love to a woman without protection. It is a risk that I can never take—for all the obvious reasons. But a virgin who has never known another man cannot be tainted.' He took her fingers and drifted them over his groin, enjoying seeing her eyes widen as he hardened instantly beneath them. 'And a virgin who is on the pill cannot give me an unwanted child.'

Isobel snatched her hand away. 'So you really hit the jackpot with me?'

He gave a low laugh as he recaptured her hand and brought it up to his lips. 'You wanted to know why I found sex with you more exciting than with anyone else and I've told you. Don't ask the questions, Izzy, if you can't bear to hear the answers.'

'You're impossible,' she whispered.

'And you're...' His eyes narrowed as he kissed each fingertip in turn. 'Well, right now you are looking positively *decadent*.'

Her indignation melted away as he slid her fingers inside the moist cavern of his mouth. It was as if even his most innocuous touch could weaken all her defences. 'Am I?'

'Extremely.' He drifted the now damp fingers to the faint indigo shadows beneath her sleepy tawny eyes. 'But you also look worn out, *kalila*.'

She loved him touching her like that. She loved him touching her pretty much anywhere. 'Mmm?'

'Mmm. So why don't you just relax?' He brushed back the heavy spill of curls which had fallen down around her face. 'Go on, Izzy. Relax.'

With a little sigh, she let her head drift back against the sofa as he continued to stroke her hair, just as if she were some cat that he was petting.

Distantly, as her weighted eyelids whispered to a close, she could hear the sound of water splashing. For one crazy moment she could have sworn that she heard someone *whistling*. But then the emotion of what had just happened and the stupefying endorphins it had produced made Isobel drift off into a glorious half-world of sleep.

She was woken by the distinct smell of sandalwood and the lightest brush of lips over hers, and when she blinked her eyes open it was to see Tariq standing over her. His black hair was glittering with tiny droplets of water and he was wearing a stark and beautifully cut tuxedo. He must have showered and changed in his office's luxury bathroom, she thought dazedly.

The crisp whiteness of his silk shirt contrasted against the glow of his olive skin, and his black eyes positively *gleamed* with energy and satisfaction. He looked like a perfect specimen of masculinity, she thought—all pumped up and raring to go. As if, for him, sex had been nothing but a very gratifying form of exercise.

She stared up at him. 'What's…what's happening?'

Tariq swallowed down a surge of lust. She looked

so damned sexy lying there that part of him wanted to carry on where they'd left off. To do it to her again— only more slowly this time, and on the comfort of a couch. But wouldn't some kind of natural break be better—for both of them? Wouldn't that allow them to put some necessary perspective on what had just happened—and allow her not to start reading too much into what could be a potentially awkward situation?

'You know I have to go to the party at the Maraban Embassy,' he said softly. 'You were nagging me about it before we…'

Isobel kept the stupefied smile glued to her lips. *He was still planning on going to the party!*

'Yes. Yes, of course. You must go.' She struggled to sit up a little, but Tariq made matters even worse by leaning over her and stroking a strand of hair away from her lips with the tip of his thumb. For a moment his thumb lingered, tracing its way around the sudden tremble of her lips.

'I'll get my car to drop you off home,' he said.

'No, honestly. I can get the—'

'Bus?'

'Well, yes.'

'Without your panties?' His rueful gaze drifted across the room to where her ripped knickers were lying in a crumpled little heap of silk. 'I don't think so, *anisah*. So go and quickly run a brush through your hair, and then we'll go.'

It was rather a grim end to an eventful afternoon, and one which made Isobel question the wisdom of what she had just done. Quickly she availed herself of his bathroom, dragging the Titian curls into some sort of order and straightening her clothes before they went down in the elevator to his waiting car.

There was no back seat kiss, no telling her that she was the most gorgeous woman he'd ever met and that he would spend the evening thinking about her. Instead all proprieties were observed as Tariq spent the short journey to the Maraban Embassy tapping on the flat, shiny screen of his laptop.

When the car pulled up and he looked up he seemed almost to have forgotten who he was with.

'Izzy,' he said softly.

She looked at him, aware that he looked impeccably groomed in comparison to the rumpled exterior she must be presenting. Was he regretting what had happened? Wondering how he could have allowed himself to get so carried away in the heat of the moment? Well, she didn't know how these things usually worked, but she was determined that he should have a let-out clause if he wanted one.

Batting him a quick smile, she pointed to the car door, which was already being opened for him. Let him see that she was perfectly cool about what had happened.

'Better hurry along, Tariq,' she said quickly. 'Leave it much later and you'll have missed all the canapés.'

CHAPTER SIX

'I JUST WANTED to check that you got home okay. The party at the Embassy went on longer than I thought. In fact it was a bit of a bore. I should have stayed right where I was and carried on with exactly what I was doing.' There was a pause before the distinctive voice deepened. *'I'll see you in the office tomorrow, Izzy.'*

With an angry jab of her finger Isobel erased the message on the answer-machine and made her way out to her tiny kitchen, where the morning sunshine was streaming in. It was a strangely unsatisfying message from the man she'd given her virginity to—Tariq must have left it late last night, after she'd gone to bed. But what had she expected? Softness and affection? Tender words as an after-sex gesture? Why would he bother with any of that when she'd practically *begged* him to have sex with her?

She stared at the piece of bread which had just popped out of the toaster and then threw it straight into the bin. She wasn't in the mood for breakfast. She wasn't in the mood for anything, come to think of it, except maybe crawling right back under the duvet and staying there for the rest of the week. She certainly wasn't up for going into work this morning to face her boss after what had happened in the office last night.

She closed her eyes as a shiver raced over her skin, scarcely able to believe what she'd done. Taken complete leave of her senses by letting Tariq have wild sex with her, pressed up against the wall of his office. After years spent wondering if maybe she didn't *have* the sexual impulses of most normal women, of wondering if her mother had poisoned her completely against men, she had discovered that she was very normal indeed.

Behind her eyelids danced tormenting memories. Was that why she'd behaved as she had? Because a lifetime of longing had hit her in a single tidal wave? Or was it simply because it was Tariq and subconsciously she'd wanted him all along?

She shuddered. She'd been like a woman possessed—urging him on as if she couldn't get enough of him. It had been the very first time she'd ever let a man make love to her, and she'd been so greedy for him that she hadn't wanted to wait. She felt the dull flush of shame as she acknowledged that she hadn't even been ladylike enough to hold out for doing it in private—in a *bed!*

Yet she *knew* what kind of man he was. Hadn't she seen him in action often enough in the past? She'd lost count of the times she'd been dispatched to buy last-minute presents for his current squeeze—or bouquets of flowers when he was giving chase to a new woman.

And what about when he started to cool towards the object of his affections, so that he became positively arctic overnight, usually three to four weeks into the 'relationship'? She'd witnessed the faint frown and the shake of his head when she mouthed the name of some poor female whose voice was stuttering down the telephone line as she asked to speak to him. She'd even seen him completely cold-shoulder one hysterical blonde who'd been lying in wait for him outside the Al Hakam building. Then had had his security people bundle her into a car and drive her away at speed. Isobel remembered watching the woman's beautiful features contorted with rage as she glared out of the back window of the limousine.

Time and time again she had told herself that any woman who went to bed with Tariq needed her head examined—and now she had done exactly that. Was she really planning to join the long line of women who had been intimate with him and then had their hearts broken into smithereens?

She stared at her grim-faced reflection in the mirror. No, she was not.

She was going to have to be grown-up about the whole thing. Men and women often made passionate mistakes—but *intelligent* men and women could soon forget about them. She would go in to work this morning and she would show him—and herself—how strong she could be. She would surprise him with her maturity and her ability to pretend that nothing had happened.

So she resisted the urge to wear a new blouse to work, putting on instead a fine wool dress in a soft heathery colour and tying her hair back as she always did.

Outside it was a glorious day, and the bus journey

into work should have been uplifting. The pale blue sky and the fluffy clouds, the unmistakable expectancy of springtime, had lightened people's moods. The bus-driver bade her a cheerful good morning, and the security man standing outside the Al Hakam building was uncharacteristically friendly.

The first part of the day went better than she'd expected—but that was mainly because Tariq was away from the office, visiting the Greenhill Polo Club in Sussex, which he'd bought from the Zaffirinthos royal family last year.

She juggled his diary, answered a backlog of e-mails, and dealt with a particularly persistent sports journalist.

It was four o'clock by the time he arrived back, and Isobel was so deep in work in the outer office that for a moment she didn't hear the door as it clicked open.

It was only when she lifted her head that she found herself caught in the ebony crossfire of his gaze. His dark hair was ruffled, and he had the faint glow which followed hard physical exercise. He looked so arrogantly alpha and completely sexy in that moment that her heart did a little somersault in her chest, despite all her best intentions. She wondered if he'd been riding one of his own polo ponies while he'd been down at Greenhill, and her imagination veered off the strict course she'd prescribed for it. She'd seen him play polo before, and for a moment she imagined him astride one of his ponies, his powerful thighs gripping the flanks of the magnificent glistening animal…

Stop it, she told herself, as she curved her lips into what she hoped was her normal smile. No fantasising—

and definitely no flirting. It's business as usual. It might be difficult to begin with, but he's bound to applaud your professionalism in the end.

'Hello, Tariq,' she said, her fingers stilling on the keyboard. 'Good day at Greenhill? I've had the *Daily Post* on the phone all morning. They want to know if it's true that you've been making approaches to buy a defender from Barcelona. I think they were trying to trick me into revealing whether the football club deal is still going ahead. I told him no comment.'

Tariq dropped his briefcase to the floor and frowned. He'd been anticipating…

What?

A blush *at the very least!* Some stumbled words which would acknowledge the amazing thing which had taken place last night. Maybe even a little pout of her unpainted lips to remind him of how good it had felt to kiss them. But not that cool and non-committal look which she was currently directing at him.

'I'll make you a coffee,' she said, rising to her feet.

'I don't want coffee.'

'Tea?'

'I don't want tea either,' he growled. 'Come over here.'

'Where?'

'Don't be disingenuous, Izzy. I want to kiss you.'

Desperately she shook her head, telling herself that she couldn't risk a repeat of what had happened. He was *dangerous.* She *knew* that. If she wasn't careful he would break her heart—just as he'd broken so many others in the past. And the closer she let him get the greater the danger. 'I don't want to kiss you.'

He walked across the office towards her, a sardonic smile curving his lips as he reached for her, his hand snaking around her waist as he pulled her close. 'Well, we both know that's a lie,' he drawled, and he brushed his lips over hers.

Isobel swayed, and for a moment she succumbed—the way women sometimes succumbed to chocolate at the end of a particularly rigid diet. Her lips opened beneath his kiss, and for a few brief seconds she felt herself being sucked into a dark and erotic vortex as he pressed his hard body into hers. Her limbs became boneless as she felt one powerful thigh levering its way between hers, so that she gave an instinctive little wriggle of her hips against it.

Until common sense sounded a warning bell in her head.

Quickly she broke the contact and stepped away from him, her cheeks flushing. She cooled them with the tips of her trembling fingers. 'D-don't.'

'Don't?' he echoed incredulously. 'Why not?'

His arrogant disbelief only made her more determined. 'Isn't it obvious?'

'Not to me.'

'Because…because I don't want to. How's that for clarification?'

Tariq's gaze ran over her darkened eyes and the telltale thrust of the taut nipples which were tightening against her dress. His lips curved into a mocking line as he transferred his gaze to her face. 'Really?' he questioned softly. 'I think the lady needs to get honest with herself.'

Stung by the slur, but also aware of the contradictions in her behaviour, Isobel shook her head. 'Oh, Tariq—please don't look at me like that. I'm not saying that I'm not attracted to you—'

'Well, thank heavens for that.' He gave a short laugh. 'For a moment I thought my technique might be slipping.'

'I don't think there's any danger of that,' she said drily. 'But I've been thinking about last night—'

'Me, too. In fact I have thought of little else.' His voice softened, but the blaze in his black eyes was searing. 'You're now regretting the loss of your innocence? Perhaps blaming me for what happened?'

She shook her head. 'No, of course I'm not blaming you. I'm not blaming anyone,' she said carefully. 'It's just I feel I'm worth more than a quick fumble in the office—'

'A *fumble?*' he interrupted furiously 'This is how you dare to describe what happened between us?'

'How would *you* describe it, then?'

'With a little more poetry and imagination than that!'

'Okay. That…that amazing sex we had, pressed up against the wall of your office.' She sucked in a deep breath—because if she didn't tell him what was bugging her then how would he know? 'And you then treating me like a total stranger in the car before waltzing off to your fancy party at the embassy.'

Tariq narrowed his eyes with sudden comprehension. So *that* was what this was about. She wanted what all women wanted. Recognition. A place on his arm to illustrate their closeness—to show the world their togetherness. But wasn't she being a little *presumptuous,* in the circumstances?

'I didn't touch you because I knew what would happen if I did—and I had no intention of walking into the party with the smell of your sex still on my skin. No.' He shook his head as he saw her open her mouth to speak. 'Let me finish, Izzy. It would have been inappropriate for me to take you to the party,' he added coolly. 'For a start, you weren't exactly dressed for it.'

'You mean I would have let you down?'

'I think you would have felt awkward if you'd gone to a party in your rumpled work clothes, post-sex. Especially to a diplomatic function like that.'

'I'm surprised you know the meaning of the word *diplomatic,*' she raged, 'when you can come out with a statement as insulting as that!'

'I was trying to be honest with you, Izzy,' he said softly. 'Isn't that what this is all about?'

His question took the wind right out of her sails. She supposed it was. She had no right to be angry with him just because he wasn't telling her what she wanted to hear. If he'd come out with some flowery, untrue reason why he hadn't taken her to the embassy, wouldn't she have called him a hypocrite?

'Maybe last night should never have happened,' she said in a small voice.

Ignoring the sudden hardening of his body, Tariq thought about the mercurial nature of her behaviour. Last night she had been *wild* and today she was like ice. Was she testing him to see how far she could push him? She had turned away from him now, so that he got a complete view of her thick curls tied back in a ribbon and a dress he'd seen many times before. Nobody could accuse Izzy of responding to their lovemaking by becoming a vamp in the office. She was probably the least glamorous woman he'd ever met.

Yet the strange thing was that he wanted her. Actually, he wanted her more than he had done yesterday. The contrast between her rather unremarkable exterior and the red-hot lover underneath had scorched through his defences. The memory of how she had yielded so eagerly wouldn't leave him. But it was more than a purely visceral response. Her freshness and eagerness had been like sweet balm applied to his jaded senses. Hadn't she given him more than any other woman had ever done—surrendering her innocence with such eagerness and joy?

And yet what had he done for her? Taken that innocence in as swift a way as possible and offered her nothing in return. Not even dinner. He felt the unfamiliar stab of guilt.

'What are you doing tonight?' he said.

The question made Isobel turn round. 'It's my book club.'

'Your book club?'

'Six to eight women,' she explained, since he'd clearly never heard of the concept. 'We all read a book and then afterwards we sit round and discuss it.'

He knitted his brows together. 'And that's supposed to be enjoyable?'

'That's the general idea.'

'Cancel it.' The answering smile he floated her was supremely confident. 'Have dinner with me instead.'

Shamefully, she was almost tempted to do as he suggested—until she imagined the reaction of her girlfriends. Hadn't she let them down enough times in the past, when Tariq had been in the middle of some big deal and she'd had to work right through the night? Did he really expect her to drop everything now, just so he could get a duty dinner out of the way before another bout of sex?

She thought about everything she'd vowed. About not leaving herself vulnerable to heartbreak—which wasn't going to be easy now that she *had* taken such a big leap in that direction. But even if she had made herself vulnerable she didn't have to compound it by being a total doormat.

'I don't want to cancel it, Tariq—I'm hosting in my apartment. There's two bottles of white wine chilling in the fridge and we're reading *Jane Eyre*.'

Damn *Jane Eyre,* he thought irreverently—but something about her resistance made his lips curve into a sardonic smile.

'What about tomorrow night, then? Do you think you might be able to find a space in your busy schedule and have dinner with me then?' he questioned sarcastically.

Her heart began thundering as she stared at him. Wasn't that what she'd wanted all along? The cloak of respectability covering up the fact that they'd had sex without any of the usual preliminaries? Wouldn't a civilised meal prevent their relationship from being defined by that one rather steamy episode—no matter what happened in the future? Because the chances were that they might decide never to have sex again. Maybe in a restaurant, with the natural barrier of a table between them and the attentions of the waiting staff, they could agree that, yes, it had been a highly pleasurable experience—but best kept as a one-off.

Isobel nodded. 'Yes, I can have dinner with you tomorrow night.'

'Good. Book somewhere, will you? Anywhere you like.'

His expression was thoughtful as he walked through to his inner sanctum. Because this was a first on many levels, he realised.

The first time he'd ever had sex with a member of his staff.

And the first time a woman had ever turned him down for a dinner date.

CHAPTER SEVEN

'THIS IS THE LAST kind of place I'd have thought you'd choose,' said Tariq slowly.

Isobel looked up from the laminated menu, which she already knew by heart, and stared at the hawk-like beauty of the Sheikh's autocratic features. 'You don't like it?'

He looked around. It was noisy, warm and cluttered. Lighted candles dripped wax down the sides of old Chianti bottles, posters of Venice and Florence vied for wall-space with photos of Siena's football team, and popular opera played softly in the background. He could remember eating somewhere like this years ago as a student, at the end of a rowdy rugby tour. But never since then. 'It's…different,' he observed. 'Not the kind of place I normally eat in. I thought you might have chosen somewhere…'

'Yes?' Isobel raised her eyebrows.

'Somewhere a little more upmarket. The kind of place you'd always wanted to go but never had the chance.'

Isobel put the menu down. 'You mean somewhere

like the Green Room at the Granchester? Or the River Terrace? Or one of those other fancy establishments with a celebrity chef, where you can only ever get a table at short notice if you happen to *be* someone? All the places *you* usually frequent?'

'They happen to be very good restaurants.'

She leaned forward. '*This* happens to be a good restaurant, too—though you seem to be judging it without even trying it. Just because you don't have to take out a mortgage to eat here, it doesn't mean the food isn't delicious. Actually, I thought *you* might like to try somewhere different and a bit more relaxing. Somewhere you aren't known, since you often complain about rubbernecking people staring at you.' She sat back in her chair again and shot him a challenge with her eyes. 'But maybe you like being looked at more than you care to admit—and anonymity secretly freaks you out?'

He gave a soft laugh. 'Actually, I'm rather enjoying the anonymity,' he murmured, and glanced down at the menu. 'What do you recommend?'

'Well, they make all their own pasta here.'

'And it's good?'

'It's more than good. It's *to die for.*'

His gaze drifted up to the curve of her breasts, which were pert and springy and outlined by a surprisingly chic little black dress. 'I thought women didn't eat carbs.'

'Maybe the sorts of women you know don't,' she said, thinking about his penchant for whip-thin supermodels and feeling a sudden stab of insecurity. 'Personally, I hate all those dietary restrictions. All they do is make people obsessed with eating, or not eating, and their whole lives become about denying themselves what they really want.'

Tariq let that go, realising that he was denying himself what *he* really wanted right at that moment. If it was anyone other than Izzy he would have thrown a large wad of notes down on the tablecloth and told the waiter that they'd lost their appetite. Then taken her back to his apartment and ravished her in every which way he could—before sending out for food.

He realised that he was letting her call the shots, and briefly he wondered why. Because he'd taken her innocence and felt that he owed her? Or was it because she worked for him and his relationship with her was about as equal as any he was likely to have?

'Perhaps we'll have a little role-reversal tonight. How about you choose for me?' he suggested.

'I'd love to.' She beamed.

She lifted her head and instantly the waiter appeared at their table, bearing complementary olives and bread and making a big fuss of her. For possibly the first time in his life Tariq found himself ignored—other than being assured that he was a very lucky man to be eating with such a beautiful woman.

As he leant back in his chair he conceded that the waiter had a point and Izzy *did* look pretty spectacular tonight. For a start she'd let down her hair, so that corkscrew curls tumbled in a fiery cascade around her shoulders. Her silky black dress was far more formal than anything she'd ever worn to work, and it showcased her luscious curves to perfection. A silver teardrop which gleamed at the end of a fine chain hung provocatively between her breasts. And, of course, she had that indefinable glow of sexual awakening...

With an effort, he dragged his gaze away from her cleavage and looked into tawny eyes which had been highlighted with long sweeps of mascara, so that they seemed to dominate her face. 'I take it from the way the waiter greeted you like a long-lost relative that you've been here before?'

'Loads of times. I've been coming here since I first started working in London. It's always so warm and friendly. And at the beginning—when I didn't have much money—they never seemed to mind me spending hours lingering over one dish.'

'Why would they? Restaurants never object to a pretty girl adorning their space. It's a form of free advertising.'

Isobel shook her head. 'Were you born cynical, Tariq?'

'What's cynical about that? It happens to be true. I'm a businessman, Izzy—I analyse marketing opportunities.'

She waited while the waiter poured out two glasses of fizzy water. 'And did you always mean to become a businessman?'

'As opposed to what? A trapeze artist?'

'As opposed to doing something in your own country. Doing something in Khayarzah. You used...'

He frowned as her words trailed off. 'Used to what?'

'At school.' She shrugged as she remembered how sweet he had been to her that time—how he'd made her feel special. A bit like the way he was treating her tonight. 'Well, I hardly knew you at school, of course, but I do remember that one time when you talked about your homeland. You spoke of it in a dreamy way—as if you were talking about some kind of Utopia. And I suppose I sort of imagined…'

'What did you imagine?' he prompted softly.

'Oh, I don't know. That you'd go back there one day. And live in a palace and fish in that silvery river you described.'

'Ah, but my brother is King there now,' he said, his voice hardening as he acknowledged the capricious law of succession and how it altered the lives of those who were affected by it. 'And Zahid became King very unexpectedly, which changed my place in the natural order of things.'

Isobel looked at him. 'How come?'

'Up until that moment I was just another desert sheikh with the freedom to do pretty much as I wanted—but when our uncle died suddenly I became second in line to the throne. The spare.'

'And is that so bad?' she prompted gently.

'Try living in a goldfish bowl and see how *you* like it,' he said. 'It means you have all the strictures of being the heir, but none of the power. My freedom was something I cherished above everything else…' Hadn't it been the one compensation for his lonely and isolated childhood? The fact that he hadn't really had to account for himself? 'And suddenly it was taken away from me. It made me want to stay away from Khayarzah, where I felt the people were watching me all the time. And I knew that I needed to give Zahid space to settle into his Kingship in peace.' There was a pause. 'Because there is only ever room for one ruler.'

'And do you miss it? Khayarzah, I mean?'

He studied her wide tawny eyes, realising that he had told her more than he had ever told anyone. In truth, his self-imposed exile had only emphasised his feelings of displacement, of not actually belonging anywhere. Just like the little boy who had been sent away to school. As a child he'd felt as if he'd had no real home and as an adult that feeling had not changed.

'Not really,' he mused. 'I go back there on high days and holidays and that's enough. There's no place for me there.'

Isobel sipped her drink as the waiter placed two plates of steaming pasta before them. His last words disturbed her. *There's no place for me there.* Wasn't that an awfully *lonely* thing to say? And wasn't that what she'd thought when she'd seen him lying injured in hospital—that he'd looked so alone? What if her instinct then had been the right one?

'So you're planning on settling down in England?' she questioned, and then gave a nervous laugh. 'Though I guess you already are settled.'

There was a brief pause as Tariq swirled a forkful of tagliatelli and coated it in sauce. But he didn't eat it. Instead, he lifted his eyes to hers, a sardonic smile curving his lips. It was always the same. Or rather women were. Didn't matter what you talked about, their careless chatter inevitably morphed into thinly veiled queries about his future. Because didn't they automatically daydream about *their* future and wonder if it could be a match with his? Weren't they programmed to do that, when they became the lover of a powerful alpha male?

'By "settling down", I suppose you mean getting married and having children?' he questioned.

Isobel nodded. 'I suppose so.'

Tariq's lips curved. She *supposed* so! 'The perfect nuclear family?'

'Well—'

'Which doesn't exist,' he interjected.

'That's a little harsh, Tariq.'

'Is it?' Black eyes iced into her. 'You experienced one yourself, did you?'

'Well, no. You know I didn't. I told you that I never knew my father.'

'And it left a gaping hole in your life?'

'I tried never to think of it that way,' she said defensively. 'Holes can always be filled by something else. It may not have been a "normal" family life, but it was a life.'

'Well, I never knew a "normal" childhood, either,' he said, more bitterly than he had intended.

'Can I…can I ask what happened?'

He stared at her, and she looked so damned sweet and soft that he found himself telling her. 'My mother almost died having me, and after I was born she was so ill that she needed round-the-clock care. Zahid was that bit older, and a calmer child than me, and it was decided that my needs were being neglected. So they sent me away to boarding school when I was seven. That's when I first came to England.'

Isobel frowned. She hadn't realised that he'd been so young. 'Wasn't there anywhere closer to home you could have gone?'

He shook his head. 'We have a completely different system of schooling in Khayarzah—it was decided that a western education would be beneficial all round.' He read the puzzlement in her tawny eyes. 'It meant that I would be able to speak and act like a westerner. More importantly, to think as a westerner thinks—which has proved invaluable in my subsequent business dealings. It's why the Al Hakam company has global domination,' he finished, with the flicker of a smile.

But, despite his proud smile, Isobel felt desperately sad for him, even though she could see the logic behind his parents' decision. She had been the daughter of a school nurse and knew how illness could create chaos in the most ordered of lives. Sending away a lively little boy from his mother's sickbed must have seemed like a sensible solution at the time.

Yet to move a child to live somewhere else—without any kind of family support nearby—and what did that child become? A cuckoo in the nest in his adopted country. And surely he must have felt like an outsider whenever he returned to his homeland? Tariq had spoken the truth, she realised. He *didn't* have any place of his own—not in any true sense of the word. Yes, there were the apartments in London and New York, and the luxury houses on Mustique and in the South of France—but nowhere he could really call *home*. Not in his heart.

'So you don't ever want children of your own?' she questioned boldly.

At this the shutters came down and his voice cooled. 'Not ever,' he affirmed, his gaze never leaving her face—because she had to understand that he meant this. 'My brother has helpfully produced twin boys, and our country now has the required heir and a spare. So my assistance with dynasty-building is not required.'

A shiver ran down her spine as his unemotional words registered. Was that what he thought fatherhood and family life was all about...*dynasties?* Didn't he long to hold his own little baby boy or girl in his arms? To cradle them and to rock them? To see the past and the future written in its tiny features?

She looked at his face in the candlelight. Such a strong and indomitable face, she thought, with its high slash of cheekbones, the hawk-like nose and wide, sensual mouth. But behind the impressive physical package he presented she had discovered a reason for the unmistakable sense of *aloneness* which always seemed to surround him.

Yet this notoriously private man had actually confided in her. Surely that had to mean *something?* That he trusted her, yes—but was there anything more than that. And was it enough for her to face risking her heart?

She drifted her eyes over his hands—powerful and hair roughened. On the white silk cuffs of his shirt gleamed two heavy golden cufflinks. She could see that they were Khayarzah cufflinks, with the distinctive silhouette of a brooding falcon poised for flight. And somehow the bird of prey reminded her of him.

Restless and seeking…above the world, but never really part of it.

Had he seen her looking at them? Was that why his hand suddenly reached out and caught hold of hers, capturing her wrist in his warm grasp and making it seem tiny and frail in comparison? His thumb brushed over the delicate skin at her wrist and he gave a brief smile as he felt the frantic skitter of her pulse.

'Stunned into uncharacteristic silence by my story, are you, Izzy?'

'It's some story,' she admitted quietly.

'Yes.' He looked down at her untouched plate. 'You're not eating.'

'Neither are you.'

'Delicious as it looks, I'm not feeling particularly hungry.'

'No.'

Across the candlelit table, their eyes met. 'Perhaps some fresh air might give us a little *appetite*.'

Isobel blinked at him in bewilderment. 'You want to go for a walk?'

His smile was wry. He'd forgotten that she had every right to be naïve, for she knew nothing of the games that lovers played… 'Only as far as the car. I thought we could go to my apartment. There's plenty of food there.'

Isobel's heart began to pound as his lazy suggestion shimmered into the space between them. She hadn't thought a lot beyond the meal itself. Somehow she had imagined that she might be going home alone to her little flat, as if the whole…*sex*…thing had been nothing but a distant dream. She'd told herself that would be the best for both of them, even if her commitment to the idea had been less than whole-hearted.

But then Tariq had opened up to her, taking her into his confidence. It had felt almost as intimate as when he'd been driving into her body. How could she possibly go home alone when she thought about the alternative he was offering her?

He was gesturing for the bill, seeming to take her silence for acquiescence, and the waiter was coming over to their table, his face creased in an anxious frown.

'You no like the food?' he questioned.

'The food is delicious,' Tariq replied, giving Isobel's hand a quick squeeze. 'I just find my partner's beauty rather distracting. So we'll just have the bill, please.'

Isobel saw the man-to-man look which passed between Tariq and the waiter, and for a moment she felt betrayed. Suddenly she had become someone else—not the woman who'd been frequenting this place for years, but someone dining with a man who was clearly way out of her league.

The waiter moved away, and Isobel tried to wriggle her fingers free. But Tariq wasn't having any of it.

'What's the matter, Izzy?'

'Just because you want to go to bed with me, it doesn't mean you have to tell lies!'

'Lies?' he questioned, perplexed.

'I am *not* beautiful,' she insisted.

'Oh, but you are,' he said unexpectedly, and then he did let go of her hand. Instead, he moved to cup her chin, running the tip of his thumb over it. 'Tonight you look very beautiful, sitting there, bathed in candlelight. I like your hair loose. I even like your eyes flashing with defiance. In fact, I can't quite remember ever seeing a woman look quite as desirable as you do right now, and it's making me ache for you. And you feel exactly the same, don't you?'

'Tariq!'

'*Don't you?*'

She met the mocking gleam in his ebony eyes. 'Yes,' she whispered.

'So pick up your handbag and let's get out of here—before I do something really crazy like hauling you to your feet and kissing you in front of the entire restaurant. Now, that really *would* provide fodder for the tabloids.'

She was trembling with anticipation as they went outside, where Tariq's chauffeur-driven car was sitting purring by the kerb. Climbing into its sumptuous interior, she waited for him to pull her into his arms. To kiss her as she so badly wanted to be kissed.

But he didn't. In fact he slid his body as far away from her as possible, and when he saw her turn her head he must have read the disappointed expression in her eyes because he shook his head.

'No, Izzy,' he said sternly. 'Not here and not now. I think we have demonstrated the wilder side of passion, and I think I've made it clear that once I start touching you all bets seem to be off. Tonight we will have the slow burn of anticipation and I will show you just how pleasurable *that* can be.'

Even when they reached his apartment he simply laced his fingers in hers and led her along the long corridor to his bedroom. Once there, with dexterous efficiency, he began to slide the clothes from her body. Only this time he hung her black silky dress over the back of a chair and did not tear off her panties.

When at last she was stripped bare, he peeled back the silken throw which covered his bed and laid her down on it.

'I want to see you naked,' he murmured appraisingly, as his gaze travelled slowly down the length of her body.

She watched as he undressed, the breath dying in her throat. His body was taut and magnificent—and he made no attempt to hide the heavy length of his arousal. But when at last he was completely naked, and maybe because he felt the trembling of her body, he frowned.

Smoothing back the cascade of Titian curls, he looked deep into her eyes. 'You are nervous?'

'A little.'

'But there is no reason to be, *habiba*.' He brushed his mouth over hers. 'For tonight there will be no pain—only endless pleasure.'

She gave herself up to his kiss at last, glad to lose herself in its seductive power. And grateful, too, for the clamour of her senses, which responded instantly to his expert touch and drove all nagging thoughts from her mind.

It was only afterwards that they came back to haunt her. When all passion was spent and they were lying there, Tariq's hand splayed possessively over the damp fuzz of curls at her thighs and her head slumped against his shoulder.

No pain, he had said—only pleasure.

But he had been talking about the physical pain of having surrendered her virginity to him. Not the infinitely more powerful pain she suspected might be about to be inflicted on her heart.

CHAPTER EIGHT

THE OFFICE DOOR clicked quietly shut, and Tariq's distinctively soft voice whispered over Isobel's senses.

'So what has it been like without me, *kalila?* Did the office grind to a halt without me? More importantly... did you miss your Sheikh while he was away?'

Isobel looked up from her work, trying to steel herself against the impact of seeing Tariq for the first time in almost a week. Having to fight back the urge to do something stupid—like leaping up and throwing herself into his arms.

He'd been to New York on business, and along the way had taken delivery of a new transatlantic jet. He'd also announced the expansion of the Al Hakam Bank in Singapore, but was still refusing to confirm reports that he was in the process of buying the famous 'Blues' football team. Consequently, his face had been pictured on the front pages of the financial press—and Isobel had secretly pored over them whenever she had a spare moment. It had felt slightly peculiar to look at the hard and handsome face which stared back at her amid the newsprint. And to realise that the man with the hawk-like features and noble lineage was actually her lover.

Now he leaned over her desk, a vision of alpha-sex-iness in a dark grey suit and pristine white shirt. His olive skin made him look as if he had been cast in gold, and his black eyes gleamed as they surveyed her ques-tioningly.

'Tariq,' she said slowly, laying down her pen and put-ting the churned up feeling in her stomach down to his tantalising proximity. 'You know perfectly well that the office always runs smoothly in your absence. In fact, there's a quiet air of calm around the place. People are that bit more relaxed when the big boss isn't around.'

He gave a slow smile as he loosened his tie and dropped it in front of her like a calling card. She sounded as unruffled as she always did when she spoke to him in the office—her cool air of composure barely slipping. Why, nobody would guess that the last time they'd seen each other she had been giving him oral sex in the back of his darkened limousine. Demonstrating yet another new-found sexual skill which she seemed to have adopted with her usual dexterity.

And he had reciprocated by sliding his fingers be-neath her skirt and bringing her to a shuddering or-gasm just moments before he'd left the car to catch his flight to JFK.

Yet to look at her now she seemed light-years away from his fevered and erotic memory of her. She looked restrained and efficient—almost *prim*.

To Tariq's surprise, any fears he'd had that she would become cloying or demanding had not been realised.

Despite being such a sexual novice, Izzy seemed to have no problems juggling her dual roles as his lover and PA, and was as discreet as anyone in his position could have wished for.

He frowned. The only downside was that she seemed to be getting underneath his skin in a way he hadn't anticipated. By now he should have been growing a little bored with her—because that was his pattern. Once the gloss of new sex had worn off, predictability tended to set in—and three weeks was usually long enough for him to begin to find out things about a woman which irritated him.

But Izzy was different, and he wasn't quite sure why. Might it be because she knew him better than almost anyone? Working so closely with him over the years had given her glimpses of the private person that he would never have allowed another to see. Sometimes it felt as though she had already stripped away several layers to see the man who lay beneath. Was that what gave sex with her its extra dimension of closeness? Or was it just the fearless way she responded to him? The way she looked straight into his eyes while he was deep inside her? As if she wanted to see into his soul with those big tawny eyes of hers. Sometimes it unsettled him and sometimes it did not—but it always excited him.

He watched as she picked up his discarded tie and began to roll it into a neat silken coil. 'So, did you miss me?' he repeated.

Isobel put the tie down and looked at him. What would he do if she told him that she *always* missed him? That she wished she could suddenly become one of his ties, so that she could wrap herself round his neck all day and stay there? He would run a million miles away—that was what he would do. Declarations of adoration were not what Tariq wanted, but she could see perfectly well from his darkening eyes just what he *did* want.

She rose from her desk and walked towards him, aware of his gaze on her and conscious of the fact that her thighs were bare above her stocking tops. She'd dressed with deliberate daring for the office this morning, knowing that he was bound to want her as soon as he arrived—and determined to feed into the fantasies he had assured her on the phone last night had been building all week.

She might be new to all this, but some survival instinct had made her turn herself into the best lover she could possibly be. Because wasn't that her default method? To do something to the best of her ability? Didn't that usually mean security? If you became so good at something then you wouldn't be replaced.

Only this wasn't a new job, or a new project which was going to enhance her life. This was all about a relationship—it was strange new territory. Her mother's often repeated warnings still came to her from time to time, but how could she take them seriously when she was looking into the glittering hunger of Tariq's black eyes and feeling the lurch of her heart in response?

'Of course I've missed you,' she said softly.

'How much, on a scale of one to ten?'

'Well…' She pretended to think about it. 'How about seven?'

'Seven?'

'Eight, then. Nine! *Tariq!* Okay—ten!'

'You're wearing *stockings,*' he breathed in disbelief.

'Well, you've nagged me often enough about my tights.'

'With good reason. Let me see.' He lifted up her skirt and expelled a small appraising sigh. The tops of the dark silk stockings had been embroidered with deep turquoise and green, so that it looked as if some peacock had wrapped its feathers enticingly around her thighs and left them there. 'You know that there are consequences to dressing like that?' he questioned unsteadily.

'What kind of consequences might they be?'

'Can't you guess?' he breathed, as he placed her hand on the fly of his trousers.

'T-Tariq.'

'I want you, Izzy.'

'You always want me,' she whispered back, her fingertips caressing the thick, hard shaft.

He swallowed. 'And is it mutual?'

'You know it is.'

He caught her by the shoulders and looked down into her widened tawny eyes. 'Then why don't you show me how much you've missed me?' he questioned unsteadily. 'Because I have missed you too, *kalila.*'

She savoured his unsteady words as she rose up on tiptoe to kiss him, revelling in the sheer pleasure of being in his arms again. She closed her eyes as his practised fingers began to reacquaint themselves with her body. At times like this, when he could reduce her to boneless longing within seconds, it was easy to imagine that a unique bond existed between them. Was that because they seemed to have the ability to anticipate each other's needs—despite the disparity of their experience—or was it because they simply knew each other so well?

Or was it something far more commonplace? He'd told her candidly that making love without having to wear a condom was the biggest turn-on he'd ever known. For him, that was a brand-new experience, and that was rare enough to excite a man who'd been having sex since he was a teenager. She'd tried telling herself that Tariq's reaction to her was purely physical. Because if she looked the truth straight in the face then surely there was less likelihood of her getting hurt?

If only her own feelings were as straightforward. If only she hadn't started to care. Really care. She wondered if it was normal for a woman to become a little more emotionally vulnerable every time her man made love to her. For her to start wanting things she knew she wasn't supposed to want—things he'd specifically warned her against. Things that Tariq was renowned for never delivering—and especially to a woman like her. Stuff like commitment and happy-ever-after.

'Izzy?'

She closed her eyes, letting go of the last of her troubled thoughts, allowing pure and delicious sensation to take over instead. 'Yes,' she whispered, as he pushed her down onto the floor and sank down beside her. 'Oh, yes.'

His fingers were on her flesh now, stroking open the moist and heated flesh at the very core of her, and he was saying, *'Luloah...'* softly and fervently beneath his breath, something which Isobel had learnt meant 'pearl' in his native tongue.

'You taste of honey,' he said on a shuddered breath, his mouth high on her thigh.

'Tariq—' His tongue had reached the most sensitive part of her anatomy, and Isobel gave a little gasp of pleasure as she felt its delicate flick. Glancing down, she could see the erotic image of her boss's black head between her legs, and the sheer intimacy of it only increased the sensations which were beginning to ripple through her.

Her head fell back as an unstoppable heat began to build, and she trembled on the brink as he teased her with his tongue.

'Tariq,' she gasped again, clutching at his shoulders, her fingers biting into him.

'What?' he drawled against her heated flesh.

Tariq, I think I'm falling in love with you!

But her passionate thoughts dissolved as a feeling of intense pleasure washed over her—strong enough to sweep away everything else in its wake. Wave after wave of it racked her trembling body—and just when she thought it couldn't get any better he thrust deep inside her.

'You feel so *good,*' he said unsteadily.

'So...do you.'

He thrust even deeper, his breaths becoming long and shuddering. 'And I've been wanting to do this to you *all week.*'

She heard his voice change and felt his body tense,

watched him splinter with his own pleasure. She loved the helplessness of his orgasm, feeling in those few heightened moments of sensation that he was really hers.

Afterwards, they lay wrapped tightly in each other's arms, until Isobel lifted her head to free some of the hair which was trapped beneath his elbow.

'You know, we're going to have to stop meeting like this,' she murmured.

Tariq laughed , drawing his fingers through the spill of her curls and marvelling at how *uncomplicated* all this seemed. His mouth settled into a curve of satisfaction. He could walk in from a trip and within minutes have her writhing and compliant in his arms. There were no demands made, nor questions asked. What could be better than that?

'I think this is a very good place to meet.' He yawned. 'You've brought a whole new meaning to the expression "job satisfaction".'

But Isobel wasn't really listening. Now that her euphoric state had begun to evaporate she was remembering what she'd been thinking at the height of their lovemaking. About loving him.

She stared at the ceiling, her heart beginning to pound with fear. *Love?* Surely she wasn't crazy enough to waste an emotion like that on a man who very definitely didn't want it? Who had explicitly warned her against it? And hadn't her mother done the very same? She'd managed to convince her daughter that love was rare—and Isobel knew it was an impossibility to expect it from a seasoned playboy who shied away from commitment.

Uncomfortably, she wriggled, wanting to get away, to try and soothe her confused thoughts into some kind of order. 'Tariq, we can't lie here all day.'

'Why not? We can do anything we like.' He touched his lips to hers. 'I *am* the boss.'

She pulled away from him—but not before he had caught hold of her, his eyes narrowed. 'Something is wrong, *kalila?*' he queried softly. 'You are angry with me because we have had yet another *fumble* on the floor of the office?'

Isobel smiled. 'I can hardly blame you for wanting instant sex when I was a willing participant. I just happen to know that there's a whole pile of things which need your attention. And we *are* supposed to be working.'

Yawning, he rose to his feet and held out a hand. 'By the way—I've brought you a present from New York,' he said as he pulled her to her feet.

'Oh?' She felt her heart skip a beat. 'It's not my birthday.'

"That's a little disingenuous of you, Izzy.' Walking over to his briefcase, he slanted her a lazy smile as he withdrew a slim leather case. 'Don't you like presents?'

She wasn't sure—her feelings were pretty mixed when it came to presents from Tariq. She wanted to be the first and only woman he'd ever bought a gift for. Not to feel as if she was just one in a long line of women who smiled their acceptance of whatever glittering trinket he had bought them. *But she was. That was exactly what she was.*

She wanted to tell him that she didn't need presents. Because she knew him too well and she knew how he operated. Her counterpart in New York had probably been dispatched to choose something for her—just as she had chosen such gifts for his lovers many times before. She had probably even consulted him to find out what the budget for such a gift should be.

But she kept silent. She was curious and scared, knowing that she was in no position to make highly charged pronouncements because of what the outcome might be. Because mightn't he just shrug his shoulders and walk away?

So she took the box he handed her and flipped open the clasp with fingers which were miraculously steady. The first irreverent thought which crossed her mind was that she was pretty low down on the price scale. After five years of choosing various sparklers for Tariq's women, she could see instantly that her own offering would not have caused a stratospheric hole in his wallet. No diamonds or emeralds for *her.*

But in a stupid way she was glad. Precious jewels would have been all wrong on someone like her: they would have felt like some sort of *payment* and they wouldn't have suited her. Instead Tariq had bought her something she might actually have saved up for and bought for herself.

Lying on a bed of blue-black velvet lay a shoal of opals, fashioned into a dramatic waterfall of a necklace. Isobel drew it out of the box. The stones were dark grey—almost black—but as the necklace shimmered over her fingers she could see the transformation of each gem into a vivid rainbow.

'Do you like it?' questioned Tariq.

Isobel blinked. 'It's the most beautiful thing I've ever seen,' she whispered.

'I chose it myself,' he said unexpectedly. 'I liked the element of surprise. In some lights it looks quite subdued—while in other aspects it's amazingly vibrant.' His eyes narrowed and his tone was dry. 'A little like you, in fact, Izzy.'

Isobel suddenly became extremely preoccupied with the jewellery, swallowing down the glimmer of tears which were hovering at the back of her eyes. He'd chosen it himself. To her certain knowledge he'd never done that before—not in all the time she'd worked for him. So did that *mean* anything? She couldn't help the wild leap of her heart. Did such an unexpected gesture mean that his feelings for her might be growing and changing? Dared she…dared she *hope* for such a thing?

'You do like it, Izzy?'

His question broke into her thoughts and she lifted her head. 'I do like it. In fact, I *love* it.'

'Good.' There was a pause. 'I thought you might want to wear it tomorrow night.'

She heard the studied casualness in his voice. 'Why? What's happening tomorrow night?'

'My brother is in town.'

She blinked. 'You mean your brother, the *King?*'

'I only have one brother,' he answered drily. 'He flew my sister-in-law to Paris for their wedding anniversary.

Francesca hasn't been back in England in nearly a year, so they've decided to come on to London. Our embassy is throwing a formal dinner for them tonight—which I shall have to attend. But tomorrow they want to meet up privately. You've spoken to Zahid on the phone so many times that I thought you might like this opportunity to meet him.'

Carefully, she put the necklace back in its case and smiled. 'I'd love to meet your brother,' she said.

'Good.' Tariq walked through to his private office, calling out over his shoulder, 'I'll let you have the details later.'

Isobel waited until the door had closed behind him, then stared at the jewellery case in her handbag, a strange cocktail of emotions forming a tight knot at the pit of her stomach. She might be going out of her mind, but try as she might she couldn't quite subdue the sudden flare of happiness which rose within her. Hand-picked jewels and meeting his brother were surely remarkable enough to merit a little analysis. Was it possible that, deep down, Tariq was willing to move this relationship on to something a little more tangible?

Cold reason tried to swamp her as she remembered the emphatic way he'd told her that he didn't ever want commitment, or a family of his own. But measured against that was the terrible loneliness he'd experienced as a child. Maybe now he was coming to realise that people could change—and so could circumstances. That what they had was good. That it didn't have to peter out after a few weeks—that maybe it could endure and grow. Was that too much to hope for?

But she felt as if she were on shifting sands—her hopes quickly replaced by a strange feeling of foreboding as she remembered something she'd read somewhere.

She clicked open the box to stare at the multi-hued fire of her brand-new necklace, and frowned. Because weren't opals supposed to be awfully *unlucky?*

CHAPTER NINE

'YOU LOOK FINE, Izzy. Really.'

For the umpteenth time Isobel smoothed damp palms down over her thick mass of curls, aware that she was probably mussing her hair up instead of flattening it. She frowned at Tariq. What kind of a recommendation was that? 'Fine' wasn't the kind of description she wanted when she was about to meet the King of Khayarzah and his English bride Queen Francesca. Not when she felt so nervous that her knees were actually shaking.

'That's a pretty lukewarm endorsement,' she said.

His black eyes gleamed as he captured one of her fluttering hands and directed it towards his mouth. 'I thought honesty was our mantra?'

'Maybe it is, but sometimes a woman needs a little fabrication.'

'No need for fabrication, *kalila,*' he said. He brushed her a brief kiss as their car drew to a halt outside the glittering frontage of the Granchester Hotel, but if the truth were known he was finding this very feminine need for reassurance a touch too *domestic* for his taste. Had it been wise to extend this invitation? he wondered. Or was Izzy now reading far more into it than he'd intended her to read? Maybe he should have made it clearer that there was no real significance behind the meeting with his brother. 'You look absolutely stunning,' he drawled. 'Didn't I tell you exactly that just an hour ago?'

Yes, he had, Isobel conceded. But a man said all kinds of things to a woman when he had just finished ravishing her in the middle of his big bed...

Their spontaneous lovemaking had left her running late—but maybe it was better not to have had time to fret about her appearance when she'd been nervous enough already. She was wearing a new dress in grey silk jersey, and its careful draping did amazing things for her figure. She'd teamed the dress with high-heeled black suede shoes, and on Tariq's instructions had left her hair hanging loose. She'd wondered aloud if the wild cloud of Titian curls was not a little too much, but he had wound his fingers through its corkscrew strands and told her that it was a crime to hide it away.

Her only adornment was the opals he had brought her back from America, and they sparkled rainbow light at her throat and dominated the subdued palette of her outfit. *The gems he'd chosen for her himself...* How could such beautiful gems possibly be unlucky? she asked herself, her fingertips reaching up to touch the cool stones as a doorman sprang to open the car door.

The private elevator zoomed them up to the penthouse suite, and when the door was opened by a man who was unmistakably Tariq's brother all Isobel's expectations were confounded.

He had the same hawk-like features as Tariq—and

the same knockout combination of ebony hair and glowing olive skin. But he was casually dressed in dark trousers, and although he was wearing a silk shirt he was tieless. Isobel had been expecting to be greeted by a servant, so her curtsey was hastily scrambled together and ill-prepared. But King Zahid smiled at her as he indicated that she should rise.

'No formality,' he warned. 'That is my wife's instruction, and I dare not disobey!'

'Why, Zahid—you sound as if you are almost under the thumb,' mocked Tariq softly.

'Perhaps I am. And a very beautiful thumb it happens to be,' murmured Zahid.

'You've changed,' observed Tariq, creasing his brow in a frown. 'You'd never have admitted to something like that in the past.'

'Ah, but everything changes, Tariq,' said Zahid. 'That is one of life's great certainties.'

For a moment the light of challenge sparked between the eyes of the brothers, and for a moment Isobel caught a glimpse of what the two men must have been like as children.

'Come this way,' continued Zahid, leading them into an enormous sitting room whose floor-to-ceiling windows overlooked the park.

And there, with a baby on her knee and another crawling close by on the floor, was the English Queen Francesca, her dark hair tied back in a ponytail and a slightly harassed smile on her face. She had a snowy blanket hanging over one shoulder, and was holding a grubby white toy polar bear, at which the sturdy baby on her lap kept lunging.

Isobel blinked. The last thing she'd expected was to see a queen in blue jeans, playing nursemaid!

'No, please don't curtsey, Izzy—we're very relaxed here,' said Francesca with a wide smile. 'But if you want to be really helpful you could pick up Omar before he tries to eat Zahid's shoe! Azzam has already tried! Darling, I do wish you'd keep them out of reach.'

Rather nervously, Isobel bent to scoop up the black-haired baby, aware that one of these precious boy twins was the heir to the Khayarzah throne. A robust little creature, Omar was wearing an exquisite yellow romper suit which contrasted with his ebony curls. He took one long and suspicious look at the woman now holding him, then gave a shout as he began to tug at her hair.

Isobel giggled as she extricated his tiny chubby fingers, all the nerves she'd been feeling suddenly evaporating. You couldn't possibly feel uptight when you were holding a cuddly bundle like this. He was so *sweet!* She risked a glance at Tariq, but met no answering smile on his face. In fact his expression suddenly looked so *glacial* that she felt momentarily flummoxed. But at least he was now directing the chilly stare at his brother instead of her.

'Don't you have any nannies with you?' Tariq asked Zahid coolly.

'Not one,' answered Zahid, giving his wife a long and indulgent look. 'Francesca decided that she wanted us to have a "normal" family holiday—just like other people.'

'And you agreed?' questioned Tariq incredulously.

'Actually, I find that I'm enjoying the experience,' said Zahid. 'It's useful to be "hands-on".'

'I want our children to know their parents,' said Francesca firmly. 'Not to be brought out like ornaments, for best. Zahid, aren't you going to offer our guests a drink?'

Isobel saw Tariq's face darken. Clearly he did *not* approve of the babies being present, and she noticed that he kept as far away from his nephews as possible. She wondered how he could possibly ignore such cute little black-haired dumplings, before deciding that it was *his* problem and that she was just going to relax and enjoy herself.

In fact the evening went much better than she could have hoped. She took turns cuddling both Omar and Azzam, and ended up kicking off her high-heeled shoes and helping Francesca bath the twins in one of the fancy *en-suite* bathrooms. Her dove-grey dress was soon splattered with drops of water, but she didn't care.

They grappled to dress the wriggling boys in animal-dotted sleepsuits, and then brought them in to the men to say goodnight, all warm and rosy and smelling delicious. But she noticed that Tariq's embrace was strictly perfunctory as each baby was offered up to him for a kiss.

She tried not to be unsettled by his rather forbidding body language as she and Francesca carried the babies through to the bedroom and laid them down in their two little cots. For a while they stood watching as two sets of heavily hooded eyes drooped down into exhausted sleep, and then—as if colluding in some wonderful secret—both women smiled at each other.

Francesca bent to tuck the polar bear next to Azzam, then straightened up. 'You know, we've never met any of Tariq's girlfriends before,' she said.

Isobel wasn't quite sure how to respond. She didn't really *feel* like his girlfriend—more like an employee, with benefits. But she could hardly confess that to the Sheikh's sister-in-law, could she? Or start explaining the exact nature of those 'benefits'? Instead, she smiled.

'I'm very honoured to be here,' she answered quietly.

Francesca hesitated. 'Sometimes Zahid worries about Tariq. He thinks that surely there's only so much living in the fast lane one person can do. It would be nice to see him settle down at last.'

Now Isobel felt a complete fraud, because she knew very well that Tariq had no intention of settling down. Not with her—and not with anyone. He'd made that more than clear. Because when a man told you unequivocally that he never wanted children he was telling you something big, wasn't he? Something you couldn't really ignore. And if she'd been labouring under any illusion that he hadn't meant it—well, she'd discovered tonight that he had. With his stony countenance and disapproving air, he'd made it pretty clear that children didn't do it for him.

And if Zahid and Francesca thought that her appearance here was anything more than expedient—that she and Tariq were about to start playing happy-ever-after—well, they were in for a big disappointment.

'I don't know whether some men are ever quite ready

to settle down,' she told the Queen diplomatically. 'He isn't known as the Playboy Prince for nothing!'

Francesca opened her mouth as if she wanted to say something else, but clearly thought better of it because she shut it again. 'Come on,' she said. 'Let's go and eat dinner. I want to hear all about life in England—the fashion, the films. Who's dating who. What's big on TV. I get a whole load of stuff off the internet, of course, but it's never quite the same.'

And Isobel nodded and smiled, feeling an immense sense of relief that the subject of Tariq's inability to commit had been terminated.

Dinner was served in the lavish dining room which led off the main room, its table covered in snowy linen and decorated with white fragrant flowers. Heavy silver cutlery reflected the light which guttered from tall, creamy candles, and the overall effect was one of restrained luxury and taste.

'This looks wonderful,' said Isobel shyly, realising that this was the first time she'd been given an insider's experience of Tariq's royal life.

'A dinner fit for a king!' said Francesca, and they all laughed as they took their places around the table.

The evening passed in a bit of a blur. Isobel was aware of being served the most amazing food, but it was mostly wasted on her. She might as well have been eating bread and butter for all the notice she took of the exquisite fare. She could hardly believe she was here with Tariq—meeting his family like this. It had the heady but disconcerting effect of almost *normalising* their relationship—and she knew that was a dangerous way to start thinking. Just because you really wanted something, it didn't necessarily mean it was going to happen.

So she joined in as much as she could, though she felt completely lost when the two brothers began speaking in their own language.

'They're discussing the new trade deal with Maraban,' confided Francesca.

Isobel put her knife and fork down. 'Do you speak any Khayarzahian?' she questioned.

'Only a little. I'm learning all the time—though it's not the easiest language in the world. But I'm determined to be fluent one day—just as my sons will be.'

'They're such beautiful babies,' said Isobel, a sudden note of wistfulness entering her voice almost before she'd realised.

'Not getting broody, are you?' Francesca laughed.

It was perhaps unfortunate that the brothers' conversation chose that precise moment to end and Tariq glanced up. He must have heard what they'd been saying, Isobel thought, her skin suddenly growing cold with fear. He *must* have done. Why else did he fix her with an expression she'd never seen before? A calculating look iced the ebony depths of his eyes which made her feel like some sort of gatecrasher.

'Of course I'm not!' she denied quickly, reaching for a glass of water and horribly aware of the sudden flush of colour to her cheeks. Why was he looking at her like that—with his eyes full of suspicion? Did he think she was trying to ingratiate herself with the monarch and his wife? Or did he think she really *was* getting broody?

One moment she had been part of their charmed

inner circle—warmed by its privileged light—and now in an instant it felt as if she had been kicked out and left to shiver on the darkened sidelines.

By the time the evening ended her feeling of despondency had grown—though she managed to maintain her bright air of enjoyment until the car door had closed on them and they were once more locked within its private space.

She settled back in the seat, unable to shake off the feeling of having been judged and found wanting, aware that Tariq did not slide his arm around her shoulder and draw her closer to him. And suddenly she was reminded of that very first time she'd had sex with him. When she'd been driven home—knickerless and confused—after first dropping him off at the Maraban Embassy.

Back then she had been painfully aware of him keeping her at a distance, and he was doing it again now. Even though in the intervening weeks they had been lovers it was almost like being transported back in time. Because nothing had really changed, had it? Not for Tariq. She might be guilty of concocting fast-growing fantasies about how hand-chosen pieces of jewellery meant that he was starting to care for her—but that was just wishful thinking. Like some young girl who read her horoscope and then prayed it would come true.

'You seemed to be getting on very well with Francesca,' he observed, his voice breaking into her thoughts.

'I hope I did all right?' she questioned, telling herself that any woman in her position would have asked the same question.

'I thought you carried it off superbly.'

'Thanks,' she said uncertainly.

But Tariq leaned back in his seat, unable to dispel the growing sense of unease inside him. The whole evening had unsettled him, and it wasn't difficult to work out why. Zahid in jeans—with no help for the children—and in a hotel suite which looked as if it had just been burgled.

He shook his head in faint disbelief. It was scarcely credible to him that his once so formal and slightly stuffy older brother was now like putty in the hands of his wife.

But it hadn't just been the sense of chaos which had unsettled him. Something about their close family unit had opened up the dark space which was buried deep in Tariq's heart. Watching his brother playing with his children had reinforced his sense of feeling like an outsider. Always the outsider.

He shot Isobel a glance, remembering the way their gazes had met over the dark curly head of his nephew. Had that been wistfulness he'd read in her eyes as she'd held the baby in her arms? Was she doing that clucky thing which seemed to happen to all women, no matter how much they tried to deny it? Especially if they knew that a man was watching them…

But why *shouldn't* she long for babies of her own? That was what women were conditioned to do. The most unforgivable thing would be for a man who didn't want children to waste the time of a woman who *did*.

He saw that her eyes were now closed. Her cheeks looked as smooth as marble. Her grey dress and the new opals were muted in the subdued light of the car. Only her magnificent mane of hair provided glowing life and colour. And suddenly, in this quiet place, all the things he usually blotted out came crowding into his mind.

He hadn't given any thought to the future. He hadn't planned this affair with Izzy—it had just sprung up, out of the blue, and been surprisingly good. But sooner or later something had to give. It wasn't for ever. His relationships never were. And the longer it went on, then surely the more it would fill her with false hope. She might start seeing a happy-ever-after for them both—which was never going to happen. Wasn't it better and more honest to end it now, before he really hurt her—a woman he liked and respected far too much to ever want to hurt?

He realised that she had fallen asleep, and although a part of him wanted to lean over and wake her with a kiss he reminded himself that this wasn't a fairytale.

He was not that prince.

Gently, he shook her shoulder, and her big, tawny eyes snapped open.

'Wake up, Izzy,' he said softly.

'What's the matter?' Groggily, she sat up and looked around. 'Are we nearly home?'

It was her choice of word which helped make his mind up. Because for them there was no 'home' and there never would be. She had her place and he had his—and maybe it was time to start drawing a clear line between the two.

'I'm going to get the car to drop me off,' he said softly. 'And then the driver will take you on to your apartment.'

Isobel snuggled up to him. 'Don't be silly,' she murmured. 'I'll come home with you.'

There it was again—that seemingly innocuous word which now seemed weighted down with all kinds of heavy meaning.

'Not tonight, Izzy. I have to take a conference call very early tomorrow, and it's pointless the two of us being woken up.' Lightly he brushed his lips over hers before drawing away—before the sweet taste of her could tempt him into changing his mind—glad that the limousine was now drawing up outside his apartment. 'And, thanks to you, I got very little sleep last night.'

Feeling stupidly rejected, Isobel nodded. In a way, his explanation made things worse. It made her feel as if she was *wanting* something from him and he was withholding it.

Or was she simply tired and imagining things? Maybe it would be better all round if she *did* go home alone. She could have an undisturbed night's sleep, and tomorrow morning she would wake up bright and cheerful.

And everything would be the same as it had been before.

'Yes, we could probably *both* do with a good night's sleep,' she said, keeping her voice resolutely cheerful. 'I'll see you in the morning.'

But as Tariq got out of the car she saw the sudden shuttering of his face, and she couldn't shift the sinking certainty that something between them had changed.

And changed for the worst.

CHAPTER TEN

SO IT WAS TRUE.

Horribly, horribly true.

Isobel's fears that Tariq was *cooling* towards her were not some warped figment of her imagination, after all. She was getting the cool treatment. Definitely. She recognised it much too well to be mistaken.

She hadn't spent a night with him in almost a week even though he'd been in the same country—the same city, even. Every night there was another reason why he couldn't see her. He was eating out with a group of American bankers. Or meeting up with a friend who'd just flown in from Khayarzah. And even though his reasons sounded perfectly legitimate, Isobel couldn't shift the certainty that he was avoiding her.

These days, even when he came into the office, he seemed distracted. There was barely a good morning kiss. No smouldering look to send her pulse rate soaring and have her anticipating what might happen later. It was as if the Isobel she had been—the woman he desired and lusted after—was disappearing. She felt as if the old, invisible Isobel had returned to take her place.

As if a switch had been flicked in Tariq's mind and it would never be the same again.

She tried telling herself it was because he was busy—but deep down she suspected a different reason for his distance. After all, she'd seen it happen countless times before, with other women. One minute they were flavour of the month, and the next they were like unwanted leftovers, lying congealed on the side of the plate.

The question was, what was she going to do about it? Was she going to sit back and let him push her away—gradually chipping at her already precarious self-esteem—until she was left with nothing? Or was she going to be proactive enough to reach out and take control of her life? Should she just face up to him and ask whether they were to consign their affair to memory?

Until she realised that Tariq's apparent lack of interest was the least of her worries. And that there were some things which were of far more pressing concern…

She told herself that the nausea she was experiencing was a residual from the brief burst of sickness she'd had, caused by some rogue fish she'd eaten. That the slight aching in her breasts was due to her hormones, nothing else. She was on the pill, wasn't she? And the pill was blissfully safe. Everyone knew that.

But the feeling of nausea began to worsen, and so did the aching in her breasts. And then Tariq said something which made her think that perhaps she *wasn't* imagining it…

It happened that weekend, when she was staying over at his apartment. It seemed ages since they'd spent two whole days together, and she loved being there when they didn't have work the next day. It was the closest she ever felt to him—as if she was a real girlfriend, rather than a secretary who had just got lucky.

It was early on the Sunday morning that he made his observation. Half-asleep, he had begun to kiss her, his hands to caress her breasts, and she had given a little sigh and nestled back against the soft bank of pillows.

'Izzy?' he murmured. 'Have you put on a little weight, do you think?'

She stiffened beneath the practised caress of his fingers. 'Why?' she blurted out. 'Do you think I'm getting fat?'

'There's no need to be so defensive.' He blew softly onto the hollow of her breastbone. 'You're slender enough to carry a few extra pounds. Men like curves—I've told you that before.'

But his words only increased her sense of anxiety, and she was almost relieved when the phone in his study began ringing and he swore a little before going off to answer it. It was the one phone he never ignored—the private line between him and his brother's palace in Khayarzah.

Isobel could hear him speaking in a lowered voice, so she took the opportunity to head for the bathroom down the corridor—the one he never used. Her heart was racing as she closed the door, and the terrible taste of fear was in her mouth. And she knew that she could no longer put off the moment of truth.

She flinched as she saw the image which was reflected back at her in the full-length mirror. Her face was paper-pale and her eyes looked huge and haunted, but it was her body which disturbed her. Like most women, she was not usually given to staring at her naked self, but even she could see that her breasts looked swollen and the nipples were much darker than usual.

Was she pregnant? *Was* she?

For a moment she lowered her head, to gaze at the pristine white surface of the washbasin. She remembered how unequivocal Tariq had been about not wanting children—and clearly it hadn't been an idle declaration. Hadn't she witnessed for herself how cold he could be when he was around them? Why, he'd barely touched Omar or Azzam the other day—he'd seemed completely unmoved by their presence when everyone else had been cooing around them.

She wanted to sink to her knees and pray for some kind of miracle. But she couldn't afford to have hysterics or to act rashly. She needed time to think, and she needed to stay calm.

Quickly, she showered and put on jeans and a shirt, feeling the slight tug as she fastened the buttons across her chest.

The silence in the apartment told her that Tariq had finished his conversation, and in bare feet she padded along the corridor to find him standing in his study. He was staring out of the window, his powerful body silhouetted against the dramatic view.

When he turned round, he didn't comment on the fact that she had showered and dressed. A couple of weeks ago he would have growled his displeasure and started removing her clothes immediately, but not now—and a wave of regret washed over her for something between them which seemed to be lost.

'Is anything wrong?' she questioned.

He stared at her, his eyes focussing on her pale skin and anxious eyes, and a heavy sense of sadness enveloped him. What had happened to his smart and wisecracking Izzy? He felt the heavy beat of guilt, aware of the enormity of what he had done. In typical Tariq fashion he had seen and he had conquered. Selfishly, he had listened to the voracious demands of his body and taken her as his lover, refusing to acknowledge the thoughtlessness of such an action.

She had been too inexperienced to resist the powerful lure of lust when it had swept over them so unexpectedly. *He* should have known better and *he* should have resisted. But he had not. He had done what he always did—he had taken and taken, knowing that he had nothing to give back.

And now he was left with the growing suspicion that he was going to lose the best assistant he'd ever had. For how could they carry on like this, when much of her natural spontaneity seemed to have been eroded by the affair?

He could tell that something had changed. It was as if she was walking on eggshells. He noticed that she kept biting back her words—which usually meant that a woman was falling in love with him, that she was weighing up everything she said for fear of how he would interpret it. And all these negative feelings would snowball—he knew that, too. How could he possibly face her in the office if her reproachful looks were to continue and the gap between them widened daily?

'Tariq?'

Her soft voice broke into his troubled thoughts. 'What?'

'I wondered if anything was wrong.'

'Wrong?'

She looked at him questioningly, telling herself that it was her business to know what was going on in his life. But deep down she wanted to clear that scary look of distraction from his face. To have him *talk* to her. Properly.

'The phone call you've just had from Khayarzah?' she elaborated. 'I hope everything's okay with your brother?'

With an effort, he focussed on the conversation he'd just finished. 'Zahid wants my help with a relative of ours.'

'Oh?'

'A distant cousin of mine, from my mother's side,' he explained. 'Her name is Leila, and she's in trouble.'

Isobel's face blanched as she wondered if the gods were taunting her. Because hadn't that expression always been a euphemism for a particular *kind* of predicament in which a woman sometimes found herself? Was it possible that a cruel fate was about to inflict not one but *two* unplanned pregnancies on the al Hakam family?

'Trouble?' she questioned hoarsely. 'What kind of trouble?'

'It seems she's decided she wants to junk university and go off to America to be a model. Can you imagine?' He gave a grim smile. 'Zahid thinks that she needs to be shown the error of her ways, and he thinks that I may just be able to sort things out.'

'I see.' Isobel nodded. Was she imagining the relief on his face—as if he was anticipating an adventure which would fully occupy him for the foreseeable future? As if he was pleased to have a *bona fide* reason to unexpectedly leave the country? 'Why does he think that?'

'He says that my uniquely western perspective might help persuade her. That I've seen enough of that kind of world to convince her that it's all starvation and cigarettes and people who will try to exploit her.' He shrugged. 'Nothing that need concern you—but I'm going to fly out later tonight, if you could make sure the new jet is ready for me?'

Two things occurred to her at the same time. The first was that he still came and went exactly as he pleased—becoming her lover had not curtailed his freedom in any way at all. And the second was that she knew there was no way she could announce her momentous news. Not when he was about to go on some mission of mercy for his brother. Not when she hadn't even had it confirmed. And until she did then surely there was always the chance that it was nothing but a false alarm?

But her decision didn't give her any peace of mind. She was still left with nagging doubts. Tariq was leaving to go back to his homeland, and suddenly she didn't know where her place in his life should be. She struggled to a find common ground.

'Did…did your brother and his wife enjoy themselves in London last week?' she asked.

'I assume so.'

'They didn't mention it?'

He raised dark brows. 'Should they have done?'

'Just...well, I thought it was quite a fun evening, that's all.'

'Indeed it was.' He gave a brief smile, preoccupied with his forthcoming trip and pleased to have something to take his mind off the damned tension between them. 'But they have a hectic life, you know, Izzy. Pretty much wall-to-wall socialising wherever they are.'

It was the hint of aloofness in his tone which made Isobel stiffen. That and the patronising sense that she had stepped over some invisible line of propriety. As if she had *dared* to look on the King and his wife as some sort of equals, instead of people she'd been lucky enough to meet only on a whim of Tariq's.

'Silly of me,' she said lightly.

There was a pause as she forced herself to acknowledge the tension which had sprung up between them and which now seemed there all the time. She didn't know when exactly it had happened, but it wouldn't seem to go away. Like a pebble dropped into a pond, the ripples carried on for ages after the stone had plopped out of sight.

She knew what was going on because she'd witnessed it countless times before. Tariq was beginning to tire of her and he wanted the affair to be over—with the least possible disruption to *him*.

She thought of how the situation might pan out. He might decide to stay longer in Khayarzah than he'd intended. Or he might slot in lots of extra trips abroad which would seamlessly and physically separate them. And when they finally came face to face back in the office so much time would have passed that it would be easy to consign the whole affair to history.

Easy for him, perhaps—but not for her. She hadn't done this kind of thing before. Unlike him, she was *no good at pretending*.

Wasn't it better to face the truth head-on—no matter how difficult that might be? To confront reality rather than trying to airbrush it away? Wouldn't that at least go some way to restoring her pride and making sure she didn't whittle away at her self-respect until there was nothing left but an empty husk?

She forced a smile. 'Tariq, I've been thinking.'

Something in her tone made his eyes narrow. 'Oh?'

Her heart was hammering, but she forced herself to look directly into his eyes. 'I'm due a lot of holiday—and I was wondering if I might take the chance to use up some of my entitlement while you're away? Fiona's pretty much up to speed, and she's perfectly capable of running your office.'

Tariq stiffened as he heard the sudden formality of her tone. Holiday *entitlement*. Fiona *running his office*. He met her tawny gaze and felt a brief spear of something like pain as he realised what she was doing. Izzy was clever, he conceded. Clever enough to sense that he was cooling towards her.

'Is that really necessary?' he said.

It was a loaded question. She knew it, and he knew it too. Isobel nodded her head. 'I think so. I think we need to give each other a little space, Tariq. This... *affair* has been pretty amazing, but I suspect it's run its course—don't you?' She stared at him, willing him to say no. Longing for him to pull her into his arms and tell her she was out of her mind.

Tariq looked at her and felt a wave of admiration underpinned by a fleeting sense of regret. For, although he knew that this was the perfect solution, he was going to miss her as a lover. But relationships never stayed static. Already he could sense that she wanted more from him. More than he could ever give. And if he allowed her these weeks of absence mightn't she come back refreshed and able to put the whole thing behind her? Couldn't they go back to what they'd had before? That easy intimacy they'd shared before they had allowed sex to complicate everything?

Briefly, he acknowledged the stab of hurt pride that she should be the one to end it. But why *shouldn't* he be the one on the receiving end of closure for a change? Mightn't it do him some good?

'I think you could be right,' he said slowly.

'You do?' Could he hear the disappointment which had distorted her voice?

He nodded. 'I do. Maybe it's better we stop it now before it impacts on our working relationship.'

'Oh, absolutely,' she agreed, gritting her teeth behind her smile. Wanting to lash out at him for his naïveté. Did he really think it *hadn't* impacted on their working relationship already?

'And you deserve a break,' he said, his gaze drifting over her face. 'Why don't you get some sun on your cheeks? You look awfully pale, Izzy.'

Dimly, she registered his words, and they gave her all the confirmation she needed. He thought that a short spell in the sun was all she needed to bring her back to normal. Oh, if only it was that easy. A strange dizziness was making her head spin. For a moment she felt icy-cold beads of sweat pricking her forehead and the sudden roar of blood in her ears.

'Izzy?' He was grabbing hold of her now, hot concern blazing from his black eyes. 'For heaven's sake! What's the matter?'

His fingers were biting into her arms, but she shook them off and pulled herself away. Gripping onto the edge of the desk, she sucked in deep breaths of air and prayed she wouldn't pass out.

Tell him.

'Izzy?'

Tell him.

But the words wouldn't come—they stayed stubbornly stuck at the back of her throat and she swallowed them down again. I'll tell him when I know for sure, she thought. When he gets back.

'I'm fine, Tariq. Honestly. I just feel a little off-colour, that's all. Must have been something I ate. And now, if you'll excuse me for a minute, I'd better see about your jet. And then I'll ring through to Fiona and have her sit in on our meeting.'

She waited until she'd spoken to the airfield, and then calmed an excited Fiona's nerves, telling her that of *course* she could cope with running Tariq's office.

And it was only then that Isobel slipped along to the thankfully empty sanctuary of the bathroom, where she was violently sick.

CHAPTER ELEVEN

IT WAS CONFIRMED.

The blue line couldn't be denied any longer—and neither could the test Isobel had done the day before, or the day before that. Because all the tests in the world would only verify what she had known all along. And all the wishing in the world wouldn't change that fact.

She was pregnant with Prince Tariq al Hakam's baby. The man who had told her in no uncertain terms that he had no desire to have a baby was going to be a father.

Feeling caged and restless, she stared out of the window at the red bus which was lumbering down the road below. It was stuffy and hot in her tiny flat, but she felt too tired to face walking to the nearest park. She'd been feeling tired a lot recently...

Little beads of sweat ran in rivulets down her back, despite the thin cotton dress and the windows she'd opened onto the airless day. Somehow summer had arrived without her really noticing—but maybe that wasn't so surprising. In the two weeks since Tariq had flown out to Khayarzah she certainly hadn't been focussing on the weather.

Her thoughts had been full of the man whose seed was growing inside her—and she had a strange feeling of emptiness at being away from work. For once she couldn't even face going down to the cottage, where the memories of Tariq would have been just too vivid.

She'd always thought there was something slightly pathetic about people who haunted the office while they were supposed to be on holiday, and so she hadn't rung in to work either. Fiona would contact her soon enough if she needed her help, and so far she hadn't.

Which made Isobel feel even emptier than she already did. As if she had made herself out to be this fabulous, indispensable addition to the Al Hakam empire when the reality was that she could quite easily be replaced.

And she had heard nothing from Tariq. Not even an e-mail or text to tell her he was alive and well in Khayarzah. If anything proved that it was all over between them, it was the terrifying silence which had mushroomed since his departure.

There had been times when she'd been tempted to pick up the phone, telling herself that she had a perfect right to speak to him. Wasn't he still her boss, even if he was no longer her lover? But she wasn't a good enough actress for that. How could she possibly have a breezy conversation with him, as if nothing was happening, when inside her body their combined cells were multiplying at a frightening speed?

And what would she say? Would she be reduced to asking him whether it was *really* over between them—and hearing an even bigger silence echoing down the line?

No. She was going to have to tell him face to face. She knew that. And soon. But how did you break the news that he was going to be a father to a man who had expressly told you he didn't want children? And not just any father—because this wasn't just any baby. It was a *royal* baby, with *royal* blood coursing through its tiny veins—and that would have all kinds of added complications. She knew enough history to realise that the offspring of ruling families were always especially protected because royal succession was never certain. Wouldn't that make Tariq feel even more trapped into a life he had often bitterly complained about?

But that's only if he accepts responsibility for the child, taunted a voice inside her head. *He might do the modern-day equivalent of what your own father did and walk away from his son or daughter.*

Dunking a camomile teabag in a mug of boiling water, she heard the ring of her doorbell and wondered who it might be. The post, perhaps? Or some sort of delivery? Because nobody just dropped by in London on a weekday lunchtime. It could be a lonely city, she realised with a suddenly sinking heart—and this little flat was certainly no place to bring up a baby.

A baby.

The thought of what lay ahead terrified her, and she was so distracted that she'd almost forgotten about the doorbell when it rang again—more urgently this time. Her thin cotton dress was clinging to her warm thighs as she walked to the door, and she was so preoccupied that she didn't bother to check the spyhole. When she opened the door, the last person she expected to see on her step was Tariq.

She gave a jolt of genuine surprise, her tiredness evaporating as she feasted her eyes on him. She had thought of little else but him since he'd been gone, but the reality of seeing him again was a savage shock to the system. His physical presence dominated his surroundings just as it always did, even if the heavily hooded ebony eyes were watchful and his mouth more unsmiling than she'd ever seen it. He was wearing a shirt— unbuttoned at the neck—with a pair of faded jeans. He looked cool against the day, and the casual attire made him look gloriously touchable—the irony of that did not escape her.

'Tariq,' she said breathlessly, aware of the thunder of her heart. 'This is a…surprise.'

He nodded. A surprise for him, too, if he was being honest. He hadn't intended to come and see her, and yet he'd found himself ordering his driver to bring him to this unfamiliar part of London.

He'd spent a brutal two weeks chasing around Khayarzah looking for his damned cousin, and the office had felt strangely empty when he had returned to find that Izzy was still away. Not that there was anything wrong with Fiona, her replacement. She was a sweet girl, and very eager to please. But she wasn't Izzy. His mouth hardened.

'Can I come in?'

'Of course you can.'

Tariq walked in and she closed the front door behind

him. It was the first time he'd ever been there, and he walked into the sitting room and looked around. It was a small room, and much less cluttered than her country cottage. A couple of photos stood on the bookshelf. One was of her standing in a garden aged about eight, squinting her eyes against the bright sunlight. One of those images of childhood you saw everywhere. But he had no such similar pictures of his own. There had been no one around with a camera to record his growing up. Apart from official ones, the only photos he had been in were those big group ones from school—when his darkly olive complexion and powerful build had always made him stand out from the rest of his year.

He turned round as she walked into the room behind him. Her thick red curls had been scraped back and tied in a French plait, and her eyes looked huge. She looked so fragile, he thought—or was that simply because he hadn't seen her for so long?

He frowned. 'I thought you'd have been back at work by now.'

How formal he sounded, she thought. More the time-watching boss than the man who had shown her such sweet pleasure. 'You did say that I could take three weeks. And it's only been two.'

'I know exactly how long it's been, Izzy.'

They stood facing each other, as if trying to acclimatise themselves to this new and unknown stage of their relationship. It felt weird, she thought, to be alone with him and not in his arms. To have a million questions tripping off the edge of her tongue and be too afraid to ask them.

Tell him.

But the words still refused to be spoken. She told herself that she just wanted to embrace these last few moments of peace. A couple more minutes of normality when she could pretend that there was no dreaded truth to be faced. Two minutes more to feast her eyes on the face she'd grown to love and which now made her heart ache with useless longing.

'Did you find your cousin?' she questioned, raking back a strand of hair which had flopped onto her cheek.

Tariq watched as the movement drew his attention to the lush swell of her breasts, and he felt the first twisting of desire. 'Eventually,' he said.

'And was she okay?'

'I haven't come here to talk about my damned cousin,' he said roughly.

'Oh?' Her voice lifted in hope. 'Then what *have* you come here to talk about?'

He looked at the soft curves of her unpainted lips and suddenly wondered just what he was fighting. Himself or her? 'Nothing.'

'Nothing?' Her eyes were wide with confusion. 'Then why are you here?'

'Why do you think?' he ground out, his black eyes brilliant as temptation overpowered him and he pulled her into his arms. 'For *this*.'

Isobel swayed as their bodies made that first contact and she felt the sudden mad pounding of her heart. Conscience fought with desire as he drove his mouth down on hers, and desire won hands down. Her lips opened and she made a choking little sound of pleasure as she coiled her arms around him. Because this was where she wanted to be more than anywhere else in the world. Back in the arms of Tariq. Because when she was there all her problems receded.

'Oh, *yes!*' Her helpless cry was muffled by the hard seeking of his lips. His urgent hands were in her hair and on her cheeks, and then skating down the sides of her body with a kind of fevered impatience, as if he was relearning her through touch alone. And greedily she began to touch him back.

Tariq groaned as she began to tug at his belt. She was like wildfire on his skin—spreading hunger wherever her soft fingertips alighted. He could have unzipped himself and done it to her right there. But he'd spent too many nights fantasising about this to want to take her without ceremony—and too many days on horseback not to crave the comfort of a bed.

'Where's the bedroom?' he demanded urgently.

Tell him. Before this goes any further, you have to *tell him.*

But she ignored the voice of protest in her head as she pointed a trembling finger towards a door. 'O-over there.'

Effortlessly he picked her up, as he'd done so many times before, pushing open the door with his knee and going straight over to the bed, putting her down in the centre of it. Isobel felt the mattress dip as he straddled her, one knee on either side of her body. With fingers which were not quite steady he began to unbutton her dress, and Isobel held her breath as he pulled it open. But he seemed too full of hunger to study her with his usual searing intensity, and maybe he wouldn't have noticed even if he had, for his black eyes were almost opaque with lust. Instead, he was unclipping her bra and bending his head to capture one sensitised nipple in his hungry mouth.

'I feel as if I have been in the desert,' he moaned against the puckered saltiness of her skin.

'I th-thought you had?'

'Not that kind of desert,' he said grimly.

'What kind, then?'

'*This* kind,' he clarified, his lips on her neck, his fingers hooking inside her little lace panties. 'The sexual kind. A remote place without the sweet embrace of a woman's arms or the welcome opening of her milky thighs.'

Even if they lacked emotion, the words were shockingly erotic, and Isobel lifted her head to give him more access to her neck, her fumbling fingers reaching for the buttons of his shirt and beginning to pull them open. He had come back, hadn't he? And he still wanted her. It was as simple as that. Had he found it more difficult than he'd anticipated to simply let her go?

Hope began to build in time with the growing heat of her body. She helped him wriggle out of his jeans and then the silken boxer shorts, which whispered to the ground in a decadent sigh. His shirt joined her dress on the floor and she looked up at him, strangely shy to see his powerful olive body naked on *her* bed. He seemed larger than life and more magnificent than ever—like a Technicolor character who had just wandered into a black and white film.

He moved over her, and she drew in a deep breath of anticipation. She knew his body so well, and yet she was a stranger to his thoughts. Should she tell him now? When they were physically just about as close as it was possible to be without—

'Oh!' she moaned as he entered her. Too late, she thought fleetingly, as sweet sensation shot through her body and the familiar heat began to build. Take this pleasure that you weren't expecting and give him pleasure in return. Let him see that there can still be sweetness and joy. And then maybe, maybe…

'God, you're tight,' he moaned.

'It's because you're so big,' she breathed.

'I'm always big,' came his mocking boast.

'Big*ger,* then.'

But words became redundant as he began to move inside her, his mouth on hers as she met his every powerful thrust with the welcoming tilt of her hips.

It was the most bittersweet experience of her life. Amazing, yes—because sex with Tariq always was—but tinged with a certain poignancy, too. She was aware that things were different between them now, that nothing had been resolved. Aware too of what she still hadn't told him. And all those facts combined to heighten every one of her senses.

She felt her climax growing. The beckoning warmth which had been tantalisingly out of reach now became a blissful reality. She felt the first powerful spasm just as he gave his own ragged cry, his movements more frantic as her arms closed around his sweat-sheened back.

And she was falling, dissolving, melting. Past thinking as the world fell away from her.

Minutes passed, and when she opened her eyes it was to find Tariq leaning on one elbow, his hooded eyes enigmatic as he studied her.

'Amazing,' he observed after a moment or two, a finger tracing down the side of her cheek as she sucked in a deep breath of air. 'As ever.'

'Yes.'

'You didn't ring me, Izzy.'

'I could say the same thing about you.' She looked straight into his eyes. 'Did you think I would?'

His mouth quirked into an odd kind of smile. He'd thought that her cool evaluation of their relationship having run its course had been a clever kind of bargaining tool. Had she realised that no woman had ever done that to him before? That the tantalising prospect of someone finishing with him was guaranteed to keep him interested? 'Of course I did,' he replied truthfully.

Isobel shifted restlessly. The warmth was ebbing away from her body now, and she knew she couldn't put it off much longer. Yet some instinctive air of preservation made her want to gather together all the facts first. 'Why did you come here today, Tariq?'

He smiled. 'I thought I'd just demonstrated that—to our mutual satisfaction.'

Her own smile was tight. So that had been a *demonstration,* had it? In the midst of her post-orgasmic glow, it was all too easy to forget his arrogance. 'For sex?' she queried. 'Was that why you came?'

'Yes. No. Oh, Izzy—I don't know.' He shook his head

and gave a reluctant sigh, not wanting to analyse the powerful impulse which had brought him to her door today. Couldn't she just enjoy the here and now and be satisfied with that? 'Whatever it is, I've missed it.'

'If it's just sex you can get that from plenty of other women,' she pointed out.

'Then maybe it isn't just sex,' he said slowly. He lifted her chin with the tips of his fingers and she was caught in the brilliant ebony blaze of his eyes. 'Maybe what I should have said is that I've missed *you*.'

Isobel's heart missed a beat, and all the wistful longings she had suppressed as a matter of survival now came bubbling to the surface. 'You've said that before,' she whispered. 'When you've come back from a trip.'

'Yes, I know. But it was different this time—knowing that you weren't going to be here. Telling me that it was over made me realise that I could lose you—and I don't want to.'

Her heart crashed against her ribcage. 'You don't?'

'No.' He brushed his lips over hers. Back and forth and back and forth—until he could feel her shivering response. 'What we have together is better than anything I've had with anyone else. I'm not promising you for ever, Izzy, because I don't think I can do that. And I haven't changed my mind about children. But if you think you can be content with what we've got…. Well, then, let's go for it.'

His words mocked her. Taunted her. They filled her with horror at what she must now do. *Let's go for it.* That was the kind of thing a football coach said during the half-time pep talk—not a man who was telling you that you meant something really special to him. And Isobel realised what a mess she had made of everything. Despite her determination not to follow in her mother's footsteps, she had ended up doing exactly that. She had hitched her star to a man who was unavailable. In Tariq's case it wasn't because he was married but because he was emotionally unavailable. And in a roundabout way he'd just told her that he always would be.

I haven't changed my mind about children.

So now what did she do?

Feeling sick with nerves, she sat up, her unruly curls falling over her shoulders and providing some welcome cover for her aching breasts.

'Before you say any more, there's something I have to tell you, Tariq.' She sucked in a shuddering breath, more nervous than she'd ever been as he suddenly tensed. She met the narrowed question in his ebony eyes. 'You see…I'm going to have a baby.'

CHAPTER TWELVE

THE SILENCE IN THE room emphasised the sounds outside, which floated through the open window. The faint roar of traffic a long way below. The occasional toot of a car. A low plane flying overhead.

Isobel stared down at Tariq's still figure, lying on the bed, and ironically she was reminded of the time when he'd lain in hospital. When he'd looked so lost and so vulnerable and her feelings for him had undergone a complete change.

But he wasn't looking vulnerable now.

Far from it. She watched the expressions which shifted across his face like shadows. Shock morphing into disbelief and then quickly settling itself into a look which she'd been expecting all along.

Anger.

Still he did not move. Only his eyes did—hard and impenetrable as two pieces of polished jet as they fixed themselves on her. 'Please tell me that this is some kind of sick joke, Izzy.'

Izzy trembled at all the negative implications be-hind his response. 'It's not a joke—why would I joke about something like that? I'm...I'm going to have a baby. Your baby.'

'No!' He moved then, fast as a panther, reaching down to grab his jeans before getting off the bed to roughly pull them on, knowing he couldn't face having such a conversation with her when he was completely naked. Because what if his traitorous body began to harden with desire, even as an impotent kind of rage began to spiral up inside him as he realised the full extent of her betrayal?

He zipped up his jeans and tugged on his shirt. And only then did he advance towards her with such a look of dark fury contorting his features that Isobel shrank back against the pillows.

'Tell me it isn't true,' he said, in a voice of pure venom.

'I can't. Because it is,' she whispered.

Tariq stared at her. She had known that he never wanted to be a father. She'd *known* because he'd told her! He'd even told her just now. After they'd...they'd...

'How the hell can you be pregnant when you're on the pill?'

'Because accidents sometimes happen—'

'What? You *accidentally* forgot to take it, did you?'

'No!'

'How, then?' he demanded hotly. *'How,* Izzy?'

Distractedly she held up her hands, as if she was surrendering. 'I had a mild touch of food poisoning after I ate some fish! It must have been then.'

'Must it?'

Abruptly he turned his back on her and went over to

stand beside the window, staring down at the busy London street. When he turned back his face was a mask. She had never seen him look quite like that before— all cold and empty—and suddenly Isobel realised that whatever feelings he might have had for her, they had just died.

'Or was it "accidentally on purpose"?' he said slowly. 'When did it happen?'

'It was…' She swallowed. 'It was around the time when I met Zahid and Francesca.'

'You mean the *King* and *Queen?*' he corrected imperiously, unknown emotions making him retreat behind protocol—despite his conflicting feelings towards it. He remembered the way she'd held Omar that night. The way she'd looked at him over the mop of ebony curls with that soppy soft look that women sometimes assumed whenever there was a baby around.

'What? Did you look at Francesca?' he questioned. 'See another ordinary Englishwoman very much like yourself? Did you look around you and see all the wealth and status at her fingertips and think: *I wouldn't mind some of that for myself?* After all, you also had a royal lover—just as Francesca had once done. The only difference is that she didn't get herself pregnant in order to secure her future!'

If she hadn't been naked she would have lunged at him. As it was, Isobel got off the bed and grabbed at her dress to hide her vulnerability—the outward kind, anyway. For her heart was vulnerable, too—and she felt as if he had crushed it in his fist.

'I can't b-believe you could think that!' she stuttered

as she started doing up the buttons, her shaking fingers making the task almost impossible.

'I suppose I can't really blame you,' he mused, almost as if she hadn't objected, a slow tide of rage still building inside him. 'Most women seem hell-bent on marriage—and the more prestigious the marriage, the better. And you can't do much better than a prince, can you?'

'You must be joking,' she hissed back. 'You might be a prince, but you also happen to be an arrogant and overbearing piece of—'

'Let's skip the insults, shall we?' he snapped, as he tried to get his head around the fact that in her belly his child grew. *His child!* A child he'd never asked for nor wanted. A child he would never be able to love...that he didn't know *how* to love. 'I thought you were into honesty, Izzy? Except now I come to think about it you haven't been very honest all the way along, have you?'

She stared at him uncomprehendingly. 'What are you talking about?'

'Just how long have you known about this pregnancy?'

She met the accusation which blazed from his face. 'For a couple of weeks,' she admitted.

A strange light entered his eyes. He looked like someone who had been trying to solve a puzzle and had just found the last missing piece stuffed down the back of the sofa. 'When we were in bed—the morning I got the phone call from Khayarzah about Leila—you knew you were pregnant then, didn't you?'

She shook her head. 'I didn't *know.* I had my suspicions, but I wasn't sure.'

'But you didn't bother to tell me? Even today you kept quiet. You let me come here and…' She'd let him lose himself in the refuge of her arms. Lulling him into sweet compliance with the erotic promise of her body.

'We had *sex,* Tariq!' she declared brutally. 'Let's not make it into something it wasn't!'

She could see the faint shock which had dilated his eyes, but his reaction was breathing resolve into her and Isobel felt something of her old spirit return. Was she going to allow him to speak to her as if she was some worthless piece of nothing he'd found on the bottom of his shoe? As if she counted for nothing?

'I didn't tell you because I knew how you would react,' she raged. 'Because I knew that you'd be arrogant enough to think it was all some giant conspiracy theory instead of the kind of slip-up that's been happening to men and women ever since they started fornicating!'

His eyes bored into her. 'I'm assuming that marriage *is* what you want?'

Isobel's eyes widened. Hadn't he been listening to a word she'd been saying? 'You must be *mad,*' she whispered. 'Completely certifiable if you think that I'd ever want to sign up for life with a man like *you.* A man so full of ego that he thinks a woman will get herself deliberately pregnant in order to trap him.'

'You think it's never been done before?' he scorned.

'Not by me,' she defended fiercely, closing her eyes as a wave of terrible sadness washed over her. 'Now, please go, Tariq. Get out of here before either of us says anything more we might regret.'

His impulse was to resist—for he was used to calling the shots. Until he realised that this wasn't the first time Izzy had called the shots. It had been her, after all, who'd had the courage to end the relationship. And, yes, he had been arrogant enough to think that she might just be playing a very sophisticated game to bring him to heel.

But Izzy didn't do game-playing, he realised. She hadn't told him she thought she was pregnant because she'd feared his reaction—and hadn't he just proved those fears a thousand times over? He looked at the haunted expression on her whitened face and suddenly felt a savage jerk of guilt.

'I'm sorry,' he said suddenly.

Her eyes swimming with unshed tears, she looked at him. 'What? Sorry for the things you said? Or sorry that you ever got involved with me in the first place?'

He flinched as her accusations hit home. 'Sit down, Izzy.'

She ignored the placatory note in his voice. He thought he could spew out all that *stuff* and that now she'd instantly become malleable? How dared he tell her to sit down in her own home? 'I'll sit down once you've gone.'

'I'm not going anywhere until you do. Because there are things we need to discuss.'

She wanted to tell him that he had forfeited all rights to any discussion with his cruel comments. But she couldn't bring herself to do that. Because Tariq was her baby's father. And didn't she know better than anyone how great and gaping the hole could be in a child's life if it didn't have one?

'And we will,' she said, sucking in another deep breath, her hand instinctively fluttering to her still-flat belly. 'Just not now, when emotions are running so high.'

Tariq watched the unfamiliar maternal movement and something tugged at his heart. To his astonishment, he found that he wanted to ask her a million questions. He wanted to ask whether she'd eaten that day, whether she had been sleeping properly at night. He'd never asked for this baby, and he didn't particularly want it, but that didn't mean he couldn't feel empathy for the woman who carried that baby, did it?

He looked at her with a detachment he'd never used before. She *did* look different, he decided. More delicate than usual, yes—but there was a kind of strength about her, too. It radiated off her like the sunlight which caught the pale fire of her hair.

He should have been gathering her in his arms now and congratulating her. Laying a proprietorial hand over her belly and looking with pride into her shining eyes. If he had been a normal man—like other men—then he would have been able to do all those things. But he knew that all he had was a piece of ice where his heart should be, and that was why they were just gazing at each other suspiciously across a small bedroom.

But this was no time for reflection. Whatever his own feelings, this had to be all about Izzy. He had to think practically. To help her in any way that he could.

'You obviously won't be coming back to work,' he said.

Impatiently, she shook her head. 'I hadn't even thought about work.'

'Well, you don't have to. I want you to know that you don't have to worry about anything. I'll make sure you're financially secure.'

Now she observed him with a kind of fury. What? Buy her off? Did he think that she'd be satisfied with that as compensation for the lack of the marriage she'd supposedly been angling for? She thought of her own mother—how she had always gone out to work and supported herself. And hadn't Isobel been grateful for that role model? To see a woman survive and thrive and not be beaten down because her hopes of love had not materialised?

'Actually, I've decided that I want to carry on working,' she said. 'And besides, what on earth would I do all day—sit around knitting bootees? Plenty of women work right up until the final weeks. I'll...I'll look for another job, obviously.'

But she was filled with dread at the thought of going from agency to agency and having to hide her pregnancy. Who would want to take on a woman in her condition and offer her any kind of security for the future?

'You don't need to look for another job,' he said harshly. 'You could come back to work for me in an instant. Or I could arrange to have you work for one of the partners, if you don't think you could tolerate being in the same office as me.'

Isobel swallowed. She thought of starting work for someone new, with her pregnancy growing all the time.

She wasn't aware of how much other people at the Al Hakam corporation knew about their affair. After all, it wasn't the most likely of partnerships, and Tariq hadn't exactly been squiring her around town. Would people put two and two together and come up with the right answer? Would her position be compromised once any new boss knew who the father of her baby was?

She stared at him, wondering what kind of foolish instinct it was which made her realise that she actually wanted to work for *him*. For there was a certain kind of security in the familiar—especially when there was so much happening in her life. At least with Tariq she wouldn't have to hide anything, or pretend. Tariq would protect her. Because, despite his angry words of earlier, she sensed that he would make sure that nothing and nobody ever harmed her, or her baby.

'I think I could just about tolerate it,' she said slowly.

She met his eyes, knowing that she needed to believe in the words she was about to speak—because otherwise there could be no way forward. She had thought that if she quietly loved him then he might learn how to love her back—even if it was only a little bit. She had thought that maybe she could change him. But she had been wrong. Because you couldn't change somebody else—you could only change yourself. And Tariq didn't want love—not in any form, it seemed. He didn't want to receive it, and he didn't want to give it either. Not to her—and not to their baby.

'We must agree to give each other the personal space we need,' she continued steadily. 'The relationship is over, Tariq—we both know that. But there's no reason why we can't behave civilly towards each other.'

He was aware of an overwhelming sense of relief that she wasn't going to be launching out on her own. But something in the quiet dignity of her statement made his heart grow heavy with a gloomy realisation. As if somehow there had been something wonderful hovering on the periphery of his life.

And he had just let it go.

CHAPTER THIRTEEN

'THE PRESS HAVE been on the phone again, Tariq.'

Tariq looked up to see Izzy hovering in the doorway of his office, lit from behind like a Botticelli painting, with her hair falling down over her shoulders like liquid honey. Although she was wearing a loose summer dress and still very slim, at four months pregnant there was no disguising the curving softness of her belly. A whisper ran over his skin. For weeks now he had been watching her. Trying to imagine what his child must be like as it grew inside her.

And now he knew.

Aware of the sudden lump which had risen in his throat, he swallowed and raised his brows at her questioningly. 'What did they want?'

Isobel stared at the brilliant gleam of the Sheikh's black eyes, and the faint stubble on his chin which made him look like a modern-day pirate. Had she been out of her mind yesterday when she'd told him that he could accompany her to the doctor if he wanted to see her latest scan? What crazy hormonal blip had prompted *that?* She'd been expecting a curt thanks, followed by a terse refusal, but to her surprise he had leapt at the opportunity, his face wreathed in what had looked like a delighted smile. A most un-Tariq kind of smile. And then he'd acted the part of the caring father as if he actually *meant* it—clucking round her as if he'd spent a lifetime looking after pregnant women.

In fact, when he'd been helping her into the limousine—something which she'd told him was entirely unnecessary—his hand had brushed over hers, and the feeling which had passed between them had been electric. It was the first time that they had touched since their uneasy truce—and hadn't it started her senses screaming, taunting her with what she was missing? Their eyes had met in a clashing gaze of suppressed desire and she had felt an overwhelming need to be in his arms again. A need she had quickly quashed by climbing into the limousine and sitting as far away from him as possible.

She sighed with impatience at her inability to remain immune to him, then turned her mind back to his question about the press. 'They were asking why the Sheikh of Khayarzah was seen accompanying his assistant to an obstetrician's for her scan yesterday.'

'They saw us?'

'Apparently.' Her eyes were full of appeal. 'Tariq, I should have realised this might happen.'

Maybe she should have done. But to his surprise he was glad she hadn't. Because mightn't that have stopped her from giving him the chance to see the baby he had never wanted? He still didn't know why she had done that—and he had never expected to feel this overwhelming sense of gratitude. Perhaps he should have realised himself that someone might notice them, but the truth was he wouldn't have cared even if he'd known that a million journalists were lurking around.

He hadn't cared about anything except what he was to discover in that darkened room in Harley Street, watching while a doctor had moved a sensory pad over the jelly-covered swell of her abdomen.

Suddenly he'd seen an incomprehensible image spring to life on the screen. To Tariq, it had looked like a high-definition snowstorm—until he had seen a rapid and rhythmical beat and realised that he was looking at a beating heart. And that was when everything had changed. When he'd stopped thinking of Izzy's pregnancy as something theoretical and seen reality there, right before his eyes.

His heart had lurched as he'd stared at the form of his son—or daughter—and the doctor had said something on the lines of the two of them being a 'happy couple'. And that had been when Izzy's voice had rung out loud and clear.

'But we're not,' she had said firmly, turning to look at Tariq, her tawny eyes glittering with hurt and challenge. 'The Sheikh and I are not together, Doctor.'

Tariq had flinched beneath that condemnatory blaze—but could he blame her? Didn't he deserve comments and looks like that after his outrageous reaction when she'd told him about the baby? Even though he had been doing his damnedest to make it up to her ever since. Short of peeling grapes and bringing them into her office each morning, he was unsure of what else he could do to make it better. And he still wasn't sure if his conciliatory attitude was having any effect on her, because she had been exhibiting a stubbornness he hadn't known she possessed.

Proudly, she had refused all his offers of lifts home or time off. Had turned up her pretty little nose at his studiedly casual enquiry that she might want to join him for dinner some time. And told him that, no, she had no desire to go shopping for a cot. Or to have her groceries delivered from a chi-chi London store. Pregnant women were not invalids, she'd told him crisply—and she would manage the way she had always managed. So he had been forced to bite back his frustration as she had stubbornly shopped for food each lunchtime, bringing back bulging bags which she had lain on the floor of her office. Though he had put his foot down about her carrying them home and told her in no uncertain terms that his limousine would drop the bags off at her apartment.

Now, as she walked into his office and shut the door behind her, he realised that the Botticelli resemblance had been illusory—because beneath her pale and Titian beauty she looked tired.

'We're going to have to decide what to say when the question of paternity comes up,' she told him, wondering why it had never occurred to her that people would want to know who the father of her baby was. 'Because it will. I mean, people here have been dropping hints about it for ages, and that journalist was on the verge of asking me outright about it today—I could tell he was.'

His voice was gentle. 'What do you want to do, Izzy?'

She gave a short laugh. 'I don't think what I *want* is the kind of question you should be asking, Tariq.'

What she wanted was the impossible—to be carrying the child of someone who loved her instead of resenting her for having fallen pregnant. Someone who would hold her in the small hours of the morning when the world seemed a very big and frightening place. But those kinds of thoughts were dangerous. Even shameful. Because wasn't the truth that she still wanted Tariq to be that man—even though it was never going to happen?

To Isobel's terror, she'd discovered that you didn't just fall out of love with a man because he'd spoken to you harshly or judged you in the worst possible way.

'I don't know what I want,' she said quietly.

He stared at her, and a flare of determination coursed through him. He was aware that he could no longer sit on the sidelines and watch, like some kind of dazed ghost. Up until now he had allowed Izzy to dictate the terms of how they dealt with this because he had been racked with guilt about his own conduct. He had given her the personal space she had demanded, telling himself that it was in her best interests for him to do so. He had scrabbled deep inside himself and discovered unknown pockets of patience and fortitude. He had acted in a way which a few short months ago would have seemed unimaginable.

But it was still not enough. Not nearly enough. Close examination of her bleached face made him realise that he now had to step up to the mark and start taking control. That to some extent Izzy was weak and helpless in this situation—even though she had shown such shining courage so far.

He stood up, walked over to her, and took hold of her elbow. 'Come and sit down,' he said, guiding her firmly towards the sofa. 'Please.'

Her lips trembled and so did her body, responding instantly to his touch, and silently she raged against her traitorous hormones. But it was a sign of her weariness that she let him guide her over to the sofa.

Heavily, she slumped down and looked up at him. 'Well?'

He sat down beside her, seeing the momentary suspicion which clouded her eyes as, casting around in his mind, he struggled to find the right words to say. Clumsy sentences hovered at the edges of his lips until he realised that nobody really gave a damn about the words—only about the sentiment behind them. 'I want to tell you how sorry I am, Izzy. Truly sorry.'

She shook her head. 'You've said sorry before,' she said, blinking back the stupid tears which were springing to her eyes and which seemed never far away these days.

'That was back then—when neither of us was thinking straight. When the air was full of confusion and hurt. But it's important to me that you understand that I mean it. That in the cold light of day I wish I could take back those words I should never have said. And that I wish I could make it up to you in some way.'

She stared at him, thinking how strange it was to

hear him sounding so genuinely contrite. Because Tariq didn't *do* apology. In his arrogance he thought he was always right. But he didn't look arrogant now, she realised, and something in that discovery made her want to meet him halfway.

'We both said things we shouldn't have said,' she conceded. 'Things we can't unsay which are probably best forgotten. I'm sorry that I didn't tell you about the baby sooner.'

'I don't care about that. Your reasons for that are perfectly understandable.' There was a pause. The heavy lids of his eyes almost concealed their hectic ebony glitter. 'There's only one thing I really care about, Izzy—and that's whether you can ever find it in your heart to forgive me?'

She bit her lip as hurt pride fought with an instinctive desire to make amends. Because wasn't this something she was going to have to teach her baby—that forgiveness should always follow repentance? And there was absolutely no doubt from the stricken expression on Tariq's face that his remorse was genuine.

'Yes, Tariq,' she said softly. 'I can forgive you.'

He stared at her, but her generous clemency only heightened his sense of disquiet. It made him realise then that if they wanted some kind of future together he had to go one step further.

But it wasn't easy—because everything in him rebelled against further disclosure. Wasn't it his ability to close off the painful experiences in his life which made him so single-minded? Wasn't it his reluctance to actually *feel* things which had protected him from the knocks and isolation of his childhood? Success had come easily to Tariq because he hadn't allowed himself to be influenced by emotion. To him, emotion was something that you blocked out. Because how else could he have survived if he had not done that?

Yet if he failed to find the courage to confront all the darkness he'd locked away so long ago then wouldn't he be left with this terrible lack of resolution? As if he could never really get close to Izzy again? As if he was seeing her through a thick wall of glass? And what was the point of trying to protect himself from emotional pain if he was going to experience it anyway?

'There are some things you need to know about me,' he said. 'Things which may explain the monster I have been.'

'You're no *monster*,' she breathed instantly. 'My baby's not having a monster for a father!'

'There are things you need to know,' he repeated, even though his lips curved in a brief smile at her passionate defence. 'Things about me and my life that I need to explain—to try to make you understand.'

He frowned. He struggled to put his feelings into words—because in a way wasn't he trying to make *himself* understand his own past?

'I've never had a problem with the way I live,' he said. 'My work life was a triumph and my personal life was…manageable. I was happy enough with the affairs I had. I liked women and they liked me. But as soon as they started getting close—well, I wanted out. Always.'

Isobel nodded. Hadn't she witnessed it enough times

before experiencing it for herself? 'And why do you think that was?' she questioned quietly.

'Because I had no idea how to relate to people. I had no idea how to do real relationships,' he answered simply. 'My mother was so ill after my birth that I was kept away from her. My father was run off his feet with the ongoing wars with Sharifah—so my relationship with him was pretty non-existent, too. And the nurses and nannies who were employed to look after me would never dare to show *love* towards a royal child, for that would be considered presumptuous. Children only know their own experience—but even if at times I felt lost or lonely I did not ever show it. In that strongly driven and very masculine environment it was always frowned on to show any weakness or vulnerability.'

Vulnerability. The word stuck to her like a piece of dry grass. It took her back to when she'd seen him lying injured on the hospital bed—for hadn't it been that self-same vulnerability which had made her feelings towards him change and her heart start to melt? Hadn't it been in that moment when she'd started to fall in love with Tariq? When he'd shown a side of himself which he'd always kept hidden before?

'Go on,' she said softly.

'You know that they sent me away to school in England at seven? In a way, my life was just as isolated as it had been in the palace. For a while I was the only foreign pupil—and I was the only royal one. And of course I was bullied.'

'You? Bullied? Oh, come on, Tariq! As if anyone would dare try.'

He gave a wry smile. 'There are more ways to hurt someone than with your fists. I was certainly excluded on a social level—never invited to the homes of my classmates. My saving grace was that I made every sports team going and I had first pick of all the girls.' He shrugged as he realised that was about the time when he had begun to use the veneer of arrogance to protect him. 'Though of course that only increased the feelings of resentment against me.'

'I can imagine.' She sighed as she looked at him, longing to take him in her arms but too scared to dare try. Still afraid that nothing had really changed and that he would hurt her again as he had hurt her before. And besides, if he really meant it then didn't he have to come to *her?*

He saw the fear and the pain which clouded her face, and it mirrored the aching deep inside him. A terrible sense of frustration washed over him as he looked into her tawny eyes.

'Oh, Izzy—can't you see that I'm a novice at all this stuff? That for the first time in my life I don't know what to do or what to say? I've never dared love anyone before, because I didn't want to. And then when I did—I didn't know how to.'

She blinked at him, unsure whether she'd just imagined that. Love? Who'd said anything about love?

'Tariq?' she questioned, in confusion.

But he shook his head, determined to finish what he had begun, and it was like opening up the floodgates and letting his heart run free.

'In you, I found something I'd never known with

any other woman. Even before we became lovers you gave me an unwitting glimpse of what life *could* be like. Those days I spent in your cottage—I'd never felt so at peace. It felt like *home*,' he realised wonderingly. 'A home I'd never really known before. Only it took me a long time to realise what was staring me in the face.' He paused. 'Just like something else which was there all the time—only I was too pig-headed to admit it. And that's the fact that I love you, Izzy. Simple as that—I just do.'

Still she didn't dare believe him—because she sensed that there would be no coming back from this. That if she discovered his words were nothing but a sham then her pain would never heal. But the light which gleamed from his ebony eyes cut through the last of her resistance. It broke through the brick wall she had erected around her heart and made it crumble away as if it were made of sand.

She lifted her fingertips to his lips.

'I love you,' he said fiercely. 'And if I have to tell you a thousand times a day for the rest of our lives before you will believe me, then so be it—I will.'

A little awkwardly, given the bump of the baby, she scrambled to her knees and sat on his lap, facing him, her hands smoothing over his face, touching his skin with a trembling delight. 'Oh, Tariq. My sweet, darling Tariq.'

'I love you, Izzy,' he said brokenly. 'And I was a stubborn fool to have tried so hard *not* to love you.' He stared at her, willing the tawny eyes to give him the only answer his heart craved. 'Just tell me it's not too late.'

'Of course it isn't,' she whispered, as she dragged in a great shuddering breath of relief. 'I think we've managed to save it in the nick of time. And thank goodness for that—because I love you too, Tariq al Hakam, and you'd better believe it. I've loved you for a long, long time, I think. Since the time you lay injured—or maybe even before that. Maybe it just took your brush with death to show me what already lay deep in my heart. And I love the baby that grows beneath my breast— *your* baby.'

He stared at her, her soft understanding suddenly hard to take. 'You are too sweet, Izzy. Too kind to a man who has done nothing but—'

'No!' she contradicted, her firm denial butting into his words. 'I'm just fighting for what is mine—and you *are* mine, Tariq al Hakam. You and this baby are all mine.'

'*Our* baby,' he said fiercely.

She touched her lips to the palm of his hand, seeing the last of the pain and regret leave his eyes as they were eclipsed by love. And she felt her heart soar as the bitterness of the past dissolved into the glorious present. 'Our baby,' she agreed.

He caught her against him and brought her head close to his. 'Beautiful, Isobel,' he whispered against her soft cheek. 'Outside and in, your loveliness shines like the moon in the night sky.'

'Poetry, too?' she questioned unsteadily. 'I didn't know you did poetry.'

'Neither did I. But then, I could never really see the point of it before.'

'Just kiss me, Tariq,' she whispered urgently. 'Kiss me quickly—before I wake up and discover this is all a dream.'

His lips grazed hers, slowly at first, and their eyes were wide open as they watched themselves kiss. And then hunger and passion and love turned the kiss into something else, and Izzy's breath began to quicken as she pressed her swollen breasts against him.

'Wait a minute,' he said, dragging his lips away and hearing her little sigh of objection. Carefully disengaging himself, Tariq got up from the sofa and went over to his desk, where he bent over and spoke into the intercom. 'Fiona, can you hold all calls, please? Izzy and I don't want to be disturbed for the rest of the day.' He turned and dazzled her with a blazing look of love. 'Do we, darling?'

In the outer office, Fiona couldn't believe it. Sheikh Tariq al Hakam had just called Isobel Mulholland *darling* and asked that they be left alone for the rest of the day! It was the sort of *unbelievable* statement which was impossible for her to keep to herself, and she went straight down to the water-cooler to tell anyone who would listen.

But perhaps that was what Tariq had intended.

Rumours were soon spreading like wildfire through the building, and by five o'clock the evening newspapers were all carrying the news that the Playboy Prince was going to be a daddy.

EPILOGUE

IT WAS A SOURCE of enormous frustration to Tariq that Izzy refused to marry him—no matter how many times he asked her.

'Why not?' he demanded one morning, exasperated by what he perceived as her stubbornness. 'Is it because of all those stupid accusations I made when you told me—when I said you'd deliberately got yourself pregnant in order to trap me?'

'No, darling,' she replied with serene honesty—because those days of fury and confusion were long behind them. 'That has absolutely nothing to do with it.'

'Why, then, Izzy?'

Isobel wasn't quite sure. Was it because things seemed so perfect now? So much the way she'd always longed for them to be that she was terrified of jeopardising them with unnecessary change? As if marriage would be like a superstitious person walking on a crack in the pavement—and bad luck would come raining down on them?

It had become a bit of a game—which Tariq was determined to win, because he always won in the end.

But winning was not uppermost in his thoughts. Mostly he wanted to marry Izzy because he loved her—with a love which had blown him away and continued to do so.

'You'll be a princess,' he promised.

'But I don't *want* to be a princess! I'm happy just the way I am.'

'You are an infuriating woman,' he growled.

'And you just like getting your own way!'

His lips curved into a reluctant smile. 'That much is true,' he conceded.

He asked her again on the morning she gave birth to a beautiful baby daughter and he felt as if his heart would burst with pride and emotion. The nurse had just handed him the tiny bundle, and he held the swathed scrap and stared down at eyes which were blue and wide—shaped just like her mother's. But she had a shock of hair which was pure black—like his. Wonderingly, he touched her perfectly tiny little hand and it closed over his finger like a starfish—a bond made in that moment which only death would break.

His eyes were wet when he looked up and the lump in his throat made speaking difficult, but he didn't care. 'Why won't you marry me, Izzy?' he questioned softly.

Slumped back against the pillows—dazed but elated—Isobel regarded her magnificent Sheikh. This powerful man who cradled their tiny baby so gently in his arms. Why, indeed? Because she was stubborn? Or because she wanted him to know that marriage wasn't important to her? That she wasn't one of those women who were angling for the big catch, determined to get his ring on her finger? That she loved him for who he was and not for what he could give her?

'Doesn't it please you to know that I'm confident enough in your love that I don't need the fuss of a legal ceremony?' she questioned demurely.

'No,' he growled. 'It doesn't. I want to give our girl some security.'

And that was when their eyes met and she realised that he was offering her what her mother had never had. What *she* had never had. A proper hands-on father who wasn't going anywhere. Here was a man who wasn't being forced to commit but who genuinely *wanted* to. So what was stopping her?

'I don't want a big wedding,' she warned.

He bit back his smile of triumph. 'Neither do I.' But her unexpected acquiescence had filled him with even more joy than he had thought possible, and he turned his attention to the now sleeping baby in his arms. 'We'll have to think about what to call her.'

'A Khayarzah name, I think.'

'I think so, too.'

After much consultation they named her Nawal, which meant 'gift'—which was what she was—and when she was six months old they took her to Khayarzah, where their private visit turned into a triumphant tour. The people went out of their way to welcome this second son and his family into their midst—and Tariq at last accepted his royal status and realised that he had no wish to change it. For it was his daughter's heritage as well as his, he realised.

It was in Khayarzah one night, when they were lying

in bed in their room in the royal palace, that Tariq voiced something which had been on his mind for some time.

'You know, we could always try to find your father,' he said slowly. 'It would be an easy thing to do. That's if you want to.'

Isobel stirred. The bright moonlight from the clear desert sky flooded in through the unshuttered windows as she lifted her eyes to study her husband.

'What on earth makes you say that?'

Expansive and comfortable, with her warm body nestling against him, Tariq shrugged. 'I've been thinking about it ever since we had Nawal. How much of a gap there would be in my life if I didn't have her. If I had never had the opportunity to be a father.'

'But—'

'I know he deserted your mother,' he said softly. 'And I'm not saying that you have to find him. Or that even if we do you have to forgive him. I'm just saying that the possibility is there—that's all.'

It was his mention of the word *forgive* which made Isobel think carefully about his words. Because didn't forgiveness play a big part in every human life—their own included? And once her husband had planted the seed of possibility it took root and grew. Surely she owed Nawal the chance of meeting her only surviving grandparent...?

Tariq was right. It *was* easy to find a man who had just 'disappeared' twenty-five years ago—especially when you had incalculable wealth and resources at your fingertips.

Isobel didn't know what she had been expecting—

but it certainly wasn't a rather sad-looking man with grey hair and tawny eyes. Recently widowed, John Franklin was overjoyed to meet her and her family. His own personal regret was that he and his wife had never been able to have children of their own.

It was a strange and not altogether comfortable moment when she shook hands for the first time with the man who had given life to her over a quarter of a century ago. But then he saw the baby, and he smiled, and Isobel's heart gave an unexpected wrench. For in it she saw something of herself—and something of her daughter, too. It was a smile which would carry on down through the generations. And there was something in that smile which wiped away all the bitterness of the past.

'You're very quiet,' observed Tariq as they drove away from John Franklin's modest house. 'No regrets?'

Isobel shook her head. What was it they said? That you regretted the things you didn't do, rather than the things you did? 'None,' she answered honestly. 'He was good with Nawal. I think they will be good for each other in the future.'

'Ah, Izzy,' said Tariq. 'You are a sweet and loving woman.'

'I can afford to be,' she said happily. 'Because I've got you.'

Their main home was to be in London, although whenever it was possible they still escaped to Izzy's tiny country cottage, where their love had first been ignited. Because maybe Francesca had been right, Tariq conceded. Maybe it *was* important that royal children knew what it was like to be ordinary.

He didn't buy the 'Blues' football team after all. It came to him in a blinding flash one night that he didn't actually *like* football. Besides, what was the point of acquiring a prestigious soccer team simply because he *could,* when its acquisition brought with it nothing but envy and unwanted press attention? He wanted to keep the cameras away from his beloved family, as much as possible. Anyway, polo was his game.

Real men didn't prance around in a pair of shorts, kicking a ball.

Real men rode horses.

* * * * *

COMING NEXT MONTH FROM
HARLEQUIN
Presents

Available December 17, 2013

#3201 THE DIMITRAKOS PROPOSITION
Lynne Graham
Tabby Glover desperately needs Greek billionaire
Acheron Dimitrakos to support her adoption claim over his
cousin's child. His price? Marriage. But as the thin veil between
truth and lies is lifted, will this relationship become more than in
name only?

#3202 A MAN WITHOUT MERCY
Miranda Lee
Dumped by her fiancé *via text*, Vivienne Swan wants to nurse her
shattered heart privately...until an intriguing offer from Jack Stone
tempts her from her shell. He is a man used to taking what he
wants, and Vivienne is now at his mercy!

#3203 FORGED IN THE DESERT HEAT
Maisey Yates
Newly crowned Sheikh Zafar Nejem's first act is to rescue heiress
Analise Christensen from her desert kidnappers and return her
to her fiancé...or risk war. But the forbidden attraction burning
between them rivals the heat of the sun, threatening everything....

#3204 THE FLAW IN HIS DIAMOND
Susan Stephens
When no-nonsense Eva Skavanga arrives on Count Roman
Quisvada's Mediterranean Island with a business arrangement,
Roman's more interested in the pleasure she might bring him.
Perhaps Roman could help her with more than just securing her
family's diamond mine...?

HPCNM1213RA

#3205 THE TYCOON'S DELICIOUS DISTRACTION
Maggie Cox

Forced to rely on physio Kit after a skiing accident confines him
to a wheelchair, Hal Treverne has no escape from her intoxicating
presence. But unleashing the simmering desire beneath her
ever-so-professional facade is a challenge this tycoon will relish!

#3206 HIS TEMPORARY MISTRESS
Cathy Williams

Damian Carver wants revenge on the woman who stole from him,
and her sister Violet won't change his mind...until he needs a
temporary mistress, and Violet's perfect! But sweet-natured Violet
soon turns the tables on his sensuous brand of blackmail....

#3207 THE MOST EXPENSIVE LIE OF ALL
Michelle Conder

Champion horse breeder Aspen has never forgotten
Cruz Rodriguez, so when he reappears with a multimillion-dollar
investment offer, Aspen's torn. She may crave his touch, but his
glittering black eyes hide a deception that could prove more costly
than ever before!

#3208 A DEAL WITH BENEFITS
One Night with Consequences
Susanna Carr

Sebastian Cruz has no intention of giving Ashley Jones's family's
island back, but he does want her. He'll agree to her deal, but
with a few clauses of his own—a month at his beck and call...
and in his bed!

**YOU CAN FIND MORE INFORMATION ON UPCOMING HARLEQUIN® TITLES,
FREE EXCERPTS AND MORE AT WWW.HARLEQUIN.COM.**

HPCNM1213RB

REQUEST YOUR FREE BOOKS!

2 FREE NOVELS PLUS
2 FREE GIFTS!

YES! Please send me 2 FREE Harlequin Presents® novels and my 2 FREE gifts (gifts are worth about $10). After receiving them, if I don't wish to receive any more books, I can return the shipping statement marked "cancel." If I don't cancel, I will receive 6 brand-new novels every month and be billed just $4.30 per book in the U.S. or $4.99 per book in Canada. That's a saving of at least 14% off the cover price! It's quite a bargain! Shipping and handling is just 50¢ per book in the U.S. and 75¢ per book in Canada.* I understand that accepting the 2 free books and gifts places me under no obligation to buy anything. I can always return a shipment and cancel at any time. Even if I never buy another book, the two free books and gifts are mine to keep forever.   106/306 HDN FVRK

Name	(PLEASE PRINT)

Address	Apt. #

City	State/Prov.	Zip/Postal Code

Signature (if under 18, a parent or guardian must sign)

Mail to the **Harlequin® Reader Service:**
IN U.S.A.: P.O. Box 1867, Buffalo, NY 14240-1867
IN CANADA: P.O. Box 609, Fort Erie, Ontario L2A 5X3

Are you a current subscriber to Harlequin Presents books and want to receive the larger-print edition?
Call 1-800-873-8635 or visit www.ReaderService.com.

* Terms and prices subject to change without notice. Prices do not include applicable taxes. Sales tax applicable in N.Y. Canadian residents will be charged applicable taxes. Offer not valid in Quebec. This offer is limited to one order per household. Not valid for current subscribers to Harlequin Presents books. All orders subject to credit approval. Credit or debit balances in a customer's account(s) may be offset by any other outstanding balance owed by or to the customer. Please allow 4 to 6 weeks for delivery. Offer available while quantities last.

Your Privacy—The Harlequin® Reader Service is committed to protecting your privacy. Our Privacy Policy is available online at www.ReaderService.com or upon request from the Harlequin Reader Service.

We make a portion of our mailing list available to reputable third parties that offer products we believe may interest you. If you prefer that we not exchange your name with third parties, or if you wish to clarify or modify your communication preferences, please visit us at www.ReaderService.com/consumerschoice or write to us at Harlequin Reader Service Preference Service, P.O. Box 9062, Buffalo, NY 14269. Include your complete name and address.

HARLEQUIN®

Presents®

Revenge and seduction intertwine…

**Miranda Lee brings you her stunning novel,
packed with power, temptation and excitement!**

Don't miss
A MAN WITHOUT MERCY
January 2014

His out-of-hours invitation…

Dumped by her fiancé *via text*, Vivienne Swan
wants to nurse her shattered heart privately…until
an intriguing offer from Jack Stone tempts her from
her shell. But is Vivienne playing with fire? Jack's a
man used to taking what he wants, and now she's
at his mercy!

HP13208